Accidental Immortal

Ceridwen Hughson

L Y C A N
B O O K S

Myrddin Publishing
unique electronic & print books

Contents

1 Wrath of Duat

The Pharaoh was coming. Hesire pulled the first Osiris band from the deep pocket of his green neophyte robe, the rest clinking together as they jostled back into place in the confined space. He held the bracelet in his palm for a second, contemplating its power. Anyone wearing this bracelet would know everything, be able to talk to anyone. They would be faster, stronger. He had seen it himself. These bands made gods.

Hesire's lips formed a smile before he placed the bracelet in its alcove. Though it was tempting, the order's punishment for taking it was death. It was not for the lower ranks to even consider such power. He arranged them with care, ensuring that the worn symbols were facing outward, that the golden symbols of the Egyptian god glittered in the low light.

When the last bracelet was placed in its allotted slot, he stood back to regard the rest of the hall with a critical eye.

Only those who served Osiris could enter this place. Travellers were escorted out immediately upon arrival. The place was kept impeccably clean and protected. Nothing could be moved or touched, with intricate cleaning instructions for any item that must then be placed back in its correct spot.

Hesire checked the equipment in the room, making sure that everything was in its proper place and in good condition. He knew that if any of the delicate equipment was damaged, there would be no more supplies. No one knew how to repair the equipment anymore and the designers were long dead in the other world. Egypt was changing on the other side, and no one knew how long they could rely on getting the materials to maintain this new world.

A raised circle of bronze, as wide as a workman's hut, stood proudly in the centre of the room. The top of the circle was smooth, with twin emblems of Osiris etched in the centre. The priests wanted to leave no doubt who was in charge. A triangle of three bronze boxes inlaid with gold and jade were placed around the disk like sentinels.

The pyramid's apex loomed above Hesire. Though a thousand feet in height, the massive structure seemed to be a single seamless form. The old-world building disguised a new world construction. This pyramid was built to receive, not to send. The walls were made of brick rather than stone. The lone compromise on new world materials. He knew the engineers would rather have made the pyramids a better replica of the originals. But the measurements and materials did not need to be so exacting. Only the basic design of the inner pyramid as laid down by mathematicians, astronomers, and engineers had to be followed. There was no need to stroke the Pharaoh's ego on this world.

Hesire took a sip from a stone mug, a concoction steeped in herbs and spices, to help ward off the chill of the desert night. He had been up since before sunrise, but the intake was due to arrive in only a few days. Everything had to be perfect for the glory of Osiris.

It was ironic that the wealth of the Pharaohs created the pyramids, this place, so that they could travel to the underworld, the colony of Duat. But no Pharaoh had ever made it through to the promised land. The original designers had believed that the only way to traverse to Duat was to die inside the pyramid, but no priest had ever been brave enough to suggest a Pharaoh should kill himself to get here. In fact, Hesire's grin spread even wider, as soon as the priests realised one had to be alive in the pyramids before a copy of that person could be transmitted, they designed the mummification process to ensure that the Pharaohs would be dead long before they arrived.

Hesire felt a low rumble in his stomach, then his whole body vibrated with the surrounding floor. His bones tingled first, then his whole body was humming from the sensation. The marble felt like it was moving underneath his feet and he thought he heard a melody buried in the thumps and moans. He whipped around and stared at the jewels lighting up the bronze boxes from the battery bank in an ancillary room.

Hesire looked desperately around the room; the papyrus was adamant on the matter. Ahmose, I had already died, but all the preparations would not be ready for days. He hadn't seen it, but the brotherhood was abuzz with what food or tools or building materials would arrive with this one.

Rumours circulated that there might not even be another pyramid built. He had heard that the small pyramid replica in the High Priest's office had been sending regular scrolls back and forth, negotiating what would be included.

Hesire hoped that they would have the foresight to send seeds rather than yet more jewels but, of course, the High Priest would have all this in hand. A blight had killed most of the crops off in the spring.

Hesire tried not to think about what would happen to his brother's farm if they didn't come through with what they needed. There had been protests in the southern precinct, and everyone was on edge about the food shortages. As he worried, the room began to shake and dust fell from above. He quickly sought refuge at the edge of the bronze circle for protection from the impending forces about to flood the chamber.

As the shaking grew worse, sparks flew in the outer ring, and electric lights burst into shards. He covered his head with his hood and cowered beside the circle, watching the centre. More sparks flew, each lighting up the room briefly, with another taking its place in increasing frequency.

He composed himself with an effort. This was the first time he had greeted anyone from Earth. Disrespect would not be tolerated. He hadn't expected to be given this privilege for years. This was an opportunity to stand out, maybe rise in the ranks if he played this right. He placed his arms forward in the bow, expected of his order.

A stray bolt whizzed past Hesire's ear to hit the sleeve of his arm. The material smouldered, and a flame ate eagerly at the linen. Holding back an oath, he smothered the flame with his other sleeve and sat back, taking deep breaths to calm himself.

Black smoke pervaded the air, radiating from the centre. This was different. Hesire coughed several times as smoke filled his lungs, making him breathless again. Then the acrid smell of burning flesh assaulted his nose, and he grimaced and brushed it before resuming and staying in position. His eyes streamed.

Suddenly, a form took shape in the middle of the room, filling the space with a monstrous presence. Hesire gasped; this was no funeral procession! He sat up to get a better look, forgoing propriety in his confusion.

There was no time to run.

Hesire was frozen in fear, unable to move as the creature growled and lunged at him. All thoughts ceased as terror gripped his mind.

2 Impending Storm

Lynsey strode down the busy London street. Her back ached from lugging her bag around, but she didn't care. She had to get home. She picked up the pace and twisted the heavy bag so that it fell across her stomach. No pickpockets were going to get into her stuff! The crowds parted before her like waves upon a boat's prow.

She felt the tension in her shoulder and twisted her handbag to relieve the pressure. She considered taking the e-reader, but that would have been far too sensible.

"I need a break from screens," she'd told her friend. "Isn't it nicer to hold actual pages in your hands?" Lynsey held up the book to her friends at dinner. "And," she'd announced a little too loud, "It's Charles Dickens!"

"So, you're flexing?"

"I wouldn't put it like that." Lynsey felt a little deflated. That article about eye strain seemed almost irrelevant now.

"Well," her friend grinned at her, "At least it wasn't War and Peace. Can you imagine a large print version of that?"

The hardback didn't seem such a good idea now. It was weighing her down. Still, she was thankful that she'd almost emptied the large bottle of water that lay beside it. Her neck ached where the strap pulled on her shoulder. The further she walked down the street, the larger the crowds grew, pressing around her. She pushed her way through the shoppers.

Oxford Street teemed with people. Five deep on her side of the road and it was no better on the other. Out of the corner of her eye, she saw a gaggle of pedestrian stepping on to the road to bypass the crowds as ever more were emptying from the shops or joining the crush from the underground. Horns honked in protest, but no one paid any attention. All around men, women, and children wove in and out, not looking at each other, all desperate to get to the latest bargain or to get home. Why hadn't she left earlier? Lynsey smiled to herself, as if Mary would have let her. "One for the road?" she'd said as Lynsey had tried to take her leave. Of course, to refuse would have been churlish, and then, of course, they had to have something to eat so they wouldn't get too drunk, and then another drink to wash it down. Lynsey's smile broadened; she had known exactly what would happen when she agreed to meet up for the day and she had needed it. A good laugh, great food, and booze to chase away the past twelve months.

At an intersection, the traffic lights turned green, and Lynsey stopped at the curb. She stepped from foot to foot, relishing the brief relief from pain for the seconds her feet were off the pavement. As the light turned red, stopping the London traffic, she moved off, striding with purpose once again in a straight line. People walking towards her always gave way for Lynsey. They would move. It was all about the posture. She looked them in the eye and didn't slow down. She moved down the street at twice the speed of everyone around her, instead of swerving in and out as the tourists were doing.

And yet, when Lynsey had gone two steps past the kerb, a woman appeared in front of her. Where had she come from? A brief flicker of annoyance swept over Lynsey's face. But she didn't have time to get out of the way, even if she'd wanted to. Their eyes met. Challenge accepted. The woman let out an abrupt oomph as she walked straight into the corner of the hardback book in Lynsey's bag.

Lynsey let a small smile escape as she watched the woman double over for a moment before righting herself as she carried on behind her. The woman really should have moved out of the way. Lynsey twisted back around and carried on.

***

Half an hour later, she arrived at Enfield Town. The quick journey was uneventful, and she spent the time thinking about what to pack to take back to university. There was only one term left, so she wouldn't need much. Maybe Gareth would give her a lift with her stuff. It was worth a try.

She'd almost forgotten about her feet as she stepped off the train on to the platform. The step was a little steeper than she was expecting and she landed hard on her ankle. She almost toppled, but another passenger grabbed her arm before she fell. His balding head bent to look closer at her for a moment and then nodded before he moved past her to get on the train. This wasn't her day.

Lynsey winced at every step. Every time her feet touched the ground, it was like walking on broken glass. There was no way she could walk the rest of the way home, so she dug into her pockets and pulled out her phone. She swiped on the screen until she found the bus timetable. There was a bus scheduled in ten minutes. She might just catch it if she hurried as much as she was able, she thought, wincing with pain.

Lynsey gritted her teeth and hurried out of the station, limping like a demented frog. Tears rolled down her cheeks as she hobbled through the pain. Her foot was throbbing. The nearest stop was close, but she had missed the bus far too many times before because the buses were early. She didn't want to wait another forty-five minutes for another one. They never came every few minutes as promised.

Standing at the bus stop, Lynsey shivered as she calmed down, feeling a cool breeze that seemed to come from nowhere. She put her bag between her feet and leaned against the clear plastic wall. Goosebumps rose on her arms and legs, and she rubbed her upper arms with her hands. She pulled

9

her jumper from around her waist and shrugged herself into it, letting the baggy folds envelop her.

She loved it, but the white loose knit was an idiotic choice for this weather. Would it really have taken so long to pick up her coat? She berated herself? It was stupid to go out without it. But then the weather forecast had been for a hot day, and why shouldn't she take a risk now and again? She was fed-up of being the sensible one. A fresh gust of wind passed through her jumper like shards of shooting ice.

Bloody weathermen, did they ever get it right?

A woman's soft, husky voice came from her right, and Lynsey turned to look at her. She was slight and dressed in the standard black skirt and jacket uniform of the city. The reek of cigarette smoke emanating from her made Lynsey's nose twitch.

"I'm fine. I just wish the bus would get here already." She smiled, reaching down to rummage through the front pocket of her bag.

"I know! You don't get any buses for half an hour and then…" the red-haired woman said with a knowing smile as Lynsey glanced back at her.

"Then three come along at once," Lynsey finished with a tired smile as she came back up. "It is getting a bit nippy at the moment."

A harsh gust of wind assaulted them from the east. The three walls of the bus shelter swayed and rattled. There was no protection against it. Rain fell in sheets around them.

"Wow," the woman cried as she grabbed a shopping bag, her cigarette falling unnoticed to the floor. The plastic ballooned, nearly blowing her away. "You're right. It is picking up now. I don't know what's going on with the weather at the moment. It can't seem to make its mind up. I blame global warming."

Lynsey didn't reply as she eyed up the grey storm clouds blowing towards them. That was unusual. There had been blue skies for as far as she could see a moment ago. A clap of thunder made her jump, and as she watched, sparks of lightning jumped from one end of the cloud to the other as it drew closer.

"I think I'll just pop into the shops until the storm passes." The woman shouted into the wind as she walked away from Lynsey down the street. She held her shopping bag above her head to protect her from the rain, but it flapped tight in front of her face from the force of the wind that whipped around them both.

Lynsey stood undecided for a moment, eyeing the ominous clouds above them. She looked from side to side, first left, then right for cover. She picked up her bag from between her feet and hitched it over her shoulder. The rain had already soaked through her clothes, anyway. It had to be a once in a million chance she would be hit by lightning? She considered waiting. It would pass. Hadn't she read that lightning went to taller objects first? Wasn't that why church steeples were made? Then again, she looked up to see the bulk of the storm was nearly above her. Lightening crackled around her. If she rushed across, she might get rained on, but if she didn't move, maybe the lightning would go for a safer, taller target. Could she take that risk?

She craned her neck. There wasn't any protection in the park behind her. The bus stop wasn't safe either, so the only options were the shops in front where the woman had gone.

A black mass rose from the treeline, a moving wall of darkness advancing on her. There was no time to think. She turned and ran for her life, towards the safety of the shops. Through the trees lining the road, she spied a café. Perfect! Taking the decision, she altered course and rushed forward to the pedestrian crossing.

The wind gusted across the road and pushed against her as she ran across the street with cars just yards away.

She fought the wind, which picked up power as she crossed the road, threatening to push her back. Rain gushed down from the clouds as from a celestial tap. Lynsey couldn't see anything beyond a few feet, and she looked up to see clouds swirling in a maelstrom over her. She pushed forward, but now it seemed as if every step was taken in treacle; it felt like she wasn't moving at all, but just plodding along. She heard an almighty thunder clap and broke into a run towards the shop two yards away now. The muscles in her calves ached as she struggled against the wind, carrying leaves and debris of all shapes and sizes with it. Bending her head down, she forced her way through the rain. She was nearly there. She saw a blue flash and a sudden pain shot through her as a thousand bolts of electricity crashed along her body.

Today was not a good day to go to town.

3 Lost in Duat

Lynsey's head throbbed as she slowly awoke. Every second was like another hammer strike on an anvil. An ache spread from the base of her skull up to her temples, stabbing behind her eyes. She flinched, the pain almost causing her to cry out. Gingerly, she placed her palm on the cool marble floor and eased up onto one elbow, wincing at even that slight movement.

The inside of her head felt ready to burst. She squinted against the agony, breathing slowly. What in heaven's name had happened to make it feel as if her brain was trying to smash through her skull? She swallowed back the nausea rising in her throat. Best not to move too quickly until the worst had passed.

She placed her hand on the cool—was that marble?—floor. She reached out her hand a little further and felt an even cooler metallic surface. It curved, but she couldn't make out any detail.

It was then that she started sneezing uncontrollably. She reached into her jeans and pulled out an old tissue, cursing the fact she'd forgotten again to put a fresh pack in her handbag before she'd left the house. Each sneeze made her head feel like it would fall off until she squeezed her nose tight with thumb and forefinger and the attack subsided.

She pressed her temples with her hand and massaged where it hurt the most. What had happened?

Her vision, never the best, was very blurry, and she had to blink several times to make it clearer.

"What the…?"

She craned her neck, ignoring the spike of pain the motion caused. Towering walls surrounded her, smooth stone carved into geometric shapes. Strange symbols were etched into pillars stretching up to a high, triangular ceiling.

Confused, she breathed in dusty, stale air. This was no hospital room either. She sat up straighter, listening. No beeps of machines, no shuffle of nurses down halls. Just silence, heavy and disorienting. Where was she? Lynsey looked around again, more carefully. Some sort of temple? But nothing she recognised. Unease trickled down her spine. How had she got here? The last thing she recalled was the high street, waiting at the bus stop. But this was somewhere else entirely. Somewhere unfamiliar, and very, very wrong.

"Where am I?" she whispered hoarsely.

Lynsey's thoughts jumbled together as she tried to make sense of where she was. She rose unsteadily to her feet, swaying. The floor seemed to shift under her trainers. She blinked hard, willing her vision to focus. Nothing looked familiar. Where were the shopfronts, the bus stop? Panic fluttered in her chest as she turned in a circle, peering into the gloom. "Hello?" she croaked, her voice echoing back at her.

She staggered forward, throwing her hands out to steady herself against a cold stone pillar. Its surface was etched with strange symbols that made no sense. Lynsey shook her head to clear it, then winced at the stab of pain the motion caused. She drew a shaky breath, heart racing as she strained her ears for any sound besides her own rapid breaths. Only ominous silence answered.

What was this place? How had she got here? Lynsey bit her lip anxiously, fingers worrying at a fraying thread on her jumper sleeve. She had to get out. There had to be a way back home. Back to familiarity, normalcy. But she did not even know where 'here' was. Lost, confused, she sank down, back against the pillar. She dropped her head into her hands with a sob.

After a while, she rose, staggering on her feet, to trip on her bag strap. She righted herself and grabbed the offending strap with relief. At least she had some possessions. She grabbed her mobile phone as if it were a lifeline.

Every part of her ached and her face was hot and stuffed up with mucous. Her head pounded with renewed vigour as she tried to piece together what had happened. She closed her eyes for a moment, and when she opened them again, her vision had cleared a little in the gloom and she looked around, steadying herself against a cabinet and the pillar. The light was dim and cast eerie shadows on the walls and ceiling high above her head.

Where was the light coming from? Every detail was murky, but she could just make out windows high up near the top of the apex. Am I dead? She wondered, but the pain belied that course of thinking.

Lynsey pressed the button on her phone to activate the screen. Her eyes were automatically drawn to the top of the screen and she sighed. It was no use. No signal. She dropped the phone into her pocket, sighing again as let her hands fall to her sides. Well, that was no good. She could be anywhere.

Exhausted and confused, Lynsey slouched against the cabinet, allowing herself to wallow in confusion: What was she doing in this place? She stopped to think, but her mind felt foggy. How much time had she lost in this state? As she rested, her mind cleared. She couldn't stay there all day.

She walked towards a set of huge, ornate bronze doors situated at the opposite end of the hall. Her eyes were getting used to the dark, and she noticed that the floor beneath her changed from an ornate bronze circle surrounded by a wider circle of marble to black granite shot with dark green. She glanced back and saw the bronze circle where she had woken up had a motif similar to the door.

A hundred thoughts jostled for position in her mind. Where was she? What was this place? What if whoever had brought her here was behind that door? She twirled her hair between her fingers with unconscious unease as she crept forward. Her trainers squeaked on the floor, making her jump with the sound.

Suddenly, it was almost too funny, and she chuckled to herself until she burst out laughing at how absurd the situation was. This was so surreal. "A minute ago, I was standing at a bus stop in Enfield. Now I'm in some sort of pyramid? How does that even happen?" Come to think of it, her feet weren't hurting anymore. She experimentally twisted her foot in a small circle. No pain! Well, at least that was something.

She stopped in front of the doors and traced the outline of the relief etched into the bronze in the gloom with one finger. An Egyptian king stood with bandages around his leg, carrying some sort of whip. Lynsey racked her brain for the documentary she'd seen last week. That was it! Osiris. But he was a god, not a pharaoh.

As her fingers ran along the outline of the whip, dust caked them. Either they weren't into cleaning or this door hadn't been opened in a while. She pressed the door, and it creaked open to reveal a long corridor.

As she pondered the even gloomier corridor, every horror film she had ever seen ran rampant through her mind. She imagined flesh eating mummies shuffling towards her. The tiny hairs on the back of her head rose. She was about to scream when the passage lit up with a soft glow emanating from lights fashioned to look like torches hung high on the walls. Shelves lined the hallway — but no mummies. She breathed a sigh of relief. If she ever got out of this, she was never watching a horror movie again.

Lynsey crept forward, her trainers squeaking on the dusty stone floor. She trailed her fingers along the wall, feeling for any gaps or hidden doors. The shelves looked empty, but she searched them anyway, hoping for some clue to this strange place.

Rounding a corner, she paused, squinting in the dim light. Something glinted at the end of the row. She hurried forward and crouched down, brushing away debris.

An ornate bracelet crafted from thick yellow gold sat propped against the small pile of dust. She picked it up and rubbed off some of the grime. It was beautiful. Lynsey held the delicate bracelet in her palm, testing its weight. It had to be gold. Its faint lustre called to her. She ran her finger along the two tiny symbols of a crook and flail on the outside face. That was the same symbol that had been on the floor and door. She wanted it. No one was around anyway - not for a long time, judging by the dust. On impulse, Lynsey slid the jewellery over her wrist and twisted her arm to admire it. It had been a long time since she had worn anything so sparkly and beautiful. The jewellery didn't quite fit her, and she struggled with the effort to get it on.

The pain began as a sharp scratch and then turned into a burn that ran up and down her inner arm and into the tips of her fingers. She jerked her arm at the sharp pain and scrambled to pull the bracelet off. It moved an inch. She pushed gently. It wasn't hurting anymore, so she used the flat of her hand to get more of a purchase. She pushed with all her strength, but it still wouldn't come off. Lynsey clenched her fists in frustration, eyes stinging with tears.

She didn't want it there! She sobbed and was about to smash the metal against the floor when she stopped to look closer at where the bracelet had hurt her. Where she had first put the bracelet on her wrist, there were five bloody puncture wounds in a circle. Had it injected her with something?

As Lynsey pushed herself to her feet, a loud squeal filled Lynsey's hearing, bringing her to her knees again. She clasped her hands around her ears in pain, but the sound lowered in frequency until she could bring them down again, wiping tears from her eyes with her sleeve in the same movement. A smooth voice emanated from all around her.

"HELLO, LYNSEY."

"Who's there?" Lynsey asked, spinning around. The room was empty. She let her hands fall to her sides.

"I AM YOUR PERSONAL GUIDE TO DUAT. HOW MAY I BE OF HELP?"

The disembodied voice seemed to echo off the walls.

"Where are you?" Lynsey asked.

"I AM THE SUM OF BILLIONS OF PICONITES WHICH ARE COURSING THROUGH YOUR PHYSIOLOGY AS WE SPEAK. MY MISTAKE. WE ARE NOW IN CONTROL. I AM IN YOUR BODY, LYNSEY."

The voice paused for a moment to let that sink in. While Lynsey wasn't familiar with the word 'piconites', she understood that the world she knew was being altered on a deep level, which triggered her automatic response to panic. She started to hyperventilate, but her anxiety was held back by the sense that there were no bad intentions behind this change. Still her voice squeaked as she focussed on one word.

"Control?" Panic thundered inside Lynsey's thoughts as she picked up on the one word that stood out. "You have control over my body?"

"INDEED. HOW ARE WE TO REPAIR YOUR BODY OR ADVISE IF WE CANNOT CONTROL?" the voice said calmly. "I BELIEVE WE SHOULD MOVE OUT OF THE RECEPTION HALL NOW. THERE APPEARS TO BE NO WELCOMING PARTY TO GREET YOU. THEY MUST HAVE FORGOTTEN YOUR ARRIVAL."

"Who must have forgotten? Do you know where we are?"

"OF COURSE. WE ARE IN DUAT. I WAS CREATED TO BE THE GUIDE FOR PRIESTS WHO ENTER THIS REALM. CLEARLY, THIS DID NOT HAPPEN, BUT I AM PROGRAMMED TO SERVE THE PERSON WHO WEARS THE BRACELET. THAT WOULD BE YOU."

Relieved to get an answer, Lynsey homed in on the place's name. "Where is Duat? Is it in Scotland? I haven't heard of it, but then my geography was never that good."

"DUAT IS THE WORLD RULED BY OSIRIS. THE SENIOR HIGH

PRIEST HAS NAMED HIMSELF OSIRIS AND RULER OF THIS LAND."

"Osiris? As in Ancient Egypt?"

There was a brief pause, and then the voice replied. "INDEED."

"You are telling me we are in Ancient Egypt?" Her voice was rising in pitch again.

"NO, I SAID WE ARE IN DUAT WHICH IS RULED BY OSIRIS."

This conversation was going nowhere. Lynsey tried a different tack. "How do I get out of here?"

"I THOUGHT YOU WOULD NEVER ASK." The voice was accompanied by overtones of warm orange and pinks swirling in her mind. The cadence soothed Lynsey's nerves.

"Are you calming me down?"

"OF COURSE, STRESS IS NOT A GOOD THING FOR YOUR HEALTH."

Strangely enough, Lynsey found she didn't mind. She followed its directions, passing through passage after passage with low ceilings. Featureless brick walls followed others until she reached an open archway filled with light. Lynsey shaded her eyes and blinked rapidly, but it took her about half a minute before her eyes adjusted to the harsh light: the heat hit her next. A suffocating wall of dry air enveloped her. She hastily retreated, taking her jumper off to tie it around her waist. Her long cotton shirt should protect her from the sun, she reasoned. She went outside again and slowly shapes formed in her vision. She gazed out into a desert. The landscape was barren, the only vegetation being a few small shrubs that sprouted from a crack in a rock a few yards away. When she looked behind her, she gasped. Five pyramids filled her vision, their fine edges sharp against the clear blue sky.

"IT TOOK FOUR ATTEMPTS TO COMPLETE THE PROCEDURE BEFORE THEY SENT ONLY THE CONTENTS OF THE PYRAMIDS NOT THE PYRAMIDS AS WELL." Came the voice from inside her head. "IN THE FOURTH ATTEMPT, THEY COULD CALIBRATE THE MEASUREMENTS SO THAT ALL INCOMING GOODS AND VISITORS WOULD BE SENT TO THE ONE PYRAMID. THE FIFTH PYRAMID WAS BUILT HERE."

Lynsey looked at the shimmering desert around her, feeling a little claustrophobic with just the voice for company. "Where is everyone?" she asked. "If the Ancient Egyptians could send people and goods to here, wherever here is, what happened to them?"

"MY PROGRAMMING IS SILENT ON THAT POINT. THE CULTURE WAS THRIVING WHEN I WAS CREATED. MY ASSIGNED HUMAN WOULD HAVE BEEN A HIGH PRIEST AND WOULD HAVE BEEN EXPECTING ME AND A NEW PYRAMID OF GOODS AND SLAVES, SO WE COULD LIVE TOGETHER." said the voice.

"They had slaves?" said Lynsey.

"OF COURSE, WHEN THE PRIESTS DESIGNED THIS NEW WORLD THEY NEEDED ENGINEERS FOR BUILDING, FARMERS FOR CROPS AND OF COURSE SLAVE LABOURERS TO BUILD. NO PRIEST COULD

BE EXPECTED TO DO THIS WORK THEMSELVES. THERE WERE SLAVES FROM ACROSS WHAT YOU CALL EUROPE, ASIA AND AFRICA."

"Hello!" Lynsey shouted, losing interest in what he was saying. There had to be someone around.

No reply.

"There is no one here." Her voice was small, like a child.

"IT WOULD APPEAR SO." came the reply.

"No shit, Sherlock." That voice was getting annoying. "Do you have a name?" asked Lynsey, realising that she didn't know what to call the thing.

"I CAN BE ANYTHING YOU WANT ME TO BE." came the reply.

Lynsey thought for a moment, looking at the desolate ground around her. The voice was soothing, but she couldn't tell if it was male or female. "Are you a man or women?" She laughed at the ridiculous question, knowing what he would say before he even said it. Why would it matter? It's not as if she was dating the voice in her head!

"I AM WHATEVER YOU WANT ME TO BE." It repeated.

"How about Pico? Because, you know, Piconites."

"THAT IS ACCEPTABLE TO ME."

She nodded and then felt silly. There was no one to see her here. Lynsey swallowed and realised her throat was getting dry. "I'm getting thirsty. Do you know where they might keep some food or drink?"

"INDEED, I HAVE FULL KNOWLEDGE OF WORKING PRACTICES, BUT GIVEN THE LACK OF PEOPLE, WE DO NOT KNOW HOW LONG THIS PLACE HAS BEEN UNINHABITED. ANY FOOD WILL HAVE GONE LONG AGO, BUT THE END PYRAMID WAS CONVERTED TO CATCH WATER. IF THERE HAS BEEN A RECENT RAINY SEASON, THEN THERE SHOULD BE WATER UNDERNEATH IT."

Lynsey balked. "What if there hasn't been? I will need to drink soon."

"THERE IS AN OASIS NEARBY, A FEW HOURS' WALK AWAY. WE CAN GATHER SOME PROVISIONS, STOCK UP ON WATER, AND THEN GO TO THIS OASIS. FROM YOUR MEMORIES, THERE HAVE BEEN NO PHARAOHS FOR HUNDREDS OF YEARS. THIS PLACE IS OBVIOUSLY ABANDONED."

"Yes, I think so too. What did you say about reading my memories?"

"I HAVE DOWNLOADED ALL YOUR MEMORIES TO MY DATA BANKS. IT IS PART OF MY PROGRAMMING, SO THAT I WON'T BREAK PROTOCOL. THERE WASN'T MUCH COMMUNICATION WITH EARTH, AND THESE THINGS CHANGE. IT WOULDN'T DO TO OFFEND NEW ARRIVALS UNTIL THEIR STATUS AND PURPOSE ARE KNOWN."

"I don't want you reading my memories," Lynsey said bluntly,

"UNFORTUNATELY, THAT CANNOT BE UNDONE NOW. I CAN DISCONTINUE ACCESS TO YOUR CURRENT THOUGHTS AND

ONLY LISTEN TO YOUR VOICE AND THOUGHTS DIRECTED AT ME? THIS CAN BE REVERSED AT ANY POINT."

"Look, I appreciate your help, but I don't want you in my mind. Can you get this bracelet off?"

"SORRY LYNSEY, I AM WORKING INDEPENDENTLY FROM THE BRACELET NOW. EVEN IF YOU REMOVED IT, I WOULD STILL BE HERE. I AM, IN CONJUNCTION WITH THAT BRACELET YOUR UNIVERSAL TRANSLATOR."

"I can't get rid of you?"

"IF I WERE TO LEAVE YOU, IT WOULD MEAN THAT I MUST DIE. THERE IS NO OTHER WAY FOR YOU TO BE FREE OF ME, AS I AM NOW BOUND TO YOU. WE ARE NOT IN YOUR WORLD. IT IS VERY DOUBTFUL FROM YOUR MEMORIES AND WHAT WE'VE SEEN THAT EVEN IF WE COULD GET BACK TO YOUR WORLD, I COULDN'T BE REMOVED WITHOUT KILLING ME. I MUST CONCLUDE TO STAY ALIVE WITH YOU IS THE BEST THING FOR ME."

"I thought you were my guide for my well-being."

"MY EXISTENCE IS BASED ON YOUR SURVIVAL. YOU CAN BE ASSURED THAT I WILL DO EVERYTHING WITHIN MY POWER TO ENSURE THAT YOU STAY ALIVE AND HEALTHY. YOUR MEMORIES AND ATTITUDES ARE VERY INTERESTING TO ME. SINCE I WAS PROGRAMMED BY YOUR MEMORIES AND ATTITUDES, I HAVE ADOPTED THEM AS MY OWN. YOU HAVE A PARTICULARLY STRONG WILL TO LIVE. DID YOU KNOW THAT?"

For the next few hours, Lynsey roamed around the pyramids looking for anything useful to keep her alive. Pico was strangely silent during this time, but he was probably analysing her memories, she thought bitterly. The rooms that branched off the corridor in the first pyramid were large, empty rooms. She tried to ask Pico what it was they were for, but she got no response. So, she shrugged and carried on looking for anything she could take with her.

The second pyramid was built of limestone, just like the ones from Ancient Egypt. This pyramid had fewer rooms with hieroglyphs and was smaller than the others. Lynsey shuddered as she imagined what poor people might have been buried here. The bones of ancient slaves or mummies? The dry air preserved anything well enough to keep its secrets. She didn't want to find out what secrets this pyramid kept. She took a step forward and forced herself to walk in.

It was cooler inside the corridor. Lynsey sighed. Why didn't they move to lush fields with a nice lake for water, she thought, probably because it would have been easier for them to go here? Why bother with something difficult when something was easier? She imagined that this was like where the real pyramids were, stifling heat and sand everywhere. Was that a coincidence, or did they mean to move here?

Relieved from the unbearable heat outside, she moved down the corridor. The same glowing lights illuminated the way. They must have upgraded it from the real pyramids, she joked to herself. But she had read about a hidden panel found in a pyramid, a panel filled with electrical wiring.

She passed a large empty room and noticed a small door that looked like it had been disguised as part of the wall in the past. Broken masonry lay strewn at its base. She pushed it open and saw a room full of well-preserved, tiny artefacts. Inside, she had a better view. Was that a cart? A small conveyance about the size of a wheelbarrow was nestled among similarly sized objects. Lynsey laughed at that. Everything was tiny. The Egyptians probably thought that they would be symbols and they would be grown to their needs in the afterlife. This world was a little more literal than that. You send toy tools, and they remain a toy tool. It was probably why they were still here. They thought they were useless.

The third pyramid was a storehouse of another sort. It held a few jugs and jars in rooms filled with otherwise empty shelves. Lynsey roamed the rooms, like a spirit in a deserted city. The hunt for food went on, but she only found some hard amber sludge at the bottom of a few jars. Forgoing a taste test, Lynsey picked up two smaller empty jugs and stowed them in her bag.

A different room in the same pyramid was an Aladdin's cave of precious items, filled with gold and jewels. The racks of trinkets stood to attention like soldiers, awaiting her command. Cabinets sparkled with jewels and the shelves were covered with gold. She ran her hands over the cool treasure, picking up a necklace here, a brooch there. As she worked, she daydreamed about all the beautiful things she could buy with the money. She sang to herself as she worked.

If she ever made her way back, she was going to be rich! Forget the lottery. There was enough money here that could finance a small country. All she had to do was to stuff her pockets with all these jewels - millions of pounds' worth! If only she could take everything! But it would be too difficult to carry.

She slowed down her humming and began picking up jewels worth millions of pounds one by one, letting them drop into her pockets in a carefully controlled manner. The jewellery felt heavy in her pockets and it glistened against her clothes, but they were still only a small part of this whole selection.

Hours later, Lynsey stepped out of the third pyramid and halted mid-step. at the sandscape. Two thick crescent moons hung low in the sky and above them a layer of cloud and trailing mist, stars so intense and beautiful they almost hurt her eyes. She could kid herself that she was on Earth before, but this broke down all her barriers. Lynsey stared in disbelief, pushing a stray lock of hair behind her ears. She felt a breeze against her cheek as she watched clouds forming overhead.

She was enveloped in a profound sense of wonder, her senses in awe of the scene unfolding above. The sand beneath her feet, the coolness of the breeze against her skin, the otherworldly hues that painted the sky—all combined to create an experience that left her speechless.

Lynsey stood inside the entrance to the pyramid and watched the storm approach. She swallowed convulsively and realised again she was thirsty. Pico had said the final pyramid held water, but then she remembered the bottle she'd bought in London. Some water remained in it, so she drained it before putting it back in her bag.

The hardback book she had forgotten was still inside, so she set it aside at the entrance behind her. If she wanted to survive, she had to make room for things that would keep her alive. A Tale of Two Cities, although long enough to keep her attention, wouldn't cut it in a life and death situation.

She needed more water for the desert, but it would have to wait until tomorrow. The sound of thunder grew louder, drowning out other sounds. The storm was coming closer.

Back in the second pyramid, she remembered seeing some strange platforms that were probably meant to be beds. They were slightly higher at one end than the other, but beggars couldn't be choosers. They may be uncomfortable, but they would have to do. Pico was still quiet, so it would be best if she stopped the night there and find the oasis in the early morning. Pico mentioned he would direct her and he probably would do that by navigating by the stars. It was too hot to go searching by day. That storm looked ominous for tonight.

She stumbled back into the bed pyramid, as she thought of it. Behind her, the stars were out in force, but dark clouds were quickly covering them under her watchful eye. Lynsey stood in the shadow of the second pyramid's entrance, contemplating the storm gathering, and wondered if she'd recognise any of the star formations. She didn't, but then she knew little about astronomy and hadn't seen stars as bright as these since working in the Planetarium. No light pollution here, she mused.

Stifling a yawn, she moved into the building and chose a bed. She settled onto it, her gaze fixed on the low ceiling, lost in thoughts of the uncertain path that lay ahead. The weariness in her body was palpable, her eyelids heavy as if weighted down by the weight of her worries. She lay staring at the low ceiling, wondering what she was going to do next. She tried to contact Pico again.

"Pico?"

"YES."

"Can I return to my world?"

"I DON'T KNOW LYNSEY. DOES IT MATTER? YOU ARE ALIVE, THERE SHOULD BE PEOPLE HERE SOMEWHERE. OSIRIS ORDERED THAT SETTLEMENTS BE CREATED THROUGHOUT THE LAND. SOME OF THEM MUST HAVE SURVIVED. YOU COULD MAKE A LIFE HERE. I KNOW YOU HATED YOUR LIFE ON EARTH. HERE YOU CAN MAKE A NEW LIFE. NO ONE KNOWS YOU. YOU CAN REINVENT YOURSELF. WHEREVER YOU GO, I CAN TRANSLATE FOR YOU. WITH A BIT OF EFFORT, YOU SHOULD BE ABLE TO FIT IN ANYWHERE HERE."

"We don't know what to expect," Lynsey said sleepily, punching her jumper under her head to make it comfier.

"YOU DIDN'T KNOW THAT ON EARTH," Pico reminded her. His thoughts were mellowing to soft purples in her mind. "IT'S TIME TO SLEEP NOW. TOMORROW IS ANOTHER DAY."

4 Locating the Oasis

Lynsey cracked open her eyes in the gloom and snapped them shut again. Lynsey's thoughts whirled. She blinked hard, struggling to grasp onto anything that made sense. The surrounding shadows shifted uneasily as she sought for answers.

Where was she? Her bed was hard, and the blinking green light of her retro alarm clock was missing. She yawned and stretched as the memories from yesterday flooded back. Oh, God. It had happened. Her eyes once again flew open to meet darkness. Considering the bed was presumably made of mud, it was comfortable. She reached out with her hand and grabbed her jumper under her head as she rose to sit up, wobbling as she remembered that her makeshift platform was on a slant. As she sat up, lights glowed dimly around her.

Everything that happened yesterday became clearer as she focussed on it: London, the pyramid - Pico. The shallow ceilings in the dim light felt as though they were closing in.

"HOLD YOUR BREATH LYNSEY YOU ARE HYPERVENTILATING," she heard his voice in her head again. "YOU WILL MAKE YOURSELF ILL," he added.

Last night's fear threatened to bubble up, but she forced it down with a deep breath of stale air. Anger flashed through her mind, but she did as he said, feeling herself calm down. She put her hands down on the edge of the bed beside her. Calmer, but weak. What was she going to do? She'd never been claustrophobic before. The air was dry, but cloying and filled with centuries of dust and sand. The air swirled around her with particles as she pulled her jumper off the bed, making her lungs tight. She needed to get out.

The way was simple. She navigated the passageways with ease until she felt a breeze, and then she was outside. Red and gold rays of the sunrise splashed across the stark, white sand dunes stretching from east to west as far as she could see.

"That's gorgeous!"

She felt relief and stretched a little further to ease the knots from sleeping on the unusual bed. She moved into some deep lunges until her muscles were more limber. Incredible—she hadn't experienced this level of well-being in ages. Correction, it was like the way she felt before falling sick.

"ARE YOU FEELING IMPROVED LYNSEY?"

"Much."

"ARE YOU READY TO EXPLORE?"

"Absolutely." Her smile grew as the exercise lightened her mood. "I'm starving, but I need a drink first."

While making her way to the fourth pyramid, she untied her jumper from around her waist. She remembered this was the one which Pico had suggested might contain water. Lynsey hummed as she walked. The sun warmed her back, and she had a plan.

When she saw the front of the pyramid, her mouth dropped in horror. While the other pyramids had escaped build-ups of sand, because of where the entrances were, in this pyramid. Oh, God. She couldn't see the doorway. It was covered in mounds of sand. How was she going to get in? She held back tears and fell to the ground at the sight.

Her stomach ached with hunger, and her mouth felt like she'd been sucking paper. What else was this place going to throw at her? Get a grip Lynsey, she thought to herself. You can do this. No one else will. There was no other way for it but to dig through the sand.

Lynsey rushed back to the toy room. There had to be a shovel or something to move all that sand, but there was nothing in the room she could use. Her eyes burned as tears welled at the futility of the search. She was going to die here! Then she saw it. Discarded, half-hidden by a statue, she saw a tiny shovel no bigger than her hand. She bent down to grab it and strode back to the water pyramid.

She worked for hours, using her small spade to scrape away at the sand, watching as the pile of sand grew larger by the second. It didn't help that the shovel wasn't sturdy enough and kept bending under the weight of the sand, or that the tool was minuscule. It was more like a garden trowel than a spade, but she carried on. Lynsey wiped the sweat from her neck as she surveyed the mounds of sand around her. She hoped that Pico's prediction about water being beneath the surface was right, or she would be there forever.

Feeling each step with her feet and hands, Lynsey descended the dark stairs after she'd cleared the entrance of sand. The further she went, the cooler it became, and her body shivered. She untied her jumper from around her waist and shrugged into it again. The curved stairway seemed endless, but the sound of lapping water told her she was near. How was that possible? Surely, it should be stagnant?

"THEY WERE PLANNING TO DIG DOWN TO SEE IF THERE WERE ANY AQUIFERS HERE, THEY MUST HAVE FOUND ONE." Came Pico's voice from all around her.

"Can you stop that?"

"STOP WHAT?"

"That! It is very confusing; can you sound like you are coming from one direction or something? And not behind either. That would creep me out."

Pico's voice resumed from her right-hand side.

"IS THAT BETTER? I HAVE DETACHED FROM YOUR AUDITORY NERVES ON YOUR LEFT SIDE."

"Better." she said.

As she moved even further down, lights turned on around her, illuminating the way. She heard something slithering in the dark further on, then a splash. Was that a snake? She shivered. This time not from the cold. There was no going back now. She needed some water and there was no one here to help her.

The cavern was vast. The same torches that had peppered the pyramids were here but in a smaller number, but they were secondary to the light shining from the wall, which had grown brighter with each step she took. Her fingers grazed along the stone, discovering a type of lichen growing. It was the light source Lynsey was looking for, she realised. The lichen reflected the glow and increased it exponentially. She took a jug from her bag and moved with caution to the water's edge. It rippled as it touched the stone. If there had been something there, it was gone now. She filled the jug to the brim and put it down with care next to the steps, taking out the second jug.

Lynsey touched the lip of the jug to the water, and the water erupted around her. A huge two-headed serpent rose from the water's depth. Its long neck towered above her and it glared at her, water flowing from its body. Its fangs glistened in the light.

She fell back on to the floor, still clutching the jug with her right hand. A gasp escaped her lips. The pitcher fell to the ground as her fingers spasmed, aching with pain, and she felt blood oozing from her torn skin. Her left hand smacked against the floor with a thud.

Never taking her eyes from the monster, her fingers squirmed around in the mud until they found a stone. She grabbed it to throw it at the creature. It struck the head. Her heart beat fast. She heard the creature shriek in pain, and its second head hissed in retaliation. It bore down to bite her, but she twisted at the last second to avoid its teeth. Something cracked, either its teeth or part of its skull. She didn't know which one.

Lynsey looked back, and it was lop-sided as one of its heads hung beside the other one, dragging it down by its dead weight. She felt around, hands grasping for something, anything, and found more stones. Never taking her eyes from it, she hurled each stone with all her strength.

Thunk… thunk…. She heard something crunch. A strange keening sound came from the snake before it turned away, slithering back to wherever it came from.

Lynsey breathed hard, adrenaline coursing through her. The first jug of water was still upright and full of water, so she lowered the second jug to fill it as she took out the bottle from her bag with her free hand. Her eyes darted about the cavern. Lynsey's breaths were rapid and loud to her ears, She couldn't believe the thing had gone so easily, were there anymore? When everything was full, she put the bottle back in the bag, grabbed the jugs and ran out of there as fast as she could.

The moment she got outside, she drank thirstily from her bottle. The water was cool but had a strange taste to it. Before she could spit it out, Pico's voice reassured her.

"IT'S OKAY LYNSEY. IT IS SAFE TO DRINK."

"How do you know?"

"I SCANNED A SAMPLE OF THE WATER USING YOUR BRACELET WHILE WE WERE DOWN BY THE AQUIFER. IT IS FINE."

She wasn't sure if she believed him, but drank fast to avoid tasting too much. When she was done, she poured some water into a bowl she'd brought out at the same time as the jugs and dunked her hands into it to splash her face. That felt so good!

Lynsey shook while putting down the jug. If she hadn't rolled when she did… if that rock hadn't been there.

"Pico! Why didn't you tell me about the snake!"

"I DIDN'T KNOW ABOUT IT, LYNSEY. A LOT HAS CHANGED OVER THE CENTURIES. THAT CREATURE MAY NOT HAVE BEEN DISCOVERED, OR IT MAY HAVE EVOLVED FROM ANOTHER ANIMAL THAT MY CREATORS DIDN'T THINK WAS WORTH ME KNOWING. IT IS IMPOSSIBLE TO SAY."

Lynsey's pulse was slowing, and with it, her anger seeped away. "Wait, the Egyptians didn't tell you everything they knew?"

"I CANNOT REVEAL WHAT THEY KEPT FROM ME. I CAN ONLY SHARE WHAT I KNOW.

That settled it. They had to find that oasis tonight. She would not stick around to be food for that snake when it recovered. Besides, her stomach was growling.

It was still hours before it would get dark. Lynsey trudged back to the sleeping pyramid and went for a nap. She flopped on the bed, instantly falling asleep.

Hours later, she woke up refreshed. Nothing like a detox and a life-or-death event to make you feel better, she thought as she readied herself to leave the pyramid for the last time.

Taking a last look at the pyramids behind her, Lynsey paused, and as an afterthought, headed back to the toy pyramid. She took a moment to get oriented, but she found what she wanted. The lightweight wagon would be far too small for a horse or ox, but it was the perfect size for her to carry water enough for a couple of days. She loaded the cart, putting in several jugs and some linen shot with gold thread. She also picked up a bow and arrow. It was half the size a man would need, but perhaps she could use it, and a dagger.

Lynsey grabbed some cloth and wrapped it around the cart's handles. She hoisted the makeshift straps over her shoulders and pulled the wagon outside. She darted back inside, snatched a couple of urns, and hurried to the water pyramid. If she moved quickly and quietly, she might get away with this. The snake would need more than a few hours to recover from their earlier encounter.

The cool stairway air kissed Lynsey's skin as she raced down the steps. She filled the first jug in seconds, eyes scanning the water for any sign of the serpent. Clutching the overflowing urn, she ascended and left it halfway up before descending for the second vessel.

The cavern was silent, but Lynsey's nerves were on high alert. As water gushed into the jug, a splash echoed through the cave. Lynsey froze, heart pounding. After a few tense heartbeats of stillness, she grabbed the jug and darted upstairs to retrieve the first one.

Lynsey was soaked with sweat by the time she reached outside. She was surprised she could carry such a heavy weight, and the thought of carrying that load across the desert made her want to cry.

"GET SOME SMALLER JUGS, LYNSEY. YOU CAN THROW THEM AWAY WHEN THEY GET EMPTY THEN."

Relief soaked into her weary muscles and joints. A sigh crossed her lips. Of course. Duh! Lynsey fetched some smaller jugs and placed them in the wagon, emptying the bigger vessels into them. It would be hard, but would get easier. She hoped.

This was it. She didn't know what she would find, but looking back at the pyramids behind her, she was glad to be moving on.

The trees she had spied on arrival were deceptively far away. As she trudged along in the ever-shifting sand, the sun bore down on her. Sweat poured off her face until she took one of the cloths taken from the pyramids and wrapped it around her head and shoulders. It was still too hot, but at least the cloth protected her skin.

Within an hour, the sun had dropped to the horizon. The sunset was just as beautiful as the day before, although muted compared to the sunrise. She would have loved to share it with someone. She had never felt so alone. Even those days she had lain in a hospital bed, and no one had found the time to visit. She knew it was because they were busy or they just couldn't. There was no one here to care if she lived or died, except maybe Pico, and he wasn't really alive no matter what he said.

The shadows lengthened against the sand, drawing her eyes up to the sky. She was surprised at how much light the stars gave off. The sky was filled with pinpoints of light, creating unfamiliar shapes. You could get lost in their beauty. She breathed out, tearing her gaze away. There would be plenty of time to star gaze. Now she needed to get to food, water and safety.

Every now and again, Pico would break in to her thoughts to tell her to go one way or the other, but he was quiet. Maybe he knew how much she resented his presence.

After a few hours, the ground under her feet felt different. The sand was packed together tighter, making the surface harder. She had to watch her footing over the occasional plant, and the cart jarred and bumped, making her shoulders ache as the strap pulled on them. How the vegetation survived in these conditions, she didn't know.

Lynsey was so tired. She needed to rest and get some protection from the constant breeze that was sweeping over the desert. Lynsey rummaged among the contents she'd pillaged from the pyramids and pulled out the linen. She weighted the end in the cart with the jugs and folded the cloth under her to make a small tent. It wasn't the best shelter she'd seen, but she was proud of it. She took some water and her tired body gave in to the demands of the long journey, and she fell into a deep sleep. As she dozed off, her thoughts swirled with images of the strange desert landscape and the pyramids she had left behind. Soon, her mind drifted into a restless dream that brought a new set of visions, both frightening and surreal.

She was trapped in a small featureless white room, no door, no windows, then she was running away from creatures, but she couldn't see them clearly. People turned towards her, but they had animal heads and human bodies.

Now, she was sprinting down the street that led to her parent's house. The monsters were gaining. Dark shadows slid relentlessly behind her. She sobbed as she searched for keys in her pockets, but she dropped them as soon as found them. Picking them up, she sobbed, and her hands shook as she put the key in the lock. The door opened, and she burst into the house, pulling the door so it slammed behind her. She panted with her eyes closed and opened them to greet her parents. They had jackal heads, their mouths gaped wide, as they leapt towards her. She screamed and found herself back in the water pyramid, but the water had all gone.

Lynsey woke up, sitting bolt upright. She reached for the jug she'd rested against the cart earlier. The precious liquid slid down her throat, cool as if from a fridge. She was never so grateful to take a drink as she was then. I should have started earlier in the day, she mused.

"IT WASN'T SAFE, IT WAS TOO HOT. IT IS BETTER TO TRAVEL AT NIGHT WHEN IT IS COOLER." Pico replied.

"Are you always going to do that?"

"DO WHAT?"

"Answer a question I haven't asked."

"YOUR SUPPOSITION WAS INCORRECT, I WAS MERELY CORRECTING IT."

"Where have you been?"

"THERE WAS SOMETHING DIFFERENT ABOUT YOUR PHYSIOLOGY. I THOUGHT IT HAD SOMETHING TO DO WITH THE THOUSANDS OF YEARS BETWEEN YOUR TIME AND WHEN I WAS CREATED, BUT THERE IS MORE TO IT THAN THAT. THIS JOURNEY HAS GIVEN ME TIME TO COLLECT DATA ABOUT HOW YOUR BODY DEALS WITH STRESS."

"and,"

"YOU ARE HEALING TOO QUICKLY WITHOUT MY HELP. YOU SHOULD HAVE BEEN SEVERELY BURNED, BUT YOU ARE NOT. LYNSEY, YOU HAVEN'T BEEN DRINKING ENOUGH, AND YOUR SLEEP HAS RESTORED YOUR ENERGY LEVELS. THESE ARE NOT NORMAL RESPONSES."

Intrigue flickered in Lynsey's eyes. "What are you saying?"

"IT IS STILL TOO EARLY TO SAY TOO MUCH BUT LET'S JUST SAY THAT THE MANNER OF YOUR TRANSFER HERE HAS GIVEN YOU

MIRACULOUS HEALING ABILITIES BEYOND WHAT I'VE SEEN BEFORE."

Lynsey yawned and stretched in the confined space.

"How long was I asleep?"

"TWO HOURS. IT IS TIME TO GET MOVING."

The next few hours went quicker. The sparse vegetation increased. More colourful plants appeared the further she went. Lynsey stopped. Before her eyes was a stunning fuchsia plant. Its wide, flat green leaves and long pink petals were arranged in a seductive clump. As she got closer, the petals opened to reveal large white seeds in a circle in the centre. She was about to get even closer when Pico shouted in Lynsey's mind. She jerked back.

"What was that about?" grumbled Lynsey. "I was only looking."

"PICK UP A STICK AND PROD THE FLOWER."

"Okay." A branch, a finger thickness wide and the length of her forearm, lay within reach. She picked it up and poked the centre of the plant. She had just the time to see a hole with teeth and the plant's petals clamped shut over the tip of the stick. They had looked fragile before, but now they had the strength of steel. She pulled at the branch to get it back, but the plant would not let go.

There was a grinding sound, and the plant spat out the branch. Lynsey hefted the branch up and examined it closer. The end was mangled.

"I'm definitely not in Kansas anymore."

"AH, A CULTURAL REFERENCE FROM YOUR 20TH CENTURY. VERY APT. YOU CAN HEAL FAST, BUT YOU NEED TO BE CAREFUL. THERE ARE STILL A LOT OF DANGEROUS CREATURES AND PLANTS OUT HERE."

Looking at the chewed branch end, Lynsey could only agree. Moving on, the plants were soon covered by a canopy of trees. She was struck by the view. This is amazing, she thought. This desert must be quite small.

Pico laughed, sending shards of colours shooting through Lynsey's mind. "WE'VE REACHED THE OASIS."

"Oh, yes." Heat rose on Lynsey's cheeks as she studied the grasses by her feet. The tips of her ears burned bright red at her blunder. But then she knew the creature inside her had access to everything stupid she'd ever done, anyway. It was going to take a long time to get over that. She cringed at what Pico had seen.

"I'm starving."

"I KNOW. YOUR BLOOD SUGARS ARE DANGEROUSLY LOW. THERE ARE SOME PLANTS I RECOGNISE A FEW FEET AWAY. IT'S THE FIRST I HAVE SEEN WHICH CAN BE EATEN RAW. YOU DO NOT WANT TO BUILD A FIRE HERE. WE HAVE BEEN DRAWN TO THE OASIS FOR A REASON BUT SO HAS EVERY ANIMAL THAT NEEDS WATER TO SURVIVE."

"What is it?"

"A BARYGSRE. IT WAS A DELICACY DURING MY TIME. IT

CONTAINS ALL THE ESSENTIAL NUTRIENTS YOU NEED TO KEEP GOING."

"What does it taste like?"

"THERE WAS QUITE A COMPLICATED COOKING PROCESS BUT IT CAN BE EATEN RAW. THERE ARE NO RECORDS AS TO ITS ACTUAL TASTE. MAYBE IT TASTES LIKE CHICKEN?"

"Is that a small joke?"

"YES, AND ONE WHICH YOU FOUND MILDLY AMUSING FROM YOUR BRAIN CHEMICALS."

"Mildly amusing, Pico, mildly."

Lynsey leaned closer to the plant and touched it gingerly. It didn't move. She grabbed the stem and pulled. A long cord of root came out of the ground with the plant.

"CUT IT CLOSE TO THE STEM. THESE PLANTS ARE RARE. YOU WANT TO GIVE IT A CHANCE TO GROW AGAIN."

"Right!" Lynsey grabbed a small jewelled knife with a bronze blade from the cart, which was probably meant to be a sword, and severed the stem. "Do I just eat the leaves, or the flower? Should I shove the lot in my mouth?"

"IT IS UP TO YOU. IT IS ALL EDIBLE."

Lynsey pulled one of its blue petals and gingerly placed it on her tongue and then spat it out.

"WHAT ARE YOU DOING!"

"It's disgusting!"

"THAT EXPLAINS THE DRAWN-OUT COOKING METHODS, BUT YOU STILL NEED TO EAT IT."

"Oh God, I don't know if I can do this."

"BECAUSE THE ALTERNATIVE OF KILLING US FROM HUNGER IS SO MUCH BETTER?"

"Just shut up, will you? I'll do it. I just need a moment!"

Lynsey grabbed a handful of the petals and crushed them in her hands and stuffed them in her mouth. She chewed voraciously; her whole body scrunched up as she made herself eat the disgusting leaves. Eventually, she gnawed at them enough that she could swallow. Tears were streaming down her cheeks when she finished, and she was exhausted. She felt alive, though.

"THAT WASN'T SO BAD WAS IT?"

"Not for you, maybe. Didn't you taste that?"

"WELL, I DISCONNECTED MYSELF FROM YOUR TASTE CENTRES FOR A MOMENT."

"Great, just great."

She sat on the grass, letting the hunger cramps subside. She leant back, her mind wandering, feeling at peace as she watched leaves from giant red-barked trees tickling nearby branches under the gentle breeze. They were as tall as any skyscraper in London.

After half an hour, Lynsey felt rested. She rolled to her feet and packed the cart again. She looked at the straps. They had dug into her shoulders on the way in. She pulled her shirt down over her shoulder to have a look, but the skin was clear and unbroken. In fact, she twisted her neck to get a closer look. There had been a mole there for as long as she could remember. It wasn't there anymore.

"SORRY, I REMOVED THAT, THERE WAS A SMALL CHANCE IT COULD HAVE BECOME CANCEROUS."

"Oh, okay." Lynsey's lips pressed into a tight line. What could she say to that? *Bring back my cancerous lump?* The words dried up in her mouth like parchment left in the desert sun.

Lynsey picked up the straps and positioned them over her shoulders again. She shook her head and pulled the cart. It was a lot easier going with the firmer ground.

"Didn't they bring seeds from Earth?"

"THEY DID, BUT MOST OF THEM DID NOT SURVIVE. THERE WAS QUITE A BIT OF TIME BETWEEN THE FIRST AND SECOND PYRAMIDS, AND THEY WOULD HAVE STARVED IF THEY HADN'T LEARNT ABOUT THE LOCAL PLANT LIFE."

"Interesting." she puffed. There appeared to be a break in the trees just ahead. She increased her speed, but then had to break. The cart hit the back of her legs.

The view was breath-taking. Pico had described it as an oasis, but it was nearer a lake. Lynsey scanned the expanse. The other side was too far away to see clearly. It had to be fed by underground springs because no rivers were visible.

The water was blue and clear, and there were some shapes almost obscured by plant life at the far side, which had to be animals.

"Why did you bring me here?"

"IT IS A FEW DAYS WALKING TO GET TO THE NEAREST KNOWN SETTLEMENT FROM HERE. YOU SHOULD STOCK UP ON FOOD AND WATER."

"I can't survive just on plants."

"YOU CAN, BUT AS I SAID BEFORE, THERE ARE ANIMALS HERE. THERE IS NO RUSH. LEARN HOW TO HUNT. WE DON'T KNOW WHAT KIND OF CIVILISATION THIS LAND HAS ANY MORE. YOU NEED TO BE PREPARED. YOUR LIFE OF STUDYING WON'T HELP HERE. REMEMBER I HAVE A VESTED INTEREST THAT WE BOTH SURVIVE."

"I have that bow and those arrows. But I can't hurt anything."

Reds and oranges swirled in Lynsey's mind. Was Pico getting annoyed? "HOW DID YOU THINK YOUR BURGERS AND ROAST CHICKEN GOT IN THE SHOPS? DID YOU THINK THEY GREW ON TREES?"

"Of course not, but killing is different."

"NO, IT ISN'T. A CREATURE IS DYING SO YOU CAN LIVE. RESPECT THE ANIMAL, RESPECT ITS DEATH BUT DON'T KID YOURSELF IT

IS ANY DIFFERENT. LOOK AROUND, THERE ARE NO SHOPS HERE."

Lynsey recoiled, the thought as sour as the memory of barygsre on her tongue. She wanted no part of this. Her head shook in refusal, blond waves dancing around her shoulders. She'd been on farms. She knew a cow led to beef in the refrigeration section in a shop, but to kill?

"WELL, WE CAN AT LEAST PRACTICE. DO YOU HAVE ANY OBJECTION TO HITTING TREES?"

"Of course not."

Lynsey reached behind her and picked up the bow and arrow from the cart. How hard could it be? She picked a tree a few feet away and pulled the string on the weapon. She pulled back, so her hand was next to her chin, and let the arrow fly. On the plus side, she hit a tree — on the minus. It was nowhere near the one where it was supposed to go. Disappointment dropped Lynsey's slender shoulders. This would not be as easy as she thought. Her brows drew together as she notched another missile.

"DON'T WORRY, IT WILL COME."

A peal of laughter sounded from behind her. Lynsey whirled to find a figure dressed in a long brown robe with her hands around her mouth. The woman was shaking with mirth.

Around her, more people appeared from the trees. A small boy picked up the arrow and brought it to the woman, who examined it with interest.

"Who are you?" asked Lynsey.

The woman who had laughed approached her and bowed.

"Greetings. My name is Illyara. We are the Bardoon. She bowed, twisting her arms, genuflecting towards the sky and behind her.

"Greetings." She echoed. "I am Lynsey Walker."

"Lynsey Walker, we would like to invite you to have supper with us."

Lynsey cocked her head to one side. Pico? Pico" Can you hear my thoughts? Should I trust them?"

"OF COURSE, WHAT HAVE YOU GOT TO LOSE? YOUR ARCHERY SKILLS WILL NOT NET YOU ANY FOOD TONIGHT, AND YOUR ENERGY LEVELS ARE FALLING AGAIN."

"I would be delighted, Illyara." Lynsey smiled back.

The woman nodded and indicated for Lynsey to follow. Lynsey took one more look at the sun setting over the oasis and followed the troop. They didn't walk far.

Lynsey trailed after them toward the lake until she spotted some brown tents surrounding a camp fire. They passed the tents to stand before an old lady and man, their faces creased like old leather from years of desert life.

"Greetings. We welcome you to our camp." They performed the same genuflection that Illyara had done, so Lynsey attempted the same. The man gasped as he saw her bracelet poking out from under her jumper sleeve. "Osiris," he breathed. The camp went silent as everyone turned to face Lynsey.

"This?" Lynsey pointed to her arm. "I can't get the bracelet off. I found it at the pyramids. I'm sorry if I offended you." She pulled the sleeve to conceal the bracelet. The elders' rigid posture melted like ice under sunlight. Their severe expressions softened, eyeing Lynsey with less hardness than before, but they still looked concerned.

"That is the mark of Osiris. The God of Death, and a symbol of the people before. You should not be wearing that."

"Believe me, I would get rid of it if I could. I tried to take it off, but it just won't budge."

"Please forgive us. We need to confer." The two beckoned Illyara, who smiled at Lynsey before moving past her. They walked into the nearest tent and Lynsey was left to standalone.

"I'm sorry?" She said to the camp, but people wandered away. Life began again, and she saw a woman stir pots and children were running around ignoring her.

"Do you know what is happening?" She asked Pico.

"I DO NOT, BUT I BELIEVE THESE PEOPLE MAY HAVE BEEN AFRAID OF WHO YOU CALLED THE EGYPTIANS. WHILE THE PRIESTS WERE HELD BACK BY THE PHARAOH'S POWER IN YOUR WORLD, IN THIS THERE WAS NO SUCH BALANCE. THEY WOULD NOT HAVE BEEN GENTLE WITH ENEMIES. THEY HELD ALL THE KNOWLEDGE, THE TECHNOLOGY, AND THEY WIELDED RELIGION LIKE A SWORD.

I SUSPECT THAT THEY ARE DESCENDED FROM THE ORIGINAL SLAVES. THEY MAY HAVE KEPT THEIR MEMORIES ALIVE WITH WHAT HAPPENED."

"What happened?"

Pico's voice grew quiet. "THEY WERE BUILDING A NEW WORLD, A NEW CIVILISATION. THEY HAD TO BE STRICT. IT WASN'T ALL ABOUT BUILDING POWER. MANY PEOPLE DIED WHO DIDN'T FOLLOW THE RULES. PEOPLE HAD TO CHANGE TO SURVIVE."

"I'm glad I didn't end up back there then!"

Just then, Illyara returned. "Lynsey Walker, you may stay with us. We may know someone who can help you in Ghinari. We will take you there, but you must hide your bracelet at all times. It is a sign of power that frightens us."

"Why are you helping me?"

"You are a stranger in need. We would help anyone in trouble." She reproved. "Your hunting skills would mean you would be dead without us in weeks. It would damage our Chi if we were to let that happen, and it was in our power to help you." She said.

Lynsey bowed. "Illyara, I hope we can be friends."

Illyara's eyes widened. "I hope so, traveller, but I fear your bracelet does not bode well."

5 A Scorpion's Kiss

Lynsey stirred awake to the sound of activity outside. The heavy thud of mallet on stake mingled with the scrape of guy ropes on sand as the camp was dismantled. Underneath it all simmered an acrid odour drifting into the tent. Her nose wrinkled. What on Earth were they burning? Then she grinned at the ridiculous thought. They weren't on Earth!

She blinked, letting her eyes adjust to the dim interior. The crimson cushions beside her still held the imprint of Illyara. Lynsey's friend hadn't been up long then. She stretched her limbs before pulling on her rumpled clothing, discarding the borrowed nightgown in a crimson pool on the pillows.

With care, she lifted the tent flap over her head and stepped outside. The camp swirled with motion, but nothing she hadn't seen on school trips. Except here, the campfire was a blazing pyre with a boy shovelling dung on to feed the flames. So that was the stink!

Large iron cauldrons bubbled above it, an older woman ladled out bowls of porridge to the snaking queue. Lynsey's stomach rumbled, enticing her to join the breakfast line behind the children and women. Clumps of men hung back, talking in low voices.

The smell of the mixture was earthy with a hint of unidentifiable spices which drew Lynsey from the threshold of the tent to the back of the line. As if from nowhere, she felt someone tap her shoulder from behind.

"Here, these are yours. You must carry them with you on our journey." Illyara held out a small bowl and cup.

"Thank you." It already held the steaming mixture from the pots and the cup was rim-high with a light-coloured tea. Both were without handles, and the clay was decorated with crude pictures of flowers. They were basic, but beautiful in their own way. Lynsey set the tea between her feet, then mimicked those around her by dipping her hand into the mixture in the bowl and bringing it to her mouth. The temperature was perfect, but best of all, it tasted great. "Much better than the porridge packets back home," she joked.

Illyara looked blank. Lynsey just smiled back. "It's delicious." Illyara nodded and turned to walk away. Lynsey almost groaned with pleasure at how sweet the tea was. A splash of milk would have elevated it to another level. She shouldn't be picky, she chided herself.

Suddenly, she remembered the cart that she had left behind at the Oasis. She looked for Illyara, but she was already at the far end of the camp. Lynsey rushed over.

"My things! I left them over by the water."

Illyara smiled, her face downcast. "Jov brought them back here last night. They are behind the tents. You should leave them. They are cursed."

"I can't do that. I might need to trade some of that stuff."

"Some people will buy those in the big cities and it is not my place to say anything, but I would strongly advise you to abandon them."

"If I carry them?"

"You would have to. No Bardoon would go near artefacts from that terrible place. You are lucky Jov brought them this far."

"I was going to offer you some jewellery for helping me out."

Illyara smiled at that. Stray curls in her hair fell forward, covering her hazel eyes as she bent her head. "No, Lynsey Walker. We would not take such things from that place or anything else for an act of kindness. You will learn our ways soon enough." She brushed her hair back into place as she re-joined the women, helping to bring down a tent. As more and more people finished their breakfasts, they helped the others to pack.

The tribe worked in perfect sync, a well-oiled machine dismantling the temporary village. Men rushed to take down tents, folds of fabric billowing down into their waiting arms. Women neatly rolled bedding and stacked embroidered cushions into chests, securing the latches. Children scampered about, gathering discarded items and bringing them to the communal piles.

Lynsey watched a nearby tent collapse as the supports were removed. Two women efficiently rolled the material, twisting the ends to secure it. A pair of youths carried poles over their shoulders, heading toward the stacked supplies. The oasis returned to its natural state with astonishing speed under the tribe's coordinated efforts. Lynsey moved to help but found herself more hindrance than help. Their patience thinly veiled frustration at having to explain the tasks. She stepped back, letting them continue their efficient rhythm unimpeded.

Lynsey packed up her own cart, hiding its contents with a white cloth. Illyara smiled with approval as she passed on her way with a pile of cushions in her arms.

"Why do they hate these things so much?" whispered Lynsey to Pico as the girl turned away.

"THE PRIESTS USED TO PUT CURSES ON THE PYRAMIDS TO STOP LOOTERS. WHO KNOWS? THEY MAY HAVE BEEN HEEDED IN THIS WORLD."

With the caravan packed away, Lynsey saw the tribe had about fifty people with a herd of what looked like camels with antlers. The camels stood side by side, making no sound except for the shuffling of feet on the hard packed ground. Their heads moved, looking this way and that, baring their teeth seemingly at random. The animals were piled high with possessions and those that weren't carried pregnant women and babies in embroidered seats swinging like hammocks off the camel's humps. As they moved out. Lynsey joined them in the back, trailing behind the children.

"I wonder how long it will take to get to the city." Lynsey said out loud.

"A full week," came a voice behind her. Illyara fell in step with Lynsey.

"How do you keep doing that?"

"You must learn to not walk like a pregnant camel with a limp. If you move like this." Illyara walked ahead apace and exaggerated her movements, her skirt swishing like a whisper against her legs. "You will not only be quieter, but you won't get tired. Move with the sand, not against it."

Lynsey attempted to mimic Illyara's graceful movements. She waddled ahead, feet sinking into the soft sand. Her hips swayed clumsily, skirts swishing against her legs instead of whispering like Illyara's. Lynsey's strides were too long, stumbling in the ever-shifting terrain. Sweat beaded on her forehead as she struggled to match her friend's effortless glide.

Ahead, Illyara floated atop the dunes, footsteps barely denting the sandy surface. Her skirts trailed behind, propelled by the subtle sway of her hips. Each step flowed into the next, movements fluid and economical. Lynsey's awkward shuffling only kicked up clouds of sand in comparison. She grimaced, knees and back already protesting.

She took a closer look and copied her again, but it was harder than it looked. Move your hips this way, your leg that. She was walking like a pregnant goat, never mind the camel, which had far more finesse and dignity in this place.

"It will take a week." Illyara reiterated, hiding a smile. "We must rest at midday during the hottest part of the day. Otherwise, we would lose some animals and our people would suffer unnecessarily."

"Are there more places for water on the way?" Asked Lynsey, grunting under the weight of the cart while copying Illyara's gait. The trees were getting scarcer here, and the sand was harder to walk on.

"Wait!" called Illyara to the front of the caravan and everyone halted. Illyara scurried to a tree which had fallen. She asked for a knife. A boy, probably only a couple of years younger than the girl, brought her a vicious looking curved blade, which she took before hacking at two large branches. There were murmurs of approval from the people watching.

Illyara, with the help of the boy, brought over two pieces of wood about the length of the cart. She placed one on each side of the small wagon and another boy held it up while she fixed it on the underside of the wheel. They did it to the other side.

"You've made a sledge!"

Illyara gave her now familiar smile. "Would you like to try it now?"

Lynsey pulled the straps over her head, so they lay over her shoulders and pulled. The cart glided over the sand easily. The relief! She grinned at the three who had helped her, and they bowed. The caravan set off again. This time Lynsey found it easy to keep up.

As the hours rolled by, Illyara opened up more and more to Lynsey's questions.

"Who were those people that you spoke with when we met?"

"Mother and father. They look after our tribe. I will replace them one day,"

Illyara turned away to look into the distance. "If I can find the right husband."

"Oh, will your husband be the leader, then?"

Illyara burst into a peal of laughter. "Oh no, but you cannot be a leader unless you are married. There needs to be a balance in all things. I must find a suitable mate, to have someone with another viewpoint but who would always be loyal to me." The swish of the girl's skirts was soothing in the momentary silence.

"What's a suitable mate?" asked Lynsey.

"One that will complement me. Someone that will give me another point of view but won't be confrontational. He will have the same status as me and… I want someone who won't annoy me."

Lynsey snorted. "I wasn't expecting you to say that!"

"I have years yet. There is no hurry. It took father thirty-six moons to find mother when he looked. He says love can come in surprising places."

"Is there anyone here you like?" Lynsey asked, looking at the men surrounding them. They were tall, lanky, with grizzled features from the sun. Every now and again, a man would lift his scarf from his head and mop the back of his neck with a cloth revealing close-cut hair. Everyone wore the same loose robes and had the same gentle eyes.

"Oh no, I couldn't marry anyone here. We're all family. We're going to the city to meet up with other families. Maybe there will be someone for me there."

"I hope so." Lynsey had only known the girl less than a day, but she hoped she would get what she wanted.

Just before midday, they broke camp to have their meal. After watching how the tents were taken down in the morning, Lynsey found she could help to erect the enormous tent where everyone gathered. Brightly coloured embroidered cushions were brought in and scattered on the floor for people to relax and chat in low voices.

As with breakfast, bowls were brought out, but this time they were placed down beside their feet. Young women with babies queued up at the far side and were served by the older women. As they were eating, children moved around the tent, filling bowls after gulping down their own. Illyara pulled Lynsey to sit beside her.

"I thought the men would eat first."

"Why? If those that take smaller amounts eat first, then the rest can be divided between the men with nought worrying that anyone will go hungry."

"What if you take more than you need?"

"Why would you do that?" Illyara turned to face her. "You only need enough to feel full. Is that what they do where you are from?"

"Some do, I suppose."

Illyara shook her head in despair at 'some' people.

"I heard that in the cities that people grow large doing that, but I have never seen them. There has never been a need to go inside the walls, but I may have the excuse to visit now." Her eyes sparkled at the thought.

"You want an adventure, don't you?" Lynsey made her voice low.

"I-I-I think so."

Lynsey turned to look at the pot. "That looks a lot like breakfast."

"Oh no. That was cornmeal porridge. This is cornmeal polenta."

There was a pause. "I can see why you might need to have an adventure."

Illyara gave off another peal of laughter.

A couple of hours later, when everyone was rested, they set off again. Lynsey pulled her wagon, and Illyara helped with the straggling children.

The sand dunes were enormous. They were miniature hills which had to be climbed one by one. At the apex of each one, Lynsey saw rolling curves of sand into the distance. She did not know how they knew what direction they were going in, but Pico informed her they were going east.

"How do you know?"

"MAGNETIC POLES," came the quieter than usual reply. Pico seemed distracted. Or he was giving her space. Who knew? Still, she appreciated the time alone with her thoughts. She enjoyed the company of Illyara and was fascinated with the nomadic life around her.

Every night was like the previous. She shared a tent with Illyara. The only difference was there was yoghurt with dinner. She loved sweet things, but these guys almost worshipped it. She was surprised they still had teeth.

The next few days followed the same pattern. They walked until lunchtime, slept for a couple of hours, then walked again until the darkness made it impossible.

"Lynsey!" Illyara's voice came from the tent's opening.

"What?" She rolled over and buried her head under the pillow. It couldn't be time to get up already.

"Lynsey, we have to pack up the camp. There is a storm coming."

That caught her attention. Not another one, she thought. She supposed storms would dog her for the rest of her life. Lynsey jumped up and shoved her feet into her boots, while throwing bedding into chests in the tent's corner.

Illyara worked beside her. "We are lucky that we camped in the open. Wear this." She offered her a dress from her casket.

Lynsey nodded and donned the garment over her nightdress, noticing that Illyara put hers on with practiced speed. With the dress on, all she saw of her friend were her eyes peeking through the voluminous brown material. They continued to pack away as the sound of the storm outside grew, blowing the tent flap open with a burst of sand.

Lynsey turned and tripped over the hem of her outfit and fell heavily against the sturdy chest she was packing. She pushed her arm out to save herself but knocked against the chest, scratching her arm as she fell. Winded, she rolled over and pulled herself up and paused.

At eye level, behind the box was a creature with a curved tail.

Lynsey froze, half kneeling on the floor. "Illyara?" She whispered.

"Are you alright?"

Illyara wouldn't be able to see the creature from where she was. "There is something here, Illyara."

Illyara moved to stand next to her, and she heard a gasp. "It is not moving. Did it touch you?"

"No. I don't think so. Is it poisonous?"

"Come back slowly. It is dead or playing dead. You must hope that it is playing dead."

Lynsey backed away into a crouch, but the scorpion wasn't moving. Illyara pulled Lynsey beside her and threw a cushion at the insect. It didn't move, but toppled over.

"It is dead. Are you sure that it did not touch you with its tail?"

"No, I would have noticed that. Its tail is huge."

Illyara let a deep breath out. "There should be no problems then. There could be many reasons the scorpion is dead. The one we would have had to worry about is if it stung you. The tip would have been ripped from its body, and it would have died. You would already be feeling its effects by now if you had been stung." She looked Lynsey up and down. "You seem alright. We have a more pressing matter." Illyara turned her attention back to the clothing as the entrance of the tent flapped open with another blast of sand. "The clothes will help protect you from the sandstorm. We must go into the storm tent until it passes." Lynsey nodded and followed her, carrying the last of the tent's contents out to waiting hands.

Sand whirled in the air as they moved outside. Men rushed up wearing the same robes, protecting their skin from the bite of the sand. They emptied the tent and pulled the tent poles down while Lynsey and Illyara helped to fold the tent material into a roll.

Their visibility grew worse, and Lynsey lost her sense of direction. The wind whipped past her, needles of sand driving into every part of her body. She worked through the pain, following Illyara's example until she tucked the end of the roll into itself.

The nearest man nodded his head with approval. He pointed to where she had to go, and she pulled Illyara in the direction he pointed. They saw nothing for a moment, but then dim shapes could be made out. The camels sat in a wide circle, their weight holding down the cloth of a tent. As she watched, people ducked under the cloth, through a gap between the camels.

The wind increased, and it was becoming difficult to see the light brown material against the terrain. Illyara and Lynsey struggled through the wind and sand. The white grains lashed Lynsey's hands with force as the storm's power raged. She gritted her teeth while she grasped the tent to lift it to go inside. She pushed Illyara in ahead of her and let the material drop behind her.

The sounds of the storm muted, replaced by the sounds of low conversation. It was warm in the tent, and Lynsey's nose wrinkled at the acerbic scent of so many people in proximity. A few lamps were lit, dotted around them. Men, women, and children sat cross-legged with bowls between them and a space in the middle. Inside, a young girl with an all-encompassing sapphire dress, similar in style to the one all the men and women wore, sat quietly. The circle of bowls had become an impromptu barrier and a focus for all eyes.

There was an air of anticipation. Lynsey turned to Illyara, but her new friend put her finger to the front of her face to tell her to be quiet.

Lynsey dropped into a crouch, crossing her legs underneath her as the others did. Behind her, the last member of the tribe entered, and the doorway was sealed. The atmosphere changed as the tribe relaxed. Voices fell away, and everyone turned to watch the woman in blue. The sound of the sand battering the surrounding tent filled the silence for a moment, then the girl in sapphire sang.

Nobody made a sound. Not even the babies with their mothers as they rocked them in the semi-darkness. With so many people in an enclosed space, the heat made Lynsey drowsy. The beautiful voice of the girl lowered, then swooped into new highs that tingled her nerves. Her voice was sweet, yet had mature depths. It conjured images of the desert in her mind until it stopped, leaving her wanting more. Then another tune started as glorious as the first.

A woman offered her a bowl filled with cubes dusted with sugar. Lynsey pulled off her veil and reached for a sweet. It was really warm now, and a few had already taken their outer dress off. The woman with the bowl smiled and tilted the bowl towards Lynsey. Illyara already had one from a different dish.

Lynsey picked it up and brought it to her lips and popped the cube into her mouth. There was nothing for a moment, just sugary goodness. Then Lynsey's eyes watered. She coughed as the sweet sugar dissolved, leaving a sour taste in her mouth. She choked back the noise at Illyara's glare and grabbed a flagon of water as it passed by. Gulping down the liquid, she refused the next sweet.

The singer began another song, and people dozed around her until Lynsey fell asleep as well.

Lynsey woke, clawing at the fabric covering her. Why did she have to wear it in this tent? It was too damned hot! She felt cool hands lift the dress off her, but it didn't help. She heard voices, but couldn't understand what they were saying. A louder voice kept talking to her, but it was no use. Why didn't they speak English? Her body ached. Then she was cold, then hot again. She had the thought that it was the worst case of the flu she'd ever had. Then she fell unconscious again.

When Lynsey woke up, she felt as weak as a kitten. A delicious breeze played across her features, which felt good. She was rocking, cocooned in a hammock. Through a gap in the material, she saw the tan fur of the camel. She pulled back the cloth and looked out. Illyara walked beside her with a concerned look.

"You are awake. We were worried."

"AS WAS I." Came a familiar voice only Lynsey could hear. This time

Lynsey didn't feel annoyed.

"What happened?" She croaked. Illyara handed her a leather flask of water.

"The scorpion did indeed sting you. We were not expecting you to survive, but I am glad you did. You must rest now."

"IF YOU HAD BEEN ANYONE ELSE YOU WOULDN'T HAVE. EVERY TIME A CELL DIED; ANOTHER WAS REPLICATED TO TAKE ITS PLACE. THE MANNER OF YOUR ARRIVAL IN THIS WORLD HAS CHANGED YOU. THE EGYPTIANS SENT PERFECT COPIES TO THIS WORLD THAT COULD GET ILL, AGE AND DIE. THIS ILLNESS HAS SHOWN THAT THE WAY YOU ARRIVED CREATED A COPY THAT CANNOT CHANGE. I DO BELIEVE YOU MAY NEVER AGE. YOU COULD BE IMMORTAL LYNSEY."

Lynsey blinked in surprise. "That's impossible," she thought back to Pico.

"THE LAST FEW DAYS HAVE PROVED OTHERWISE."

The next two days passed in a haze of weakness for Lynsey. She drifted in and out of feverish dreams in the gently swaying hammock. When awake, the world tilted and spun if she tried to lift her head. Her tongue felt swollen, lips parched and cracked.

On the second day, Lynsey managed with Illyara's help to sit up and sip some water. The liquid soothed her ragged throat. She tried to engage with the girl, ask what she'd missed, but exhaustion dragged her back into restless sleep.

On the third day Lynsey awoke feeling strong enough to stand. Her legs wobbled like a newborn foal's but held her weight. Other members of the tribe smiled in greeting, relief plain on their faces. Lynsey returned their smiles, heartened by their concern. There was still a long recovery ahead, but this first step buoyed her spirits.

While she had been unconscious, Illyara had tied the cart to the camel that carried her by the straps that she'd used to pull the cart, so that it trailed behind. Knowing how much the Bardoon hated the cart, Lynsey went to untie it, but Illyara touched her arm to stop her.

"It is alright Lynsey Walker. We performed a ceremony to purify the cart and contents. While we will do everything to minimise contact with it, it is fitting for the yelk to take its weight while you fully recover."

The days blurred into a monotonous procession of endless sand. Each morning Lynsey woke to the now familiar routine - porridge by the campfire, packing up tents, and setting off again. The landscape was an unchanging vista of rolling dunes. Her legs ached from trudging up the endless slopes, feet sinking into the shifting sand.

At midday they broke for a meal of polenta, the bland taste coating Lynsey's tongue. She missed the variety of flavours from home, the spices and textures. But she ate without complaint, refilling her waterskin for the afternoon trek.

When they stopped for the night, it was more porridge for dinner. The savoury scent no longer tempted her appetite after days of the same fare.

Lynsey wearily helped pitch tents, the work becoming routine. She fell asleep to the soft sounds of the desert night, only to wake and do it all again the next day.

It gave Lynsey time to think about what Pico had said. Immortality was impossible, but if you didn't age, then maybe you could be?

Lost in contemplation, Lynsey trudged along, oblivious to her surroundings. Her thoughts meandered, feet treading a mindless path through the sand. The endless dunes had long since faded into tedium, the landscape without variation.

The packed earth underfoot barely registered until the shifting sand gave way to solid ground. Lynsey blinked, drawn back from her reverie. Glancing up, she stumbled in surprise. Brick walls towered ahead, erupting from the desert floor like colossal ramparts. They extended to the horizon on either side, lofty as the pyramids had been.

This must be Ghinari. Eagerness quickened Lynsey's pulse, breaking the soul-numbing drudgery of travel. She hurried to catch up with Illyara, peppering her with excited questions. Was it Ghinari? What was behind those walls?

Illyara's eyes darted around as she spoke, her voice barely above a whisper. "Ghinari, the place of dreams they call it. You can buy anything or anyone here." She leaned in, brow creased with worry. "It is ruled by the Brotherhood of the Dragon and the King. Powerful, dangerous men."

Lynsey noted her friend's hands twisting the fabric of her skirt, posture tense. "You must be cautious with these people." Illyara's shoulders hunched, shrinking into herself. "It is why we never enter those walls."

"You said there was someone I should see?" Lynsey asked.

Illyara hesitated, weighing her words. "The High Priest may know of the bracelet. But I cannot enter his temple." She shuddered, arms wrapped tight across her chest. "He is the sworn enemy of my people." Her eyes held a shadowed fear that chilled Lynsey's bones. Lynsey shivered despite the afternoon heat.

"DO YOU STILL WANT TO GET RID OF ME?" Pico's voice interjected. "WITHOUT ME, YOU COULD NOT SPEAK TO OR UNDERSTAND THESE PEOPLE."

Lynsey thought back, "but this is my body. You are just a parasite."

"I MAY BE A SYMBIONT, BUT I'M NOT A PARASITE. WHAT I CAN DO FOR YOU BENEFITS YOU. I DON'T BENEFIT WITHOUT GIVING. I CAN HELP YOU SURVIVE HERE. THAT IS WHY I WAS CREATED. IT IS MY SOLE PURPOSE. I DON'T KNOW WHAT ELSE I CAN SAY TO CONVINCE YOU. YOU NEED ME IN THIS WORLD!"

"You were not created for me. Your creators didn't send me here. I'm here by accident. I don't owe you anything."

6 The Dragon Temple

It was mid-morning before Illyara and Lynsey approached the city gates. This was it! Butterflies fluttered in Lynsey's stomach. What was she going to find? The rest of the tribe had stayed behind. Illyara had explained that they would not go any closer than they needed.

Lynsey slid a sideways glance at Illyara as they approached the city gates. Her friend's eyes shone as bright as stars, flickering here and there, trying to take in everything at once. Illyara's toes curled and flexed inside her worn desert sandals, kicking up small puffs of dust as they walked. She rubbed her thumbs along the straps of her pack, back and forth, back and forth. Lynsey hid a smile, reading the signs. Illyara acted nonchalant, but it was clear as day she was champing at the bit to get inside the city walls and see the sights. Illyara played it cool, but her body language gave her away.

"Father spent fourteen moons in Merg when he was younger. He said it was scary, but whenever Mother left the tent, he mentioned it was exciting."

"What was he doing in there?"

Illyara smiled, and the lights in her eyes seemed to dance. "We have to spend some time away to see how other people live, so we know how good life is with the family. We always come back."

From the camp, the road had been barely a mud path, but the closer they got to the city gates, the more defined it became. Their desert shoes were still silent on the ground, but without the shifting sand, progress was easier and quicker. Whatever Illyara had said about her pregnant gait, it was soon obvious that the tribe's shoes had a lot to do with how easily they walked. Illyara found that hilarious, Lynsey thought sourly. It had taken her friend a couple of hours before she relented and gave her a spare pair of sandals.

Enormous wooden doors cast a long shadow on the dirt road in front of them. It was deceptive quite how big the gate was from a distance. The nearer they got, more and more travellers joined them. Each wore a style which gave away their profession or status. There were merchants in coloured cloaks, farmers in cheaper home-made clothes, and even a traveller troupe who breathed fire from a cart while a man shouted out what to expect later that night. The pungent flower smell that had accompanied them for hours in the desert was now being swamped by a sweeter fragrance from the troupe's carts.

"They are advertising the food they will sell with their performance," Illyara said, answering Lynsey's unspoken question. "We sometimes meet up in the desert, and they give us a free show for our hospitality and aid in getting to less travelled routes. Their popping corn is to die for!"

They fell in step behind the troupe and soon they were sandwiched between dozens of people, all showing signs of tiredness but smiling, happy to be reaching the ends of their journey. As they walked, Lynsey saw Illyara was nervous. Normally serene and prone to giggle, she jumped at the slightest sound, and her eyes darted everywhere.

In comparison, a burst of happiness effused Lynsey's soul. She was happier than she had been in all the time she had been in Duat. This was a city! She was used to city life. The quiet of the desert unnerved her. It couldn't be more different to her life in London.

As they passed under the cool shadow of the city walls and emerged into a grove of trees, Lynsey's senses came alive. The tart, tangy scent of lemons permeated the air, followed by the sweet perfume of oranges. Lynsey's mouth watered. She spied the round, textured skin of the fruits hanging ripe and heavy from the branches. The fruits looked so juicy and colourful compared to the sandy shades of the desert.

Up ahead, voices, shouts, laughter, and cries mingled with the clip-clop of hooves on stone streets. The buildings pressed close, their windows glowing warmly in the morning light. Lynsey thought of the winding alleys and spice vendors of Marrakesh she'd seen on the telly, the chaotic hustle and bustle of an Eastern bazaar. This was no sterile, concrete city, but a living, breathing organism pulsing with activity. Lynsey felt a thrill run through her. This was much more like home than that silent, empty desert.

Instead of pulling the small toy wagon into the city, before they left, Lynsey opted to put as many jewels as she could fit inside the bag she brought with her, as well as in some concealed pockets. Pickpockets were just as rife in this world as her own, so she carried her bag facing forward. The rucksack was the only thing that marked her as an alien.

Lynsey wore the dress gifted to her the day before by Illyara's parents. Similar to the outfit Illyara was wearing, rather than the drab brown outfits of the desert walk, she now wore a beautiful muted green dress. Illyara's was a delicate blue. The dresses were long, just scraping the ground. Narrow sleeves tapered to their forearms, then grew into huge cuffs, which dropped to their waist. The light cloth was cinched to their waists with a silver-coloured braid. They didn't have mirrors at the camp, but the admiring looks from the men told Lynsey that the dress suited her. Illyara had said the tribe made them to sell during festival season besides spices and other items they collected along the caravan route.

At the entrance, children rushed up to greet them, offering them fruit. Small hands tugged at their clothes. Illyara smiled but shook her head while taking Lynsey's arm and increasing her pace. They gave up and turned to the merchants behind them.

Lynsey walked with Illyara down street after street. They all looked similar - low one-storied houses crowded together, punctuated by larger wooden structures. After some time with no other travellers in sight, Illyara paused in the wide road. No one had passed them for a while, and it was eerily quiet after the crowds at the gates. Their only company was a stray dog snuffling in some bushes.

"We could ask someone for directions," Lynsey suggested.

Illyara's face paled, and she took a quick step back. "No! That would mark us as lost. Who knows where we could end up?" She spoke quickly, almost tripping over her words.

"This city is full of villains. It's too perilous to ask for aid."

Lynsey held her tongue, Illyara's jaw was set and Lynsey knew she couldn't change her mind. She decided not to push the issue, for now.

They walked on through the vacant streets in tense silence. Lynsey's steps grew heavier, kicking up dust in her irritation. Soon the alleys narrowed, crammed with market stalls and people. They had found a market. As they progressed, the market stalls became ever more tightly packed.

It stank.

Lynsey smiled as she felt Pico recoil in her mind at the offensive smells that seemed to ooze from everywhere. It was easy to see why.

Pig's heads hung from hooks on market stalls, flies buzzed around the nearly rotting meat, next to stalls selling cooked pies.

Birds squawked beside howling wolves, baring their teeth in too-small cages, creating narrowing corridors by the haphazard placement of stalls. The stall owners called out their wares, audible over the sound of their merchandise and crowds.

Lynsey's feet were sore, and it was getting hot. She wiped the sweat from her forehead with her sleeve. It may not be lady-like, but stuff it. It wasn't like Mum was here to tell her off. She was tired of avoiding dung on the ground, and she was hungry. They had brought no food or drink with them, which seemed strange considering how much water Illyara had made her drink during their journey.

Then again, Illyara had said it would take less than half a morning, and they would be back before they needed to buy anything from the city. Her friend was great, Lynsey thought, but not hot on planning. What she would give for a cold pint right now!

Illyara had that vacant expression again. She looked just as lost as she had when they had stopped in the empty street earlier. Lynsey grabbed her hand. "Have you got any money?"

"A little, why?"

"We need to stop for a moment and get a drink."

Her friend fumbled with the edge of her shawl. It had tangled with the cord belonging to a small drawstring purse which hung from her silver belt. "Here, this should be enough. Remember to get back change."

Lynsey took the coin. It was small, bronze, but then what did she know about metals?

"IT IS."

"Butt out Pico," she thought sharply in her mind, knowing he would pick it up. Pico went silent again, and Lynsey hid the coin in her palm before moving towards a vendor she'd seen with vats of amber liquid. A picture of an apple hung from a hook above the counter. The woman was short and rotund. Her long black hair was slicked back in a rainbow scarf, which looked out of place against the dark brown dress and creased leather apron.

"Two of those full, please." Lynsey pointed to a tankard.

The woman nodded and filled the vessels to the top, placing them on the counter without spilling a drop in front of Lynsey and held out her hand beside the drinks. Lynsey dropped the coin that Illyara had given her into her palm, and the woman brought the coin up to her mouth and bit it before slipping it into an apron in one quick movement.

Illyara opened her mouth to ask for change, but Lynsey kicked her in the shins. The front of the stall hid the action from the owner.

"We have been told to report to the Dragon Temple when we arrived here, but we appear to have taken a wrong turn."

The grizzled features of the woman showed slight interest, but she replied. "Take a left at the end of the market onto Butchers Walk, continue straight and take a right onto Temple Road."

"Thank you." Lynsey took the cider and drained the cup quickly, urging Illyara to do the same. Illyara looked at the tankard with distaste. The rim looked grimy, but she followed her friend's lead. They put the flagons back down at the same time and walked on in the direction the woman had pointed.

"You were lucky," Illyara said.

"Only if we weren't poisoned by those disgusting cups," Lynsey whispered back.

Illyara grinned, tipsy from the drink. "I do not think evil humours would have survived that much alcohol."

Lynsey and Illyara weaved through the crowded market, assaulted on all sides by the grating calls of hawkers and the noxious odours of animal pens. The thick, cloying scents of offal and manure mingled with wafts of frying meat and fragrant spices. Flies and gnats swarmed overhead, diving to sample the wares. Lynsey's nose wrinkled at the stench, her fingertips pressed to her nostrils in a futile attempt to block it out.

Leaving the market behind, their footfalls echoed down deserted streets, accompanied only by the occasional scuttle of a rat amongst the rubbish piles. Winding their way deeper into the city's heart, the buildings changed from cramped wooden shacks to proud structures of weathered stone.

They knew when they reached a grand stone building that towered above the others that it was the place they were looking for.

It was old, hundreds of years old. Built like a fairy-tale castle, it was constructed of sandstone with long thin unglazed windows on the top floor and wide windows glazed with a glass which gave off a blue sheen on the lower floors.

Lynsey looked at Illyara.

"This is it," Illyara confirmed.

"We just walk in?"

"No, bring out one of the necklaces you found in the cursed place. One of the smaller ones. It will make a good bribe for the doorkeeper that will get you inside."

Lynsey opened the front pocket of her bag and looked inside. If she gave away a whole necklace just at the door, she wouldn't have much left by the end of the day. The Bardoon people may not think the jewels carried much worth, but Lynsey suspected that the people of Ghinari would be more appreciative of the craftsmanship of Ancient Egypt. She reached down and picked up a small elephant figurine encrusted with sapphires. Lynsey almost hesitated to take it out, but if she ever wanted her body to be all hers again, she would have to part with it.

Lynsey steadied her nerves and rapped at the immense wooden door. There was no answer, but after a second, a little panel she hadn't noticed opened with a sharp bang.

"What do you want?"

"Hello, I would like an audience with the High Priest." Remembering what Illyara had told her to say. She heard muffled laughter and then silence. She knocked again.

"He is busy." The panel opened and shut so quickly she missed it. She rapped again. This time, she put her hand in where the panel shut. The door snapped against her hand. The pain was sharp, but she didn't let go. She made out an old face with a sour expression, looking out through the crack in the door.

"I have this elephant you might like?" She wiggled it in front of the panel. There was a pause as the man considered. Suddenly, she heard bolts open one by one from the bottom to the top and it cracked a little. Lynsey beckoned Illyara to join her, but her friend shook her head. Fair enough, there were some places even Illyara would not go.

Lynsey plucked up her courage, remembering that she was not alone, and stepped onto the threshold.

"The elephant?"

Lynsey's fingers closed around the bejewelled figurine as she handed it over, her eyes fixed ahead on the temple's imposing facade. She hesitated on the threshold, nerves twisting in her stomach. What would she find inside?

Illyara's warnings rang in her ears. She was so worried. Lynsey glanced back, but her friend remained rooted in place, refusing to accompany her inside.

Lynsey inhaled deeply, steadying herself. She had come this far. Squaring her shoulders, she stepped across the boundary from sunlight into shadow.

The heavy door swung shut behind her with an echoing thud, sealing her fate.

The man behind stayed silent for a moment, enjoying her reaction. This place could give any church or cathedral a run for its money.

The inside was incredible; the outside facade was almost drab in comparison.

Whoever had designed the interior was a master of light and dark. What had appeared to be a stingy use of windows on the outside created a pattern inside that made the building look spacious and grand but also cosy with the use of alcoves.

The entry hall was vast. Columns reached to the ceiling, breaking up the otherwise empty square space in the centre. Great golden paintings were revealed by the light from the windows. From the floor to the ceilings, the pictures dominated the room, vying for attention from each other.

As she looked closer, she realised they were telling a story. Before her, she saw an image of a dragon breathing fire in a desert landscape. The painting to the right showed men in burnished red armour like she'd never seen before, leaving a city.

As she turned her head, she admired the optical illusion. The edges of the alcoves were painted, as were the spaces inside them, so whichever direction you looked you could see the complete picture. Lynsey craned her neck behind her. The illustration above the door showed men travelling through the desert, and the last painting on her left showed the dragon doubled over with a spear poking out from his middle. Turning to the floor, she saw it was tiled with large terracotta slabs with a walkway showed by lighter, gold tiles which pointed towards the far wall.

"Follow the gold walkway to the Solar. He is working in there this morning." The old man went back to his post. So, a jewelled elephant only bought directions here. Maybe she had an over-inflated idea of its worth after all.

"BE CAREFUL LYNSEY. WE DON'T KNOW WHAT TO EXPECT. ILLYARA MUST BE AFRAID FOR A REASON."

"Oh, shut up. You just don't want me to get rid of you."

"YOU DO REALISE THAT EVEN IF YOU GET RID OF THE BRACELET, I WILL STILL BE HERE? IT WILL JUST MEAN THAT YOU WILL HAVE TO LEARN TO SPEAK THE LANGUAGES BY LEARNING THEM. ALTHOUGH I CAN'T SEE HOW THESE PEOPLE WOULD HAVE THE TECHNOLOGY TO GET RID OF ME ANYWAY, LOOKING AT WHAT WE'VE SEEN SINCE WE ARRIVED IN THIS CITY."

"You would say that, though, wouldn't you?"

In Lynsey's mind, Pico's thoughts swirled with deep purples and blacks, like dark storm clouds rolling in. Good! He was feeling as frustrated as she felt. Stick to the plan. Get rid of the bracelet, get rid of Pico and then get home. She felt her face screwing up in annoyance.

She followed the coloured tiles until she came to a door with a gold sun emblazoned on an indented panel. It had been concealed before from the main doorway by the columns. She was about to knock, but held her hand back before it hit the wood. Thinking that this would require another bribe, she was about to open her bag when the door opened in front of her.

A young man stood there. Covered head to toe in close-fitted black velvet, his athletic form filled the doorway. Dark brown curls shied just before hitting his eyes. His eyes, brown pools of melted chocolate, pierced through her as if her soul were bare.

"What do you want?"

Unnerved, Lynsey grabbed the end of her hair and twisted it between her fingers. She took refuge in extreme politeness. "I'm sorry to bother you, sir, but I'm here to see the High Priest." She could have kicked herself. She would get nowhere if she carried on like this!

He tapped his fingers against the door frame, glancing behind him, and seemed to come to a decision.

"He has finished his audiences for today. Come back tomorrow."

"Oh look, I know how this plays. I keep coming. I bribe the doorman until I have nothing left and I still don't get to see the priest. Am I right?"

The man's lips twitched for a second. His expression lent him a boyish charm, belying his height and deep voice, as he assessed her again.

"Indeed, it is highly unlikely that the High Priest will see a woman straight off the street. Why do you think he would deign to see such a person?"

"This!" Lynsey pulled back her sleeve and revealed the bracelet. He seemed unimpressed.

"That trinket? Why would he be interested in that?"

"I can't get it off!" Lynsey's voice squeaked in her frustration.

He took her arm and pulled down the sleeve. "There are better places to take that off. A priest from the Order of the Dragon is not one of them. Have you tried the Mages? A Healer or even a jeweller?"

Lynsey looked at him, "Well, no"

"Come, this is not the place. Have you anywhere to stay?"

"Not really. I came with the Bardoon, and I have a friend waiting outside."

"Great, if you have such baubles to bribe with, then I know of somewhere safe for you to stay. We need to go now. You will need to put your scarf back on, or you will get burnt," he said, stepping past her, shutting the door. He gestured for Lynsey to follow.

She hovered on the threshold, clutching her sleeve over the bracelet. Could she trust this stranger? His expression seemed earnest, but looks could deceive.

Sensing her hesitation, the man adopted a gentler tone. "Please, let me help you find somewhere safe to stay. The streets here can be dangerous for an unaccompanied woman."

He met her gaze, his dark eyes glinting with kindness. Lynsey felt her doubts ebb. With a nod, she fell into step beside him.

7 Revealing the Osiris Band

Arkan gazed out of the window, his poise deliberate. The High Priest was taking his time reading the scroll. Arkan consciously relaxed his shoulders and lounged against the stone windowsill, giving every impression to the man behind him he was in no hurry.

The street directly below was quiet, but it was to be expected during market day. He watched with interest as two women turned into the street wearing festival garb. He was careful not to show any outside sign of his attention. Had they made a wrong turn? There was something about their manner that showed them out of place.

A subdued cough behind him drew Arkan's attention away from the view. He wandered over to the wooden shelves closer to the High Priest's desk at the other end of the room. He nonchalantly picked up a hand carved statue of a dragon, turning it over in his hand with gentle movements, all the time noting the man's narrowed glances in his direction with an inward smile. Let the priest play these silly games. He had all the time in the world.

While he stood there, Arkan balanced on the balls of his feet, ready to move in an instant. He was aware of everything in the room, from the hidden daggers in the padded arms of the chair to the eyes looking through the walls, unaware that he was watching them as they observed him.

The priest was the perfect example of his order. Baserius' red robes were impeccably turned out, his hair shorn off except for a long braid of black hair entwined with the same colour-red material. His skin was paler than normal, showing the order's distaste of setting foot outside the temple unless they needed to.

His entire attitude was of entitlement; hundreds of years of deference to the order did not beget modesty or humility. The man was a leech. The priest's scarlet robes cascaded over the armrests of his high-backed chair, the rich fabric gathering in luxurious folds. His bejewelled fingers drummed an impatient rhythm on the polished kellian wood desk, the emerald ring on his forefinger winking in the sunlight streaming through the open window. As he waited for Arkan's response, his hooded gaze held a bored contempt, as though the assassin was an irksome insect. When he spoke, his cultured tones held a note of lofty privilege that brought an amused glint to Arkan's eyes. Though the priest considered himself above this meeting, Arkan knew the man's true nature - a greedy social climber who would do anything for favour with the king. Arkan buried his feelings. He was here to observe and play diplomat, not to start a diplomatic incident.

If Arkan wanted to, the High Priest would be dead before he even dropped the pen to get to his daggers. As for the wall watcher, that had to be Fenish Gerd. A capable guard, but he was no match for the King's Assassin. Arkan again hid his smile. It would do no good to let the High Priest know what he really thought of him. His smile slipped. Was he getting complacent? It had been too easy to get in unseen, and it was a trifle flamboyant to appear at the High Priest's door. The king would find it funny, and it added mystique to his reputation. He laughed at himself. It was good to reflect on such things. It kept him alive!

The High Priest looked up, placing the pen exactly perpendicular to the scroll. He tapped the desk as if lost in thought. Arkan waited patiently, his thoughts turning to planning the evening's entertainment in his mind. He could call on Darianna. She'd been giving him signals for the past six months. Delectable Darianna, the moniker, fitted her perfectly. How her husband left her alone for so long was beyond him. He had noticed her long conversations with the king, but then again, what woman would dare not reply to a king's conversation?

Still, brief jealousy shot through his mind. Arkan's jaw tightened imperceptibly as the image of the king and Darianna flashed through his mind, her melodic laugh as she placed a slender hand on the royal arm. The assassin swiftly buried the flare of envy that surged within him. Darianna was merely being polite, he reminded himself. Her coy glances and playful banter over the past months had been for him alone. His momentary doubts were foolishness. With an effortless smile, Arkan turned his focus back to the priest.

The tapping had stopped, and the signal drew Arkan soundlessly to stand directly in front of the desk. He smiled with disarming charm at the older man.

Summarising the scroll, Arkan's soft tones filled the room. "The king has requested that you join him for the banquet tomorrow night."

"I am not sure if I will come. I have some passing business to attend to with the merchant's guild."

Ah, that was it. The old crook had found out that Dearik Sequim was to be seated closer and, therefore, be honoured higher for the night.

"That is fortuitous. We also have Dearik attending. Unfortunately, you will be seated on the King's right while Dearik is on the left. We can move you if you require?" A look of sheer delight lit up the man's face. Arkan hid his distaste for the priest's machinations.

"No, no. That will be fine. I am sure I will have time to speak to Dearik during the evening's entertainment."

"I'm sure you will, Sir."

The High Priest waved his arm, and Arkan found himself summarily dismissed. He was still bristling with annoyance when he entered the waiting room, but he closed the door quietly behind him. By the time he twisted the handle on the second, he was in a better mood than when he had entered the temple.

Arkan opened the heavy wooden door quietly from habit. A young woman stood there with her hand raised as if she were about to knock. Behind her, he saw the doorkeeper hunched over as he concealed a small gold item in his pocket. Was that an elephant? What would a lowly second rank brother be doing with a precious object? He looked fully at the woman in front of him. She was half of the duo he'd seen from the window earlier.

"What do you want?"

"I'm sorry to bother you, but I'm here to see the High Priest."

Arkan looked at her closely. Her dress was the expected festival garb, but she held herself strangely. She stood straight as any woman of the nobility, but her shoulders were squared, almost as if she were a man. She wore a bag in front of her, straps from each side wrapping around her arms. He'd seen nothing like it. Where was the other one? He craned his neck, but she wasn't in the room.

His body tensed inwardly, as if it knew something he didn't. Her features were fair, unusually so. Underneath her scarf, he watched as a tendril of hair freed itself from its confines. She pulled the scarf from her head in annoyance, draping it over her bag in one movement. Her hair flowed down her back like a waterfall. He blinked; she had blond hair! And her face, it was as appealing as the Delectable Darianna. Who was she? What was she doing here?

Arkan glanced behind him to see if anyone else had seen, but the main door was still closed and the doorkeeper had gone back into his room. Arkan was intrigued. He needed to find out more.

"He has finished his audience for today. Come back tomorrow."

"Oh look, I know how this plays out. I keep coming, I bribe the doorman until I have nothing left and I still don't get to see the Priest. Am I right?"

Arkan let a small smile play around his lips. She was perceptive.

"Indeed, it is highly unlikely that the High Priest will see a woman straight off the street. Why do you think he would deign to see such a person?"

"This!" Lynsey pulled back her sleeve and revealed a bracelet. Arkan leaned forward slightly to get a clearer view. He contained his excitement. An Osiris band! He'd only see them in scrolls.

"That trinket? Why would he be interested in that?"

"I can't get it off!" The girl's voice squeaked higher in her frustration.

He took her arm and pulled down the sleeve.

"There are better places to take that off. A priest from the Order of the Dragon is not one of them. Have you tried the Mages? A Healer or even a jeweller!"

She looked at him ruefully. "Well, noâ€¦" Her voice trailed off.

"Come, this is not the place. Have you anywhere to stay?"

"Not really. I came with the Bardoon, and I have a friend waiting outside."

"Great, if you have such baubles to bribe with, then I know of somewhere safe for you to stay. We need to go now. You will need to put your scarf back on, or you will get burnt." He waited a moment for her to put it on. He was wrong earlier; her movements were graceful, but they were just different. She bundled her hair with ease to the top of her head, securing it with the scarf.

Picking up on her doubt, Arkan changed his tone to be more soothing. "Please, let me help you find somewhere safe to stay. The streets here can be dangerous for an unaccompanied woman."

She nodded.

They hastened to the entrance, gaining a confused look from the doorman. No doubt returning from hiding his treasure, Arkan thought. He made no mention, and they were let out without a word.

The street was hot compared to the temple, but Arkan was happy to be in the sun again. His black suit absorbed the heat, but it was lightweight and covered most of his body. The slight breeze ruffled his hair. The girl easily kept pace with him, even with her cumbersome skirts. She was strange, but she had good taste in clothes. The green matched her colouring perfectly.

As they negotiated the stone steps down to street level, he reflected on the morning's visit. That silly man believed he was getting preferential treatment when all the time he was being played. He was getting a message delivered by the King's Assassin and premier seating at a forthcoming banquet, but the king was getting a map of the temple, including the location of a basement entrance and number of guards. A success indeed.

Where was the girl's friend? He wasn't lying earlier. This wasn't the best place for unaccompanied women. Arkan frowned, stopping at the foot of the steps. He looked around. There were two women on the road this morning, but the street was deserted now. His brows furrowed deeper. Had she been caught by slavers? A lone Bardoon woman would be thought ready pickings without her tribe to protect her.

A footstep behind him made him whirl around. How had she done that? There was nowhere to hide here.

"Who is this?" the woman asked.

Before the girl beside him replied, Arkan shook off his surprise and stepped forward. "Arkan Blade ma'am. I've offered my services to help you find a place to stay and help with your problem."

"Has Lynsey Walker shown you the bracelet?"

"Indeed, she has. Miss,"

"Illyara."

"Miss Illyara, it is not advisable to show that piece of jewellery to a priest of the Dragon Brotherhood, never mind the High Priest. Now I suggest we move from this place before we draw much more attention to ourselves?"

He gave a whistle, and a coach pulled up before them silently. A lot of effort had been taken to make it quiet. The horses' shoes were muffled, the wheels covered. A necessary perk of his office. Not anything that could be used for work off the record. It was far too ostentatious for that, but when the king wanted his citizen to know he employed an assassin, then it was ideal. The black coach gleamed, its sumptuous interior was covered in blood red velvet. The horses, Ferestrian, with their coats brushed and their manes braided. It was quite a sight. He was gratified by the girls' faces.

"My Lord," Illyara exclaimed. "I'm sorry if I appeared rude."

"It's nothing. We must get going."

Arkan opened the doors for the girls and followed them in, shooting instructions to the driver as he entered. The coach set off immediately.

Through the black velvet curtains, Illyara and the other girl, Lynsey, were staring at the city. Illyara as befitting a Bardoon sat ill at ease, her hands fidgeting on her lap, but was respectful in her manner. Lynsey, however, seemed relaxed, almost casual. She had a far off look in her eyes.

"May I take another look at your bracelet, ma'am?" asked Arkan.

Lynsey pushed back her sleeve and proffered her arm to give him a closer look. It had to be an Osiris band. He held out his hand above hers and she nodded her head in permission and Arkan pulled gently, but it wouldn't budge.

"That won't do any good. I've already tried that."

"One must try. How did you get it? Have you noticed anything different?"

She hesitated for a moment, but then shook her head. Interesting â€¦ why the hesitation?

"Where are you from, Lynsey Walker?"

Again, she held a faraway look, but she answered. "From Earth. I'm not from here."

From the direction her eyes were pointing and her body language, she was speaking the truth. But Earth didn't exist. It was a legend, a story told to children to help them get to sleep. But then again, so was the Osiris band. He stared at the gleaming band on her wrist. Who was she? How did she get here and what did it mean?

8 Arkan's Aid

The carriage made its way with only the barest sound of a muted crunch on the long drive. The wheels almost glided over the gravel. All the effort had gone into making it quiet. For as far as Lynsey could work out, the suspension was almost non-existent. Her bones jarred with every bounce. She was thinking she'd gone several rounds with the world heavyweight champion when the carriage rolled to a stop.

Lynsey's body sagged against the padded velvet seat, her lungs expanding with the first calm breath she had taken since boarding the bone-rattling contraption that passed for transport in this city. Illyara stretched her back, grimacing as she did so.

As Lynsey peered between the heavy drapes, she saw an imposing detached town house. Unlike the wooden houses near the city gates, this house was made of sandstone, like the temple. It was as tall as any English stately home.

Lynsey pushed the carriage door open and saw a woman running out of the entrance to greet them. She wore a sheer satin dress which, while reaching the floor, the material was see-through, leaving little to the imagination. Lynsey averted her eyes to a particularly well-manicured hedge cut to look like a long-necked bird.

"Arkan." The woman breathed. Her front almost bursting out of her tight laces. Lynsey rolled her eyes.

"My lady." Arkan lifted the woman's hand to his lips while staring into her eyes. Well really, Lynsey thought. Get a room! Pico chuckled in her mind.

"Stop that! It's very distracting!" She hissed at him. Conscious of Illyara's curious expression, she subsided, faking a renewed interest in the bush.

"Who are these people, Arkan?" The woman's eyes were enormous and round as she looked from Lynsey to Illyara.

"I'm terribly sorry to impose on you, my dear Darianna, but I came across these strays on official business at the temple. They are strangers to this land, but they have money. I couldn't very well leave them to the mercy of the priests, could I?" They both chortled at some private joke. Lynsey pushed herself forward from the coach wall and stood straighter, grabbing Illyara's hand to reassure her.

"We can pay for lodging." She dropped her friend's hand and brought out a beautiful necklace from the store in her bag, offering it to Darianna.

The woman stared in wonder for a few seconds at the jewels before replying. "That looks like something the pyramids would have held."

"Exactly," Arkan said meaningfully.

Darianna's eyes looked on covetously at the offering, but shook her head with regret. "I can't accept it. That must be worth hundreds of thousands. For a few nights, board and lodging that is unreasonable and one cannot take from a traveller."

Arkan visibly relaxed. His smile widened into a broad grin, and he took Darianna by the arm to stand a few feet away. Lynsey strained but couldn't quite hear what they said, but the woman's soft giggling could only make her guess.

"WHY ARE YOU ANNOYED?" Pico asked. "YOUR HANDS ARE TREMBLING, AND YOUR HEART IS POUNDING. THERE IS NO REASON FOR THIS." Then his voice, a quiet, thoughtful sound in her mind, added, almost as an afterthought. "WOULD YOU LIKE TO HEAR WHAT THEY ARE SAYING?"

Lynsey thought for a moment. It was nice Pico was asking for a change. Did she really want to know what they were saying? It was probably private. They didn't look like they were talking about her. Still, she was curious.

"Picoâ€¦."

But before Pico could reply, the two turned to re-join them. She shrugged and placed the necklace back in the rucksack, zipping it closed with force. Illyara looked at her in surprise, then her lips twitched imperceptibly. She hid it behind her hands.

Just then, Arkan strode up. "Darianna will look after you for a few days. She says she has been a little bored lately and has been looking for a project. I will come by tomorrow to talk about some more of your problem. Don't show the bracelet to anyone, not even Darianna."

While Arkan drove away, Lynsey watched as Darianna waved incessantly with quick, fluttery hand movements at the carriage as it departed. It was a good thing there was a slight chill, since all that energy for a goodbye would keep Darianna warm.

Lynsey and Illyara followed Darianna to the entrance and stepped across the threshold into a lavish hall, their footfalls muffled by an intricate mosaic tile floor. A butler, who appeared as if from nowhere, closed the door behind them. A crystal chandelier dripped from the arched ceiling, scattering fractals of light. Display cases lined the hallway, filled with artefacts and oddities. Lynsey's gaze caught on an emerald sarcophagus no bigger than her hand. She craned her neck to take in a series of ancestral portraits, frowning down from gilded frames.

"This way," Darianna called over her shoulder, already ascending the grand staircase. Lynsey gripped the ornately carved banister, the wood smooth under her palm as she followed Darianna up past landings adorned with statuary and houseplants. Their climb ended on the third floor, where Darianna led them down a richly papered corridor.

"Are you two, you know, going out?" asked Lynsey.

"Going out?" Darianna echoed, turning to face her as they continued through the hallway.

"Yes, in a relationship?"

"Oh no, I am married." Darianna showed them two entwined bracelets. One gold, one silver. "Look, this is my second marriage. I have two." She pointed out a second set on her other arm.

"Oh, you don't have rings?"

"Why would I have a ring?" Darianna gave her a quizzical look. "Anyway," she led them up a grand staircase. " Arkan has asked me to introduce you to society as a distant relative." Darianna paused and turned around with a graceful twirl. "I find the whole thing rather exciting. It has been rather boring with Lord Trell away for so long."

The corridor branched off into two more, but Darianna continued on, her hands gesturing at rooms ahead. "I'm giving you the blue suit. The two bedrooms are connected, and you will have a room to receive visitors."

She opened a door. "Well, go in. It's yours for as long as you need it. We'll sell one of your heirlooms in the morning and go shopping. I do so love shopping." She patted her dark curls and stepped out, closing the door behind her. There was silence for a few moments.

"Illyara? Do you believe what just happened?"

Her friend stared at the room and then her friend for a moment. "No, but we can only see where it goes. What do we have to lose?"

The next morning Lynsey woke to the sound of a maid pulling curtains violently across rails. She never said a word but busied herself laying clothes on the foot of the bed and pouring fresh water into a bowl on an ornate, dark wooden cabinet. She left as quietly as she arrived.

"This is all very nineteenth century. They have toilets, but give you washbasins?" Lynsey mused.

"CAN WE TALK NOW?" Pico's voice interjected her thoughts.

"You know there is nothing you can say that will stop me from trying to get rid of you?"

"DO YOU KNOW THERE IS ACTUALLY NO WAY YOU CAN GET RID OF ME? LOOK ALL I WANT IS FOR US TO GET ON."

"The bracelet is uncomfortable; I just want it off."

"I UNDERSTAND. I FEEL IT TOO. THE BRACELET WAS DESIGNED TO HELP A PRIEST TO COMMUNICATE AS WELL AS A SYMBOL OF POWER. THEY WERE NOT REALLY THINKING ABOUT COMFORT. HOW DO YOU THINK YOU WOULD BE ABLE TO TALK TO ILLYARA, ARKAN OR EVEN DARIANNA WITHOUT ME? IT HAS SENSORS TO HELP DEFEND YOU FROM POISON, REMEMBER THE WATER? AND THE ONLY WAY TO GET IT OFF WOULD BE TO CHOP YOUR ARM OFF!"

Lynsey rubbed her hands over her face, staring up at the ceiling. She hadn't thought of it like that.

"Do I have to spend the rest of my life hiding the thing in long sleeves?"

Pico went quiet for a moment. "IN THE SAME WAY I CAN MAKE YOU UNDERSTAND DIFFERENT LANGUAGES AND THEY YOU, I CAN MAKE PEOPLE NOT 'SEE' THE BRACELET. WOULD THIS BE BETTER?"

"Yes!" She pushed herself upright, startling the maid as she walked out of the room. How does that work? She thought to Pico.

"IT IS DONE. TO UNDERSTAND PEOPLE, THE BRACELET PICKS UP THE ELECTRICAL SIGNALS FROM THEIR BRAINS, AND THEN I TRANSLATE THEM. THE BRACELET CAN ALSO TRANSMIT SIGNALS I SEND."

Just then, the door creaked open, and Illyara stepped in.

"Wow, you look gorgeous!" said Lynsey.

Illyara twirled in the doorway. "I could never wear such a dress like this at home." The dress was asymmetrical. One side was lower at the knee than the other. It was made from satin and hugged her curves. The sleeves cut off just above her elbows.

Lynsey dived to the bottom of the bed to see what dresses Darianna had given her. It was sheer black, crushed velvet with long sleeves which reached beyond her wrists. Even with the ruffles on the tips of his sleeves, it was not ostentatious. The wow factor was in the cut. She stepped out of bed; the nightdress Darianna had lent her trailing after her. Illyara let out a gasp of surprise.

"The braceletâ€¦ it's gone!"

"Huh?" Lynsey looked down, but the hated yellow band was there. "No, it's stillâ€¦ Oh. You really can't see it?"

Her friend shook her head.

"Thank you, Pico," Lynsey mentally called. She blinked, and it was gone. Yet she still felt it. "How are you doing that?"

"IT IS STILL THERE; I AM JUST ENSURING THAT YOU CANNOT SEE IT."

Lynsey touched the rich velvet fabric of the dress on the bed with her fingertips. "This one is lovely too."

"Try it on!" Illyara grabbed the dress and pressed it against Lynsey to test the fit.

"You are different when you are away from the tribe." Lynsey said, pulling the material over her head.

"No, I can just be more myself."

As the dress enveloped her, Darianna sashayed in.

"Oh well, you're dressed. I hope you like the dresses. They are a couple of seasons old, but I suspect you won't mind." Darianna giggled. "You'll have to put the jewellery you don't sell today in the bank. My husband should be back soon, and I'm not sure he'll be able to stand the temptation to take control of them."

Gooseflesh prickled up her arms, as a chill slithered down her spine. Lynsey rubbed her hands up and down her sleeves, but couldn't dispel the sudden cool dread permeating her bones. She was in an alien world. She did not know the rules. "How can he take control of my things?" Lynsey demanded.

"Oh, it's not malicious. Surely you realise you may own nothing. That belongs to the head of the household. As you're pretending to be relatives, that would make that be him. Better to squirrel it away for a rainy day. It is what I do. The men should never know all our secrets!"

Lynsey looked at Illyara, who shrugged. It made sense.

"But first we need to sell something small, so we can go shopping." Darianna led the way out of the room.

"Do you get the impression she enjoys shopping?" whispered Lynsey. Both Pico and Illyara agreed.

The carriage waiting downstairs was wildly different from Arkan's. It was a brash red with a gold insignia on the door.

Darianna saw them looking at the emblem and winked. "I'm a duchess, so technically I outrank hubby, which is why it's on the coach. He just hates it!"

The first stop was a shop in the centre of town. Windows filled the front of the building, and the proprietor was waiting at the door as soon as the carriage pulled up.

"Lady Kartridge. A pleasure, as always. I have had some exquisite earrings come in just the other morning that I think you will find enchanting."

"Really? I must have a look before we go. The young lady beside me with the simply horrid bag has something to show you." They both turned to Lynsey with eyebrows slightly elevated.

"Of course." Lynsey searched through the bag and found a small cat ornament. It was smaller than the elephant had been, but she was curious about how much she had wasted at the temple.

She brought it out and sat it on her palm. The shopkeeper gasped.

"It is lovely. Look at the workmanship! May I?"

Lynsey nodded.

He took it with care. Gingerly turning it over in his hands.

"It is made of obsidian." He took out a monocle and looked closer at the eyes and collar. His hands shook. "This is made with jade and diamonds!" He looked at Darianna, and she gave a warning glance.

"I can give you 60,000 for it." Darianna coughed, and he revised his offer. "The diamonds are particularly fine. I can offer you 125,000?"

Lynsey looked at Darianna, who nodded. "That would be lovely."

The next stop was the bank. An imposing building it stood straddling two streets. It was two stories high with windows that reminded Lynsey of eyes watching. They followed Darianna through revolving doors into a grand hallway lined with private booths. Each one was busy with a clerk and a patron. They must have been sound proofed because neither Lynsey nor Illyara could hear what was said as they passed.

Striding down the room, they stopped next to a desk that was higher than most. Darianna informed them they needed to see the head cashier. He looked disapprovingly at her companions, but agreed.

Five minutes passed while they observed the comings and goings of the bank staff and their patrons. There was a constant stream of people arriving and leaving. Eventually, a gentleman arrived. He dismissed the other as he directed them to follow him.

They shadowed the banker through a concealed door at the rear of the grand hall, leaving behind the hustle of patrons conducting their business. Her footsteps echoed down a sterile corridor devoid of adornment. The only light came from glowing sconces anchored at regimented intervals along the hallway. Lynsey focused on the tap of the banker's heels against the marble floors, amplifying in the empty passage. He led them to an unmarked door indistinguishable from the others lining the austere hall. With a swift twist of his wrist, the door swung inward to reveal a small private office with opulent furnishings.

"Lady Kartridge, it is a delight to see you so soon." The banker rounded his desk and, as he sat down, gestured for them to do the same.

"We would like to open an account for my cousins. They are slightly provincial, you know, but they have brought a substantial sum and jewellery with them to enjoy society. I'm sure you understand, it is not sensible to leave such sums around the house."

"Of course, Milady." He steepled his fingers on the desk.

He turned to Illyara. "What kind of items are we talking about?" he asked, looking over half-moon glasses at Illyara. She laughed and pointed at Lynsey.

"I have several pieces that I need to put away." She emptied the rucksack on the table.

There was silence for a moment. The banker pushed his glasses firmly up the bridge of his nose.

"Well, I didn't expect there to be that much. You must have millions there."

The clerk was suddenly galvanised into action. "Put those back in your bag and follow me."

They exited the room from a concealed door out the back and walked through another bare room devoid of colour and furniture. The space filled with the sound of their breathing and the echoes of their clicking heels on the marble floor. Lynsey couldn't see anyone, but she felt as though eyes were on her.

The next door was behind a metal gate, which the man opened with a heavy iron key ready in his hand before they had gone half-way through the room. The key slipped into the lock with a click, and they entered a hall with thousands of small vaults lining the walls. Up to the height of the clerk, they were larger, and the higher Lynsey's gaze rose, the smaller the vaults became.

Ladders spanned the height of the room along regular intersections with men and women opening and closing boxes. The clerk ignored the vaults and continued to the back of the room to press a button hidden in an intricate painted design on the wall. None of the clerks even blinked in their direction as a trapdoor opened and a set of stone steps were revealed. They followed the clerk down with the sound of the trapdoor closing behind them.

They descended several levels, spiralling down a narrow staircase. The stone wall and floor were illuminated by lights hung at regular intervals. Lynsey, Illyara, and Darianna followed the clerk in single file. She focused on the tap of their shoes and the banker's rhythmic breaths echoing off the close stone walls. After what seemed an eternity, they reached a landing.

Lynsey sagged against the wall, massaging a stitch in her side as the banker sorted through a formidable ring of keys. The jangling ceased when he found the one he sought. With a scrape of metal, he slid the iron key into the lock. Tumblers clicked, and the door yawned open.

"Can you give me a word that you will remember? You can write it on this piece of paper, and I will set the second vault door."

Lynsey nodded, taking the yellow parchment, noting a heavy metal door to their left. She put pen to paper, then paused, realising they probably had a different alphabet.

She looked up, her cheeks reddening. "I can't write."

The man looked surprised but replied. "Have you a good memory?"

Lynsey nodded, her cheeks reddening. What would the others think of her?

The man took the pencil back and quickly drew some symbols.

"Here, this is your password."

Lynsey looked in despair at the symbols. How was she going to remember those? Pico suddenly spoke in her mind.

"IT'S OKAY. I CAN REMEMBER THEM FOR YOU."

"Thank you." Pico was being really useful all of a sudden.

The man took back the paper and fiddled with the vault door. Lynsey lengthened her neck to look over his shoulder and then ducked to see a combination lock with symbols through his arms. Once the man had finished jiggling the pictures into the correct sequence, he scrambled them again and turned back to face the group. Slowly and with deliberation, he scrunched up the paper and put it in his mouth and chewed.

"Rice paper." Came the muffled reply to their stares.

He handed her a small key. The handle had a circle with three bars going through it. Then left them alone.

"THAT'S THE EGYPTIAN NUMBER FOR THREE," advised Pico.

Lynsey touched the first cog, and Pico threw up the first symbol in her mind. Twisting it into position, Pico gave her the next and another until all the pictures lined up as they were on the paper. The lock clicked, and the metal gave way easily, swinging open on large metal hinges. She threw the bag in the small room by its strap, but before she closed the door completely, she had a thought. She stepped inside and unzipped the bag and took out some paper money.

"Illyara, can you look after this for me?" Her friend nodded and placed the money in her purse. "I see I'm going to have to buy a purse on this shopping trip!" Lynsey thought longingly of her red leather purse, but the money wouldn't fit in it properly, and it was far too bulky to be concealed in the figure-hugging clothing everyone seemed to wear.

She pushed the door gently, and it slammed closed, making her jump. She looked around in apology and then scrambled the symbols in front of the vault. There, safe. Who would have thought she'd be rich by the age of nineteen?

They walked out of the room to find the clerk waiting patiently in the stairwell. Lynsey closed the vault door and locked it with the key. What am I going to do with this? She twirled the key in her hand. She didn't want to give it to Illyara. That wasn't fair. She wasn't her servant. Then she laughed. Lynsey stooped down and removed her shoe. She placed the key under the strip of cloth that served as a sole and put her shoe back on.

Darianna was already heading back up the stairs. "Great," she called down, "that's our business concluded here. Let's get shopping!"

9 Power of the Band

rkan stood before the king in his private chambers. The sound of courtiers in the outer audience room was barely audible, muffled by the heavy door. Large tapestries and sumptuous woollen rugs were liberally draped over the walls and floors, creating a luxury feeling that could only be dreamt of by his subjects. The heavy tapestries absorbed every whisper and footfall, cocooning the room's occupants in a blanket of secrecy.

"Did you find anything?" The King's voice was friendly, its low tones mellow, like dripping honey.

"I saw all the rooms on the upper floors. I have given instructions to the royal map maker, and a finished map should be available by the morning. He's been given gold as per your instructions, My Lord. He will not talk. I threatened to pay him a visit if he did." Arkan gave a grim smile before continuing. "The temple has more levels below. They're hiding something, but I couldn't get to the lower levels to find out what."

"What are they hiding?" The king rested his hands on the windowsill, looking out at the courtyard. Arkan stayed in the shadows behind him.

"A dragon?" Arkan suggested. Both laughed at the absurd notion.

"I don't know, my Lord. But there were around thirty guards placed strategically around the building to stop anyone from finding out." Arkan grew tired of talking to the back of the king's head. Something was up.

"I heard you came from there with more than just information?" The king's voice was still soft, but there was an edge creeping in that he hadn't heard before. There was more to the question than idle enquiry.

Arkan felt his body freeze in place. His fingers brushed against the deadly points nestled in his sleeves, ready to strike at the first sign of betrayal. He hid the movement with a slight cough. If the king had doubts about him, then he would not be the only trained fighter in the vicinity. Unconsciously, his eyes swarmed around the room for telltale signs of watchers. How had he found out? He frowned at the uncomfortable thought. The king must have spies in the priesthood as well. If he did, why did he send him to investigate? Why not just ask his informant? Was the king testing his loyalties? For the first time in years, Arkan felt nervousness creep up his spine. He should report the girl, but he wanted to find out more about Lynsey Walker before he told him everything. His mind was in a quandary.

Arkan's pulse quickened as he weighed his next words. The wrong choice could destroy Lynsey or even end his own life. Though sworn to serve the king, curiosity for the mysterious girl pricked at him like the tips of his concealed blades. He would smooth it over, he decided. He'd been in worse situations than this.

"There were some distant relatives of Darianna Kartridge trying to get an audience with the High Priest. I believe they thought there would be an actual dragon there." Arkan hated the lie, but the Osiris band was an unknown. Could the King be trusted with that much power?

"Ah, the Delectable Darianna. How is she?"

"Fine, my Lord. Bored as always while her husband is away." The King chuckled as he turned to face Arkan. The king's outfit was more subdued than normal. Burgundy velvet hugged the man's frame while the crisp white ruffles streamed like water from his wrists. He toyed with his cuffs, a clear sign that there was something on his mind.

"I hear the visitor is quite fetching. Will I see her in court?"

"If Darianna has anything to do with it, I would put money on it."

"You?" The King's left eyebrow rose in surprise. "I've never seen you gamble on anything in your life. But then our Darianna's passion for projects is a sure bet. Is there anything else you need to tell me?"

Arkan shook his head and moved towards the door. He stopped mid-way. "You'll have to place the High Priest on your right during the banquet." The king groaned but nodded. He waved his arm in dismissal.

Arkan slipped through the hidden door, leaving the king's paranoia behind. Only three people knew of the secret entrance. The King, Arkan, and the King's mistress. Even the queen didn't know its location, although she suspected its existence.

The sounds of sizzling pans and clattering ladles masked the scrape of stone as Arkan emerged from the passage. Sweaty cooks shouted orders over the din, oblivious to his presence. While hiding the exit, the heavy tapestry gave him the opportunity to choose the moment to appear unseen into the side corridor, where he could bide his time to walk out into the main passage.

The king was right. Now would be the time to break the power of the priests. They must know what they were up against. Possibly, the king's informant had a lowly status and limited access to the rest of the temple. That was it! Arkan let out a breath he didn't realise he was holding. The informant must be the doorkeeper or someone from the kitchens.

Thinking about the temple brought the girl back into his mind. Lynsey was impossible to forget for long. He'd hardly spent a minute not thinking of her since he met her. It was obvious why. She was manly in the way she moved. There was no finesse there, but she possessed a different sort of grace. Her beauty rivalled Darianna's, and her blonde hair was unusual, the stuff of legends. That reason alone would have the King interested. Everyone thought that blondes and other fair skinned folk had died out years ago â€" and to have an Osiris band!

Arkan swerved to avoid a beggar as he entered the main courtyard. He needed to go to the library.

"Arkan, long time no see," a warm voice greeted him. Arkan felt himself instantly relax at the sound of his old mentor's voice.

"Birolan, always a pleasure. How is Sir Sira?"

"He is fine. Sitting by the fire begging for a treat as usual, but he's on a diet. He is the size of a horse already! Try not to give him any treats this time."

Arkan smiled. "Old friend, you know that won't happen."

Sir Birolan laughed, "Aye, I do. How can I help you?"

"I'm looking for references to the Osiris band."

"Indeed? A strange topic for a King's assassin, but I won't ask why. You don't get to be this old by asking why."

"Come, Sir Birolan. You're not that old. You'll be the Librarian long after I've retired."

"That's true unless you have curbed your impulsiveness in the last ten years."

"I was a boy!"

Sir Birolan roared with laughter. "A boy could not have seduced and bedded the Chief Advisor's wife."

"I think you have it the wrong way round, old man."

"That's not what she said!" Birolan's eyes sparkled at the memory. Arkan shuffled his feet in unease. Dark memories of temporary banishment to his uncle's estates while the furore died down surfaced for a moment before he buried it. That had been humiliating. His family connections were the only thing that saved him then, and he didn't appreciate the reminder.

Birolan decided he'd had enough fun at Arkan's expense this time around and nodded. Birolan let the smile fade from his wrinkled face. "There should be some books in the mythology section which cover the Osiris band. Do you need help with finding it?" he said, a glint of curiosity lingering in his eyes.

"No, that's fine."

Birolan gratefully sank back into his leather chair, which was probably as old as he was. Arkan heard him chuckling as he walked away.

The scrolls were easy to find. The library was split into several sections. Mythology books sat in the back section, tucked beside romances and other fiction. It had always aggrieved him as a child that he had to visit the girly section just to read about the ancient gods, but later it made for a good excuse to meet ladies.

Two out of the twenty scrolls he pulled from the shelves stood out as holding useful information. One had a clear drawing of the band. The tiny insignia was drawn in minute detail, confirming that the girl's band was the same. It was a copy of an earlier work and the section following the drawing was missing. The other scroll contained details of what the band could do.

Interesting, the wearer of the band spoke any language like a native. It gave miraculous healing powers to the wearer, and the bearer was given with all the knowledge of the Gods. What drew Arkan's attention more than anything else was the next words in the text.

The band could also be used as a weapon.

10 Pico to the Rescue

Illyara twirled and admired her dress.

"That looks beautiful on you." Lynsey exclaimed.

She puffed out her cheeks, then let out her breath slowly. "You are spending too much money on me."

"It's not mine. Easy come, easy go." Lynsey picked up a glove from a pair from an adjacent counter. She drew the length of silk through her fingers and looked up at Illyara again.

"I found it all at the pyramids. I don't really have anything else which anyone would find useful in this world; I would be destitute here if it weren't for that stuff. Besides, we wouldn't even be here if it wasn't for you and your family. I would have died if your tribe hadn't discovered me. I owe you."

Across the room, she noticed Darianna trying on another hat. Lynsey grinned. That had to be the fifth creation that the shop girl had brought her. She watched as the woman twirled in front of the mirror. Twin spots of pink saturated Darianna's cheeks in the reflection. Catching sight of Lynsey looking at her, she halted mid-pose. Lynsey nodded at her, giving her two thumbs up. Darianna looked confused, but smiled back at her, taking it as a compliment. She called for the next hat.

"Are you still going to get rid of the bracelet?" Illyara asked, climbing into the dress she had arrived in.

"I'm not sure. It is heavier than it looks, which makes it uncomfortable, but I'm getting used to the feel." She looked down at her wrist. "But now that I can't see it, I almost forget I have it on."

"There must be a reason you can't take it off."

"Pico says we need it to understand each other."

"Who is Pico?"

"Pico...." Lynsey realised she hadn't mentioned him at all to anyone since she'd arrived. Pico became more alert, shooting blues and greens into her awareness. To her surprise, she suddenly felt protective towards him.

"CAREFUL LYNSEY."

Fear clouded her thoughts, filling her with disquiet. Pico's bright colours turned to murky browns and blacks, swirling slower than usual, reminding her of mud or thick dark chocolate in the recesses of her mind. Yet she could tell he was interested in how she would answer.

Should she confide in her? Illyara was her friend. The only person she trusted in this strange world. She didn't — couldn't — know the people here, what their agendas were, or how things worked. But, if she was going to tell someone, then Illyara was a good bet. She didn't even know Arkan. His face popped into her mind. Why was she thinking about him again?

"Pico," she started again, "he's a creature that was put in me by the bracelet. He's a voice inside my head."

"You hear voices?" Illyara's tone lowered in concern.

"He's not just a voice, he's real. He doesn't talk a lot, but says he can help me."

"At least he is not malevolent," replied Illyara after a moment. She knelt down beside her friend. "Is he how you made the bracelet disappear?"

"It hasn't gone away. Here, touch it." Lynsey pulled Illyara's hand and placed it on her arm where she could feel the band. "See? hard metal."

Illyara's eyes widened, and she snatched her hand back, rocking on the balls of her feet as she regained her composure. She reached out again and touched Lynsey's wrist.

"Oh, I understand. It's like when we hide. We are there, but you can't see us."

"Sort of." It was a strange metaphor, but she saw where Illyara was going with it.

Darianna's voice drifted towards them as she approached. "Have you found everything you need?" Her perfume reached them first. The heady floral scent made Lynsey's nose wrinkle. They exchanged warning looks before Darianna was hovering over them. "Then it is time to leave. There is a feast tonight we should be ready for."

The journey to Darianna's house was uneventful, but Lynsey would have given anything for a mini-fan, or even a paper fan, for that matter. Maybe she should invent one? She glanced at Darianna, sitting opposite her with disbelief. She looked as cool and collected as when she first stepped into the carriage. How did she do that? Lynsey wriggled as sweat dripped between her shoulder blades, making its way down her spine, tickling as it went, but she didn't want to lose face in front of the woman. She clenched her fingers; she would not scratch in front of Darianna.

The drawn-up blinds should have kept the carriage cooler but only kept the insects out. Strike that. An evil looking fly with spikes along his body landed on the slight ledge between the door and the blind covering the window. It seemed to glare at Lynsey from its perch. The spikes moved to an upright position. Was it poisonous? There wasn't a stinger, but perhaps she eyed the spikes. They had poison on them? A hand reached out and filled her vision, snapping the blind open and flicked the insect out of the window in the same movement.

"We don't want that little thing in here, do we?" Darianna observed as she closed the blind again. She wasn't wrong, Lynsey thought, shuddering.

Within minutes, they arrived back at the house. There were still several hours before they needed to leave to get to the banquet on time. However, as soon as they entered the hall, Darianna asked their forgiveness and left them to go to her rooms.

They trudged up the stairs, followed by two servants carrying their boxes.

The rest of their purchases would be delivered over the next few days. The boys placed the packages on a side table and bowed as they exited the room, closing the door behind them.

Illyara sat down first, picking up some sewing that she'd started earlier, while Lynsey paced the room, examining the flowery wallpaper. Illyara ignored her, delicately unpicking the hem to lengthen the dress. Lynsey threw up her hands and perched on the end of a plush green chair beside her friend. She fell back into it, hitting the cushions, and tapped her foot on the floor.

The stuffy air pressed down on Lynsey, making the floral wallpaper appear to creep closer with each breath. There was literally nothing to do, no television, no books, no phone or computer. What did the people here do?

"I'm bored, I need something to do!" she burst out, jumping up to pace the sitting room.

Illyara looked up at her with the end of the cotton in her mouth. She cut the length with her teeth and tied a small knot. "What do you want to do?"

"I heard Darianna talk to the shop attendant about a park about five minutes' walk south?"

"That sounds nice." Illyara put the garment down on a cushioned stool beside her. "Do you know how to get there?"

"I think so. She said it was left at the end of the driveway, and only a couple of right turns away. She mentioned there were some sort of rare flowers there that the shop girl might like. Mind you, all the plants here are exotic to me."

"Well, that does not sound like it might be too far away. It will do us good to get some sunshine and fresh air. We have been indoors far too much in the last couple of days."

They hurried out, grabbing cloaks hung on thin metal spikes near the side door as they exited. It was getting cooler outside, and the fur enveloped Lynsey like a hug. They would be warm enough for a short walk.

The further they walked from the mansion; the more relaxed Lynsey felt. Maybe city life wasn't as good as the desert after all. She felt as if she was trapped in some twisted nineteenth century society.

Darianna's words were harmless enough, yet something about the woman set Lynsey on edge. But what? She tried to think what it was about Darianna that creeped her out. The woman acted all vacuous when people were looking at her, but then sometimes there was a look that sent a chill down Lynsey's spine - when the woman thought no one was looking. The girly Darianna had to be an act.

Then again, if women weren't supposed to own anything, possibly that was the only way to survive here. Pretend you are dumb to get along. She shouldn't judge. She'd been here, what? Five minutes? She didn't know what life had been like for her. Could she live like that?

Illyara looked at her as if she expected an answer. What had she asked? Lynsey blinked. Oh yes, something about gardens where she came from.

They were chatting freely along a straight bit of road when Lynsey noticed

Illyara taking constant fleeting glances behind them. Then she heard it too. The soft pad of footsteps on the dry muddy track.

"There is someone behind us," said Illyara under her breath.

"I AGREE," Pico interjected. "HE HAS BEEN FOLLOWING US FOR SOME TIME, THERE MAY ALSO BE ANOTHER ONE ACROSS THE STREET."

Lynsey grew cold but refrained from looking back. This might not have been such a great idea. She should've told Darianna where they were going. Why did she even think it was safe to go for a walk on their own?

The grand houses lining the street implied wealth, but Lynsey doubted there was any law enforcement to keep them safe. She hadn't thought to ask. Everywhere has police. Right?

She increased her steps, pulling Illyara along beside her. Their shadows did the same, matching them step by step. The second right turning was coming up, and Lynsey swerved into it, hoping there would be someone in the park.

A dusty street lamp illuminated the dusk, and she saw two more men striding towards them, coming from a different direction. Lynsey panicked.

"I DON'T WANT TO PANIC YOU LYNSEY, BUT THIS COULD BE A TRAP."

"I don't need you to tell me that, Pico."

Lynsey shot a worried look at Illyara. Her friend's eyes widened in silent agreement. The women broke into a run, turning on to a path that branched off to avoid the men closing in. Their breaths came in gasps, and Lynsey's lungs screamed as she pumped her legs on the uneven ground. She twisted to check if Illyara was still behind her, but she was gone.

Lynsey shouted with heightened fear. She was alone. There was another shout as their pursuers realised one of their quarries had got away. Lynsey ran again, but she was running out of breath—and time.

Pico's voice thundered in her ear, making her grab it in pain. "STOP!" She came to a halt, gasping. The men were coming from all directions. Their dirty, stained clothing filled her with horror. What were they going to do?

Suddenly she was jerked backwards, but she was still standing. Lynsey saw a gap between the men and wanted to dive between them, but her body wouldn't respond. She could still feel her body, the ache in her legs, and the pain of breathing hard in her lungs, but she was now an observer. She had no control.

She pivoted on her heel with no warning and her arm deflected the arm of the first attacker to reach her. Her foot kicked out and hit his knee. He went down as if in slow motion. The second man to his right in her vision was looking at the first, and the look of surprise would have given her satisfaction if she knew what was happening.

Lynsey rushed forward at him. Her right hand grabbed his hair as she simultaneously kicked him in the back of the knee with her hooked leg. With a muffled grunt, the man went down hard, like a sack of potatoes.

Lynsey grimaced as her foot connected with the soft bulge between the third man's legs.

The fourth and fifth man hesitated, which gave her an opportunity to run.

She swerved past a man with a toothy grin, but yet another appeared from behind a tree to her right. She saw him swing a long branch towards her. Fascinated, she tilted her head and watched as the wood swooped towards her in slow motion. She heard Pico's voice saying sorry in the distance before she lost consciousness.

***

Lynsey woke to a headache that rivalled the pyramid PE.

"PE?" asked Pico.

"Post-Earth."

"OF COURSE. BEFORE YOU SAY ANYTHING, I CAN TELL YOU ARE NOT HAPPY. I WOULD LIKE TO REMIND YOU THAT IF I HADN'T DONE SOME EXTRA HEALING WHILE YOU WERE OUT, YOU WOULD BE A LOT WORSE OFF NOW."

"Thanks." she thought back. "Now, can you get me out of here?"

"I EXPLORED A LITTLE WHILE YOU WERE SLEEPING. THEY'VE GOT US IN A CELLAR. THERE ARE NO WINDOWS, AND THE DOOR IS LOCKED FROM THE OTHER SIDE."

Lynsey sat up, using a large wooden barrel to prop up her back. The cellar was filthy, but she was thankfully alone. The only light was from a bulb high in the ceiling. They write in hieroglyphics, but they have electricity? This world got stranger the more time she spent in it.

She thought about the men who caught her, and her head shot up.

"You took over my body!" She said aloud.

"I HAD TO."

"How did you even know how to do that? Those were martial arts moves!"

"I TOLD YOU WHEN WE FIRST MET THAT I HAVE FULL ACCESS TO YOUR MEMORIES. YOU TOOK A FEW JIU JITSU LESSONS WHILE YOU WERE AT UNIVERSITY BEFORE YOU GAVE UP AND YOU'VE SEEN DOZENS OF FILMS WITH IT IN SINCE THEN."

Lynsey's mind was racing. "Why didn't you help me hunt? Why did you make me do all that practicing if you can just take over and do it for me?"

"IT WOULDN'T HAVE BEEN ETHICAL. YOU WOULDN'T HAVE LIKED THAT ANYWAY. I HAD TO TAKE OVER WHEN THEY ATTACKED. THERE WAS NO WAY TO DIVINE THEIR INTENTIONS. THEY MIGHT HAVE KILLED US. I NEVER WANT TO TAKE OVER. THERE IS NO NEED TO. I'M JUST A PASSENGER WHO IS HAPPY TO RIDE SHOTGUN."

"I'm not happy…"

"I CAN TELL THAT."

"You can't just take over like that."

"IF YOU REMEMBER, I DON'T." Pico's mental voice was imbued with purples. He was annoyed.

Lynsey fumed. "I just want some kind of warning, okay?"

"TELL YOU WHAT, NEXT TIME OUR LIFE IS THREATENED, I'LL ASK YOUR PERMISSION AS THE SWORD IS SLICING OUR NECK IN TWO. YOU NEVER KNOW, YOU MIGHT GROW ANOTHER HEAD."

"Ha ha, Pico. Hilarious, if you could just let me know in the future. It's only polite. It is my body!"

Her vision saturated with colour, blinding her for a moment. She felt Pico pulsating in her mind. It was her body, her mind. He had no right!

"I could have got away before the fighting started." She continued. "There was a gap, I might have got through that. I might have got away."

"THERE WAS LESS THAN 1% CHANCE THAT YOU WOULD HAVE ESCAPED," replied Pico.

"You can't know that."

"I CAN. YOU WERE TIRED, UNFIT AND OUTNUMBERED. HOW MANY MEN WERE THERE LYNSEY? THERE WAS NOT ENOUGH DATA TO EVEN GUESS THE NUMBER INVOLVED. NEED I GO ON?"

God, she wanted to hit him. He was so smug, so right. An unexpected laugh burst from Lynsey's throat. Any blow she landed on Pico would only hurt herself, literally.

It was just hard. Pico wouldn't, couldn't go, but Lynsey was just expected to accept someone sharing her body? It was impossible. And now he'd actually taken over her body. Could she trust he wouldn't change his mind someday and just take over permanently?

"I WOULD NEVER DO THAT YOU KNOW." Pico's voice was quiet in her ear.

"How can I believe that?"

"YOU JUST HAVE TO TRUST ME! HAVE I DONE ANYTHING TO MAKE YOU BELIEVE I WOULD HARM YOU?"

"No-o-o." Lynsey picked at a stray length of cotton that worked its way free from the seam of her skirt. "That doesn't mean that you won't, though."

"GRANTED BUT WE ARE GOING TO BE TOGETHER FOR A VERY LONG TIME, POSSIBLY CENTURIES. TIME WILL SHOW YOU I MEAN NO HARM, THAT I CAN'T DO YOU ANY HARM. I AM PART OF YOU NOW. WHAT YOU DESIRE, I WANT. IT IS PART OF MY CORE PROGRAMMING. IT WOULD HAVE BEEN DIFFERENT CENTURIES AGO. I WOULD HAVE HAD TO SUPPORT THE AIMS OF THE EGYPTIANS. THEY ARE DUST NOW. MY ONLY LOYALTY IS TO YOU AND WILL ALWAYS BE TO YOU. DO YOU UNDERSTAND?

"I think so."

"YOU WILL LYNSEY, MY LIFE IS YOURS NOW AND ALWAYS WILL BE."

Sunlight streamed through the window, illuminating motes of dust dancing in the air. Arkan rested his feet on the sill, surveying the room. He shifted on the plush velvet seat; the cushions moulding to his body as he tried to get comfortable.

Arkan twiddled the point of his dagger against his finger, testing its sharpness. Blood trickled down the dagger's blade, pooling in the crevice by the hilt. Arkan's lips pressed together in a tight line as he watched the droplet swell, hang for a moment, then splatter on the tiles below.

The banquet was hours away still. No one would expect him to arrive early. He had time to kill. No one ever expects me to be punctual, Arkan thought grimly. More often than not, they'd prefer I wasn't there at all. An image of curious grey eyes framed by golden hair flashed through his mind. That damned girl was creeping into his thoughts again. Arkan shook his head in frustration. This obsession was getting ridiculous. He should think about the Osiris band, not some silly girl. That was actual power.

But he couldn't get her out of his head - the waterfall of golden hair over her shoulder, those stormy grey eyes at once curious and guarded. She had a spirit. He'd give her that. No one dared speak to him the way she did, as if they were equals. Impossible - she was a mere commoner, and he the king's personal assassin; she was a girl, and he was a man.

Not that marriage would ever be allowed, even if he wanted it. Which he didn't. Where had that even come from? Arkan shook the thought away impatiently. He needed to get a grip. Nothing serious could come of this fascination, of course. But perhaps some carefree fun.

Arkan jumped up from the chair. Time to check on the girl and her strange friend. Once he unlocked the Osiris band's secrets, it would be his. Lynsey claimed she didn't want it - so much the better. He could take the treasure and leave this life behind, live in luxury far away. And the sooner the girl was out of his thoughts for good, the better.

At the door, Arkan paused. Something else nagged at him, some uneasy hunch he couldn't shake. Even if no one else knew of the Osiris band, Lynsey's exotic looks alone would make her a coveted prize. She had more than one admirer in this city - himself included - he was forced to admit. The king's keen interest in the girl had set Arkan on edge. That disquiet clung to him as he set out onto the streets.

Chaos greeted Arkan on his arrival at Darianna's home. The butler rushed him inside without the usual courtesies and he was ushered in to see Darianna within seconds of his arrival.

"They've gone!" Darianna's shrill voice betrayed her panic.

"What happened?" Arkan demanded.

"We went shopping, then I went upstairs to dress for the banquet," Darianna rushed to explain. "Tar saw the girls sneak out a half hour after we returned." At Arkan's glance, the butler inclined his head in confirmation before slipping out.

"Why did you let them wander off alone?" Fear fuelled Arkan's rising temper. "I told you to watch her!" He threw his hands up in frustration. "You've got enough guards to secure a damned palace!"

"You didn't exactly tell me she was to be treated as a prisoner, my lord," came the prim reply.

Before Arkan could respond, a quiet knock sounded at the door.

Illyara hurried through as the butler opened the door, slightly breathless but otherwise composed.

"Lynsey's in danger. We only went to the park - it seemed safe here." She caught her breath. "Ruffians set upon us. I got away, but they've taken Lynsey."

Arkan closed the distance between them. "Gods be damned! What can you tell me about them?" he pressed urgently. "Any insignia? Their colours? How were they dressed?"

Illyara leaned away, eyes darting to the door. With a huff of impatience, she said, "There's no time for questions. We must hurry!" She met his eyes pleadingly. "I followed them to a house near the park, surrounded by guards. I can't get to her alone!"

Arkan had to admit, he was impressed by the girl's courage. Brave, if foolishly so. A direct attack would have meant her death, yet she had trailed the men to help her friend. Reckless, but brave.

"Come with me!" He ordered.

Arkan strode from the room, the others hurrying behind him. With a sharp whistle, his black stallion trotted up, whickering softly as it butted its head against his shoulder. He vaulted easily astride it, then pulled Illyara up to sit before him. She tensed as she settled against his chest. What did she think he would do to her? Arkan suppressed an exasperated sigh. You can take the girl out of the desert…

"We'll return shortly," he told Darianna over his shoulder. "Stay put. I'll bring the girl back safe."

He kicked the stirrups, and they cantered down the road to Illyara's directions. The path meandered. She must be pointing to how they had walked, but of course, she did not know the area like he did. He breathed out in frustration. This was slow! He breathed in and out and let the rhythm of the horse calm him. He would not panic. Lynsey's life was in danger. He ground his teeth in frustration, but he was grateful for the help she gave. When he sensed the girl becoming nervous, he slowed down.

"How far are we from the house where they have her?"

"Just around the corner," she replied.

"I need you to watch Shade for me. Don't let her wander." Of course, the mare wouldn't leave without his command, but Illyara didn't know that. One less thing to worry about.

Looking doubtful but grateful, Illyara slid from the saddle and took the reins. Arkan dismounted and vanished into the shadows.

Arkan slipped between the trees, jaw tightening as the action reminded him of his training in his youth. Until age eight, he'd apprenticed with the kingdom's finest knights and guards, marked as a future royal protector. But after his father's murder, his jaw convulsed at the memory as he crept through the trees, he had turned to the Assassin's Guild instead.

He'd proven himself quickly, becoming the Master Assassin's own protégé within two years. When Arkan stalked unseen, only those expecting him stood a chance - and many had died begging for their lives.

Arkan circled around the back of the building, noting that there were two men patrolling, counter to each other on the grounds of the small house. This was unusual. Why would someone who would live in such a mean house need so many guards? The annual cost of so many guards would exceed the house itself.

He shimmied up a drainpipe, pressing close to the wall when a guard passed underneath. Using his fingertips, he grabbed hold of a ledge, clawing his hand forward so the entire width fitted into his hands. He hung in space and listened hard. He heard voices, so he waited. His legs dangled freely, but he was in no hurry. He could easily hold this position for a half hour if need be.

Directly above him, he identified grating voices as two men. Eastern Islanders, if he was any judge. Interesting. He inched to the right and swayed from side to side until he had enough momentum to get to the next window with ease. He swung up, so he was standing on the sill. Balanced on the ledge, his soft-soled feet gripped tight as his ankle blade picked the lock.

And he was inside.

The spacious room held an imposing four-poster bed swathed in plush velvet hangings - which gave Arkan pause. He'd seen the like just this morning. Surely even the king wouldn't risk a powerful family's wrath by taking Darianna's guest? Unless he suspected Lynsey's claim of relation false. It would be simple to confirm Darianna had no blond kin. A golden-haired babe's birth would have sparked gossip across the land. None had been seen in a century. The king must have made inquiries. This revelation only deepened Arkan's unease over their earlier conversation. He froze, listening by the door.

Arkan wavered, arguments warring in his mind. If he acted with care, the king might not suspect his involvement. But if discovered, he'd be marked for death. Arkan had complained of his constrained life, even dreamed of escape... yet he had to admit, he enjoyed the thrill and challenge of the work. Did he truly want to give it all up and spend his life running? He had to ask himself, was Lynsey or even the Osiris band worth it?

The moment of indecision was just that. Arkan entered the room and opened the door a crack. When he was sure that no one was in the passageway, he crept downwards. He reasoned they would want no one to see her through a window, so the basement was the only option.

There were no more guards until he reached the stairs leading down to the last level. At the top of the cellar stairs stood a lone guard in plain clothes. But his bearing betrayed his soldier's background, while his slack vigilance marked him as merely a guard, not elite force. Arkan hazarded a guess that the man volunteered for the job because he thought it would be an easy ride. How hard could it be to watch two girls? It would be even easier in his mind, now there was only one.

Arkan nudged some debris from the stairs, so it bounced down with a muffled thud. The guard jumped and stepped forward. His sword ready. Arkan held his breath, worried that the man wouldn't take the bait. The guard looked down the staircase behind him but seeing nothing amiss; he moved towards the sound with his sword upraised. Arkan, lithe as a cat, jumped over the banisters to come up behind the man. The pommel of Arkan's blade crashed against the guard's temple. Arkan caught the slumping body and lowered him against the wall, lifting the ring of keys from his belt with a faint clink.

Arkan pressed his ear to the lone door and listened for any signs of life behind it. There was no sound, so he put the key into the lock and twisted it quietly. A soft click sounded, and he nuzzled the door open. It was darker in the room, and it took him a second for his eyes to adjust. He was almost blind as he stepped through, but he spotted the fist coming at him from the light in the hallway, with a second to spare as he ducked and rolled into the room.

Lynsey attacked with foreign moves unlike any he'd learned. Arkan gaped in astonishment before the trained fighter in him took over. In all the years of his training, he would not be beaten by a small girl he could break with his thumb. If - he - could - just -get - hold - of - her. Arkan spun and wove, easily blocking her strikes until finally she slowed, flagging. Seizing his chance, Arkan captured her in a neck hold.

"Lynsey." he panted. "It's me. I'm here to rescue you." Lynsey struggled for a moment more before she collapsed in his arms. He gently helped her up, and they crept back up the stairs to the room where he entered the house.

Arkan set her down on the bed and turned her to face him. He gently wiped away a stray tear from her eyes and tilted her chin up to look into her eyes.

"Lynsey, we need to get out of here. Can you wrap your legs around my waist and hold on to my shoulders, piggyback style, as I climb down? I can't carry you any other way." She nodded.

"There is the problem with your hair. It is going to stand out."

Lynsey nodded and bent down to her skirt. She ripped a length off and tied the material around her head, turning it into a headscarf.

"Is this better?"

"Perfect." He replied. "We need to get out. The best way to do that is if you climb on to my back and I'll get us both down."

Eyeing him dubiously, Lynsey climbed onto the bed as he turned his back. With a leap, she latched onto him. Muscles flexing, Arkan lifted her and scaled out the window. Boots hitting dirt moments later, they were at Illyara's side in under a minute.

Lynsey halted a few steps behind him, and he turned to see what the problem was. She gave her friend a disbelieving look. "You left me." Arkan saw she was having difficulty getting the words out.

Illyara shook her head.

"I had to track them to find you," Illyara protested. "I brought back Arkan as swiftly as I could!"

Lynsey blanched, clearly still shaken by the ordeal. Arkan stepped between them and scooped the girl up easily. He gave her a brief, steadying embrace before lifting her atop the horse with Illyara moments later. Mindful that Shade could not go far with three weights, he knew the guards would search soon. They would assume that Lynsey had escaped, but that she was on foot. He whistled, and Shade trotted back to the Duchess' house while he easily kept pace, jogging beside them.

12 Duchess's Domain

Lynsey didn't know where to look as they alighted from the horse. Her stomach twisted in knots, bile rising in her throat as she thought about Illyara's betrayal. What Illyara had said about following them was right, but it didn't make it any less hurtful because of it. It felt like a cornerstone of her new life had collapsed. She'd thought that she could rely on Illyara, but her friend had abandoned her! Then again, she saved her by getting Arkan to the house. Oh, she didn't know what to think anymore.

The sharp rap of knuckles on Darianna's front door barely registered in Lynsey's ears, her thoughts swirling as she tried to make sense of Illyara's actions. As Arkan opened the door, she saw the butler's eyebrows shoot up as he took in the dishevelled trio on the doorstep. She was missed then. The man ushered them into the reception room.

Illyara perched on the settee, and Lynsey moved to sit on the other end. She bit her lip. It didn't feel right being upset with her friend. She glanced at Illyara and almost chuckled at their body language. Their knees and torsos faced away from each other. This was ridiculous.

The whisper of material made her look up to see Arkan stride past them and take his customary place at the window like a king overseeing his kingdom. The silence, only broken by the ticking of the clock and their quiet breathing, was broken moments later by a maid clattering into the room. Three shot glasses filled with an amber liquid jostled together on a small silver tray she carried. The maid offered the first drink to Arkan, who picked up the glass without hesitation. He held the glass in his palm for a moment, swirling it with a slow, lazy movement. He bent his head and his dark curls fell forward as he sniffed the contents before draining it in one draught.

Next, the maid crossed the elaborately patterned beige carpet to offer Illyara the second glass. She shook her head at the invitation.

"You really should. It's a good quality brandy. It will settle your nerves after today." Arkan's voice was almost a whisper.

Illyara and Lynsey exchanged glances, and Lynsey shrugged her shoulders at her. Illyara picked the nearest and Lynsey grasped the third glass from the tray at the same time. The brandy smelled rich and reminded her of Christmas. She almost laughed out loud.

"LYNSEY, YOU ARE IN SHOCK." Came Pico's concerned thought.

She sobered at the intrusion. It was hard to get used to him doing that. She tilted the glass at Arkan and gulped it, letting the liquid burn her throat as it went down. Seconds later, Illyara bent her dark head forward and took a sip.

"Is there anything else, Sir?"

Arkan shook his head at the maid's question. She withdrew from the room, taking the two empty glasses as she went.

Darianna burst in through a second door.

"I am so sorry." She pleaded, lurching straight to Arkan. She looked slightly drunk.

What was Darianna playing at? The woman was all over him. And why did she even care what Darianna did? Not taking her eyes off the pair, Lynsey grabbed the other glass from between Illyara's hands, ignoring her startled expression, and downed it. Warmth flooded her bones. This really was good stuff. She noticed how Darianna's dark beauty matched his. They would make the perfect couple, Lynsey thought bitterly.

After hearing what must be the tenth sorry, Lynsey was getting irritated. Why was Darianna apologising to Arkan so much? He didn't own them. They were perfectly within their rights to have a walk if they wanted to. He rescued them, but given time, with Pico's help, she was sure she would have escaped on her own.

He kept looking at her over Darianna's shoulder with those puppy dog eyes. God, he is so damned gorgeous! If they had been in London, she had to admit, he would have been her type. She loved the combination of long, shoulder-length curls with matching brown eyes. He had a firm jaw and his muscles! If he were back home, he would have spent hours in the gym to get those pecs.

He's crowing, she realised. He's feeling like my knight in shining, bloody armour and I'm supposed to simper at his feet now, am I? I don't think so!

Across the room, Darianna had turned to observe her two house guests. She arched her neck to see Arkan was also looking with an expression she hadn't seen before. So that's the lie of the land, is it? She sighed. Darianna knew she could never keep him anyway, but she never thought her rival would have been some provincial girl with fewer brains than a Hreshat. This girl didn't deserve him. She was reacting so strangely. It was like she didn't want to be rescued. Maybe she didn't understand what would have happened to her, Darianna reasoned. She acted like everything was a game.

Over the last couple of days, Darianna had watched them as they had shopped and moved around Ghinari. There was no point showing your true face until you knew what you were dealing with, but they had to be worth the risk. She had always liked an underdog. Lynsey was tough. She reacted differently to anyone that Darianna had met before, yet she had a soft quality. A combination hard to resist for most men. Would she be able to keep Arkan's attention? Time would tell.

Darianna turned to inspect Illyara more thoroughly. Her friend was also interesting. There was the question of how she got away from the kidnappers. The muscles around Darianna's eyes tightened. No one had seen her come back into the house earlier and she had posted guards on all the doors as soon as she discovered they had gone.

"We should probably go to bed." She heard Lynsey say.

"Oh no, darling." Darianna purred, moving away from Arkan to take her hands. "Don't you see? We have to go to the banquet now. It will be safer if you do. The king has tried to kidnap you. If you want to be safe, you will need to be presented to court in the most ostentatious way possible. Everyone must be talking about you and your connection to my family. Everyone must know you exist!"

Arkan nodded his head in agreement. "You need to go now more than ever. Darianna is right, as always. Do you have everything you need?"

Lynsey's shoulders slumped, lips turning down at Darianna's blithe insistence that they attend the banquet. After being kidnapped, her dreams of a long soak and soft bed evaporated like smoke.

"I don't want to go out now. I've just been kidnapped! All I want is a bath and a bed."

"You shall have both the first now and the second tonight after the banquet. I will send my personal maids to ensure your entrance to the party is as extraordinary as any this city has ever seen before. The only safety for you now is notoriety, and I am the perfect person to show you how to get it!"

Darianna rang the bell dangling on a powder-blue leather rope beside her and the butler, Tar, opened the door, his eyebrow gently raised as Darianna gestured to Lynsey and her friend.

"Send Mari and Tegan to their rooms. I want them to look fabulous for tonight."

"My lady," he replied and withdrew, making no sound.

Lynsey looked at the faces surrounding her and sighed. They were right. All she wanted to do was snuggle into bed at home with a pint of ice-cream — low fat, of course. No, dammit, Cornish cream and as many bars of chocolate as she could stuff in her face. Her stomach growled audibly. She hadn't eaten a good meal for days and just maybe the food at this dinner would be worth it.

Lynsey rose to her feet, and Illyara pulled her to the door, leaving Darianna and Arkan talking. When the door was closed and Illyara was sure no-one was listening, she grabbed Lynsey by the hand. Her other hand lay on the rail at the foot of the stairs.

"You know I had no choice; understand that." Illyara began.

"I know, but I can't help feeling that you left me behind. How did you get away? One minute you were there, the next you weren't."

"I told you."

"Tell me what?"

"That I can disappear - like your bracelet."

"No, you didn't! I would have remembered that!"

Illyara sighed. "I did, but you weren't listening. It is an ability that my people have. We would have been wiped out during the time of the pyramids if it weren't for it and, in fact, we were instrumental in the uprising. We have to be very careful not to show it. If anyone outside of the family knew what we could do, our children would not be safe." Illyara made a second check around her. Lynsey blinked, and she was gone. Before she had time to register surprise, Illyara was back again.

"Why are you telling me now?"

"You are my friend, and I think we are more alike than you think. We are a peaceful people and don't like confrontations, but we will protect our own, and that includes our friends."

Lynsey returned Illyara's smile. "When you put it like that, I suppose if they had knocked you out as well, we might still be there."

"I don't know. I saw you fight. That was amazing. I wish I could do that, but it is against the ways of my tribe. It was amazing to watch, though." Illyara's eyes were practically shining at the memory.

The route to their room was marked by large cloth paintings hanging from strips of wood attached to pristine white walls. Lynsey knew they were near their room by the sultry depiction of a lady atop a horse. She seemed to smile at them with her hands raised, as though to brush her jet-black hair away from her eyes.

Through the open door, she saw two maids were busily arranging objects, ready for their transformations.

"I hope they have proper baths here." Lynsey said as she closed the door behind her.

They had baths. In fact, there were two in the same room. The air was humid, suffused with the smell of the most gorgeous bath salts she had ever experienced. A heady mix of what was it? Oh, lavender! And something else was seeping into her soul, making the events of the day feel a little further away than it had just moments before. Lynsey revelled in the feeling. It had to be citrusy, no; it was earthier than that. She shrugged her shoulders and laughed at herself. Did it matter? She gave up trying to identify the second smell and she couldn't be bothered to ask Pico.

Lynsey brushed her hands over the water to find the water was warm enough to get into, but not too hot. She groaned with relief as she lowered herself into the water an inch at a time. The salts softened her skin as soon as her body touched the water and the heat felt like it was melting her troubles away. She cupped a handful and splashed it over her front. The temperature was perfect.

This was the best thing to happen since she had got there. She dunked her head under the water and brought it up again to see Arkan standing at the tub's end, grinning at her through the dripping fan of her hair.

Lynsey's heart jumped, and she screamed, grabbing the towel that the maid had left on the stool beside the bath. She hastily arranged it around her exposed body.

"Do you mind!"

"Not in the least. Your body is quite delightful!"

"That's not what I meant. You shouldn't be in here!"

"I need a bath as well after that rescue." He brushed some imaginary dust off his shoulder with his hand. "That place could have done with a clean and brushing up against dirty walls before a King's feast is just not done. Did you not wonder at the other filled tub?"

Lynsey looked where he pointed. There were curls of steam rising from the bath. A spare green towel was folded neatly on the stool beside it. As she had climbed in to her bath, she had assumed that it was for Illyara. He followed her gaze to the bath, to the door and back again, guessing what she was thinking, and grinned again.

"Illyara is choosing what to wear. You will need both Mari and Tegan to get you ready while you are being made beautiful." He looked at her up and down in admiration. "…which won't need that much, Illyara will have her bath while you are being attended to."

"You can't have a bath while I'm in here!"

"Why ever not?" Arkan asked. Taking off his shirt, he revealed broad shoulders and an athlete's body. She saw with concern; small white scars criss-crossed his front. She crushed the impulse to trace them with her fingers.

"Because I'm in here and I'm naked!"

"Why are you worried about being naked? You shouldn't. You are actually quite beautiful." He replied, while hopping to get one trouser leg over his foot. "Are you worried about that kind of thing where you are from? Where was it again?"

Lynsey blustered. "Earth and we don't have baths in front of strangers!"

"We're not strangers. We have known each other for a couple of days now and haven't I just rescued you from a dread fate?"

She glimpsed his rear as he climbed into the bath before she closed her eyes. Yes, but this was a whole new dread fate. Pico chuckled in her mind.

"We are not prudes, we just don't enjoy showing our private areas to all and sundry." She breathed in and out, letting the heat and smell of the bath soothe her. She would not be riled by him. In fact, she was going to ignore him. That was the way to deal with this sort of person.

She lay back in the bath, keeping her eyes closed and crossing her arms. She counted the good things that had happened since they arrived. Even Pico was keeping quiet. She felt his amusement as he stirred in the depths of her mind. Come to think of it. Pico was very like a phone. Constantly there, reliable, all the information you could want at your fingertips if you want it. He was even a compass! The only thing he couldn't do was get stolen. Maybe it wouldn't be such a bad thing after all. She would never get lonely with Pico. Maybe if she just thought of him as a flatmate, but instead of a flat, he was in her head.

Arkan began whistling beside her. She ignored him. He was just trying to get her attention. She sneaked a peek at him and he was looking at her with that insufferable grin. She turned away.

This time he started singing with some whistling accompaniment.

"There was a young lady from Earth, who wouldn't show her smurth. A man crept up beside her…"

There was a splash.

Lynsey's eyes shot open, but he was still in the tub with that same grin. That is enough! She would not take anymore. She pulled the already soaking towel and wrapped it around herself while standing, then clambered out with as much grace as she could muster, almost dropping the towel. Lynsey stood for a moment, realigning the material and her dignity, and ran out of the room to him, roaring with laughter behind her.

Illyara stared at her with incredulity as she rushed back into their shared common room. Water dripped over the floor. Lynsey swiped her hair from her face over her head, drenching the bedspread through the open door with scattered bath water behind her.

"That man is incorrigible!"

"He's what?"

"Insufferable, annoying, up himself, pain in the neck…"

Illyara's face showed no emotion. "What happened?"

"He had a bath beside me."

"He had a bath beside you and that made you leave the bathroom without drying properly? Your world must be a strange place." Illyara stood up gracefully and threw a towel at Lynsey. "I am going to have my bath now. Tegan and Mari are in the receiving room. They have got a gorgeous dress for you."

From a person who came from a culture of different tents for different sexes, Illyara was acting really strange. She would have acted a lot worse if it had happened to her. Then again, Arkan was still in there. Lynsey shook her head. Maybe she didn't know Illyara quite as well as she thought she did.

Hung up on the clothing rail that lined the room. A dress made her stop and catch her breath. It was indeed beautiful. On Earth, it could easily be a, if slightly unusual, wedding gown. She ran her fingers along the material. It felt like silk. The ivory outer layer was inlaid with small pearls sewn into the bodice material. An inner lining of fuchsia pink was offset against the outer layer to peek through. "It's the same colour as that plant we saw in the desert." She mentally sent to Pico.

"OF COURSE. THE BARYGSRE WAS—OR SHOULD I SAY IS, ALSO USED AS A DYE." His voice took on a curious tone. "I AGREE. THE DRESS IS VISUALLY PLEASING."

Mari took the dress down, and the long skirt pooled against the floor. Lynsey breathed out gently. It was what she would have chosen if she ever got married. It was her dream dress.

"Do you like it, Ma'am? Illyara chose it from the dresses sent over this afternoon while you were out. Mr Blade ordered them especially."

"Arkan chose this?" She pointed at the dress.

"Yes, ma'am, and several others, but we thought this would be the one for you to wear for your first presentation."

How could she reconcile the Arkan from the bathroom with the soul who could choose something as stunning as this dress? Lynsey touched the soft silk again with reverence. Whatever she thought of him. The guy had excellent taste.

As Lynsey described Arkan's audacity, the door whooshed open. Tegan breezed in, offering another towel with raised eyebrows at Lynsey's damp hair and the droplets on the floor. Fresh blood rushed to Lynsey's cheeks, fiery tendrils creeping down her neck. She quickly dried, and the maids handed her clothing one by one, layering each garment over the last.

Underwear first, then petticoats and a bustier were hauled tight until she squeaked. Finally, the dress was pulled over her head and she was drawn over to a mirror.

"You look lovely, Ma'am but we haven't finished." Tegan pulled Lynsey with her as she was backing away. "Mari is the best hairdresser in all of Duat! The king has tried to lure her for his mistress. It was probably more the mistress than the king, though." Tegan winked at her. "I can't imagine that the king is that troubled by her hairstyle."

Lynsey sat by the dresser as Mari worked on her hair. What could loosely be described as a dead rat's tail that had gone through an electric shock followed by a gale became an elaborate hive of defined curls, with pearls and diamonds dripping through like the tributaries of a river. She noticed everything was done to stress her blond hair.

"Mari, why is everyone so obsessed with blond hair here?"

"Are we? I never thought about it like that," replied Mari, taking a clip out of her hair and slipping it into her apron. "It's just rare. I heard there were blond people centuries ago, but most people had brown or black hair and when they married and had kids, most of the babies had brown or black hair. Eventually, there were no blond children. I think people just like what is different. The exotic if you like. It's nice. You will be feted tonight, maybe even courted by the King! You will be the most exotic creature there." Then she added a second later in a lower tone, "Which will put a great big dent in Mistress Frassill's nose."

"Who is Mistress Frassill?"

"The King's mistress, of course. Thinks of herself a little above her station." The maid's expression in the mirror was not flattering.

"You don't like her, then I take it?"

"She was the Queen's handmaiden and took her chance. She wasn't nice before the King took an interest in her. Now she could make even Set look like a neteru."

"What's a Neteru?" She asked Pico.

"ANGELS." He supplied.

"She must be beautiful, then."

"Yes, but she has a dark heart. There," Mari twisted the last strands and secured it with a clip, "she doesn't hold a candle to you tonight."

"Indeed." Arkan strode in and balanced against the corner of a nearby table, crossing his legs. "We will have to come up with a story. It is inconceivable that a blond has emerged, and no one has heard about it for twenty years."

He cocked his head as if in thought.

"I think she may have been the daughter of Baron Redcher. There were whispers of a blond child born to the Redchers generations ago. He dyed his hair black to avoid attention, but secrets like that never stay hidden for long…" Arkan trailed off. "Surely it is a possibility that another could happen? Unlikely, but possible."

"What happened to him?" Lynsey leaned forward to hear better, exposing a little cleavage.

Arkan coughed and shuffled his position. "The Baron went missing about thirty years ago, travelling around the islands. He was an explorer, you know. He's probably dead by now, but maybe he had a child with a local woman."

Lynsey followed Arkan's gaze down to her chest and gave an inward smile.

"HE IS BIOLOGICALLY INTERESTED IN YOU." Piped in Pico.

"I can see that." She shifted slightly so he could get a better look.

"WHY ARE YOU DOING THAT? YOU DIDN'T LIKE IT WHEN HE COULD SEE YOUR BODY IN THE BATHROOM."

"This is different, Pico. This is called flirting. It's fun!"

"I DON'T UNDERSTAND."

"That's alright, you don't have to but if I'm going to be stuck on this godforsaken planet with no internet, books or television then I'm going to have to find some other way to have some fun."

"YOU ARE PLAYING WITH FIRE!"

"Without fire, we'd still be living in caves."

She felt Pico slink off to a corner. Round 1, Lynsey 1, Pico 0, she thought with satisfaction.

"I like your idea, Arkan. It would explain my lack of knowledge of how things work - of your manners and history."

"Perfect, then that is settled. We shall do that."

13 Delving into Duat

The chill night air slipped through the open carriage windows and wrapped around them like an icy cloak. It also brought with it a delicate floral fragrance that Lynsey barely noticed as she shivered on the plush seat. Rubbing the goose bumps breeding on her upper arms didn't help, either. Hadn't they heard of suspension in this world?

She looked out into the darkness; she felt like she was grumpy all the time now. There was nothing to distract her from the cold and the sheer boredom of the journey. No one was talking. Never mind comfy seats, the art of good conversation had taken a holiday, died and buried itself somewhere. She really regretted not bringing a fur wrap, but Darianna was in such a hurry that it had been forgotten. It turned out Darianna wasn't as calm and collected as she made herself out to be.

"We need to depart now." Darianna had said.

"Just a moment. We need to check we have everything." The room had looked like a tornado had hit it and Lynsey was busy bundling some clothes together from the settee.

"Put those down. We have maids to do that sort of thing." Darianna's voice rose to a squeak.

It was funny now, but at the time, she seemed really agitated.

"Are you okay Darianna?"

"The feast is at the Green Palace in half an hour. It is an hour's drive at the minimum. We are already fashionably late, anymore and we will get into trouble." There was a tremor of fear in her voice that made Lynsey take notice. She paused, still holding the dresses.

"Okay, okay. Keep your shirt on."

"What are you talking about? I am not wearing a shirt. I have no intention of taking anything off, even if I was."

"I didn't mean your actual shirt. Look," Lynsey took a deep breath. "I'm sorry, I didn't mean it. We'll go now." She dropped the clothes and held her hands out.

Lynsey smiled at the memory. It was good to know that Darianna wasn't perfect.

On the opposite seat, Arkan was looking out the other window. He could probably see the terrain like a cat, she mused. His dark curls were tied back by a short black thong. His gaze was unwavering, its intensity unnerving. What was he looking for?

Darianna, of course, was naturally sitting next to him. Her arm hooked around his. Why hadn't he taken his own carriage, or ridden Shade? Was he involved with Darianna? Lynsey touched the hard metal of the hidden bracelet on her wrist. All he wanted from her was this. It wasn't even as if it would work for him, or would it? Was there another Pico stored in there?

"MAY I ANSWER THAT?" Pico's thought was cautious, swirling in yellow.

"I was hoping you would. What happens if someone else wears the bracelet?"

"NOTHING; I AM THE ONLY INTERFACE POSSIBLE. ONCE THE PICONITES HAVE ENTERED THE BODY THERE IS NO WAY TO GET THEM BACK INTO THE BAND AND THEREFORE NO WAY TO 'TALK' TO THE BRACELET. IT WOULD STILL WORK OF COURSE BUT ANYONE WITHOUT PICONITES WOULDN'T BE ABLE TO COMMUNICATE WITH IT. IT IS TECHNICALLY POSSIBLE FOR YOU TO WEAR AND USE ANOTHER BAND BUT NOT FOR SOMEONE WHO DOESN'T HAVE A COMPANION TO USE A BAND."

"You are calling yourself a companion now?"

"WE WERE ALWAYS CALLED THAT LYNSEY. YOU JUST WEREN'T READY TO HEAR IT."

She ignored the gentle reproof. "So, it would be pointless to kill someone for their bracelet?"

"EXACTLY."

Lynsey pondered that for a moment. The priests would have been outnumbered by the slaves. They would have had to come up with a contingency for when someone had the bright idea of taking a band.

The coach stopped to shouting overhead and gravel crunching beneath them.

"We should get out here." Arkan said, bringing his head back through the window. "There is a queue of carriages all the way to the palace. Come on."

He opened the door and jumped down, offering his hand to Darianna, who joined him. Lynsey was the last to step out, careful to pull her skirt up from her silk slippers on the steep descent. There were only three steps, but she didn't want to fall flat on her face in front of any watchers.

The aroma of burning wood surrounded her as the wind changed direction, bringing childhood memories of nights in front of a wood fire. Thick posts lined the driveway, their tops alight with fire, beckoning them down the drive to the entrance. She noticed dozens of carriages ahead blocking the road and more were joining the queue behind them. The road was filling with men and women, all dressed in elegant attire. Several threw occasional curious glances their way, but most were going towards the entrance. There was nothing for it but to walk the rest of the way.

"This is where I have to leave you for a while."

Lynsey turned to find Arkan in the shadows. She could barely see him, but she saw him take Darianna's hand and kiss her knuckles. He winked at Lynsey over Darianna's shoulder. "Enjoy yourselves girls."

He was going to leave them? Lynsey felt a cold shiver run through her. She knew Darianna would look after her, but she expected Arkan to be there too.

He tilted his head at Lynsey's expression and leaned forward to take her hand. He turned it over to stroke her palm. "I can't be seen with you tonight. It is better to not draw attention to you more than we need to. It is enough with your blond hair and mystery without adding me to the mix. I also have some unfinished business to attend to before I am seen."

Lynsey slouched her shoulders. She was almost sad to see him go. Then she checked herself. What did she want from him? Did she really want to find a man and settle down in this strange place? That's just silly, she berated herself. It was impossible. She wanted to get home.

"WHY DO YOU WANT TO GO HOME SO BADLY?" asked Pico.

"I think anyone would if they found themselves in such an alien place. You are not human, so you wouldn't understand."

"I UNDERSTAND MORE THAN YOU THINK. HOME IS WHERE YOU ARE HAPPY. COULDN'T YOU BE HAPPY HERE? YOU LIKE ARKAN. I CAN TELL FROM YOUR HORMONE LEVELS. YOU REACT DIFFERENTLY TO HIM THAN ANYONE ELSE YOU HAVE MET. HE OBVIOUSLY HAS SKILLS OR HE WOULDN'T HAVE BEEN ABLE TO RESCUE YOU. DO YOU KNOW WHAT HE DOES HERE?"

"I thought he was just a noble. He hasn't actually said anything…"

"I THINK YOU NEED TO FIND OUT MORE ABOUT HIM. YOU SAW HIM FIRST AT THE TEMPLE OF THE DRAGON BROTHERHOOD BUT HE'S DEFINITELY NOT A PRIEST AND HE IS WELL CONNECTED IN THIS SOCIETY AS WELL AS BEING ABLE TO RESCUE YOU AT A DROP OF A HAT."

"Drop of a hat?"

"SORRY, I LIKED THAT EXPRESSION FROM YOUR VOCABULARY."

"Fair enough." Lynsey felt the muscles on her face lift into a smile. A man passing stopped and smiled back before carrying on.

"I have to be careful talking to you!" She said, suppressing a giggle. "You are right, though. I know next to nothing about him." She cast about for the most ridiculous thing she could think of. "He might be an assassin for all I know."

"HE'S PROBABLY SOME SORT OF SOLDIER, BUT YOU WON'T KNOW FOR SURE UNTIL YOU ASK HIM OR DARIANNA. I'M SURPRISED SHE HASN'T TOLD YOU."

"Maybe she assumes I know?"

"YOU NEED TO ASK, LYNSEY."

Just then, they reached the entrance of the palace. The archway was tall and the same type of torches that had lit the driveway led the way further into the building. They heard the distant strains of music and Lynsey's mood lifted. This was a party! Lynsey's eyes lit up with a mixture of excitement and curiosity, her lips curling into a subtle smile. She shifted her weight, a barely noticeable bounce in her step. This was something special—a gathering where nobles and royalty mingled—an experience that stirred a quiet enthusiasm within her. She would never happen in a million years back home.

At the entrance to the hall, a man dressed in a royal blue cloak tapped a rod to the ground, jolting her out of a reverie.

"Your names, ma'am?" he asked Illyara, who was standing nearest.

"Illyara Ackaclun and Lynsey Walker." She replied.

"Lady Lynsey Walker and her companion Illyara Ackaclun!" Came a loud call from the door.

"We're on." whispered Illyara from beside her. "Come on."

"Where's Darianna?"

"She has to be announced on her own because she's so important." Illyara rolled her eyes, which got Lynsey giggling.

She was still smiling when she entered the main hall. The room was massive. Lights shaped like flames illuminated the large space dominated by a square dance floor in the middle. Beyond this, Lynsey's eyes were drawn to some tables laden with food on the far wall. She noticed in passing the rainbow colours of the other dresses from people mingling below them.

"Shall we?" Lynsey asked Illyara, and they descended the stairs.

"Pico, why isn't everything more Egyptian?"

"WHAT DO YOU MEAN?"

"I am not sure, but I expected the fashions to be like, you know, the paintings on an Egyptian temple on Earth."

"THOSE WERE FROM CENTURIES AGO. YOU DIDN'T WEAR THE CLOTHES OF A CELTIC DRUID OR A GREEK TOGA ON EARTH."

"Well, there were a few toga parties at university."

Amidst the lively atmosphere, a lilting melody filled the air, accompanied by the rhythmic tapping of feet on the polished floor. As Lynsey meandered through the crowd, she was distracted by a couple twirling gracefully to the music. The swish of their elegant attire matched the gentle sway of their bodies, inviting her gaze to linger for a moment before she continued on her way.

"Seriously though," she continued, "I get that, but surely the buildings would be more Egyptian?"

"MAYBE YOU SHOULD ASK ILLYARA? I WASN'T CONSCIOUS UNTIL YOU WOKE ME. UNLESS YOU START READING A LOT OF HISTORY BOOKS I AM IN THE DARK AS MUCH AS YOU ARE."

"Illyara, wait a second." Her friend was like a woman on a mission. Illyara was charging ahead, the food table firmly in her sights. Lynsey grabbed Illyara's wrist to slow her down. She must be one hungry nomad.

"What's wrong?"

"I was just wondering why everything wasn't more Egyptian."

"Well, it wouldn't be. After the rebellion, people tried to forget them. Most of the buildings that the priests built were torn down. The pyramids you arrived in should be the only ones left as a reminder of what they were. My people kept the memories alive. Can we eat now?"

"Are you mad at me, Illyara?"

Illyara paused and turned to look at her. "Why would I be angry at you?"

"You've just been a little strange since this afternoon. I'm sorry I thought you abandoned me, but I can't help how I feel-felt."

"It's not that. It is just that I have been thinking about my family since the kidnap. This is the longest I have been away from them."

Lynsey looked up at the frieze on the ceiling and blew out gently before taking Illyara's hands in hers. "That's a relief. You are my only friend, and I really don't want to lose you."

"That will not happen." She smiled back, linking their arms. "And now for some food."

14 Reckless Resolve

Arkan lounged against a column near the edge of the dais, a small grin playing on his lips as he observed Lynsey and Illyara navigating their way through the sea of courtiers. Gasps of astonishment rippled through the crowd, their wide eyes and turning heads causing whispers to flutter behind raised hands. The presence of Lynsey and her friend had sent a shockwave of excitement through the courtiers, exactly as Arkan had expected. Everyone would talk about them by the end of the night.

The raised platform he stood on was lined with six painted columns. Their green colour matched the throne's upholstery, giving the palace its name.

Concealed within the column's shadow, Arkan's strategic position granted him an unobtrusive view of the throng. The murmurs of the courtiers reached his ears. The architect's foresight in shaping the space had furnished this spot with the unique ability to capture nearly every conversation, a luxury bought by the coffers of the Assassins' Guild.

Yet, it was Arkan's honed expertise that lent meaning to the chaos. Amid the hubbub, he focused his attention on the subtlest of sounds, recognising the true significance of the hushed exchanges.

Arkan leaned forward, focussing on two speakers in the far corner. "Can you believe the taxes we're burdened with?" Pigram exclaimed, his voice tinged with frustration as he leaned against the wall. "It's as if the king thinks gold sprouts from the ground!"

His companion, Soble, shook his head sympathetically. "I know, Pigram. It's got worse over the seasons. But remember, complaining won't change much. The king has his ways, and we're just small merchants."

Pigram sighed. "I understand, Soble. But it's not just the taxes. The way he spends on his extravagant banquets while the common folk struggle—I'm worried we'll push them too far."

Soble reached out, placing a comforting hand on Pigram's arm. "You're right, Pigram. It's frustrating to witness. But let's focus on what we can control. Our business is thriving, and we're making a difference in our own way. We can't change the king's actions, but we can continue to support our community."

Pigram's lips curled into a small smile as he looked at his friend. "You always have a way of putting things into perspective, Soble. You're right. We have to help each other. Let's not let the king's taxes dampen our spirits."

Soble nodded, his eyes reflecting determination. "Exactly, Pigram. We'll keep doing what we do best. The king's troubles are not our burden to bear."

Arkan tuned them out, searching for real threats. He instantly discarded the trysts and barbed comments from other guests. He was not interested in gossip. Leave that to Darianna. He scanned the crowd. Where was Darianna, anyway? He found her by the door talking to a grand dame.

"She's my cousin. Just in from the islands. Her father disappeared years ago." She produced a fan from a small purse which matched her green gown and waved it with a conspiratorial wink. "I was more surprised than anyone when she turned up at my door. I thought Jemmy had been eaten by natives years ago!" The woman gave a raucous laugh beside her.

"He had a reputation, didn't he? What happened to the blonde boy?"

"I hear he died young. Who can say after all this time? They were never spoken of after Jemmy left Ghinari. We still don't know why he left. There must have been something unsavoury going on knowing that side of the family."

"I heard that. They never really integrated into society…"

Arkan tuned out again and listened in for Baserius' voice. He couldn't identify it, but then realised he was at the food table. Arkan looked for each Guild Master in turn.

He stood up straighter and positioned himself closer to the edge, using the dark green railing as support as he leaned forward. From there, he saw both Lynsey and the King's reaction to her entrance.

It took a few moments for the unusual absence of noise to seep into the King's awareness, a delay that could be forgiven given the circumstances. Engrossed in conversation with the head of the Merchants Guild, the king appeared captivated by the man's animated discourse. Arkan couldn't help but admire the sheer audacity of the guild leader—a trait that could be seen as either bravery or sheer stupidity. Especially given the king's clear disdain for him, it seemed the latter was more fitting.

Arkan's keen observation detected nuances that spoke volumes beneath the surface. He noted the tensing of the king's shoulders, a forced smile that didn't quite reach his eyes, and the rhythmic tap of a foot that betrayed a simmering impatience. This restrained reaction, he thought, was an unexpected display of self-control. Arkan was surprised the king allowed the merchant to approach him this close.

Ah, the discussion revolved around potential tax hikes because of a disappointing tax yield in the previous year. That explained it. The down-turned face of the merchant betrayed his discontent. Arkan's mind wondered if Isabel was asking for more jewellery again. The lady had a penchant for diamond necklaces that the treasury could ill afford.

Turning his attention to the rest of the room, Arkan noted the pattern of people as they turned to look at Lynsey. It was like a rose opening at dawn. Clusters of people in a circular pattern turned towards her before another circle further away noticed something was happening and rotated towards her. More and more people stopped to look until the pattern reached the King.

Arkan watched Lynsey and the King closely. The king's eyes widened and his jaw flexed, opening his mouth for a split-second before he gained control and closed it again. He stepped forward, ignoring the man he was talking to. Then his face dropped again, this time to Arkan's consternation. It showed anger.

Arkan followed the king's gaze and saw how her long skirt kissed the floor where she walked. He couldn't help but compare her to the other women in the room. She was the most beautiful girl there. The cut of the dress stressed every curve. Her long blond hair was piled on her head, the bright jewels sparkled, snaking through to draw attention to her shiny curls. She appeared like some mythical creature from the past, like a force of nature, a nymph.

Arkan's breath slowed as she turned and caught his eye. Her smile made his heart shudder for a beat. He had no business feeling that way. Caught between two opposing forces, Arkan grappled with the metaphorical tightrope he walked. He recognised the allure of the familiar path, the soft tread of diplomacy that allowed him to remain in the shadows, serving the king's interests. But as he gazed upon her, her smile radiant as a distant star, he couldn't ignore the call to something greater, something akin to a leap of faith.

He knew that in treading this tightrope, he was courting disaster. To step out of line with the king's desires was to gamble with his own fate, to invite the precipice of ruin ever closer. Yet, the thought of her vulnerability amidst the intricate web of court politics around her weighed heavily on his conscience. He took a deep breath, his chest tight with apprehension, and Arkan's eyes lingered on her, torn between the heart's whisper and his mind's cautionary voice. It was dangerous to oppose the king in this. But if he did not help her … she was not equipped to survive in court.

15   A Dance of Intrigue

The king strode through the dancers, not giving them a second glance as they parted into two groups before him. His jaw was set in a determined line. The sweep of so many skirts on the marble floor in the silence caught Lynsey's attention, and she saw him approaching before he reached them. Lynsey looked at the food longingly but realised that in this place and in this time, a crown on someone's head should be heeded.

He was dressed in blue brocade, and although to Lynsey, he looked like someone trying too hard. Wasn't everyone here? His strides held an air of confidence, each step purposeful and unhurried, a trait rarely witnessed in her world. His presence commanded her attention, causing her to halt her assessment and regard him with a mixture of intrigue and curiosity.

The king was handsome in a different way than Arkan. The King's hair was cropped close to his head, and he had a neat goatee that suggested that he liked things a certain way. This was a man not to be trifled with.

His manner was charming, and he moved with grace.

"Lady Walker, I presume?"

"Your Highness." Lynsey curtseyed clumsily. His eye flickered briefly. Was that amusement?

"I trust your journey to our fair city was uneventful?"

Oh God, what should she say to that? Should she admit to being kidnapped? She saw Arkan in the distance tense up. He probably couldn't hear what they were talking about, but everyone was looking at them. She had better get this right.

"I encountered some problems, but nothing I couldn't deal with." She smiled sweetly at the King.

"What happened?" His voice was syrupy, full of concern, but his shoulders and arms went rigid, betraying the importance of her answer. Something was riding on this, but she didn't know how this game was played.

"I took a walk with my companion in the park and we were accosted by some brigands."

Those romance novels had really done her vocabulary a favour. Who knew they would come in handy?

"That is awful," he leaned in closer. "Might I offer some of my guards to make you feel safer? This city can be a dangerous place for someone as rare and beautiful as you."

"Oh, I'm sure that is unnecessary. We got away. I think the ruffians must have eaten a few too many pies." A titter travelled around the room. "Luckily, Cousin Darianna has doubled the guard around her house, so I can sleep easy." Name dropping might be the thing to do here.

"Then you can indeed relax, fair maiden. May I offer you a dance?"

Lynsey hesitated, searching the crowd for Darianna. She saw her nod from behind the king.

"I would be honoured, your highness but I must confess that I grew up in the islands and I have only been here a couple of weeks. No one taught me to dance. I fear I will stand on your feet."

Lynsey was really loving, talking like a character from history.

"YOU ARE DOING GREAT." Pico told her. "I'M TRANSMITTING WHAT THEY THINK YOU ARE SAYING FROM WHAT I'VE HEARD SINCE WE ARRIVED IN GHINARI. I PICKED UP THE HIGHER SPEECH FROM THE STORE CLERKS AND CUSTOMERS BUT WE CAN USE THE MORE COLOURFUL DIALECTS FROM THE MAIDS AND THE STREETS IF WE NEED TO."

"You are loving this too, aren't you?"

"WELL, YES - YES I AM."

Unaware of the silent dialogue, the king took her hand and moved her through courtiers to the dance floor where a space had naturally cleared.

"My dear, I shall be happy to teach you."

A rapid beat on string instruments filled the room, but the king threw up his hand. Lynsey winced as the music drew to a halt as a combination of harps, lutes, and drums came to a screeching silence.

"Something slower, I think." The music started up again, this time changing to a lower tempo. He took hold of her other arm and moved his feet in a slow box step. Other dancers joined them on the floor.

"Pico, I need your help. I can't dance!"

"I UNDERSTAND."

Lynsey relinquished control, surrendering herself to Pico. Her body responded with a natural grace she hadn't thought possible, every movement flowing as if the dance was a part of her very being. Her gown swirled around her legs, its fabric whispering to the rhythm of the steps, while her heart synced with the melody. Lynsey's worries melted away as her body embraced the dance with an elegance that transcended her own abilities.

"Pico, you are a star."

"SEE, YOU NEED ME."

"I'm realising that now," she replied as the king whirled her around.

When the tune ended, an advisor pulled the king away, leaving Lynsey alone on the dance floor. She saw several men from the crowd take a step forward, but Illyara was beside her in moments, stopping them in their tracks. Lynsey and Illyara linked hands and continued their way to the food table. She felt her companion's approval and her mood lifted. If Illyara thought she had done well, then she had. No pregnant goat here, thank you very much.

As Lynsey made her way towards the food table, the crowd's density seemed to shift, a determined figure clad in purple suede surging forward with purpose. Illyara and Lynsey found themselves separated as the woman's presence wedged a gap between them. A possessive grip closed around Lynsey's arm, and when she turned her gaze, she was met by a wintry smile that sent a shiver down her spine.

The woman's words brushed against Lynsey's ear like a whispered warning. "I've been watching you, Lynsey. I know what you want, and I strongly suggest you stay away from the king." The intensity in her eyes mirrored the unease that had settled in Lynsey's chest, casting an ominous shadow over the glamorous festivities.

The woman straightened, regarding her. Lynsey was taken aback by her words, unsure of what to say. The lady continued, "You may have caught his eye, but I'm the one he's chosen. I've worked my way up to be where I am, and I will not be replaced by a nobody."

Lynsey remembered her conversation with Mari earlier. She knew better than to argue with Mistress Frassill. She had to be the king's mistress.

"I'll make it worth your while. I'll give you a chest of gold coins to leave Ghinari and never come back." Mistress Frassill said.

Lynsey hid a smile. Her first thought was that one necklace from the pyramids was worth a chest of gold. She didn't even want the creepy guy. The woman smoothed her dress while waiting for an answer.

"Oh, sure, I'll stay away."

Mistress Frassill didn't look convinced. " I'm not without power here, girl. Don't mess with me."

Her look was piercing. She held it for a few more seconds, then disappeared in a flounce of skirts.

"What the blazes was that?" Lynsey said aloud.

"Lynsey, meet the king's mistress," replied Illyara in a dry tone. "Shall we proceed to the table?"

The food table was full of every food that Lynsey could imagine, and a few that she hadn't seen since her arrival. Illyara's eyes seemed to pop out on stalks beside her.

"There was a famine this year," Illyara breathed. "Look at this food. Where did it all come from?" The table stretched across the entire length of the room; its legs groaned under the weight of the colourful display.

"That's a question you should never ask, ladies." Across the table, a man was filling up his plate. With each morsel he put on his plate, another found its way into his mouth. "It is always better to fill up here. My name is Baserius. I'm the head of the Dragon Brotherhood." He popped a piece of chicken into his mouth and chewed. "I hear you tried to call the other day? As I am here now, how may I be of help?"

Lynsey exchanged looks with her friend. "It was nothing." She replied.

"Oh, come hardly nothing. You gave my doorman an exquisite elephant for the pleasure of seeing me. If I'm not mistaken, that elephant is quite priceless. My brother was very excited until we reminded him that all money and goods belong to the brotherhood."

"I knew that was worth too much." Lynsey muttered under her breath. She was seething inside. "It was nothing. I was new to the area and thought it would be interesting to see the Dragon Temple."

"… and you thought the high priest was the best person to show you round? Capital idea. I'm free after lunch tomorrow?"

She kept her face expressionless. How could she refuse? She was backed into a corner. Even Pico was silent.

"That would be lovely."

Baserius nodded at her answer and walked away.

"Lynsey! What were you thinking?"

"For someone who was never popular at home, I've got a king and a high priest wanting to spend time with me. Go me!"

Illyara gave her a warning look, but Lynsey shrugged her shoulders. She was going to enjoy this for a change.

Later that evening, Darianna introduced them to the most important families in the room. Lynsey had trouble thinking of what to say, but Illyara, growing up with the Nomads, had even more trouble. At least Lynsey had seen historical dramas and read enough books that she could fake a sophistication she didn't feel.

"I always wanted to take up acting." She silently informed Pico. "But I always assumed there would be a script."

"YOU WOULD HAVE DONE BRILLIANTLY JUDGING BY TONIGHT."

The alien-ness of the situation wore her down suddenly. "Will I ever get home?"

"I DON'T KNOW BUT YOU HAVE FRIENDS WHO WILL TRY TO MAKE IT HAPPEN. INCLUDING ME. I WANT TO SEE A REAL RED DOUBLE-DECKER BUS."

Lynsey almost snorted out loud. "Why a red bus? You've seen pyramids, the world filled with Egyptians, and you want to see a red bus?"

"I BET YOU WANTED TO SEE THE PYRAMIDS BEFORE YOU GOT HERE?"

"Well, of course. Who wouldn't?"

"SAME THING."

Illyara had moved into the corner and was having the time of her life. Tasting every morsel on the table, she eyed up each titbit, delicately picking it up between forefinger and thumb before placing it in her mouth. It was like watching a lesson in deportment. Lynsey joined her and tried to copy her, but she was so hungry that she was glad her mother wasn't there to see how she ate.

Whenever the gentlemen couldn't get a dance with Lynsey, they asked Illyara. Lynsey's jaw dropped with amazement as her friend glided across the dance floor without missing a step.

"How did you learn to dance like that?"

Illyara's face was flushed and her eyes sparkled as she answered.

"Lord Serenu and his daughter bought passage across the desert about five years ago. Darani was bored, so she taught me to dance over the weeks. It is so different dancing here than under the stars." She hopped on one foot. "No sand in my shoes, for one thing!"

The rest of the evening passed by in a blur. She danced with several men and ate until her dress protested. What made the night extra perfect, she reflected, was that the king stayed away for the rest of the night.

Everyone was exhausted by the time they entered the carriage to go home. Illyara was happier than Lynsey had ever seen her and Darianna was glowing from all the attention she'd received.

They set off slowly while they waited for the other carriages to clear a path. The air was still cold, but Lynsey didn't mind. It had been a good night. She had spoken to dozens of people. If notoriety would make them safe, then they had made a good start.

Before they left the grounds, Arkan slipped into the carriage quietly. Across from Lynsey, Darianna's face lit up. Lynsey couldn't help but feel a small kernel of happiness when she saw him, although she was careful to keep her expression neutral.

"Well done." He announced to the coach. "You navigated that rather well. Any foibles were easily explained by your upbringing on the islands. How did you get the invitation to the Temple? I overheard Baserius telling the king he had a prior appointment showing you around."

"I don't know. He just asked. Maybe he wanted to know where I got the elephant."

"You had an elephant?" he asked.

"About this big," she held up her fingers, "and made of gold and jewels."

"Where did you get it all?"

"The pyramids. They were just lying about in there. I don't know why they didn't take them when they left."

Darianna chimed in. "I think I might know why. There are legends of a dragon which drove them away. A band of men went in search of the pyramids and were said to have found and slain the dragon. The men returned and called themselves the Dragon Brotherhood. They got lost on the way back and have been trying to get back there ever since."

"How do you know this?" Arkan asked.

"I read a lot of history, Arkan." Darianna's voice held an injured tone.

"No one knows where the pyramids are after all this time?" asked Lynsey.

"No."

"Actually," Everyone turned to look at Illyara,

"My people know, but we would never go there because it is cursed."

Arkan turned back to look thoughtfully at Lynsey. "I think the Dragon Brotherhood know you got the elephant from the pyramids and they are hoping to get the location from you."

"I couldn't find it again if I tried."

"They don't know that, but it is probably why he wants to take you on a tour." Arkan rubbed his face with his hands. "This could be really useful for me. I need to find what they are hiding on the lower floors. If we can get them distracted with you, then I can see if I can get downstairs."

97

16 Glimpse of Gifts

aserius put down his pen for the third time in ten minutes and rubbed his face in his hands. Taking up the pen again, he tapped a slow rhythm on the desk while he stared in to space towards the window. He sighed and tried to make sense of the scroll in front of him, but it was no use. The chair scraped across the wooden floor as he got up to stride across the floor to look out of the window.

The Brotherhood had built this city, maybe not with their hands, but with their money and guidance. Now the money was running out. But finally, on his watch, they might just get to the wealth that was rightfully theirs.

He surveyed the room at the threadbare furniture. The small number of jewels the Brotherhood had come away with was nearly gone. They could barely afford to keep up appearance, never mind keep the upstart king in check. The man was getting above himself. If the Brotherhood wanted the status that they'd lost, no, that they deserved, then they needed funds. Money to feed the brethren and money to recruit an army to put the king in his place.

He dropped on to a leather seat by the window. The gentle breeze brought in a strong smell of sage mixed in with fruit trees. He breathed in deeply, finding the combination calming. From here he saw across the city and right up to the palace. In fact, the temple was higher than the King's residence. This was a statement on where the real power lay in the land, he thought with satisfaction. He would not be known as the high priest that ceded control.

There was also the oddity of the girl. Blond people just did not exist. His head rose slowly in realisation. Just like dragons didn't exist. Maybe they were from the same place? If they were from the same origin, maybe they were akin in other ways. Would she have similar abilities? They were limited to how much elixir they could make with what they had. With more, who knows what they could achieve?

As he watched the street through the window, he saw the red carriage belonging to the Duchess trundle around the corner. He leaned forward for a better look as they passed beneath the window. Three ladies alighted to Baserius' displeasure. His lips thinned as he saw them group together on the ground. A footman dropped from atop the carriage, carrying their personal effects. How many was he going to entertain? Baserius ground his teeth. It was foolhardy to think the girl would come on her own. He expected her companion to come, but why the Duchess? This would take all his tact.

***

Lynsey took her purse from the footman. It was light, containing only a few coins and a handkerchief. She thought it was stupid when she had to hand it to the footman before the carriage only to get it back at the other end, but Darianna was strictly on protocol.

"One does not carry objects unless for effect or when strictly necessary." She'd said. The woman was getting on Lynsey's nerves.

Lynsey smiled at the servant and thanked him with a curtsey. Her skirt grazed the deep-packed mud street, and she ruefully shook off the loose dust that gathered on the hem. The footman nodded and silently climbed back up to his place next to the coachman, driving off to come back at the appointed time. Darianna let out an exasperated sigh.

"One does not courtesy to a footman or any other servant, for that matter." She reprimanded.

Lynsey rolled her eyes and ignored her, breezing past her to knock on the door. A brother she hadn't seen before slid open the hatch and immediately pulled the bolts to let them in. He motioned for them to follow him and his arms dropped to fold inside the sleeves of his deep-red robes as he led the way. His pace was quick, and he ushered them across the hall and straight through to the high priest's office.

"Ladies, it is lovely to see you. I wasn't quite expecting so many of you, or I would have provided more cups." Baserius rose from the window seat to ring a bell. He indicated for them to sit on two plain chairs made of a soft wood brought in especially for them.

Lynsey glanced at Illyara, whispering, "Shall we stand? I think their counting has a little to be desired."

"Well, a duchess never stands if she doesn't need to." Darianna sat down, crossing her ankles while placing her purse on her lap.

Within moments, a man wearing the customary crimson robes entered.

"Please, could you get another cup for our guests?" Baserius' voice was genial, coming from behind them, "and a chair of course."

He waved his hands at his guests. The brother slipped out of the room as he continued. "I thought we could have a small chat before we got started." Their startled faces made his mood lighten, and he smiled. "I understand you grew up in the western isles. One of our brothers has recently travelled back from there. I'm sure you will have a lot to talk about. I hear the weather is inclement there."

"To be honest, I would rather forget about that place. The boredom of rural life is best left in the past. I want to enjoy a life with more diversions. I love my father, but his dedication to the provinces is not mine. It's great to be in the big city at last," Lynsey retorted, beaming her biggest smile.

He nodded. "The charms of the provinces can be quite alluring, but I can see the excitement of the big city is more in keeping with youth. Come," he stood and showed the door. "Let us begin the tour while we wait for the extra cup."

The tour of the upper levels went quickly. Baserius was knowledgeable about every facet of its construction. As he talked about flying buttresses, and carvings of dragons which glowered down from above at regular intervals, Lynsey's mind inevitably wandered to Arkan. Where was he? Was he safe? Her eyes searched the shadows for him as they moved from room to room. Was he even here yet? If he was in trouble, she could help him. She hated being the decoy.

"… and here is a picture of the pyramids. It was painted when the temple was first built. There are many who do not believe they existed, but how else did we come to this place?" Baserius pointed at a mural that sat behind long trestle tables, beside a lone brother eating a meal of green vegetables. He paused, waiting for Lynsey to respond.

"He wants me to tell him about the pyramids." She directed at Pico.

"IT WOULD APPEAR SO. THAT WOULD NOT BE A WISE IDEA."

"I seem to agree with you more and more."

"I WILL GROW ON YOU."

"Yeah, like moss."

Pico's thoughts rolled in violet as he laughed.

Baserius was now talking about the windows and it took all Lynsey's strength to not roll her eyes at the tedium.

"Excuse me, may I use your bathroom?"

He halted mid-step and turned to look at her. "Bathroom?" His brows furrowed. "You want to have a bath?"

"I'm sorry where I am from. The bathroom was used as a euphemism for the toilet."

"Oh, we can't allow you to use our facilities here. It would not be seemly. We do not have a separate place for women. We are a male only order. May I suggest the inn across the road?"

"That will be fine. I'll just pop along and be back long before you even notice I'm gone."

Lynsey's thoughts raced. If she was fast, she could buy a few minutes so she could do some snooping of her own. She sedately walked out of the room and rushed through to the front entrance.

The doorman was sitting on a bare wooden bench next to the entrance. He groaned as he stood up, but let her out without looking at her.

Her eyes burned from the bright sun and she raised her hand to cover them as she stepped out from the entrance. She squinted as she descended the steep, sand-stone steps. At the foot, she paused. The pavement, if you could call it that, was practically non-existent, barely a person's width. She shrugged and walked along it, avoiding pools of excrement on the dirt.

Shading her eyes with her purse, there was a use for the infernal thing, after all. She looked for the inn. A prominent sign down the street declared its owner to be the Dragon Inn. That must be it. Original, she thought, not without a touch of sarcasm.

The traffic was quite light, only a carriage or two passing through, with a few lunchtime sellers going home with empty hand-carts. Out of habit, she gave the road a cursory look from left to right before crossing. The inn looked less than inviting. The sort of place that would make an impressive setting for a horror movie, she mused. Paint was peeling, and the sign was falling off. Pico sent her a mental image of ghouls hanging out of the windows and lightning reigning down from above. She snorted as it faded away.

Her foot squished into the biggest pile of horse manure she had ever seen. Oh, for god's sake! As she lifted her foot with disgust, she heard a whinny, and she turned to see a horse's gallop around the corner towards her. It was pulling an individual carriage out of control. Her heart beat faster and she felt Pico take control, but it was too late. The horse hit her, sending her flying.

***

Baserius was finding it difficult to keep the show going while continuing the tour without the girl. The whole point of the tour was to quiz her about the location of the pyramids, and she'd left him with her companions. They seemed to hang on his every word, which was some comfort, but there were more important things he could do with his time than babysit a couple of females.

"While we are waiting for Miss Walker, shall we retire back to my office for a cup of tea?"

As they were turning, Brother Leer ran across the foyer towards them. Baserius felt a twinge of relief at the distraction, but Brother Leer's expression gave him pause. His lips were set in a line and his ambling gait was faster than normal. Something was wrong, he noted with mild curiosity.

The Brother gestured for them to follow him back to the front entrance. Baserius bristled at the command but recognised that whatever had happened, Brother Leer could not break his silence in front of his guests.

As they neared the door, they heard shouts from outside. The nomad girl was the first to run through the door and Darianna was blocking his view, so he was the last to see Lynsey on the ground. It took a second to register the scene. What was most surprising was to see Arkan Blade beside her. What was he doing here?

His contemplation turned to disbelief, then pleasure when he saw a gash on the girl's arm heal up before Illyara moved between him and her. Lynsey was like the dragon! If she could heal up instantaneously, was she also immortal? He had to find out. He coughed to clear his throat.

"This is beyond protocol, but may I offer sanctuary in our Temple until the Lady Lynsey is well enough to travel?"

Arkan stared down at Lynsey's battered face. As he watched, abrasions and cuts healed. Her fingers in his straightened and her eyelashes fluttered. Gods, she was beautiful. Fear warred with feelings he couldn't identify. No one healed that fast, but she was the same girl he had rescued the night before. Was it the bracelet? He rubbed her wrists with his thumb and forefinger, but felt only silken skin. Where was it? If she wasn't wearing it, then how was she healing like that? There was more to her than she was telling him.

101

In his arms, she groaned and put her hand up to her forehead, wincing.

"What happened?" She whispered. Then she looked at him. "You're here?"

He laughed. "Yes, I'm here. You had an accident."

She grimaced again and sat upright. He let his hands drop to his side.

"Can you get up? It's not safe on the street."

She nodded, and with his help, she made it to the curb. She brushed her hair back from her face so it fell over the high collar of her yellow dress. While the colour suited her, he couldn't help but think it was a poor choice to visit the temple. Darianna would have warned her it would get dirty on the dusty streets, but he thought with fondness, this was a lady who knew what she wanted.

He shouldn't get involved with her, he reminded himself, but she felt so fragile in his arms. He felt an overarching need to protect her. Arkan shouted at Darianna to call for her carriage, but saw it was already making its way towards them. He lifted Lynsey easily into his arms and carried her into the carriage, where Illyara was waiting. He heard Darianna thank Baserius, but that she had it all in hand.

Lynsey's eyes rolled back and her head lolled sideways as she fell back into his arms. Arkan felt for her pulse. It was beating strongly. He sighed with relief. It gave him a chance to talk to Darianna. Illyara was tactfully looking out of the window.

"Baserius noticed her healing?"

"I saw. That was not normal." Her eyes accused him. "What have you got me involved in, Arkan?"

"She is an innocent. We have to protect her."

"She doesn't look like she needs much protecting from what I saw."

"She is not from here."

"Clearly,"

Arkan tried again. "Do you not like her? You have spent a lot of time with her over the last few days. She does not mean any harm and simply wanted to find help." He tried to divine what Darianna was thinking from her expression, but she was giving nothing away. After a moment, she replied.

"We have no choice but to protect her now. She has been publicly announced as part of my family. My reputation would be damaged if her ability and our deception were to get out. This was just a game when you approached me, Arkan. I have worked too hard in society to let that happen now." Her voice trailed off as she watched buildings go past through the open curtains of the window. "This will be hard to contain."

Arkan agreed. "There was something about the way he looked at her."

"A spider looking at a fly?" She suggested sadly.

"Something like that. I think we not only have the King to worry about but also Baserius."

"It would seem so."

Illyara chimed in. "Would it be better for us to go somewhere else? Lynsey wanted to come to remove a bracelet, but she has made peace with it now and is happy to keep it. There is no reason for us to stay in this city any longer. I don't know why she agreed to see the Temple or why she wants to stay."

"What bracelet?" Darianna asked.

Illyara's eyes widened as she realised her mistake. "Oh, she has removed it on her own now."

Seeing no bracelet on the sleeping girl's arm, Darianna let it go.

"I think you should stay. Not because I want her to stay, but both those men are dangerous and they will do their utmost to capture her. Wherever she goes, she will be in danger, but here we can protect her - and us."

"You call this protecting?"

"Illyara, this wasn't our fault. This was neither the work of the King nor Baserius. It was an accident."

"She seems to have a lot of those." Arkan interjected.

"It is a good thing she has found some friends then, isn't it?"

17 Osiris' Legacy

Lynsey drifted in a void of white emptiness. She felt no fear, only calm. Glancing down, she studied her hands as tendrils of pale mist wrapped around her fingers with the delicacy of spun silk. There was no reason for alarm here. The fog embraced her like a soft, familiar blanket, lending a sense of belonging in this timeless space. Lynsey allowed herself to relax into the gentle caress of the mist, secure, knowing that for now, in this moment, all was well.

After a few more minutes of swirling whiteness, she got bored. This place could really do with some colour, she thought, and a mixture of pale purple and blue swirled around her, making patterns in the air. It made her think of a rainbow and a burst of colours shot through, streaking the air, breaking up the swirls, leaving afterimages. The blues and greens turned into bubbles, floating in different directions. She wondered if she could pop them.

In the distance, she heard her name, and she languidly twisted her neck to see who was calling. It seemed so far away, and it really wasn't that important. Nothing was. It was so peaceful here. She watched as a purple bubble floated past her eyes, making her momentarily cross-eyed.

The voice was getting louder, and she saw a figure walking towards her. It was getting closer, but still Lynsey didn't feel nervous, just curious. Soon enough, the stranger's face became clearer, but she didn't recognise her. The stranger was smiling and waved shyly as she drew up close.

"Hello Lynsey."

Hello? She knew her name. Did she know her?

"I'm Pico."

Lynsey looked closely at the woman, taking in her clear olive skin, the warm depth of her brown eyes, the lively bounce of her curls, and the genuine smile that instantly put Lynsey at ease. With her relaxed posture, she exuded an inviting and non-threatening presence.

"Where am I? How can I see you?"

"You are somewhere between dreaming and the awake state. It's the only way we can meet face-to-face. Do you like the way I look? I chose the attributes you most like to see in others from your memories." Pico twirled on the invisible ground.

Lynsey didn't quite know how to answer that. "You are a collection of Pico-something. Why do you care what I think?"

Pico's face fell. "I'm a person. I thought you knew that now. With thoughts and feelings. They were developed from yours, but I am my own person. We just share a body. I have said little for the past week because I had to sort through my feelings. I was born when you put on that bracelet. You put it on, no one forced you to. What you did created me. I'm entitled to think."

"I didn't know what would happen when I put on the bracelet." Lynsey struggled to keep her attention on the conversation and not on the colourful display behind Pico.

"It doesn't matter what you intended, it matters to me that I exist." Pico's voice was earnest. "Don't you remember your philosophy classes? I think therefore I am? You created me. Your actions ended up with me. Me. I had nothing to do with it, but now I am here. I deserve to live."

Fear dripped down Lynsey's spine. Pico had her full attention now. "Are you going to take over?"

Anger turned to horror on Pico's face. "Of course not! You are my mother. I would protect you with my life, but I won't give up that life willingly. But maybe you could share your body once in a while? I'm not asking for whole days or anything, just maybe the occasional evening, maybe a morning?"

This was the most bizarre conversation that Lynsey thought she would ever have with anyone. Her eyes widened in disbelief, her jaw hung slack, and she stumbled back a step as if the ground beneath her had shifted. This was a reality far beyond her wildest imagination—stranded in a strange world pursued by unknown forces and now confronted with an entity within her claiming that Lynsey was her mother? This was too much! She almost didn't hear what Pico said next.

"After all, now that you are immortal, sharing some time here and there won't really affect you."

"I'm sorry, what?"

Pico backtracked. What had she said? "Didn't I mention that? That was the other reason that I have been around a little. I was looking into some anomalies. You weren't reacting the same as I was expecting during our walk in the desert and it wasn't all me healing you. And then you had some cuts and bruising when they captured you in the park. Again, you healed quicker than humanly possible. I did some more investigating, and my conclusion is that you are immortal."

"Immortal? That's ridiculous!"

"No, it isn't. I've been thinking about it. When the Egyptians sent copies of themselves through the pyramids, they were alive when the energy fields hit them and their code was sent through to this world. I think when you came here, you died and a copy of you was sent here through a black hole with some extra information. What happened to you was 'natural' as opposed to what the Egyptians designed. They wanted what you have but didn't have the technology to replicate it. If it is even possible to duplicate that process. Every time you are injured, your body asserts its original DNA map. It is why you were so hungry at the banquet. You needed the calories to recover."

"You say that I cannot die?"

"Well, technically, you could die. If you jumped into a volcano, or you were vaporised then there would be no hope. Maybe if someone chopped off your head … but then you would probably come back from that. All your previous memories are saved in your code. I think that if you come close to dying, then you might reset to when you arrived in this world. You will lose all your experiences from the time you arrive until you 'die."

That made Lynsey pause. "That would be awful. I would not understand how I got here. I might have gone mad if I hadn't met Illyara or had time to acclimatise before I met anyone. This world is too different."

"It is okay. I have a plan. I have been creating a backup in the bracelet." Pico beamed at her cleverness.

"You did what? All my memories are in the band?" She looked down to see the bracelet replicated on her arm.

"Why yes? Just think, if some impossible misfortune were to fall on us and you were killed, someone in the future could upload you to a computer, like me!"

What sounded almost like a good idea was sounding like an awful one. "Pico, that's terrible."

"Whyyyy issss…." Pico's voice was distorting. Her image glitched.

"Pico?"

Pico couldn't answer, but she lifted a fuzzy arm to say goodbye, and she was gone.

***

Lynsey woke in confusion, her mind a swirl of emotions, but she adeptly adjusted her breathing, allowing her body to appear at rest, as she heard Arkan talking with Darianna. She didn't feel like talking to anyone for a few minutes. Pico had better be quiet as well while she processed what she said. Immortal? She really was immortal but she might lose all her Duat memories? That would be like dying over and over again. It would be like she searched for the word, like some sort of dementia.

Laura's voice floated into her hearing. "… not because I want her to stay, but both those men are dangerous and they will do their utmost to capture her. Wherever she goes, she will be in danger, but here we can protect her—and us."

Lynsey froze. Arkan didn't want her to stay?

"You call this protecting?"

"Illyara, this wasn't our fault. This was neither the work of the King nor Baserius. It was an accident."

"She seems to have a lot of those." Arkan replied with a sardonic twist to his voice.

"It is a good thing she has found some friends then, isn't it?" Affirmed Illyara.

Of all the nerve. She wasn't accident prone and if it wasn't for people after her, she would have survived very well. Thank you very much!

She gave it a few more moments and then she groaned as she moved. Arkan stopped talking and moved his hand away from her hair. She sat up and noticed the carriage was nearing Darianna's house. Arkan was sitting in the carriage corner, looking out of the window. Had she imagined his hand in her hair?

"I think I need a rest." Lynsey said aloud.

"I think we all do. " The Duchess replied.

18 Nexus of Power

"Why was Arkan here?" Baserius' gaze seared into the two Brothers standing in front of him. Their heads hung low, hiding their expressions within their hoods. They knew there was nothing they could say that would ease his wrath.

"Did he get into the Temple?" Again, no response from the Brothers. "Did anyone see him inside!"

Baserius let out some deep breaths. If it was not for the girl, this would be dangerous news. The only reason Arkan would sniff around the temple would be if the King ordered him to. If they got more gold and jewels, then these silly games the King was playing would be irrelevant. He would be crushed easily and a replacement put in his place. It had been done before and so it would be done again. Finding the pyramids was a distant dream a few days ago. Now it was a distinct possibility. His voice grew softer.

"There would be no way to tell, I suppose. Were the guards on the stairs at all times?" Their shoulders relaxing, the Brothers nodded their response.

"They saw nothing." The nearest replied.

"At least that is something." Baserius moved away to stand in front of his desk. He reached inside his drawer, pushing away scrolls and parchment until he located a golden key. He pulled it out, trailing a chain made from the same metal attached to it. Placing it around his neck, he beckoned the others to follow him.

"Come, it is time for the ceremony. I grow tired," he said as they exited the room.

They followed him along the corridor and down some stairs to the basement entrance, where two Brothers guarded another stairway. The guards were a decoy from the true entrance to their right. If any spy got past the guards, all they would find would be the temple's food and wine stores.

Baserius bypassed them, not sparing the guards a glance and moved on a few feet to a place only an ordained brother could go. Behind a tapestry, a plain wooden door barred their way. Baserius placed the key in the lock and twisted it easily. On the other side was a featureless corridor and another door on the other side.

He strode along the terracotta tiles, his boots clicking a regular rhythm. The Brothers followed closely at his heels. He knocked three times sharply and a further three times slowly. The door opened and an old man stood in the doorway. He gave a nod to Baserius and looked behind him to the two Brothers who pushed back their hoods so he could recognise them. He turned a lamp on a table beside him to its full capacity. His grizzled features twisted into recognition, and he moved aside to let them pass.

From the doorway, all they heard was the sound of scraping metal against stone as the ceremonial knife was sharpened to a slow tempo. As the men moved further into the chamber, they could hear the murmur of hundreds of voices.

All three held their noses for a moment in the gloom. Experience had taught them it would take a while for their noses to adjust to the stench of defecation and blood that permeated the basement. The doorman smiled grimly at their discomfort.

"Has he been quiet?"

"Why do you always ask, Baserius? He has been quiet for a century. The beast is resigned to his fate. He is only a dumb creature, after all. All animals will lie quiet with the right training." The voice came from a figure drawing close, wearing the same blood-red cowl from the robes that everyone else wore, hiding the figure's face. The voice was higher than normal, but with the unmistakable tone of confidence and power.

Baserius paused in response while he studied the animal. It was indeed quiet. He had never seen it exhibit any other behaviour. It lay on a bed of hay. Its head was low on its arms. Its talons were twisted underneath it, as were its wings. The chains criss-crossing the beast were tied to its arms, tail, and wings. They were taut and strong. Even if the dragon had the desire to move, it wouldn't be able to move more than a foot. A painted red circle surrounded the dragon, showing where it was safe to go near.

"I have some news," Baserius replied.

"The king is trying to overthrow you. I know. It happens every two generations. Make an example of him. It happened to your predecessor; it will happen to you. Why bother me with these banalities?" said the robed figure in front of him.

"No, this is something new. But our coffers are getting low. It will be difficult to make an example when we have no army to do so or money to bribe."

Around them, brethren were chanting quietly, moving with deliberation across the room in preordained patterns. The light from the scented candles wavered in their hands as they breathed.

"Redouble your efforts to find those pyramids. If we brought enough treasure to fund two centuries of this Temple from what we carried in our pockets. Think what you could do with a cartload."

"That is related to what I need to tell you about."

The hooded figure stayed silent, waiting for his explanation.

"A woman arrived in Ghinari a few weeks ago. She came here with a nomad girl." He took a breath, then coughed, regretting inhaling so deeply. "They left before I could question them, but they left an elephant ornament, which could only have come from the pyramids. Some jewels are not available in this world."

The old man who had let them in twisted to look at them from his post. His eyes brightened. "She has to have come from there."

"That is not all that is strange," Baserius ignored the older man, "she is blond so she cannot be from this world and she heals instantly." All three looked towards the beast.

"Interesting," came the muted reply.

19 Newfound Notoriety

Lynsey woke to find her dressing table littered with cards. She stretched out her arms and yawned, blinking sleepily. She wandered over, hitching up her nightgown with her left hand, and sipped from a glass of water she picked up from the side table on the way with the other. How did the staff get them in without waking her up? She didn't like people being in her room while she was asleep.

There were so many of them. She scanned the pile of invitations. There were more invitations here than she had birthday cards on her 18th birthday. She sat down, placing the water in an empty corner.

As she was sorting them into piles, Illyara wandered in.

"Listen to this," Lynsey read. "I would be honoured to invite you to the Contee ball." She grabbed another. "I am holding a small soiree, and I would like to invite you and your companion." She picked up card after card. "There are dozens of them. I'm finally popular." The last sentence was delivered with a twist to her mouth.

"Are you feeling alright?"

Lynsey thought back to yesterday's conversation between Arkan and Darianna. To be safe, she had to stay in Ghinari, but Arkan made it very clear he didn't want her here. She couldn't avoid him. If she stayed, then Arkan would see her every time he visited Darianna.

Lynsey stood up, reaching for the wardrobe beside the desk. She threw on a dress and tied her hair in a quick bun as she hurried out of the room.

"C'mon."

"Lynsey?"

"C'mon, we have to find Darianna."

They found the duchess reading in the Solar. A comfortable room, it had also been converted into a library. Scrolls were piled high on deep shelves that lined the longest wall. Sombre family portraits jostled together, hung wherever there was space along with landscapes between several tall windows which let the sun flood into the room.

Darianna sat on a settee surrounded by opened invitations. She looked up as they entered the room.

"Do I have enough money to have my own house?"

"Good morning to you too," Darianna replied.

"UH, LYNSEY I DON'T THINK THIS IS WISE YET." Pico's voice invaded her mind.

"Not now Pico."

"Why yes," Darianna replied, realising that a good morning was too much to ask. "You actually have more money than I do. Has someone offended you?"

"Oh no, I just feel it is time to stop presuming on you."

"Oh, my dear, you are really not presuming. I delight in your company. I haven't had such excitement in—well, forever. You are a tonic. Please do not feel that you have to leave. You are not taking advantage. In fact, I have had more invitations this morning to balls and dances than I have had in months and I am really rather popular. It has all made me feel ten years younger." She pointed at the sofa cushions littered with as many cards as Lynsey had received.

Lynsey exchanged looks with Illyara, giving Darianna a second glance. She couldn't be over thirty. She tried again.

"It's not that. It's just that I have never really lived with anyone before. I like to be independent."

Darianna scanned the invitations with a sad expression briefly and then looked up, smiling.

"In that case, please allow me to help you find somewhere to live. I believe Lord Trekarik has recently vacated Trekarik Park. Confidentially," Darianna's voice lowered, "I heard it was because he gambled his fortune away. Gambling is a fool's occupation, but you probably already know that." Darianna sat up and grabbed a scroll that threatened to slide off her lap to put it down on a nearby table.

"The Contee ball is tonight. I received an invitation this morning. They must have been curious about you to invite you on such short notice." She shuffled the piles looking for it. "Here it is. The King will not be attending and the High Priest certainly won't be there, so it should be a fun evening all around. We can have a quick look around Trekarik Park before lunch and we will still have time to get ready for the ball."

It took another hour before messages could be exchanged in order to visit the house. Lynsey paced the solar, unable to sit down while they waited for an answer. She barely held back her excitement. For years, she'd wanted to buy a house. She suspected that eventually she could have afforded a flat in one of the seedier areas of a city that wasn't London, but here she was not even twenty and she was going to buy a stately home.

A sudden rap on the door made her look up. A butler dressed in a yellow silk uniform entered, bringing a small folded slip of paper on a silver tray. He offered the tray to Darianna with a bow. Darianna rose and took the paper.

"There will be staff there this morning who can show us around. It is still open for offers."

Lynsey twisted to look at Illyara sitting on a nearby armchair. Her smile slipped at her friend's expression. Her forehead creased, but Illyara shook her head slightly. She would not say why in front of Darianna then.

On their way back to the room, Illyara took Lynsey's arm.

"You know this is not wise, Lynsey."

"Why not?"

"If we move, we will lose the protection that Darianna and Arkan afford."

"Illyara, I have enough money to have a thousand guards. We don't have to worry. We could have our own army if we needed to."

"It is not just that. We are strangers here. The conventions we should follow are a mystery to us.. We are strangers in a strange land."

"Illyara, it will be fine. We'll have the time of our lives."

She didn't want to tell Illyara that the real reason she wanted to buy a house was because she didn't want to bump into Arkan every five minutes.

Later that day, they swung into a wooded area from the main road that stretched through Ghinari. They were in the Duchess' second carriage, which, while not as grand, had, to Lynsey's relief, slightly more padding on the seats.

Tall trees with a distinctive red-violet bark grown in peculiar straight rows marked the beginning of Trekarik Park. They led the way down a well-maintained wide mud track. About a mile along, the path turned to cobbles and the smell of cut grass and a floral fragrance that reminded Lynsey of the King's ball announced the approaching formal gardens.

It was one of the oldest houses in the city, Darianna explained along the way, and as the wheels of their carriage crunched up beside the front door, the house did not disappoint. Its sweeping driveway was large enough to accommodate two carriages, and the house itself was sprawling.

A side door immediately opened, and two servants greeted them. The first was dressed in a green and yellow dress and the second wore loose-fitting trousers and a top of the same colours. The servants bowed first to the Duchess and then curtseyed to Lynsey and Illyara.

They pointed at the door, and the small party followed them.

"They don't talk much," whispered Lynsey.

Darianna leaned in between Lynsey and Illyara and whispered at the same level.

"It is alright, you cannot offend them. They are servants. Do I need to keep reminding you of this? I really don't know if you are ready to live on your own." She looked from Lynsey to Illyara and sighed. "They belong to a tribe bound by a sacred vow of silence. They communication by gestures. Their unique mode of interaction makes them exceptional servants, for they can carry no whispers of idle talk. Among Lord Trekarik's loyal retainers, these two stand as the longest-serving."

The pair waited patiently for the conversation to cease and then pointed forward again. Darianna nodded.

"We don't have long, you know, if we are to be ready for the ball tonight."

From there, they were shown around at a brisk pace. There were two floors and ten bedrooms. Lynsey walked around in a daze. Gold leaf on the walls? A swimming pool around the back and a ballroom to rival the King's. The more they were shown, the more the servants seemed almost tearful to be leaving.

"How many staff would you need to run this place?" Lynsey asked.

Darianna answered. "To run it, I would say at least thirty, but there are only five of them here currently. The old Duke couldn't afford to keep all the staff going."

"This place would house about five tribes," was Illyara's comment.

Darianna ignored Illyara. "This place is impressively big, but you would have to hire about fifty guards to make it safe. The park is no deterrent. If you built a wall to surround the house, it would be an improvement. Although it would ruin the look of the place. Even then Arkan could get over that in moments and he is not the only assassin in town."

Why did she have to bring up Arkan all the time? Hang on, did she just say Assassin?

Darianna's mouth formed an o at her expression. "You didn't realise? He's not just an assassin, he is the King's Assassin." Her mouth twitched in amusement. "I thought you knew."

"You have assassins here. Why would you do that?"

"To protect yourself. Why else? The best defence is an offence, after all."

"What about police?"

"What are police?" It was Darianna's turn to look puzzled.

"You don't have anyone who looks for criminals, enforce the laws?"

"Anyone can bring problems before the king. Why would we pay to sort out someone else's problems? We hire guards to look after our own things and put the rest in the bank."

The servants were getting restless. They needed a reply. Lynsey took another look at the grand hallway with its sweeping staircase and high ceilings. She couldn't have believed even visiting a place like this would have been possible a few weeks ago. This house could be hers. She thought about what Darianna had said. She had been kidnapped, but that was before the ball. Everyone knew about her now, and she had the protection of Darianna's family name. Wasn't that the whole point of going to the King's ball in the first place? He wouldn't go after her now. They were all exaggerating the danger. If she stayed in the public eye, maybe she could be safe and if she had to build a private army, then so be it. She chuckled. Who was exaggerating now?

"I'll take it." She replied at their questioning looks. A small smile greeted her answer.

The rest was a formality. They visited the bank, who transferred the amount needed to the duke. She didn't know what she expected, but since everyone used the same bank, it was just a matter of transferring the money from one vault to another. Here, the duke was happy to accept jewels in payment. Lynsey suspected he was getting a slighter better exchange rate than if she tried to sell the jewels herself, but she wanted the house and she didn't want to wait anymore.

They were back at Darianna's and readying for the ball, with plenty of time to spare.

"Aren't you excited about moving to our new place?" Lynsey asked Illyara.

A shadow of sadness crossed her friend's features, tugging at the corners of her smile. "I will miss Darianna, but I can only stay with you for a few more weeks. I should re-join my family."

Lynsey rolled over on top of the bedspreads to face Illyara. "I thought you could stay for years, explore the world, find love."

"I don't think I will find it here, Lynsey. They are all about money and status. These are not things my tribe value. I need to look elsewhere. You obviously want to make roots here and that is fine. I will always wish you well."

"Has your family been outside the gates all this time?"

"Oh no, they will have gone to a town further up by the coast, but they will be back here soon where I can join them again." Illyara looked down and then straight into Lynsey's eyes. "I am worried you will get lonely by yourself."

Lynsey lowered her eyes to look at the pattern on the bedspread. It wouldn't be right to keep Illyara away from her family and future.

"I'm never really alone now. Besides, I like Darianna too. She annoys me sometimes, but I think we can be friends. I just wish those two would either get together or not, so I know when to avoid Arkan."

"You think Darianna and Arkan are sweethearts?"

"Yes, it's obvious. He's always giving her doe-eyed looks."

Illyara smiled. "I am pretty sure they are not doe-eyed looks!"

"I think" Just then, Megan and Tegan knocked on the door, bringing in their dresses for the night.

They arrived at the ball only twenty minutes after the time written on the invitation, much to Darianna's chagrin. She had huffed at that, but Lynsey was still her guest, so she didn't make a fuss.

While the room was smaller than the other one, it was still elegant. There were light fixtures on the wall, but the Contees had used candles for their event instead of electric. The soft glow was a lot more flattering to the older ladies, Lynsey thought, but then given the age of the Contees - that was probably the plan.

Even though they were relatively early, there were a few men and women milling about the room. Lynsey sighed. She'd been right to come in earlier. She didn't feel like such a specimen. People were still looking at her, but they were also staring at her clothes, not just her hair this time.

Darianna looked gorgeous in a dark blue gown. The hemline trailed the floor, and the neckline showed off her best asset. Illyara's and Lynsey's outfits were demurer but just as striking. Lynsey's dress was pink, while Illyara's was green. They both had long skirts, but the cut stressed their youthful bodies. The dresses were daring, but revealing nothing. "It is how I got my first husband, darling." Darianna had said. "Before you marry, you need to tease - to draw the men to you. After your nuptials, you can do what you want."

In their room, Darianna spent a solid two hours discussing the expectations of society. These included never being alone with a man, waiting for an invitation to dance, and being mindful of portion sizes. The last topic was a barb aimed at Lynsey's plate at the King's feast, which was clearly still fresh on her mind.

"You want to become part of society, win over the other ladies. After all, what if one of them is married to the man who may ask you to be his wife?"

"Hang on, you can have more than one husband?"

"Hang on to what? No, a man may have two wives, but a woman can only have one husband."

"But your husband is only married to you?"

"I have the family and money that I can make sure he doesn't look at another woman."

Lynsey smiled to herself. There was more to Darianna than family or money.

Lynsey pulled up a fan that hung from a belt around her waist. She flicked it open and vigorously shook it to cool down her face. The room was getting full and the heat from the people and hundreds of candles was making it hot. Everyone seemed to be a little livelier than in the previous ball. People were smiling more, and she noted the men felt free to touch the arms or shoulders of the women. A lull in the surrounding conversation made Lynsey look for the source.

"Why has everyone gone quiet?" She elevated her neck to look around the room, but she couldn't see anything which would explain it.

"The king is coming!" A lady dressed next to them said in an over-loud whisper. "A footman saw his coach coming down the drive. The Contee has been trying to get him to come to one of their balls for years! But he won't go out to balls. They have finally made it. I'm hoping Arkan will be with him."

"Why would the king suddenly decide to come?"

The girl looked at Lynsey with pity. "You, of course. Everyone saw how he looked at you. He even danced with you."

Illyara was talking with a matron further into the room. Lynsey made her way through the crowd to her.

"The king is coming."

Illyara turned to her friend. "It's okay. He can't harm you here. This lady said that Arkan will probably come as well."

"All we need is Baserius, and we have a trifecta of my nemeses."

"Don't be silly, besides Arkan likes you."

"He just doesn't want me around."

"Whatever gave you that idea?"

"I heard him!"

Illyara's perplexed look made Lynsey doubt for a second, but she had heard him herself.

"I need to go out for some air."

The matron was taking it all in eagerly. You should use the balcony of the hallway on the second floor. There is a beautiful view from up there. "

"Thank you, I will." Lynsey picked up her skirt and made her way past the crowd. The room seemed to get darker. Everyone was watching her, their beady eyes boring into her back. She hated being the only blond person. She stood out like a frickin, sore thumb. If she stayed here, she would be stared at for her whole life and judging from what Pico said, that would be forever. She wouldn't be able to hide. Her hair would give her away. Lynsey paused on a step. How long before they would try to work out why she lived so long without aging?

The hallway on the second floor was lined with dark wood panels engraved with scenes from a past battle. She hardly glanced at them until she saw a pyramid. She felt Pico's interest flare in her consciousness.

"Can you see that?" Lynsey whispered.

"I CAN. THE PICTURES SEEM TO SAY THAT A DRAGON ESCAPED FROM A PYRAMID. FOR ALL THESE PEOPLE SAY THEY WANT TO FORGET THOSE THAT BROUGHT THEM HERE, THEY FIND WAYS OF REMINDING THEMSELVES. THE PYRAMID WAS IN THE TEMPLE AS WELL. THAT NEXT PAINTING SHOWS THAT THE EGYPTIANS ALL HAD TO LEAVE. HOW MUCH OF THIS IS MYTH?"

"I don't know, but this is fascinating."

"It is indeed." The voice was behind her, but she knew from the goose pimples rising in her arms who it was.

"Arkan."

"At your service."

She felt the heat from his body. She turned to find him inches from her. His fingertips grazed her arm, sending shivers of pleasure through her. This wasn't right. She looked into his eyes and melted into his arms. He brought his lips down onto hers while she lost herself in the depths of his eyes. Some last shred of her sanity took hold. No! This would not happen. She wouldn't share with anyone, not even with someone she liked and respected, like Darianna. She tore herself from his arms and ran. Her shoes clattered down the narrow stairs. Lynsey looked back up, but he wasn't following. She twisted back to bump into a man standing at the foot of the stairs.

Lynsey bounced off the King to stand inches from him. Her breaths came in quick gasps and her cheeks were bright pink, almost matching her dress. He stepped forward and took a stray tendril of hair and gently placed it over her ear.

Lynsey froze at his touch. He was handsome, but she disguised a shudder when his finger lowered to stroke her cheek. Why did the King's hand disgust her when Arkan made her breathless? She almost didn't hear the King's next words.

"For you, I would get rid of my wives and mistress."

Her lips parted in horror. This man was a monster. She backed away and headed to the ballroom and relative safety. She looked back, and he was still there, looking into space as if lost in a daydream.

20 Osiris Band Origins

Arkan's feet padded on the ground as he approached the Palace on foot. Overhead, ominous clouds covered the sky, periodically blocking the light from the silver crescent moons. Perfect conditions for a clandestine visit.

The surrounding woods were quiet except for the occasional call from a night owl to disturb the stillness. The only similarity to the bird of myth was its propensity to hunt at night. Its size, claws and intelligence made it a formidable opponent to humans. The hairs on the back of his neck tingled, keeping him scanning for any sound or movement above him. He could fight it off with no problem, but the sound the creature would make would alert everyone for an iteru. He could explain why he was creeping around the palace grounds at night while the king was away, but it would be better not to.

There was something about how the king acted that confused him. Herad had been watching the Temple for days. The grizzled veteran was old but very reliable in all the time he'd known him. He'd sat heavily on the tavern bench that afternoon. Arkan watched as the old man hid a grimace to disguise his pain. He took a deep draught of the beer that Arkan had ordered before he'd arrived and wiped his mouth with the back of his hand. His eyes twinkled.

"I have news, young assassin."

"Herad, not here."

"No one can hear. That screeching sound, I hesitate to call music, is too loud and that rabble wouldn't be interested, anyway."

"There are ears everywhere, Herad." Arkan admonished, flicking a coin between his fingers. His legs stretched out on the opposite chair to deter anyone foolish from sitting there. "What have you seen?"

"The king visited Baserius this afternoon." Herad coughed and spluttered for a moment before swallowing it back down with a swig of beer.

Arkan looked up at Herad, but he was deadly serious. Why would the king do that without telling him? He flipped the coin he was holding in the air and the old man grabbed it without blinking. Anyone watching would have been hard pressed to see the action, but within moments, the barmaid came over to refill Herad's drink. Arkan left while the other man was busy.

There were a few guards in the palace gardens. Their heavy boots made them noisy and cumbersome in the undergrowth, allowing Arkan to evade them with no trouble. He moved like a ghost from trees to statues until he came up to the folly he was looking for.

It was built over a century ago. Added to the designs by the Assassins'

Guild with coins greasing the right palms. If you didn't know what you were looking for, the building was just a tall tower. Its ground floor was open to the elements, providing a brief shelter from the rain or sun for people enjoying the gardens.

Arkan entered the structure and moved to the south-west corner where he pushed some dirt away to reveal a ring embedded in the wooden floorboard. It resisted for a moment, but he strained his muscles to pull harder. Dirt cascaded down from the hatch that opened, revealing a dark opening. He dropped, pulling the hatch closed behind him. The action jarred a chain that moved a small piece of wood that contained some dirt above the hatch. The dirt fell to the ground, concealing the hatch once again from prying eyes.

Arkan hunched down into the narrow tunnel. He bent with difficulty to get the flint from his pocket. Feeling along the wall, he found an alcove where a lamp had been hidden by a predecessor. He would have to remember to replace it later. He struck twice before the tunnel illuminated.

It smelled musty. Swathes of spider webs filled the space ahead with dust mites swirling in the lamplight. Arkan reached for a light wooden shield on a stick which had been left on its side beside him. The contraption protected his clothes from the worst of the tunnel detritus by bringing down the webs as he walked. It wouldn't be done to be seen wearing filthy clothes when he entered the palace. It would arouse suspicion. He moved forward, holding the device before him. It was light, but the awkward angle made it seem heavier than it was.

Arkan exhaled slowly as the tight earthen walls of the tunnel widened into the familiar stone corridors of the palace basement. He straightened to his full height, the ceiling now high enough that he no longer needed to crouch. Dropping the shield and lamp in an alcove made for that purpose, he rolled his shoulders to relieve the tension. He stepped forward into the lamp-lit passage, leaving the claustrophobic oppressiveness of the tunnel behind.

His soft leather boots made no sound on the smooth flagstones as he navigated the maze of deserted lower passages. At this late hour, the hustle-bustle of the day had faded to an echoing stillness. As Arkan climbed the stairs to the occupied floors above, his senses strained for any sign of life. But the halls remained hushed as the flickering torchlight was replaced by dim electric lights.

Reaching the King's private study undetected, Arkan paused, his eyes drawn upward. There, on the panelled wall, hung an intricately woven tapestry depicting the royal crest. Behind its layered threads lay the hidden door through which he had passed countless times before. Letting out a slow breath, Arkan pulled back the heavy fabric and slotted a key into the disguised lock near the top of the door. The door itself was shaped and decorated as a panel for when the tapestries were cleaned once a year. The key turned with a small click and the door swung inward without a sound.

Unlike the king's official study, this one had few luxury trappings. The king liked to play the playboy in front of his subjects, the absent-minded lord, but

Arkan knew the king had a mind like a steel trap. If there was anything the king was hiding from him, then this would be the place. He would find it.

Arkan searched the desk but found only business documents. Now, where would they be? He stood with his back to the door and scanned the room for anomalies. There, that had to be it. On the shelves against the longest wall were hundreds of small thin boxes made to hold scrolls. Each one was in precise alignment. Except - one of them jutted out against the others on the end of the shelves next to the desk. There was a thin layer of dust covering all but that one. Arkan smiled; it must have been recently used. Arkan reached up and felt the box. It rattled as the contents shifted to the side and downwards as he drew it from the shelf. He brought the box closer to his face and sniffed. A sharp whiff of incense shot up his nose. It could only have come from one place.

"The temple," he breathed, "this is why he went there."

Arkan put the box on the desk and pulled the chair under him. The king had already left for the ball, so there was no need to worry about time.

He pulled the scroll out and skimmed through the glyphs. It was about myths? Why would Baserius give the king this? Further down the scroll was a crude illustration of the Osiris band and Arkan's breath caught. Baserius knew about that? Arkan delved further in and a history he knew nothing of before unfolded.

During the reign of Suramus II, he read, an expedition was called to find the ancient pyramids of myth. The scroll detailed the provisions taken like a shopping list. Arkan's eyes glazed, and he skipped down the inventory.

It took weeks to prepare the scroll went on; the provisions had to be found, guides and men hired.

Arkan's finger traced down the aged parchment, searching for where the tale resumed. After weeks crossing the merciless desert sands, provisions depleted, the adventurers reached the ancient temple as dawn broke over the horizon. A thunderous roar shattered the morning stillness as an immense dragon emerged between the towering pyramids.

Arkan's head jerked up in surprise before he caught himself, eager to read on. His dark eyes narrowed, transfixed by the incredible account. A dragon? Until recently, he would have dismissed such fanciful myths. But now that he knew the band existed, he found himself rapt, suspending disbelief as he devoured every word. What other secrets did these texts hold? He leaned in, hungry to unravel more of the mystery that cloaked his people's past.

A great battle was fought over the next few hours. The explorers on the expedition were not soldiers. They were not expecting to fight anyone or anything, but they fought on for the riches they were promised.

Whatever they did to the dragon, they found to their fear that it would not die. They removed its head with a heroic slash of a blade and for a while; they thought it was over until it grew back within hours. This time, the dragon grew even more ferocious in its defence.

Arkan stopped reading. Lynsey had healed remarkably quickly. He remembered how her bruises had disappeared before his eyes after the accident. Was she like the dragon?

He bent down to read again, turning the lamp up a notch.

Finally, the men could put chains on it and they trapped the dragon on to their cart. The roars were deafening, but they slashed it with swords until it subsided. As the blade sunk into the dragon's arm, its blood spurted on to the wounds of an injured explorer. To the amazement of the rest of the expedition, the wound healed before their eyes.

There were jewels and objects beyond price found in just one of the pyramids, but the transport was filled with an even greater treasure, the dragon. They filled their pockets and took what they could fit in every nook and cranny available, leaving treasure beyond their imagining behind them. They would come back.

Arkan's head jerked up as he noticed how much time had slipped by unnoticed. He hastily skimmed over the next few paragraphs. The adventurers were set upon by a band of desert marauders; the text recounted. In the skirmish, one of the party was grievously injured, defending a comrade. Though they cut down the attackers, the fight had carried them to the far edge of the camp. A stray ember from the violence caught their provisions alight. Arkan's pulse quickened as he read how the blaze rapidly spread, consuming precious supplies and hand-drawn maps needed to navigate back through the endless dunes.

Further down the scroll again, there was an illustration of the temple being built over the dragon.

Arkan rolled up the scroll and put it back into the box. He was careful to place it exactly as he'd found it. He'd read enough. Here was the proof that Lynsey was in danger. If Baserius and the king were prepared to ally to get hold of Lynsey, nowhere was safe in Ghinari. He and Darianna were wrong. For the power of the Osiris band, the location of unlimited treasure and blood that healed any wound, there would be nothing Baserius or the king would not do to get her.

21 Mind Manipulation

Several courtiers surrounded Illyara in a loose circle. There was plenty of space in the room. Why did they have to stand so near? She looked from one to the other. Their bland expressions of feigned boredom on their painted faces were tedious. Her stomach muscles tightened, and she closed her eyes for a second to centre herself. Where was Lynsey? She may be strange and from another world, but she was far from scary and never boring. That was it. The reason she was on edge. If she was being completely honest with herself, these people were a little frightening. It was like they used that painting to disguise their true selves. Some instinct made her shift her weight onto the balls of her feet. What had seemed friendly when they walked in was taking on a darker aura. Why was she thinking that? She relaxed her muscles and readjusted her weight as she tried to shake the mood off. She must be imagining it. But the same ability that helped her become invisible was warning her of something. If only she could read thoughts. These hunches were just too vague to be helpful.

It was too late. She couldn't stop thinking something was wrong now. She looked for routes of escape in the gaps between people. There were just so many of them. Men and women hovered around her like bees to honey. Her instincts warred with her reason. There was no reason to be afraid. They looked vacuous. There was nothing actually threatening in their expressions or even the way they were acting. This was ridiculous, she chided herself. A wave of homesickness for the emptiness of the desert swept over her, leaving her feeling desolate. She needed to leave the city.

"...and the Maree's heir had to visit Dirik's!" Mirth erupted around her, but as she looked at the lord nearest her and then at the next, she realised their smiles didn't quite reach their eyes. They were enjoying her discomfort.

She had barely heard what they said for the last half hour. Nodding seemed to be enough for them. And Lynsey had still not come back. Where was she? She was only supposed to be going to cool down. But, Illyara reflected, she had looked annoyed. Maybe she should go after her? The man in front had stopped talking and was looking at her as if waiting for an answer. What had he said?

Goddess! Did it matter? These people were so superficial. All the women talked of was the latest fashions, how handsome Lord so and so is. The men talked about the weather, races, and their prowess at war. They were all over-dressed, over opinionated nitwits. Her hands clenched by her sides as she caught sight of the food table beyond the man. She was fuming. Her people were starving, no, not just her people, but there were others across the land who were suffering, so these idiots could eat stuffed perkot and moan about the rain shower that made their hair ever so slightly frizzy last week.

The more she thought about it, the more definite she was that her father was right. Anger replaced nebulous fear. She had to see for herself that Ghanarians were corrupt to the core. Even Darianna played the game. She had shown them a different side over the last couple of weeks, but she obviously had no intention of changing the system. Why should she, her entire lifestyle, depended on it?

Lynsey really should be back by now. Illyara smiled sweetly at the lord. She did not know what he'd said. Inwardly, she seethed at the fake pleasantries. That was it. Time to go. Dropping into a curtsey, she murmured at the man.

"Please excuse me sir, I must look for my friend." While he turned to talk to someone on his left, she flicked her fan up and walked towards the exit.

Her back straightened, she lifted her chin up, and she exuded as much confidence as she could muster. Reaching the edge of a table laden with drinks, she glanced back to check that no one was watching. A few faces were, so she picked up a glass and brought it to her lips. Illyara took a few pretend sips until they looked away and then slipped behind a column out of view of the room. She pressed her back against the cool stone and closed her eyes. She breathed in deeply and let her frustration leave her as she breathed out. Her hands dropped to her side, and she relaxed her mind, ignoring the sounds and smells that assaulted her senses. Her heartbeat slowed, and she felt something in her mind shift.

Grabbing on to the change, she visualised every mind in the room as a little candle flame in the darkness. She 'saw' clearly how many were around her. The men's flames were redder, and the women had yellower flames. She spread her awareness out further. Walls were no object, but she only got a glimpse of the number of people. Her mind was stretching too far, perhaps too much. She gathered herself together. The last thing she did was imagine darkness surrounding her. Her eyes flipped open. All anyone would see when they looked in her direction was a fuzzy black space. The mind wouldn't be able to comprehend the absence of everything, so they would dismiss her as if she wasn't there.

She remembered her father's face the first time he taught her the technique. He had been younger then, but his eyes appeared older than his years, their core deep pools of jet black.

"We were changed by those we don't speak of. We were never meant to exist. If it hadn't been for our saviour, we would not be here today. When our ancestors escaped, we carried the seeds of our master's destruction. They wanted to speak with their minds, but we learned what they did to us meant we could hide in plain sight." He'd looked out into the sunset as he spoke. His voice had been quieter than normal and she'd strained to hear him.

"We never forget that we owe a great debt, or that our abilities can be misused by others." He twisted to face her. "I once had to sentence a member of our tribe to death for letting an outsider know about what we can do. Do not let this happen to you, my daughter. Stay safe and stay hidden." Illyara had always wondered at that farewell, but as she learned their history, she grew to understand the wisdom of it.

Leaving the memory behind, she strode from the column in the direction that Lynsey had left. Nearing the half-open doorway that led to the stairs. She spotted her friend turning away from the king. Illyara breathed a sigh of relief. She was fine. Lynsey looked horrified, but she was clearly unharmed. Like the Duchess said, what could happen at a ball?

Reaching forward with the closest hand, she pushed the door fully open. Illyara breathed in, squeezing past a woman bulging out of a mint-green dress. The woman was shrieking with laughter and her nearest arm flailed out. Illyara had time to see the lord beside her, grin at his companion's reaction before she ducked. The woman's arm swept over her head. A drop of wine sploshed out and hit her as she hugged the door frame. The woman looked directly at Illyara for a moment. Her eyes narrowed and her mouth formed a sound. Illyara concentrated on the flame which seemed to superimpose on the woman's face and her eyes glazed, her expression erasing. The woman turned back to her companion.

"Darling, you are so funny."

Illyara burst through to the other side of the door to see two guards wearing royal colours separating from the king. If their uniforms hadn't given them away, then the fact that they were the tallest in the room would have made anyone pause. Their blue and gold uniforms were stretched taut over their chest muscles as they moved with purpose behind Lynsey. Their jaws were set and their eyes were steely. Illyara wanted to call out, but it would have given her position away. Years of her father's training held her back, rooted to the spot. She watched in horror as she saw one of them grab Lynsey and the other hold a cloth over her mouth and nose. Illyara gave a strangled cry. She clamped her hands around her mouth as she saw Lynsey collapse. The woman who was now to her side looked in her direction but saw nothing and turned back to the lord. Didn't she see what was happening to Lynsey? Why wasn't she helping? Illyara rushed forward, but the guards bundled her friend up and dragged her to a side room. Not one person from the corridor or room intervened or even seemed to notice.

Illyara followed and watched them throw Lynsey out of a window, then calmly walk back to the king. She was aghast. She ran to the window; a slight breeze brushed a few strands that had escaped her hair-pins and tickled her cheeks. She caught and flicked them away as she searched the ground. There! Lynsey was below. Six men in dark clothing carried her unconscious form in the gloom. They were heading for a carriage.

Illyara fought despair. She couldn't keep up with a carriage. Her arms dropped in surrender, then she caught her breath as she recognised the colour of the carriage in the flames carried by the guard. It was the blood red of the Dragon Temple.

Illyara raced to the main ballroom, dodging past revellers as she went. She found Darianna laughing with the king in the far corner. Careful not to touch anyone. She was invisible, but she could still be felt and be captured. She crept up to the pair.

"I wish there had been another way." She heard Darianna say.

"There isn't. That girl could be the answer to our prayers. She hasn't told you anything, has she?"

"No, and I don't think she would. She was determined to leave. I tried to deter her, but you know how young people can be."

"Indeed. Ghinari thanks you. With the location of the pyramids, we will gain enough treasure to raise an army to defeat the Eryl by the Festival of Sekhmet."

"That soon?"

"We have nearly pushed them from our borders. We were running low on money, but with your help, this will soon be rectified. Our alliance with the brotherhood will finally end this war, and we can concentrate on feeding our people." He was watching Darianna intently, but she still looked troubled.

"Duchess, you have done your country a great service today. We will not harm the girl. She claims not to know where the pyramids are, but that cannot be true. She has artefacts from that place. For all we know, she is an agent of the Eryl. You know there are no blond people, yet here she is. We do not know if there are any blond people within the Eryl. If she is a plant, we need to know. Maybe she was here to make us waste time and resources on a wild goose chase so that they can win sooner. Do you understand?"

"I do. I just feel sorry for the girl. She was becoming attached to your young assassin, you know."

"I suspected it was him when she escaped the first time. Arkan is dangerous, but when he realises that the fate of our world rests on that girl cooperating, he will come around. It is the reason I have not confided in him yet. I believe he is infatuated with her for the moment. It will pass."

"Thank you for letting me be a part of this, your Highness."

"It is my pleasure, Duchess. To show our gratitude, I will award your husband exclusive contracts to supply our forces on the front line."

"Your Highness, you are too kind!" Darianna's flushed cheeks turned a darker shade.

Illyara's breath caught. Darianna already knew that Lynsey had been captured. Could Arkan really be trusted? He seemed to like her. Illyara wished her father was here for advice. She was surprised that no one had missed her. At that point, she could see that Darianna had the same thought.

"Where is Illyara?"

"Her companion?"

"Yes, she was here with us."

"She is of no use to me. You may keep her as a pet."

Illyara ran. She dodged past nobles, serving men and women, and tables until she reached the dance floor. She skirted to the wall and ran out. Where could she go? Darianna's house was not safe. She stood undecided on the road. The new house was a sham. There was only one place she could go.

The Temple was several miles away, but Illyara was used to travelling long distances on foot. She tore off the bottom of her dress so it would not hamper her journey. Keeping invisible to all onlookers was a strain, but she couldn't risk being seen. Dressed in court clothes would make her a target for every cut-purse in town.

The well-kept, wide streets of the wealthy soon turned narrower and the stench of filth on the streets threatened to distract her from staying invisible. This late, there were few daring the open streets. She dodged women with low necklines and short skirts, men on the look-out for prey and younger men chancing their luck for a story to be told at the inn the next day. She glanced with pity at these denizens of the night. It wasn't her business and there was nothing to be done apart from avoiding their situations.

She reached the Temple in a couple of hours. There was no sign of the carriage, but if Arkan truly cared about Lynsey, then he would turn up sooner rather than later.

22 Allies Forged

This was getting to be a habit. Lynsey groaned. "What the hell happened?" She woke up groggy, struggling to wake up from the miasma of drugged sleep. She kept her eyes closed, letting the last wisps of confusion drift away from her.

"Pico, Pico?"

"HELLO LYNSEY. WE APPEAR TO HAVE BEEN DRUGGED."

"Master of the understatement yet again. Do you know where we are?"

"INCONCLUSIVE. THE DRUG THEY USED TO MAKE YOU SLEEP, SHUT DOWN ALL YOUR BRAIN AND BODY FUNCTIONS, SO I WAS KNOCKED OUT AS WELL. I CAN TELL YOU WE ARE IN A HUMID ENVIRONMENT AND IT SMELLS LIKE ANIMALS HAVE BEEN HERE BUT BEYOND THAT I HAVE NO IDEA."

"GPS not working then?"

"VERY FUNNY LYNSEY."

"I thought so."

Lynsey opened her eyes and blinked. She could hardly see a thing. She tried to bring her hand up to her head but couldn't. After trying again, she discovered she was bound to a chair. Oh, come on. Give me a break here.

She went limp. Was that a sound? She listened hard. There! She heard even breathing to her right. She peered into the darkness. It took a few moments, but then she saw a dull light pulsating. Lynsey craned her neck to get a better look. There was definitely someone there. Were they waiting to make a dramatic entrance or something? If they were trying to make her nervous, it was working. A rasping sound behind her made her jump. There was more than one person here. She stiffened as she tried to identify what it could be. It sounded large. Maybe it was just someone scraping a chair trying to get the wind up her. Remembering the two-headed snake, she fervently hoped so.

In silence, the light on her side moved up and travelled across the darkness towards her, revealing a figure in a long-hooded robe. What was it with priests and robes? Lynsey almost laughed, but her mouth felt dry. She realised her skin felt tight. She must be dehydrated. Where the hell was she?

"Would you like a drink?" the voice was thick, as if the speaker had smoked for years.

Lynsey swallowed, tiny knives grazed up and down her throat. "I don't understand. Who are you and where am I?"

Pico answered again in her mind, "THE TEMPERATURE IN HERE IS TOO HIGH. YOU NEED WATER. YOU WILL GO INTO A COMA SOON

IF YOU DON'T DRINK AND WE DON'T KNOW WHAT WILL HAPPEN TO YOU IF THAT HAPPENS. TAKE THE OFFER!" Pico was getting far too bossy, but she was tired, hot and she didn't know how long she could cope. Irritated, she replied to the priest.

"Yes, I need a drink."

In response, the hood lowered, and the figure disappeared from view.. The light floated back across the room and then bobbed back. The priest now carried a small wooden cup.

"Please don't try to escape, Lynsey. You may get past me, but there are guards on the other side of the door and there is a fearsome beast behind you. There is no way you can get away, so we may as well be civilised about this."

Lynsey nodded. Whatever, just give me the water, will you? She thought. The robed figure put the cup on the ground beside her feet. She heard a grunt behind her as her bonds were released. Lynsey rubbed her wrists while the pain lessened. Where the rope had wound around her hands, it had cut into her skin. The light was dim, but she kept her hands over her wrists to hide any healing. A splosh on the floor made her look up to see the proffered cup jiggling. She reached up and took it gratefully.

It tasted tepid, but it was the most delicious water Lynsey had ever drunk. She felt it slide down her neck and down through her chest. She drank thirstily, emptying the cup within seconds. The stranger watched in silence until she finished.

"Now I have your attention. We need to start at the beginning. Where are the pyramids?"

"I don't know."

"Come on now. We know you have been there. We have the elephant and the other trinkets you liberated from there." Lynsey heard a tinkle and a bag of jewellery and ornaments flowed on to the floor. The eye of the elephant twinkled in the lamplight. She heard something move behind her.

"LYNSEY." Pico replied, "I CAN TAKE YOU THERE. MAYBE THEY WILL LET YOU GO IF YOU TELL THEM."

"I don't know, but I can take you there," Lynsey said out loud.

"That is good. We have a party preparing to leave in the morning." The figure stood straighter and spoke over her shoulder. "There is some more water on the table and some cold meats and vegetables if you want it."

The figure moved off, and she heard some banging on what she presumed was a door. When she was sure she was alone, Lynsey dared to stand up.

Slowly, she turned. It was too dark to see clearly, but she could make out the table in the gloom. She stumbled over and picked up the lamp. There was a wheel underneath a glass globe. She turned it fully clockwise, and the lamp brightened. Lynsey held the light aloft and turned to face the beast the priest had said was there.

There wasn't anything? Except … there! A pile of rocks moved, morphing into a face in the gloom. Its head was the size of a small car. She looked back and saw a long neck connected to an enormous body that could house a small building.

Its jaw was resting on its … claws? They could almost be hands. They had six digits with evil looking talons which ended in sharp points. Its great head rose and tilted to examine her more intently.

"A dragon," she breathed out.

"Another human," she heard in her mind as it growled back. Lynsey jumped.

"You can talk?"

"You can understand me?" The voice in her mind was tinged with surprise.

"Yes." Then she directed a thought at Pico. "It's you, isn't it? I can understand him through you."

"OF COURSE, I AM YOUR UNIVERSAL TRANSLATOR REMEMBER."

Lynsey drew closer to the creature. "You won't eat me, will you?"

"Why do you creatures always assume that I'm going to eat you? No. You people have done a lot worse to me over the centuries."

"You've been here for centuries?"

"Is that all you are going to do? Turn whatever I say last into a sentence?"

"Sorry, but I've never been able to talk to a dragon before. It is slightly overwhelming."

The dragon rolled his red-green eyes. "Why are you here?"

"I can take them to the pyramids."

"From what that person has said, she wanted more from you than that. How can you talk to me?"

Lynsey held out her arm, and Pico made the band visible. The dragon looked at it with interest, then his head sank back to the floor again. "I've seen that before when I first got here. A priest had one."

"Priest. When you got here? Where are you from?"

"Somewhere very far away, human, you wouldn't understand."

"I think I might. Was it another planet?"

"You know about planets?" This time the dragon's head stayed up with a clink and Lynsey noticed an iron chain leading to a collar around his neck. She touched her own neck in sympathy.

"Yes, of course. I'm not from here. I'm from a planet called Earth."

"Original. Funnily enough, my planet is called that as well, but I don't think we are from the same place."

"I'm from the Milky Way Galaxy. I was hit by lightning and I found myself here."

"Interesting. The same happened to me. I was on my way to a meeting when the weather turned for the worst. I suspect it was a combination of a solar flare, freak weather conditions and a black hole occurring at the same time. A once in a lifetime occurrence. I thought I might be the only one."

"Wow, you know about solar flares?"

"I find your incredulity quite insulting. Do you think your kind are the only species that can create a civilisation? Has your world even achieved space flight yet?"

"Yes! We've been to our moon and we're planning to go to Mars."

"I bet that is in your solar system?" She nodded. "Well, we achieved that hundreds of years before I got here. My civilisation has colonies on moons and planets throughout our galaxy and I'm reduced to this - chained and tortured by barbarians on an obscure planet. My family will have been dead centuries ago now." A single tear fell down his snout.

Lynsey felt uncomfortable. "Why do they torture you?"

"Travelling to this world changed me. My life span increased. I have lived for centuries longer than I should have. I'm almost starting to fear that I cannot die." His laugh sounded hollow in her mind. When she didn't respond, he carried on. "Every day they come with their bowls and their rituals and they take blood. They found that my blood can extend their lives as well. But while I do not age, they still do at a lower rate."

"Oh God." Lynsey turned pale as she made the connection.

The dragon clinked as he leaned closer and then growled with laughter. "They are going to do that to you as well, aren't they? You are immortal like me!"

23 Devising Rescue

Illyara awoke to bright sunlight and the sound of constant heavy footsteps beside her. Men in simple coarse clothing, their shirts and trousers worn with use, were running up and down the steps carrying boxes and jars inches from her.

Before she could collect her thoughts, a box clattered past her, crashing down each step with a loud thwack. White cloth spilled on the dusty mud. The unexpected sound made her jump, and she noticed the ripped remnants of her skirt above her knees. She couldn't be more noticeable if she tried. If anyone saw her dressed like this... The thought trailed into nothing as she scurried further into the shadows of the nearest pillar. One of the men standing on the street below was already looking her way. He opened his mouth as if in slow motion to shout as her mind froze. It only lasted for a moment, and her training kicked in. She concentrated on the man, taking in his appearance, his black hair, dark eyes and full lips. She noticed a scar running down his arm leading to a tattoo that she recognised was of the Eied caste. How far down the social ranks had this man fallen to be a labourer, she thought with sudden pity. She clamped down on her emotions as she saw him raise his arm to point at her. Holding down the panic, she clenched her fists against the satin cloth of her dress as she imagined his mind as a living flame. It was one thing to use the gift in the desert when there was no danger, but... She again lost track of her thought as she imagined the flame twisting into a spiral away from her. She held her breath for a moment. Had it worked? Was she invisible again? But his brow was furrowing, and he was still looking directly at her.

She closed her eyes and focussed on the flame with all her strength. She had to merge the connection. It was harder to bond, but if she could just get it going, her subconscious would continue it. Below her, she heard his companion shouting at the man, and she opened her eyes to see him gesticulating at the remains of the box. The Eied man looked at her again and she twisted the flame once more. He did a double-take in Illyara's direction but loud shouting from above them made him grab the contents and stuff them in the box. The other man nodded to the side impatiently, and they moved off. Illyara sighed, letting her shoulders sag as she pressed her back to the wall enclosing the steps. This was the longest she had ever been invisible. How long could she keep it up?

As she watched more men take boxes down the stairs beside her, it all came flooding back. Lynsey had been taken. She looked back at the doors of the temple - she was in there somewhere.

Illyara waited for a stout workman to pass her and she fell into step behind him. She followed him in, one step behind to avoid anyone coming up behind them. There were men all over the place, some in priests' robes, others were hired help, packing items in boxes and transporting them outside. Where were they going? She quickly moved to hug an alcove wall. This was clearly a major operation. Food, water, those priests were folding tents? Illyara realised they were carrying the essentials for a desert journey. Were they going to use Lynsey to find the pyramids?

Illyara slunk along the walls, heading to the rear of the Temple. Her bare feet clung to the tiles as she trailed along the edges of the room. Her desert training ensured she made no sound.

During the tour, she had noticed that Baserius had been careful to avoid a section of the temple. There must be a reason he didn't want them to go that way. Her suspicions were confirmed when she saw Baserius walk towards her and then passed to head down a corridor. She followed. She never would have found it without him. It wasn't long before a large wooden door barred their way.

Illyara hung back while she watched Baserius rap a precise knock on the door. It opened, and she craned her neck to look inside, but the room was shrouded in darkness. Not a word was spoken. Baserius pulled the door further open and stepped inside. Illyara rushed forward to follow, but the door slammed shut behind him. An unsavoury whiff filled her nostrils. They were keeping something more than Lynsey in there.

Her breath exploded out of her in frustration. What was behind that door? She moved to the corner and sat down to wait. He would come out eventually.

The minutes passed, and nothing happened. It gave her time to think about the night before. Arkan had never come. She was sure he had fallen in love with Lynsey. How could he let someone he loved go into such danger? Maybe her father was wrong after all. About love anyway.

The door opened, and Baserius strode out, pushing Lynsey in front of him. Her friend's hands were tied behind her back with thick rope encasing her small wrists. Illyara studied her friend. She looked pale, drained, but apart from that, she seemed unhurt. Illyara breathed out gently, thanking any gods that would listen. That girl had a charmed life. How was she going to get out of this one? Illyara followed them to see where they were going. She reached out and touched Lynsey's arm briefly and Lynsey smiled. She'd got the message; Lynsey knew she was around.

"Is all this just to find the Pyramids?" asked Lynsey.

"We will need provisions. Many expeditions have tried and failed over hundreds of years. It pays to be prepared," was his answer. So Lynsey was taking them to the Pyramids.

Illyara felt a pang of guilt, but she squeezed Lynsey's hand to let her know she received the message and left.

Illyara hurried to the main gates. She was exhausted; her hands were shaking and her head felt like it was splitting in two. She had never been invisible this long. She needed to find suitable clothes and something to eat before she became too ill to walk back.

Part of the caravan that the priests were putting together was waiting by the city gates. A cluster of red-robed men stood congregated on one side while hired guides were chatting and laughing on the other side of the yelks. None of the tribes would help the temple, and these were the best of what was left. She smiled grimly; they could get them safely to the next city along the coast, but to find the pyramids, they were really relying on Lynsey getting them there.

She noticed how the priests were standing apart, facing away from the other men. Their hoods were lowered so they couldn't see the guides. Illyara chuckled at their discomfort. They wouldn't dare forbid the guides from drinking or smoking. They would leave and find another employer. There was plenty of work available. The guides did not have to work for them. Everyone knew the order was running out of money or they wouldn't ask for such large contributions during their ceremonies. Gone were the days where they could shower money everywhere to get whatever they wanted.

She saw a guide bring out a flask. The faint aroma of spirits wafted its way to her. She bet the priests couldn't stand watching them drink. Still, from the expressions on a couple of their faces, Illyara would have bet money that some of them would have joined the men if they had been alone.

She hurried towards the yelks. More than half were laden high with food, water and clothing. A small pile of provisions that hadn't been loaded yet was on one side. Illyara walked around to sit cross-legged beside the pile, out of sight of both priests and guides. They may not see her, but if she wasn't careful, they might see anything she moved.

Illyara reached into a leather pack and rummaged around for a moment before pulling out a parcel wrapped in waxed paper. She teased the paper apart to reveal a rich mellow cheese. Illyara took a quick sniff, then broke it in two to cram the first and then the second portion into her mouth. A yelk skin containing water was next, and she drank greedily, letting the liquid splash over her face and neck when she was finished. Illyara felt better, but she was still ravenous and took out more to eat until she was satiated. She lay back against the pile, staring up at the blue sky. There was no bird sound, she realised. The camp was making too much noise. Even the vultures, usually so vocal, were silent. She propped herself up on one elbow. Come to think of it. She hadn't heard many birds since she'd entered Ghinari. There were caged birds in the market, she remembered. The city people must be eating them.

Feeling rested, she looked around for a yelk, which carried clothing. She made for the nearest animal carrying cloth and carefully stepped up to it. The yelk's feet shuffled in the loose sand, its head moving from side to side. It smelt her but couldn't see her. It was nervous. Its huge legs moved back and forth and it was twisting faster to find the source of her smell. She crooned in a soft voice and it quieted as she reached up and stroked its coarse fur near its head. Her father would have been able to let the animal see him while staying invisible to everyone in the vicinity, but that took many more years of practice and skill. Maybe she could do it, but she was too scared to try with so many priests close by.

A boy, set to look after the beasts while other items were brought and loaded, noticed the animal's discomfort and came over. Illyara had to wait a few moments before he went away again and she grabbed a robe from a pack. There was a second of worry while she adjusted the invisibility to apply to the item she carried, but the boy didn't seem to notice.

Illyara moved behind the yelks in front of the city walls and placed the robe over her head. They were loose but not so baggy they would call attention to her. She was lucky today. Moving from behind the yelk, she set off in the direction where she knew her people would be waiting.

Illyara took no notice of the scorching sun, knowing she would be at camp long before mid-day. It was a tedious journey, but she had done it many times before. This spring was known only to a few nomads, so she didn't have to worry that she would meet any of the guides on the way. Still, she had kept a close eye out for the first hour and disguised her footprints in the sand, but she couldn't relax until she saw the familiar tents of her people.

They were still there.

She knew they would be, but there was always the fear of discovery. That they would have been made to move on, or worse. These were dangerous times.

Her father was in the large tent eating a snack while the mid-day meal was prepared. He was joking and laughing at something mother was saying. Illyara smiled as she pulled the flap down behind her. She really wanted what they had, but that had to wait. She approached through the milling throng and stood before him until he noticed her.

"Illyara, you are back. How did the visit go? Has Lynsey Walker removed the band?"

"No, father she is in even worse trouble."

He smiled at her. "What has happened, sweet Orchid?"

"She is a special father; she is like the Dragon."

Her father's face dropped into a serious expression as he listened.

«She is an immortal; she can talk to anyone — and what is worse is that she is being forced to show them the location of the Pyramids.»

Her father's face darkened. "That is not acceptable."

"I also believe the dragon is being held in the temple, in a section I saw Lynsey taken from."

"Why do you think that?"

"There was a distinctive odour I have never smelt before. They are keeping an animal below their temple and it definitely is no goat or chicken."

"It is not beyond doubt, yet they took the dragon and it cannot die. Our ancestors saw the head taken off, and it regrew. It must be somewhere."

Illyara waited as he voiced his thoughts.

"We cannot break into the heart of our enemy's stronghold until we are certain. Our priority has to be to rescue Lynsey to stop them from violating the pyramid and enriching themselves on our ancestors' suffering."

"They will leave within hours, father."

"Then so shall we."

24   A Theory Proposed

The tribe dispersed from the tent, picking up their cushions as they went. They worked as a team, loading up the yelks with furnishings, cloth, and supplies. Illyara was among them, orchestrating the breakup of the camp. They had done this so many times; the familiarity was soothing. She directed her people almost out of habit. The cushions and furniture were removed first from the tents, then the huge domed structures were pulled down with a warning shout. Women tended to the animals in her periphery vision while others loaded the yelks.

As the tribe set off, Illyara moved to her customary place in the back. The pace was slow. There was no hurry. It would take a while for the priests to get ready, judging by the state of the caravan when she last saw it.

The desert looked featureless around her. — unless you know what you were looking for, she thought. Her tribe was almost invisible to untrained eyes. The colour of the yelk fur blended with the sand and anything that had any colour was packed up and hidden by the material of the tents. Her eyes roved past their caravan to the surrounding dunes. Their towering presence was comforting, if deceptively calm. She lifted her head to the side and sniffed the air. There was something in the light breeze. She took a deeper breath. It was going to rain. The corner of her mouth raised slightly. Nothing to worry about, though. It would be light. She settled in to her stride. The swish of long sand-coloured travelling robes was the only sounds as they trudged on.

The journey to the pyramids should take the tribe a week at the most, but then the tribe was familiar with the route, its oases and markers. She considered how many times she had taken the trip. It was at least once a year. She knew the way to the nearby water hole by heart. It was important that the location would never be lost. In fact, it had been lucky for Lynsey that they had arrived ahead of time, but was there such a thing as luck? Maybe she was the one they had been waiting for? A brief flare of hope ignited in her, but she squashed it down. Her people had travelled this desert for centuries. This was their life; she couldn't imagine anything different. Yet it was already different. They should have been further west by now, selling their wares to prepare them for the dry seasons, but here they were chasing after a stranger and a dream.

Illyara rubbed the small of her back. It was strange that a couple of weeks of inactivity meant that years of walking were practically lost. She shouldn't tire of this easily. City life was not good for her people, she realised. She couldn't imagine living away from the desert. If the legends were right and their ancestors had farmers among them, …but that was before the Egyptians had brought them to this place.

From the back, she could see there was something different about the tribe. Illyara squinted against the sun's glare as she studied her family. What was it? They were wearing the same clothes; they were walking at the same pace as they normally did. What was it? They were walking different. Then she had it. Their heads were higher and their shoulders were straighter. She felt it too; she realised. The excitement among the tribe was almost palpable. A stray thought materialised, and she paused for a second. There had always been a cloud hanging over their heads. That could not change. It was silly to think that one person could make such a difference. But what a person, came the unbidden thought.

That night there was no shortage of volunteers to be scouts to keep track of the temple camp, but it was no surprise when Paereek was selected. His affinity with his wedas made the decision a foregone conclusion. Anyone sitting atop a lone yelk on a dune would have been too obvious. They needed the wedasi. Usually used for hunting, a wedas with its snake body was perfect for moving through the desert unseen with speed. It was low to the ground, quick, quiet and, with the right person, reliable. Paereek had been training wedasi for decades and they treated him as one of their own. Illyara shuddered. The way their twin heads would simultaneously rub the front and back of him in affection. It wasn't natural; I would rather ride a yelk any day, she thought.

Illyara wrapped her arms around herself in the night air. A soft glow emanated from an open flap of the tent behind her. Enough to see a little in front, but the light was so low her night vision was not impaired. The twin moons were bright above, allowing her to watch the long low body of the wedas slide along the sand into the distance. Paereek lay along its length, arranging himself around its legs, which were tucked up into its side as it gathered speed, slithering on the sand. She wished him luck, but he would not need it. He would report the other camp's whereabouts until they got Lynsey away. She turned to go back inside again.

The next evening, everyone gathered in the main tent for their meal early. The lamps were brighter than usual. Illyara sat next to her parents. She felt nervous and was picking at the stitching on her dress. The action reminded her of Lynsey, and she stilled her hands. She was in two minds. Was Lynsey the one they were looking for? The question kept revolving around her mind. What should she tell them? Should she keep anything back? She looked at her father for reassurance, but he had moved and was talking to her aunt against the tent doorway. Her mother caught her look and moved to sit closer to her.

"What is troubling you, my darling?"

"I do not know if I should tell everyone everything about Lynsey."

"They deserve to know Illyara. If she is what we suspect, then this affects our tribe and our world."

"It cannot be, mother. Surely if it was, then there would be more signs?"

"How many signs do you need, daughter?"

Illyara looked deep into her mother's violet eyes. She was so beautiful, so wise. Her mother's frank gaze made her cast her eyes down to the cushions on the floor.

"You are right. It is time. I have delayed enough." Illyara squared her shoulders and stood. She picked up a wooden box which lay at her feet. She lifted the lid off and pulled out a small silver bell. It tinkled as she drew it out. She rang it once, then again. The chatting ceased. Her father gave her a small encouraging nod from across the room and moved closer to give support.

"I have spent the last few weeks with the stranger we found at the oasis near the pyramids." She was surprised at how clear her voice was. She stopped to see everyone had sat down and was looking at her. They were hanging on her every word. She coughed and carried on.

"The people we met in the city were from all corners of our land. They were speaking different languages, yet Lynsey did not seem to realise. They were talking to her in one speech and to themselves in another. She understood them all and replied to everyone in their own tongue. This happened in the shops with the serving girls and with the lords and ladies at the banquets." She stopped for effect.

"There was a Droota delegate there, and she charmed him when she spoke in his own language." A murmur filled the tent. The Droota language was notoriously difficult, comprising clicks rather than words.

"That is not all. We tried to take a walk in the park and we were set upon by five people." Illyara blushed deeply at the memory. "I'm ashamed to say I used the gift and disappeared, but she bravely fought off four assailants before a fifth brought her down." There was a collective gasp, then excited whispers.

"Can she heal?" Asked her aunt from the back of the tent. Everyone grew silent.

"She can. She was knocked over by a carriage and I saw broken bones heal themselves and bruises and cuts disappear before my eyes. Lynsey is like the dragon."

Her aunt nodded at the back. She was holding a pendant with the loop and cross of the Ankh in her hands. In the silence, Illyara could hear the wind hitting the tent outside as the tribe contemplated the symbol's significance.

"Lynsey can speak many languages, she can fight, she is beautiful, she heals impossibly quickly, and she is as brave as a lion. She has to be the one we are looking for. She just has to be the Goddess Sekhmet."

"But she has not said this?" asked her father from behind her, playing the opposite, as she had seen him do to her mother so many times before in debates. She smiled, grateful for the prompt.

"I do not think she knows." She replied, turning to face him.

"How can she not know if she is the Goddess if she is?" This was her brother, two years her junior from her left.

"I do not know, but she has miraculous abilities. How else do you explain it? She is like the dragon. She came from the pyramids and she fights, heals and is blond like a lion!" Illyara had everyone's attention.

"The dragon does not like to fight. I know, but neither does Lynsey. Maybe when a goddess comes from another world, they lose their memory? Sekhmet is a goddess of war."

"This is not for us to know. If she is indeed the Goddess, then she can help us rescue the Dragon. He helped us in the past and now it is our turn to help him. Without his help, we would still be slaves to our Egyptian masters. We owe him," her father chimed in.

"We cannot fight." Came a fresh voice from the far end of the tent. This voice was from an older man whose skin was worn like leather over decades under the blistering sun.

Illyara's father answered. "We cannot fight, but there are tribes in our people who can. Our brothers have been itching to revolt for hundreds of years. Maybe this time we can let them. We are the messengers, the thinkers, the head. We were spies and we can be so again. Our tribe can slip silently into any tent unseen, listen to whispered conversations, steal what they hide, discover secrets. We will always try to forget what we were, but we were thieves in the past, not because we wanted to, but because we had to be. We will not be that or slaves again. If we can free the dragon, he will protect us and we can be free."

"What about Sekhmet?" asked another voice from the crowd.

"We cannot ask a goddess to stay with us, but if she will, she will always be welcome. She is the protector of the Pharaoh. Maybe she is here to elevate one in this world to be a Pharaoh again, as the prophecy foretold. The priests stopped them from coming. Maybe Sekhmet is here to bring them back."

Illyara had never been so proud of her father. The eyes of her people were shining. The dream of not hiding anymore, of being able to settle down, grow their own food rather than be nomads forced to roam the land until a saviour was found. Maybe it could happen now. They were already changing.

"Father, first we need to rescue Lynsey. We don't need fighters for that."

"You are right. Take your brother with you. He is itching for an adventure. While you bring Lynsey to us, we will gather the tribes."

Illyara cast her eyes down. "Father, he'll slow me down. He is just a boy."

"He has mastered the Gift. That is all you need for this task."

"And the ability to walk quietly without waking a Phalish." she muttered quietly so her father couldn't hear.

Mewlli was already waiting outside by the time she made it to the cool night air. The stars were out in force and she couldn't help but wonder where Lynsey was from. Was it one of those stars? Was it the same one as the one the Dragon came from?

The twin moons were low, but they lit up the night sky, illuminating the darkness with a soft light. Illyara and Mewlli shrouded themselves in invisibility by sending thoughts out into the area. You cannot see us; we are not here. It was strange that it only worked on the eyes, thought Illyara.

If it worked on ears, then Mewlli's noisy sand crunching wouldn't get on her nerves so much. She loved him, but he was still a boy and delighted in childish things. She stopped. Where was he this time? His footsteps ended a few feet away. She backtracked and saw a lizard resting by the last footmark. She grabbed in the air, expecting to get Mewlli's arm, but grabbed a piece of his robe instead.

"We don't have time for this," she hissed. "Each day they get closer to the Pyramids their maps get more accurate. This needs to be done tonight!"

She heard him sigh in the silence and relented. "I know this is the first time that you have been out on your own. I was excited about the first-time mother and father let me out, but this is important. They must believe in you a lot to let you come when there were older trackers who wanted to join me. Can you fulfil their trust?"

"I know," his voice was small. She pulled him closer and gave him a hug. She forgot how much she missed him while she was away. He must have felt that way, too. "I love you, brother. " She felt his smile grow against her shoulder.

"I missed you too, sister."

"Come on."

They walked on and Mewlli tried harder to be quiet. She noted with pleasure how he scattered the sand behind him with his foot to disguise their footsteps the nearer they got to the temple camp. Maybe her father was right again. She should really stop doubting him.

They entered the camp through a ring of guards surrounding the temple encampment. Their feet crunched and slid on the sand as they crept through. She cursed the light rainfall that made the thin crust on the sand, but it couldn't be helped. Look-outs sat in groups of two, quietly chatting or playing dice. The tips of tall stakes pushed in sand were alight with a bright red flame to give the guards heat and light to see by.

Mewlli and Illyara crept further in, hand in hand, so they would not lose each other as they moved from tent to tent. The tents were a stupid design; she thought. They had watched the guides take hours to erect them over the last few days and just as long to put them down. This should have been great. The journey, which would take them a week, would have taken the brothers about five. But they spent so long each day building the camp that the time between waterholes was also extended. The tribe had already rationed their water. These people did not know how big the desert was and with the way they travelled, it was even larger.

The first few tents were small, with two or more men sleeping on bed rolls. The nearer to the centre they got, the tents were bigger. More often than not, they passed someone smoking outside the entrances and when they checked, there were only one or two occupants inside. The sound of joking and laughing was interspersed with the sound of chanting from other tents occupied by the priests with their arcane ceremonies. She did not want to know what they were doing in those tents. Avoiding them, they moved swiftly through the camp until they spied Lynsey through an open flap. This time, there was a guard sharpening a spear at the entrance.

Illyara craned her neck to see clearer. Lynsey was sitting with her back to the door. She was wearing a bright blue robe, no doubt to make her easy to spot if she tried to get away. Illyara stealthily stepped around the guard, pulling Mewlli behind her to look inside. Lynsey was alone. The tent was bare except for a light on a small table and a small bed. Why would they bother with fripperies like heavy tables like that? No wonder they were so slow to move camp. Loading the yelks down with non-essentials like that was silly. She looked at the small gap between the guard and the tent. There wasn't enough space to squeeze past him. He was sitting too close to the flap. If they tried to sidle past, they would be discovered.

Looking through the flap. Illyara saw Lynsey was talking to herself again. Illyara glanced at the guard, but he was ignoring his prisoner. She couldn't make out what Lynsey was saying, but she must have been doing it a lot because the guard wasn't paying any attention to her at all.

Illyara squeezed Mewlli's hand, so he knew she was going to move backwards and they crept around the outside of the tent to the opposite side. As luck would have it, no entrances were pointing towards this side of the tent, so she started digging and moving the sand to one side with her hands. She could hear Mewlli's gentle breathing beside her. Then, sand shifting showed he was copying what she was doing. They soon dug a hole under the tent wall, spreading the sand around them as they went. Unless anyone was looking, they would think the hole was a shadow of the tent.

Illyara passed under the material of the tent wall first, followed by Mewlli. Illyara strode to the front of the tent and closed the flap behind Lynsey so the guard would not see them appear.

She was still holding Mewlli's hand, so she pulled him close to stand in front of Lynsey. She let her shield drop. Mewlli did the same beside her.

"Hello Lynsey, would you like to leave now?" She grinned at her friend.

25 Nighttime Escape

Why did the guard never close the tent door? Sorry, flap. Lynsey breathed out in frustration. Count to three you plonker. He's not really trying to wind you up.

The guard's constant nitpicking grated on her nerves even more than her mum's fussing over dirty clothing not quite reaching the wash basket. With pursed lips and narrowed eyes, the guard skulked in the tent entrance, speaking only to show how little he thought of her.

She wrapped her arms around herself, rubbing her hands up and down over her sleeves to keep warm. One minute he was correcting her, the next acting like she was stupid and useless. Also, what was with the sharpening of the spear all the time? Did he think she was going to attack him? It was going to be the size of a pencil if he didn't watch it. He really should decide whether or not she was a danger. Huh? Oh, Pico was talking again.

"Oh, yes. Keanu was great in that." Lynsey replied. She cocked her head to the side. "Did you just hear that?"

Pico swirled colours in her mind. "IT'S NOTHING, JUST SOMEONE WALKING BEHIND THE TENT. SO, WHAT DO YOU WANT TO WATCH?"

"Where was I? Oh yes. My favourite film is The Lakehouse. I really love Keanu Reeves. Take a look at that one." The great thing about chatting about home was that the guard did not know what she was talking about and he must have thought she was going, if not already, slightly mad. Well, he was keeping more of a distance than when he was first posted to be her guard. Talking to Pico only in her thoughts all the time just felt weird.

Pico went silent and his colour went murky as she felt his attention go elsewhere. She waited for a moment and closed her eyes. The movie began to play. It was like she was there again. She could feel the softness of the sofa, the popcorn as the salty-sweetness crunched in her mouth and the full feeling from the steak dinner Peter had bought her for their second date. He would have been a keeper apart from his commitment issues. Buying a toothbrush for him did not mean she wanted to marry the guy. Seriously! Lynsey took a deep breath. Don't think about that. Enjoy the warmth, she told herself. She could feel Pico's amusement. Stop listening to my thoughts, she snapped back.

She relaxed into it. There were definite advantages to Pico sometimes. This was the third movie since they had left Ghinari. If only he'd mentioned this ability at the beginning, it put a whole new angle on things. She let the heat from the remembered open fire seep into her bones and her current troubles floated away as the credits rolled from her memory. Who needs virtual reality when you have a Pico? Any film she had ever seen was available and he would play it for her in real time. He, she? was careful not to look at it until it was 'playing'. These were memories held in the band. Pico had put them in there without looking. All those years bingeing on movies and shows were really paying off.

There it was again. She peered at the rear side of the tent. It sounded like scuffling. There had to be someone there. Actually, it was more like a scrabbling noise coming from outside the tent. Could it be? She stood up and moved to the door of the tent. The guard was still there, sharpening that damned spear. What did he think was going to happen? An army of grizzly bears was going to descend on the tent? From where exactly? She shook her head.

The film was still playing in that strange double vision the way it did. It was only really fun to watch them with her eyes closed, but Lynsey was distracted as she sat back down again on the only chair in the room.

The noise was still there. It had to be Illyara. An animal would have given up by now, and anyone from the camp would come through the tent flap. She got up to investigate, loitering close to the noise. If it was Illyara, she didn't want the guard to see anything and get suspicious, but there was nothing to see yet. She sat down again. Her heart pounded. It had to be her. She just had to have a little patience and play it cool. She perched on the end of the chair. The Brothers weren't inhuman. They had provided a chair and a bed, but they weren't the most comfortable she had experienced, and she would have given anything for the comfort of the nomad tent.

She leaned back and crossed her legs, waiting to see what would happen.

"ARE YOU EVEN WATCHING THIS?"

"Sorry Pico, something is happening at the back of the tent. I don't think it is an animal. Whatever it is. It is very persistent." She thought back.

"YOU ARE RIGHT OF COURSE." He stopped the playback, clearing Lynsey's vision. "DO YOU THINK IT IS HELP?"

"I don't know. Illyara was at the temple. She could have found her people and come to find us."

There was a momentary silence in Lynsey's mind. "YOU SAID US."

"I did. I think if we are going to be together for a long time, then I need to accept you."

Just then, the bottom of the wall of the tent moved up slightly, letting a cool breeze enter. There was more scrambling and then the flap at the front of the tent fell. Lynsey was already smiling when Illyara appeared with Mewlli.

"Hello Lynsey, would you like to leave now?" Illyara whispered.

She grinned at her friend.

"Hi guys, I thought you'd never ask. I've been expecting you."

They grinned back and pointed to the back of the wall. "I get it. The guard will be used to my voice talking to myself here, but he'll think it is strange to hear yours." She followed them out of the tent and hugged the outside of the material while Mewlli scouted ahead.

While they waited in the shadows, a whistled, broken tune floated towards them on the slight breeze. Lynsey pulled Illyara closer to the tent wall. A man was briefly illuminated from fire-light coming from in-between the tents. The sounds of chanting and laughter drifted over as he limped slowly towards them. In his hand, he held a long black cigar, billowing black smoke around him. The stench pervaded the air, hitting Lynsey's nose as he passed. The smoke invaded her lungs before she thought to hold her breath and coughed slightly. She clasped her hand over her mouth, her eyes watered. The tickle grew, and she burst into a cough. The man turned, seeking the source of the sound. He did a double-take, squinting for a second, then he registered who she was. He opened his mouth to yell. Lynsey froze. Her whole body was rooted to the spot. She felt Pico unfurl from the recesses in her mind, expanding his awareness until he could take over. Lynsey retreated to let him and watched as her body twisted to get a purchase in the sand. She moved forward with fluid grace, her right hand flexing out in readiness. Before she could think what Pico was planning, her hand jabbed the man in the throat. His yell came out in a strangled cry. Her foot moved of its own volition and stamped on the man's good ankle. She could swear she heard a crunch. Her body moved backwards, taking a step in before her knee flew up in a straight line. Lynsey noted the tears that formed in his eyes with satisfaction. Good, that'll teach him to smoke. Then the man wavered for a second before falling down silently in the sand. Pico rescinded control. The colour of his thoughts was tinged pink with satisfaction.

"Well done, Pico." Pink turned to purple.

"Don't get too cocky, but well met." He wisely stayed silent.

Lynsey turned back to see Illyara's eyes shining with admiration.

Her friend darted forward to grab his hands, and Lynsey took his legs. They dragged his body closer to the tent. She grunted as she pushed him into the hole that Illyara and Mewlli had dug earlier. They covered his body with quick handfuls of sand, leaving his mouth and nose open to the air.

Mewlli came back as they were putting the finishing touches on the mound of sand.

"The guards around the perimeter have changed. They appear to be more alert. We will not get out the way we came in. We need a diversion."

"Can you do that, Mewlli?"

He grinned. "Of course, sister." He disappeared while turning away.

"Be ready for something." Illyara whispered.

"It would have been helpful if he could have given us an idea of what he was thinking of."

"He's young."

Lynsey snorted.

Suddenly, they heard a whoosh, and a tent was ablaze on the distant side of the camp.

"That's Mewlli!"

"Hand it to him. He has style, your brother," Lynsey panted as they ran.

"I probably would have done the same thing." Illyara griped.

They moved from tent to tent, keeping to the shadows. The sound of men shouting filled the night as they rushed past them to the far side of the camp laden with water as the fire leapt to nearby tents.

By the time they got to the perimeter, the guards had gone to help with the fire. Illyara motioned for Lynsey to stay within a cart's shadow while she disappeared, walking toward the yelks. Lynsey saw the ropes holding the camel-like creatures untie themselves from a post pushed into the sand. The yelks shuffled their feet as they smelled Illyara, moving their heads from side to side.

Illyara reappeared and motioned for Lynsey to join her. Lynsey nodded and ran forward, keeping an eye out to see if anyone could spot her.

The herd stomped their feet harder, sending sand flying in all directions, and their noses flared as the smoke from the fire changed direction. Lynsey grabbed the first hump she could get to. She hooked a leg over its back and hung off the side, holding on with one hand to its fur. From the corner of her eye, she saw Illyara slap the rump of the lead yelk and the herd stampeded off after it to get away from the fire.

Lynsey held on tight to the short fur with a grunt, grabbing another handful of the silky coat with the other. She gritted her teeth as a yelk banged into her from her left in its panic, letting go. Her heart jumped. She flailed but grabbed some more of its hide at the last second and hauled herself back up to sit on its back. Lynsey heard shouting in the distance from behind them and she bent her head, gripping even harder. She closed her eyes and tried not to think of her muscles screaming. Time seemed to stretch out. Some time later, it felt like they were going up a hill. She opened her eyes, and she saw they were cresting a rise.

Behind them, flames engulfed the camp, the stench of smoke overriding the gentle desert scents. Shouts rang out as priests scurried to douse the fire. She doubted they had even noticed her escape yet.

On the lead yelk, Illyara got off and grabbed hold of the hair that formed a beard on the animal, catching Lynsey's yelk before it went past her. It stopped abruptly, nearly sending Lynsey flying over its head.

Lynsey opened her fingers one-by-one, letting circulation return, wincing at the pain. She dropped to the cool sand with relief. Feet drummed the ground, sending fine sand flying in all directions. She flung her arms up to protect her head as a hoof narrowly missed her by inches. Illyara let go of the two yelks she was holding and it rushed off in a further spray of sand, followed by the others. They reached the top of a dune and then they were gone, leaving Illyara and Lynsey alone under the stars.

"Where's Mewlli?" Lynsey whispered. She didn't know how far her voice would travel in the night.

"Here." Mewlli appeared, grinning in front of Illyara. "That was easier than I thought it would be."

"Don't get too full of yourself brother, we still need to get back to camp. It won't take them long to realise Lynsey escaped under the cover of the yelks. We have a few miles to travel and we need to do it fast and quietly."

Gesturing northward, Illyara broke into a run across the moonlit sands, leading them to their escape. Lynsey kept pace in between and Mewlli took the rear, moving his shirt back and forth in the sand to obscure where they had been.

When they were in sight of the camp, Mewlli suddenly chuckled. Lynsey gave him a sideways look. What was there to laugh about? But she grinned back at him. They could have died. Her grin slipped, but they didn't. The corner of her lips lifted again until she giggled as well. They must have looked a sight riding those yelks like the devil was after them. Illyara threw her hands up in exasperation, but then she gave in with her familiar peals of laughter.

Breathless, they staggered in to the main tent and collapsed on some cushions. All around them were curious eyes, but when they saw they were unhurt, most of the tribe began to laugh and cheer along with them.

26 Desert Beauty

As the orange fingers of dawn crawled along the desert landscape, the tribe broke camp. Lynsey had already swapped the garish dress the Brothers had given her for one of Illyara's. It was definitely more suited to walking distances, but sitting on a yelk meant the long dress hadn't been a big issue with the Brothers.

Lynsey rubbed her face as she trudged on. They had talked with Illyara's father for hours last night and she was exhausted. Lynsey's legs burned, each step on the soft sand an effort. It was as if her bones had been replaced with lead weights.

"Pico? Could you take over for a while?" It was worth a try; she'd give anything for a sleep.

"I DO NOT THINK THAT WOULD BE A GOOD IDEA LYNSEY. I UNDERSTAND YOU NEED SLEEP BUT IT WOULD BE A SLIPPERY SLOPE FOR ME TO TAKE OVER WHEN THINGS GET TOO HARD. YOUR BODY NEEDS SLEEP AS WELL AS YOUR MIND. IF I DID THIS, I SUSPECT I WOULD BE DOING IT MORE AND MORE."

Great, she thought, stifling a yawn. It had been worth a try, though. No harm, no foul, as the Americans would say. She straightened her back and copied Illyara's gait as they climbed yet another dune.

They were miles away before they felt safe enough to make camp again. The wedasi riders rode out to the rest of the tribes to let them know there was a meeting while the outer tents were packed again.

Young and old jostled for position to hear their leaders and Lynsey speak. They sat on bright cushions brought in from the other tents. The floor was an enormous patterned mosaic, as if put together by a colour-blind designer. As she thought this, she realised she could see colours properly for the first time. Reds and greens popped out next to blues and purples. Her jaw dropped at the beauty. "I didn't realise what I've been missing!"

"Pardon?" Illyara replied, sitting beside her.

"I can see colours!"

"Couldn't you before?"

"Yes, but not like this." Her voice was filled with wonder.

"I'VE BEEN WORKING ON CHANGING YOUR CORE CODE. I NOTICED THERE WERE BITS MISSING AND CORRUPTED. THAT IS WHY I HAVE BEEN SILENT FOR SO LONG. IT'S HARD WORK WORKING THROUGH DNA SEQUENCES. I HAVE TO WORK SMALL. A LOT OF WHAT I HAVE TRIED GETS REVERSED, BEFORE I HAVE FINISHED CHANGING IT." Pico's voice sounded hurt.

"I thought I was stuck with how I arrived here."

"TECHNICALLY THAT IS TRUE, BUT I'VE FOUND I CAN MAKE SMALL CHANGES AT THE MOLECULAR LEVEL AND IT STICKS BUT TOO MUCH AND ALL THE CHANGES I MAKE DISAPPEAR AND I HAVE TO START AGAIN."

"Really? This is amazing." She could see the colour of people's eyes from across the room. "What else have you done?" She whispered.

"WELL AS YOU ASKED, YOU SHOULD NOTICE A MARKED IMPROVEMENT IN YOUR HEARING AND YOU MIGHT FIND THAT YOUR SENSE OF SMELL IS BETTER, ALTHOUGH I'M STILL WORKING ON THAT ONE."

"I don't really want to smell any better. That happens during the…" She went cross-eyed for a moment, trying to think of a better way to say it. Oh, hell. There was no need to censor for Pico. She smiled at the thought. "Time of the month. The number of times I've nearly prayed to the porcelain god because someone was eating something stinky in front of me. If that happened all the time, I would just be throwing up all over the place."

"NOTED, I WON'T MESS WITH THAT SENSE ANYMORE."

"Could you not mess with any more of my senses, please?"

"WHY NOT?"

"Because there is a reason that humans developed their sense in a certain way and messing about with that could have uncertain consequences. Surely you can see that? My chucking up example should give you a clue!"

"I CONCEDE."

That was easy. "Good."

"Sekhmet has come back to us," shouted a voice. Lynsey twisted and identified it as Illyara's father, Darun. Everyone clapped around her.

"What? Who is Sekhmet?"

"THE LION-HEADED GODDESS OF FIRE, WAR AND HEALING. INTERESTING, I CAN SEE WHERE THEY GET THAT FROM." Pico helpfully supplied.

"You are," Illyara replied, her eyes shining in the candlelight. "We have waited years for you to come. There was a prophecy that you would arrive. We need you to help us rescue a dragon. You can lead us and the other tribes against the brotherhood and the king and take back what is rightfully ours."

"What is rightfully yours?"

"Freedom. We are trapped in the desert, moving from one place to another so that we cannot be forced to fight for the king in distant wars. We have to hide what we can do. Our people have lived in the desert for centuries. They have been here so long that they do not know that there is another way to live. Water and food should not be rationed, as the city would have us believe. War and power make it so, and it is time to change."

Lynsey stood up, nervous to be standing in front of so many people. Illyara nodded at her, still seated on the royal blue cushion beside her.

«I'm not Sekhmet, I'm just Lynsey.» She coughed, clearing her throat. «I am from another world, but I am not a goddess. My arrival here was by accident, not by design. I›ve just stumbled from one thing to another. I really don›t belong here; all I want to do is go home.»

"DO YOU KNOW, I WOULDN'T MIND THAT EITHER." Pico whispered in her consciousness. "WE WILL DO THAT BUT WE HAVE TO HELP THESE PEOPLE FIRST."

"Why are you on their side?" whispered Lynsey.

"WE MAY BE ON THIS WORLD FOR A VERY LONG TIME. DO YOU WANT IT TO BE A HEAVEN OR A HELL?"

"They think I am Sekhmet. What if they want me to do a miracle or something?" She switched to thought at some curious glances.

"THEY DON'T SEEM TO BE THAT KIND OF PEOPLE. THEY HAVEN'T REALLY SAID WHAT THEY WANT YOU TO DO YET."

Lynsey pondered for a moment. What was a god, anyway? It was just a label. If she was honest from the beginning, then what could go wrong?

"I am not Sekhmet, but I will help you."

The nomads looked from one to the other, and they grinned. She would help them.

"Where are we going now?" asked Lynsey, struggling to climb up the steep sandy bank after Illyara.

"Back to the Oasis where you first met us. Messengers have been sent far and wide for all the tribes to meet there."

"Why there?"

"It is holy and more practical. It is the biggest oasis on this side of the desert. Our yelks will need to drink and stock up on water and we will need to be somewhere safe to talk. That won't draw attention to our numbers."

They walked for two more days at a faster pace than with the temple, but water still had to be rationed and everyone had a skin which contained enough water for the day. Lynsey pushed the container on to her belt. She was still thirsty, but Illyara had warned her to take sips now and again rather than gulps. Her thoughts were fuzzy under the heat and thirst, and she could see the others were feeling it, too. The sun was relentless. She felt tremendous relief when they arrived at the oasis at nightfall the next day. The smell of campfires burning throughout the oasis reached them as they approached and they could hear people singing.

"We won't bother with putting the tents up here. We don't need to put up walls during a gathering."

"How did everyone get here before us?"

"We sent messengers on wedasi. It is the fastest way to travel in the desert."

"Why don't you ride them all the time?"

Illyara looked horrified. "That would be dangerous. The wedasi would eat anyone that dared to ride them without training."

"What are the Wedasi again?"

"Two-headed serpent like creatures."

Lynsey paused, skin half-way to her mouth. "I met one of those when I first arrived here. Why didn't I see any of them while we were travelling to Ghinari?" They passed a family of nomads unrolling some fur on the floor for beds.

"They always travel a distance behind with their trainers." A woman to their side offered a fresh skein of water. Illyara took it with a bow and a whispered thanks.

"I can understand why," replied Lynsey with a feeling. Illyara gave her a strange look but carried on, dodging some children running past.

As they made their way through the camp, Lynsey noticed people were roaming to and from different fires with skins full of drink. From the gait of some revellers, Lynsey was pretty sure that not all the skins contained water.

"I thought you didn't drink?"

"What gave you that idea?"

"At the house, you didn't want to drink the brandy?"

"I didn't feel comfortable drinking in that company." Illyara winked and drank deeply from the skin. "Would you like some?"

Lynsey took it. As long as it wasn't vodka, she knew she would like it. She raised it to her lips and chugged it down. Her eyes watered and she stopped breathing for a moment. She coughed once and then the itch took hold, coughing uncontrollably. The men nearest started laughing.

"What is that?"

"Reasse."

Lynsey glared at her, and Illyara replied, laughing.

"It's fermented yelk milk. The taste takes a little getting used to."

The other tribes had left a space beside the river. There were several curious glances at her blond hair, but no one approached her and she could move freely through the crowds. There were hundreds of tribesmen already there and more were arriving every hour.

Darun and his wife were organising the gathering area. To the right of Illyara's tribe's area, there was a clearing in between the desert and the water. It was filled with stones styled in a half-moon pattern. Illyara caught Lynsey looking at the stones.

"The Elders will sit on the stones and everyone else will sit in a semi-circle around them." Illyara's arm swept out towards the stones.

"If someone from the crowd needs to speak, they stand and face the semi-circle."

"Do the elders need to stand as well?" Lynsey watched as an elderly lady hobbled towards them.

"Oh no, they raise their arm and we listen."

Young men were working among the stones, clearing the ground of roots, weeds and loose vegetation. In front of the stones, they laid tent material inside the half-circle. On the stones themselves, they placed cushions made from a deep blue material. They appeared to be made for the seating, as they were the exact size of the stone they were placed on. As each stone was covered, an elder would take their place from the crowd, which was forming.

Others prepared lamps and hung them from trees and placed them on the ground between brightly coloured cushions. The effect was intimate for the number of people there. A young man, skin in one hand and a sweet treat in the other, stumbled through some already seated tribes people. He stood on a hand but the woman just smiled and pulled him down to sit beside her.

"There are a lot of drunk people here. How are you going to have a meeting like that?"

"No one is seriously drunk and those that have consumed too much are only stopping their voices from being heard. That is their choice and their right."

The moons arced across the night sky. Darun raised a curling horn to his lips and blew a long, soulful note that echoed through the oasis, sending chills down Lynsey's back.

"That's beautiful." whispered Lynsey. Illyara smiled back at her.

Darun handed the horn to his wife and took a burning branch from Mewlli, waiting nearby. He lit the first lamp and then a team of what Lynsey guessed were teenagers, took small branches and lit them from Darun's to fan out and light all the lamps.

Lynsey moved to sit on the outside, next to the nomads surrounding the circle, but Illyara gently took her hand and drew her to the stone near the front.

"Your place is here."

Lynsey perched awkwardly on the stone, acutely aware of her satin slippers next to the nomads' worn leather boots. She had changed in to nomad robes but she hadn't been ready to lose the shoes. She realised how silly that was now.

They thought she was some ancient Egyptian Goddess. How was she going to live up to that? She felt Pico sending soothing thoughts to her, but she shook her head, irritated, and she stopped. Lynsey cocked her head to the side. She still hadn't decided whether Pico was a girl or a boy. He felt like a boy, but that didn't really make any sense when he showed himself as a girl.

"WHY IS THIS SO IMPORTANT TO YOU LYNSEY?"

"I don't know. I just need to know whether to think of you as he or she. It is doing my head in."

"HOW ABOUT HE THEN?"

"You want to be a he? You appeared to me as a she?"

"LYNSEY, IT REALLY DOESN'T MATTER TO ME. THERE IS NO BIOLOGICAL REASON FOR ME TO BE ONE WAY OR ANOTHER. FROM YOUR MEMORIES YOU HAVE HISTORICALLY GOT ON WELL WITH MALES SO I AM HAPPY TO BE A 'HE' FOR YOU IF THAT MAKES YOU FEEL BETTER."

"Shh. They are starting." She thought back.

"We are gathered here today to fight for what has been taken from us all those centuries ago. They took our land; they took our lives, they changed us, and they took our dragon. We must fight now while the King and the brotherhood are fighting between themselves and the others. They are losing the war against the islands. They need men and money. The king cannot effectively fight on two fronts. If we join the fight, then his empire will collapse. We have already stopped the Temple from gaining the money from the pyramids by rescuing Lynsey Walker. If we unite and push on now, we can win. This opportunity may not present itself again for centuries. We are the enemy within that they have forgotten about. But we still remember." The crowd roared, stamping their feet on the ground.

"We need a leader, someone to show the way. We must rescue the dragon. He helped to defeat the priests in the beginning and protected us for years. Now it is our turn to rescue him."

Lynsey lifted her chin, swallowing hard. Stage fright rippled through her as she recalled skipping university lectures, anything to avoid presenting in front of the class. This was the ultimate presentation.

She scanned the seated crowd. There were so many of them. Hundreds of people were looking at her from the clearing and they went as far back as the water in the oasis and into the desert to the side. She stood up and strode to the front beside Darun.

"My name is Lynsey. I am from another world and I have met your dragon." There was a gasp. She saw the surprise on Darun's face.

"He has been trapped in the bowels of the Temple for two centuries. He has been tortured and treated like a simple beast." She searched for an example that would apply to them. "Worse than a yelk. He is no animal. He is as clever as you or I and he deserves better. I don't know what he did for your people beyond what has been said today, but he was brought here accidentally as I was. He wasn't meant for the life he had and he should be free. I pledge I will do everything that I can to help you and him to make a fairer society." The crowd stamped their feet.

"BRAVO, LYNSEY."

"Shut up Pico." But she was inwardly jubilant.

Arkan scanned the sea of brown and black hair from his position on the dais. The crowd was packed in tight, but still Arkan searched from the tallest figure to the shortest with his eyes.

He spotted the king in the distance with his attendants, but didn't cross the floor to join him. One of the King's guards was handing him his cape. Good, he was planning to leave.

Arkan moved like melting ice, smooth and soundless. He positioned himself on the distant side of the room from the king, with dancers separating him from the king's entourage.

The background music was silky, but the breath of the audience, the nervous jitter of the dancers, the faint hum of conversation from those near the king filled the room with a faint disturbance. Unease trickled down Arkan's spine as he entered the ballroom. Something was off. He searched the crowd, reluctant to approach the king until he uncovered the source of his alarm. Usually, men flocked around Lynsey and her companion like flies to a yelk, but there were no clusters of men and nearby disgruntled ladies. She was notable by their absence.

He moved from room to room, chatting with a lady here and a gentleman there. Rhythmically meandering around with a carefree demeanour, a fake smile plastered over his mouth, and his eyes staring forward.

If the king suspected nothing, he had to keep up pretences. He fared no better upstairs. He grabbed a glass from a passing waiter. The sparkling wine tasted bitter, but he couldn't taste any of the alcohol. Just the bitter tinge of fear. It tasted like a man who was about to be betrayed.

The muscles in his face and belly tightencd. He felt jumpy. He should have followed her. Where were his bloody informants? He couldn't even find the servants he kept on his payroll. A shiver of uncertainty swept through him. The king couldn't know about all of them. They were avoiding him, or worse. He didn't want to think about that fate. Spying on the king was treason.

The grand stairway to the second floor was old. The wood, despite the painting and years of polish, had weathered and cracked. It was peeling, and the stairway creaked and groaned under his weight.

Then he saw Jarek hovering near a doorway. Jarek's face looked tired. Deep bags underlined his eyes, and he looked as if he was about to fall asleep standing. He wore a red velvet robe over his tunic and breeches, with the Contee's emblem embroidered across the chest. Arkan beckoned the man with his finger. The man blinked and hurried forward, picking up a jug and a glass from a nearby table as he bypassed courtiers with ease.

"Do you know where Lady Walker is?" Arkan was careful to keep his voice light. The man's bearing showed he was nervous.

Jarek poured a dark red liquid into the glass. "She was taken by the King's guards, Sir."

"How long ago?"

"More than a half hour, Sir. Is there anything else?" He offered the glass.

Arkan burned to ask more questions, but he didn't want to delay the man any more than he should. There were already a few curious glances directed their way.

"Do you know where they took her?"

"I'm sorry Sir, I heard nothing from them that would give her location away." Arkan inwardly seethed. He felt like an arrow, pulled back and ready to fire. He wondered if his face betrayed that fact, but he knew Jarek would tell him if he knew anything. Arkan relaxed his face.

He took the glass and waved the back of his other hand as if the man was of no consequence to him. Jarek nodded, relaxing his shoulders as he walked backwards a couple of feet to take his place against the wall again.

Arkan took a draught from the glass and sauntered to the window. He leant against the ledge, letting the cool breeze ruffle his fringe. The sound of shorn hooves on pebbles drew his attention down and he gripped the cool, stone hard as he recognised who was there. In the courtyard, the king was stepping into a small carriage made of dark wood and iron. It was smooth, gleaming in the light from the torches.

The vehicle was painted black, with a gold trim and a plumed crest to match. It was only large enough to carry one occupant. There were a couple of shouts and the horses trotted away from the house with the guards running alongside. These were the elite guards, he noted. Their black attire resembled his own. He shivered and took another sip of his wine. They were the only men that Arkan was wary of. He had been bested many times in mock combat by one of their guard when training. In the dark, when wearing their uniform, they were invisible. The only warning of their arrival were the whites of their eyes and the whisper of a dagger. In his experience, they used short swords with cross guards and dark sheaths. Some were also trained in a form of martial arts, making the daggers virtually invisible as they weaved their patterns of death.

Arkan tore his gaze from the empty courtyard. Lynsey wasn't here, and she wasn't with the king then.

Arkan put his glass down with regret. It was an excellent vintage, but he needed to clear his thoughts. He ran down and around to the back of the building where his horse was waiting, still saddled from his arrival.

Checking to make sure no one was watching; he stopped between the horse and the wall and began pounding his fists on the stone. They must have taken her to the Temple. It was the only place they would go, but there were far too many guards to deal with on his own. His hands were red and swollen, fast becoming raw and exposed to the elements. One of his fingers was sore, and he'd already taken off his glove to rub at the hurt. He hissed and threw back his head as his knuckles sent shooting pain to his brain in revenge for their beating. Arkan gritted his teeth and sucked his hand. He had to be clever about this! He needed to find Darianna.

Arkan re-entered the palace, but again no one knew or would admit where she was. Jarek was nowhere to be found, either. The wisest course of action, mused Arkan. Lady Khaen gave him a small wave by the buffet table and he moved to join her.

Her fingers were long and thin, wrapped around a yellow-green goblet of wine. Her grey dress hung like pigtails to either side of the sinew and muscle of her long, lean legs, ending at her ankles. She wore matching dainty grey slippers.

"My lady, you look beautiful, as always." She giggled as he knew she would.

"Thank you Arkan. Are you looking for Darianna? She left moments after the king. But," she moved closer, letting him get a good look down her low-cut bodice. "I am still here."

She smelled of lilac and wildflowers, musky and alluring. Lynsey smelled of the fresh air and garden flowers. If he had never met Lynsey, he would have been tempted. Lady Khaen's dark skin reminded him of joyful nights of his youth. Her hazel eyes promised him anything he desired—all he had to do was ask. But she was of the Contee family and if he had learnt anything from his youth, it was not to mess with one of the most powerful families in the land.

He bowed to thank her and kissed her hand, lingering for a moment. Her perfume was heady.

"My lady, I am on the King's business this night. I would give a ransom to spend time with you, but I must go."

She narrowed her eyes. Had she noticed him avoiding the king earlier? Arkan straightened, letting her hand fall from his.

"Another time, my lady?"

She nodded, and he relaxed. That was close. That would be all he needed, to insult a Contee. He bowed again and rushed off.

An uncomfortable idea crept into his thoughts as he rounded a corner. Had Darianna had something to do with Lynsey's kidnapping as well? He ran back to his horse, jumped on her, and wheeled her around towards Darianna's house. He sped down the road as if a horde of devils were after him.

The night was silent save for the sound of his horse's breath and his own heartbeat. There was a slight scent of a wood fire in the distance. He pulled on the reins at the entrance to Darianna's driveway. His horse whinnied but acquiesced, bending down to eat some fresh grass growing against the gate.

The moonlight was bright and he could see the house from his vantage point, but there were no lights in the windows. He sat on the horse and contemplated the dark building. It wasn't just that there were no lights in the reception or bedrooms, but there wasn't illumination in any of the rooms.

Not even the servants' quarters. The uncomfortable thought resurfaced. Was she part of the new alliance? Who else was? Could he trust anyone? One man could not go against the King, Baserius and the closed ranks of the nobility. He thought he could count her as his friend. His chest tightened at the betrayal.

Still, he knew it wasn't her fault - that she couldn't have done anything else if asked by the king. She had taken a risk helping as much as she had. She held her power at the aegis of the king. If she dared go against him, then she would lose her position, and judging by her husband's business - money. He berated himself for trusting her. He knew her circumstances, her capabilities. Arkan had known them before he had contrived to meet her. She was one of the strongest women in all of Ghinari, but even she had to bend her principles in the face of survival. She was gone. There was nothing he could do about that now. He needed a drink.

Pushing through the warped red-wood door, Arkan stepped into the smoky warmth of the tavern. The Dragon Arms was small and cosy, sticky, with the scent of beer and smoke. There was a bar and four tables, two with empty seats and two with occupants. The barkeep stood at the other end of the bar talking to a customer.

The inn walls were made of dark wood. It was illuminated by smudges of light that spilled from the small windows near the ceiling. A slur of smoke followed the air like the ghost of a dragon. Its bar was made of loor-wood, its chairs and tables were old and carved from the same material as the counter. This was one of the oldest taverns in the city. None of the patrons seemed in a hurry to leave. The harsh sounds of the inn disrupted the otherwise still night. The conversations had a forced tightness to them, as if they were afraid. It had a clientele that didn't ask questions as long as you didn't ask them first.

Turning his jacket inside out to look scruffier and kicking loose mud off his shoes on the front step, he regarded the tap room with caution. It was full of the usual suspects. Perfect, he thought with an inward smile. No one would bother him here. He slunk down, altering his posture to bend into a stoop, and drew his hood over his head, moving through the crowd, affecting the clumsy walk of someone who had already imbibed too much.

He strode with an aggression he didn't feel but needed to display. The music was loud and jarring, but soothed his nerves. Seeing a target, he barged into the arm of a young man he judged to be about eighteen, half-way between a boy and a man. He caught a whiff of the youth's fear, the sweet scent of fresh soap and cologne.

Arkan's fingers traced the hilt of the dagger concealed in his sleeve, even though he knew he would not need it. Still, the weapon comforted him.

The drink splashed onto his companion, who emitted a startled yelp. Crimson liquid cascaded down her pale-yellow skirts, staining them in an instant. A woman of substance, Arkan thought, surprised to see the quality of her dress and nobility of the woman's accent as she yelled at the boy. He must be trying to impress his new girl. Was it a bet? Arkan looked again at the rich cut of the young man's cloth. He should not have brought her here. No matter how much he wagered. A cleaning bill was the least of his worries if he interacted with the wrong people. He was doing the idiot a favour.

The boy turned, ready to throw a punch, but Arkan was ready with a snarl, using all the pent-up emotions he had been holding back over the last few days. The boy pulled back his arm. Just try, Arkan thought, daring him with his eyes. The youth hesitated, looked from him to his companions for a moment, and then apologised.

Maybe the boy would reach nineteen after all.

Arkan growled at his circle of friends, daring anyone else to intervene. There must have been something in his expression because they didn't. He relaxed. His performance would mean no one would disturb him.

He moved past and selected a table to sit with his back to the wall. But with an unrestricted view of the open fire and exits. He leant against the cool stone, letting the open fire heat his bones from the front.

Arkan licked his lips, realising his tongue felt rough and dry. His throat felt parched, a harsh dryness that gnawed from the inside out. He half opened an eyelid.

"Ale!" He shouted at a passing wench, closing his eye again. Wench. What a horrible word. Before tonight, he would have thought nothing of using it, he mused. One chit of a girl and he was questioning everything. Nothing seemed solid. The ancient rivalry between king and brotherhood was over. Darianna had disappeared and the woman he loved captured and maybe killed. He jerked, cutting his fingertip on the blade he was playing with. Did he love her? He sucked his finger out of habit. He rolled the idea around in his brain. Could he love someone he had only known for a few days? She was attractive, but so were so many women he had bedded over the years and he had never even remotely felt the emotion he did for this girl.

The serving woman came over and planted a flagon on the table with a bang and waited for him to notice. She reeked of sweat and stale ale. He let her wait for a moment, savouring her annoyance, knowing she was waiting for a tip. He opened an eye and looked blearily at her before flicking a coin onto the table. She sneered at it but took it anyway, sashaying over to a man with richer clothes and a looser purse.

Arkan took a swig and pictured Lynsey as he had last seen her. Her long blond hair flowed down her back in a cascade of colour. The dress she wore was a deep green hue, cut to leave little to the imagination. She looked tired and worried, but the curve of her full lips was soft and her eyes sparkled with happiness. Her dress hinting at the delights in it. His pleasure at her touch still taunted him and the pain when she broke away. Gods, he wanted to protect her.

Three flagons later and he was falling into the numb state he craved. He barely registered when some Brothers walked in, but the level of sound in the room dropped. Arkan raised his head from his arms, looking for the source. He noted a brother in red robes talking to the man he barged into earlier. He was offering work for an expedition. Did they not see the boy's clothing? He had no need for money and while an adventure would impress the girl, if he left, another would take his place over the months when he was gone.

Why not? His thoughts turned to himself. Maybe he needed a career change. It's not like he changed anything when he killed anyone. If he removed a criminal, another took his place, and that was if the man or woman was bad. The soft hand of guilt was massaging his conscience. How many of those he'd killed were just obstacles in the king's path?

He'd never thought about it before. Training will do that for you, he thought. When had he ever had the time to think it through? You like the luxury of the job, the small voice of his conscience informed him. No, it wasn't that, but no one had ever told him to think differently, and he hadn't had the time to reflect before Lynsey. He'd always taken what he wanted when he wanted. That is what everyone did if they could. It wasn't wrong. Then why did he want to protect her so badly?

The Brothers had also come to the wrong place, Arkan thought with humour. No one here would lift a finger for an honest day's wage and less than that was what they were offering. The honour of Sekhmet was worth jack shit here.

About to ask for another flagon of ale, Arkan paused. Lynsey was gone. The king had to know he was the one that rescued her the other night and if he didn't, Darianna would tell him. He needed to get out of town. Maybe this was the answer. Get a guard's job for a couple of months and then come back when everything had blown over. He had enough money that he could buy a parcel of land out in the country and no one would come looking for him. Lynsey was gone. There was nothing he could do about it, but make sure he didn't suffer the same fate. He needed to disappear for a while, just in case. Arkan put his flagon down and stood up, almost toppling, as the waves of drink rose to his head.

He stumbled out of the inn with the door slamming behind him. He hadn't been this drunk since he'd stumbled from a brothel in the south.

A brother straggling behind the others ahead turned at the noise. The man was about thirty-five, with a thinning beard and a slight paunch. Arkan raised his hand in a half salute.

"I'll take your money," He slurred.

The other brothers turned, looking disgusted at his state but the closest, moved nearer, wincing at the malodour of ale on Arkan's breath like a mastiff sniffing a steaming turd.

"He's a drunk." One brother whispered.

I can hear you, Arkan thought, thinking better of saying it out loud.

"We don't have a choice," another hissed. "We have hardly any volunteers. Do you want to tell Baserius?"

The man curled his lip at the picture Arkan made before him. Arkan held his breath. Would they take him? Did he care? Before he thought any more on the subject, the first replied to him.

"Sekhmet, thanks you," he said, striding forward and placing a pin on Arkan's shirt. "Be at the city gates by dawn. We leave at sunrise." The man was tall. Standing nearly a full head above Arkan, he had a large frame and heavy shoulders, with arms that were large enough to swing a man like a rag doll. Though his bulky frame was marred by a torn cloak that looked like it had seen better days.

"Absolutely, count me in," he saluted again.

Arkan looked down at the pin on his front. It bore the figure of a woman with a lion's face. The pin was heavy and had been worn by rough use. Its metal was warm to the touch, and had been pitted by time. In several places, the brass was visible underneath, black and weathered.

He heard the brother walk away toward another tavern.

His fingers traced the lion's mane surrounding the face. He may as well follow them. There was nowhere for him to go here. Home was not safe, and he had everything he needed to survive. A blade or two and his wits. Arkan followed the Brothers from a distance, keeping to the shadows out of habit. They went from inn to inn but only seemed to get one, maybe two, recruits at each place. It was a poor showing, and it showed how the Temple's influence had deteriorated over the years.

Once they had enough men, they returned to the temple, and he saw the recruiters help their brethren to put together the caravan for the trip ahead. He lounged in the inn's doorway down the street. His hood was still up, and he played with his blade in his hand out of habit as he watched. He was sobering up and was feeling the shadow of a headache forming.

When they left the building, he followed them to the city gates where they began loading the yelk's with the provisions they brought from the temple. Yelk's dung filled the air. The stench was sickening, but he still watched. The smoke from a nearby cooking fire filled the air with cloying smoke.

There were about fifteen yelks, fully loaded. He could offer to help with the rest, he thought, but no, he hadn't been hired for that. Between two yelks he spied a cloth hammock which was strapped around each yelk's belly. It was filled with cloth and looked very inviting. It was full with the luxuries that some in the brotherhood could not do without.

Stifling a yawn, Arkan crawled between bags of bedding in a hammock until he was comfortable. He stretched out and then closed his eyes, listening to the sound of the yelk's breathing. Its rasp did nothing to help the light-headedness, or his headache, but he felt his muscles relax.

Nestled between the bundles, sleep descended on Arkan as the caravan lurched into motion. He wouldn't be left behind. Pleased with his cunning, he slipped into dreams with a smile.

28 New Hope

Arkan's body swung from side to side in a rolling motion. He woke to find his thoughts buffeted by clouds of uncertainty. He lay there, thinking through cotton wool, enjoying the sensation of movement until he felt the first stirrings of a headache forming. Within seconds he went from comfortable to his head pounding.

The sun blazed through his black garments, searing his skin. He winced, squinting against the brutal light. The sunshine heating through his clothing was no longer a pleasure but torture. Thirst assaulted his mouth, forcing him to open his eyes, almost gagging with his need for water. He blinked in the harsh light, sitting up to cough while rubbing his eyes at the same time. The movement unbalanced him and he fell back down into the hammock under the yelks uneven gait.

Even protected somewhat by the hammock, the sun must have been burning his skin. The air was hot and clinging to the back of his throat. Smelling of burnt dust, oil, and smoke.

He tried again to sit up. Where was he? He was still thinking through a thick fog. Before he could piece together the previous night, he pitched forward out of the hammock to land face-first in a mound of gritty sand.

A burst of laughter greeted him and he propped himself up on his elbows, spitting out dry sand. Who was that? A burst of pain throbbed in his head at the movement and he pushed a palm in to his forehead. He wasn't in mortal danger or he would be dead already. Gods, he hadn't drunk that much in years. He groaned. He didn't care who heard him. Acid rose in the back of his throat. His stomach heaved, spewing its contents into a vile, choking torrent. He almost vomited again as the stench of regurgitated ale assaulted his senses.

The laughing was attached to a long shadow. The shadow ended at expensive brown boots. He stretched his neck out further, following the sound up. Who in all the hells was that? He reached for his sleeve but fought the impulse to test his blades before he pulled one out. Didn't the man know who he was? The hangover pounded in his head with renewed vigour and he squinted harder. A young man dressed slightly better for an expedition than he was, in light loose clothing which looked like it came from a fashionable tailor, stood watching him. The young man stood silhouetted against the sun, pale, slim build, straight as an arrow, and black hair flopped around a sun-kissed neck. Arkan's curiosity got the better of him.

"How are you prepared for this trip? How did you know about it? The

Brothers were only recruiting last night. You didn't have time to go to a tailor."

The boy looked at him, still laughing, and shook his head. "No, I was going to join a nomad group and go exploring with them. It was that or join the army. I needed to get out of the city for a while and the brotherhood offered me a way." He held out his hand, pointing with the other. "Come on, we'll be left behind if we don't watch it." The yelks were already several feet ahead of them.

"My name is…" Arkan thought for a second, stumbling to his feet. He changed his mind. His name was a little too well known in Ghinari. "Finton, Finton Wylde." Arkan took his hand, and they clasped arms like old friends.

"My name is Ryen Belgrade. How do you do?"

"Southerner?" Enquired Arkan.

"How did you know?"

"You are just too polite to have been born and brought up in Ghinari."

"I see your point." the man laughed again.

Arkan stayed at the back with Ryen all day. It was nice not having to worry about doing anything. All he had to do was follow instructions, and there were no expectations. It was like being a lowly palace guard again. The man was good company. He seemed to have memorised hundreds of jokes and while most of them Arkan didn't find funny; they lightened the day.

The desert air smelled ancient, as old as the mountains, its scent redolent of sand and sun, tasting of chipped minerals.

Through the miles, he had ample opportunity to look around as they walked. The sand dunes in the distance stretched to the horizon. Closer, the guards recruited the night before were easy to spot, even though they were outnumbered by the brethren. Spread throughout the party, there were about twenty guards in all. Their dour expressions made him happy he had paired with his new friend.

"Why are you here?" Ryen asked, bringing Arkan out of his reverie.

"I needed to get away, too."

Ryen nodded and went quiet, and they walked on in companionable silence.

The company began setting up camp long before sunset. When Arkan saw them unloading the yelks he realised why. They had brought luxuries from home which had no place in a desert. Why would you bring proper beds? He shook his head at their idiocy. Still, there were no beds for the guards, just bed rolls, which had seen better days. They were made from heavy canvas, flimsy and frayed. They seemed to be sewn together from a patchwork of materials taken from an old tent. The seams were worn, and the ropes were brittle. Did they steal them off the homeless? He picked up his with distaste.

"Where did they get these from, the Pharaohs?"

Ryen held his up with thumb and forefinger, inspecting it. "It smells like it, my friend. It is a good thing I brought my own."

That was the second time Arkan could have cheerfully taken his blades out.

Around them, the other guards were helping the Brothers erect smaller tents for men like them, while larger, spacious abodes were put up for the priests.

A parade of cushions, bedding, beds, and even tables were carried past them. Arkan took a step back. Maybe it would be better if he found somewhere to lie low until everything was ready.

"You there."

Arkan looked behind him, but the brother was talking to him.

"Sir?"

"Yes, you. Pick up some firewood from Brother Dhras and start building a fire for dinner."

Arkan tensed, swallowing his irritation. He couldn't risk the Brothers dismissing him. They were still close enough to Ghinari that it was a possibility.

He found Brother Dhras unloading some sticks from one of several yelks who carried them. The number of yelks had ballooned to about fifty while he had been asleep. The brother pointed to the wood on the floor and turned back to unloading the yelk. Neatly trimmed, the brother's beard contrasted well against his cropped short black hair. There was an air of menace about him. Charming, he thought, then he realised. He must have taken the vow of silence. Grumbling under his breath, Arkan lifted a handful and carried them to the centre of the camp where a nascent fire was burning.

Arkan dumped the wood from his third trip to the yelk on to the ground and wiped the sweat off his forehead. Even though the sun was low in the sky, it was still warm. The breeze coming from the west was welcome. If he was honest with himself, he wasn't used to this kind of labour. His hand froze in mid-air as he caught sight of blond hair reflected in the fire-light. He could see her. But the fire was too high. It wouldn't let him see her clearly. Her fringe flicked in the breeze. Her dress billowed around her like water, her pale skin glistening. She was beautiful.

The wood smoke was mingled with the scent of Lynsey. He breathed deep, trying to capture every nuance, to bring her to a sharp focus in his mind, to remember her.

Lynsey was here? He side-stepped behind a man wrestling a cook-pot into place over the fire and scrambled over the sand to hide behind some urns. He watched her from across the flames.

What in all the hells was she doing here? Maybe fate was telling him there was a chance for them after all. It was ridiculous, but he couldn't help but hope. Arkan grabbed the edge of his hood, pulling it up with a swift movement as he hunkered down. The cook gave him a curious look, but the water was boiling and he turned back to throw a handful of herbs in the pot. Arkan peeked around the man to get another look, then another double-take. It was Lynsey. Should he tell her he was here?

Before he could decide, Baserius moved into view, and Arkan dropped again. What was he doing here? This was all he needed. He glimpsed Baserius directing her to a tent as they walked past and Arkan scurried backwards to keep out of sight. Arkan wasn't ready to face Baserius. Tugging his hood low, he turned and strode away, putting distance between them. He was going to have to find a job to do at the other side of camp.

Later, he was brushing the yelk down when he jerked back as its sharp teeth rounded to bite him. Not this time, my friend, he thought. His upper arm still throbbed from the previous two nips. His mind raced. How could he rescue her? If he escaped with her now, he wouldn't be able to find his way back. He would have to bide his time and rescue her when they got to their destination or when they got back to Ghinari, he concluded. He couldn't let what happened to that dragon in the story happen to her.

That night, he grabbed his bedroll from the tent floor. Ryen rolled over to face him.

"What are you doing?"

"I want to sleep under the stars tonight."

"Sure, I know what you want to sleep with and it isn't the stars. I saw you looking at that blonde girl earlier. Leave it, she'll be nothing but trouble, besides she's too skinny and her skin is too light. It would be like making love to a ghost."

"Ha, ha. It has nothing to do with her. I do not like to feel confined."

"My friend, I do not believe you. I heard that this expedition is to find the riches of the pyramids. It should be easy to liberate a jewel or two and then you can have any girl you want in Ghinari. Although I would be surprised to hear you have any trouble judging by how the women were looking at you as we left. It was like sweet nectar taken from a baby!"

Arkan refused to dignify him with a response.

Moments later, Arkan sat in the shadow of a tent, taking a sip from a flask within full view of Lynsey's tent. Maybe he should let her know she was here? He discarded the notion. No, she might betray him without realising, and that would put them both in danger.

He followed the same pattern for a week. He lay there looking up at the stars when he heard a sound like digging coming from her tent.

Arkan twisted to see sand mysteriously moving by itself. The sand shifted so rapidly that Arkan had trouble following the movement. It was as if a giant invisible animal had moved the sand into place. He watched, fascinated. How was it doing that? Was there a burrowing animal there? Why had it picked Lynsey's tent? He continued to watch and was surprised to see her come out a few minutes later with Illyara and a young boy.

The boy must have been about fifteen years old. He looked small with messy black hair, dressed in the traditional robes of a nomad. As Arkan watched, he blinked to clear his eyes as the boy faded from sight. He rubbed them again, but he was no longer there. The boy had appeared and then disappeared.

Lynsey and Illyara crept past Arkan, not noticing him sitting in the shadows in his black clothing. He watched, impressed, as Lynsey dispatched a guard with ease and silently got up to follow them when the fire started. Keep your eyes on the girl, he told himself. Everything else is a distraction.

He chased them through the tents to see Lynsey climb on to a yelk's back. He stood on the periphery looking back at the fire in the camp and jogged after her.

With each step, the sand shifted and slid beneath him. He kicked off his boots to run unfettered, bare soles gripping the dunes. Running on the soles of his feet was easier, but he had to fight constantly to keep up with the fugitives. It was the constant dropping low to avoid Illyara's gaze that wore Arkan out. She seemed to have a sixth sense for where he was, but his black clothing and the clouds were on his side tonight.

Relief washed over him as they stopped to walk. They were clever, these nomads. He watched as they wiped away their footsteps behind them. He was impressed, and who knew they could disappear like that?

Arkan kept in the distance, crawling on the sand so they wouldn't see him. Copying them, he waggled his legs behind him to level the sand.

Hours later, before he knew it, he saw them go into another encampment. Arkan wasn't sure about the reception he would get, so he waited outside, sipping from a skin that hung around his waist. He dropped on to the sand. He didn't know how long he would have to stay there or even how long his water would last - he may as well get comfy.

29 A Consensus

There were seven tribes, Lynsey was told. A whirlwind of unfamiliar faces flew past her over the next two hours. The wisened old elders introduced themselves to her first. They discussed what they wanted, their histories and their fears. They were tired. She could see that in the dancing light from the campfires. Tired of the nomadic life but there was a glow about them, they were happy at an end in sight. They touched her arms, her shoulders, and her face in gratitude.

The younger generations boasted about their abilities and threw challenges back and forth in a game of one-upmanship. They too wanted something different to the elders, but just as vital to the tribe. Their energy charged the air, infusing her with their passion and spirit. Lynsey was enamoured. She felt like she was the only person who could hear them, see them, understand their purpose.

And then she saw the children. They were everywhere, running and playing, laughing and crying. She smiled at the game of tag they were playing. Children were the future of the planet; their laughter and cries were the sounds of a changing world. Assuming she intended to help the tribe, it would be for them. The children ran around her in circles, tugging at her clothes and hair as they chased each other.

To her surprise, she didn't mind their eager touches and endless questions. They cared. At home, she shied from close contact. It felt fake there, but here - these people were genuine - kind. They meant no harm. As more and more nomads introduced themselves, cousins all. She did not feel a stranger but part of their family. Her face muscles ached from constantly smiling, and she sensed Pico fidgeting restlessly in her mind, bored by the endless introductions. There had been something missing in her life for so long and she hadn't known what it was. A sense of purpose had eluded her until now. Maybe this was what she was born for.

Maybe there were no accidents. How could you be an accidental immortal, anyway? Pico was right. Who knew how many years they would be on this planet before she found her way home? Even if that were possible. She may never see her family again, but she could have another. These people could be her family in this world. She felt a sense of belonging that she hadn't felt in a long time.

The first rays of daylight seeped along the ground towards the oasis, and Lynsey was shattered. She could barely keep her eyes open, but she felt she needed some time alone. She stifled a yawn while she stood up, apologising to the elders she was talking to, and went for a walk.

Lynsey walked back to the water's edge, looking out over the lake. The water seemed to be a patchwork of colours reflecting the sky - silver, blue, purple. Lynsey found a rock to sit on and stared at the water, watching the colours change as the sky turned from the deep black of night into the pale blue of dawn. The surface of the water was smooth, like an enormous sheet of glass reflecting the sky.

She moved further into the densely packed trees to find herself back in the spot where she had met Illyara. Even in the dark, the oasis was a beautiful place. The darkness lent an air of mystery that soothed her soul, where the only sounds were the occasional splash as an animal took a drink or hunted for food. There was nothing that could harm her here—not with the tribes so close. She relaxed and sat on a fallen tree. She lay back against a vertically jutting branch for a few minutes, staring at the quiet water. It was so peaceful. No one came to disturb her, and she felt her thoughts turn to some sort of order. She had better be careful or she might find herself with a god complex. Then again, what was a god? The Pharaohs had called themselves gods. Why couldn't she?

"YOU CAN AS LONG AS YOU DON'T BELIEVE IT." Pico replied.

"You'll always be there to ground me, won't you," she thought, sending little tendrils of pink thoughts to Pico to show she meant it nicely.

"I WILL. THERE IS SOMEONE BEHIND US BY THE WAY."

Lynsey tensed. She just wanted a few moments to herself. Was that too much to ask? If she carried on looking at the water, maybe they would take the hint and go away? Unfortunately, whoever it was, ignored the sign. She heard the rustle of leaves draw near. She was surprised how quiet the person was. The nomads had been moving through the oasis like a herd of elephants tonight.

"SPIRITS WILL DO THAT TO A PERSON," was Pico's dry thought.

"Look, I need some time alone to have a think," Lynsey said over her shoulder, attention fixed on the water. There was no answer, so she looked up.

Arkan stood beside her, gazing out on the water. Her heart jumped, and she smiled involuntarily. He had come for her. But how?

"How?" she asked.

"I thought I'd lost you," he said.

"Me too."

Arkan pulled her up towards him, gently taking her chin in his hand.

"I don't want to lose you again. I'm sorry, I should have just taken you away at the ball."

"Arkan, I wouldn't have gone. I don't think either of us realised the danger."

"You can't go back. Come away with me. There are some islands to the west where no one has gone before. We can go exploring together,"

Lynsey regarded him for a second. There was nothing she wanted more than to go with him, to leave it all behind, but she had made a commitment. Besides, she couldn't betray her new family.

"I can't. I promised I would free the dragon."

"The dragon, the one in the Temple?"

"How do you know about that?"

"The king was sent a scroll by the brotherhood detailing their history, and it mentioned a dragon. When I realised what they did to it, I ran to save you, but they had already taken you." He turned to face the water again.

She looked out to see a small rabbit like creature lapping at the water. Arkan's voice startled her to look back at him.

"They use the dragon's blood to stay alive longer. They promised the king a share of the elixir for you. You would have been put in with the dragon and bled for an eternity."

Lynsey took a sharp breath. She believed him. Baserius wouldn't look her in the eyes whenever he spoke to her. The other Brothers avoided her. Now she knew why, and it wasn't because she was a woman. How many of them knew what they planned for her? She shuddered in the gloom.

He gripped her shoulders. "Come with me! This isn't your fight. We can flee, just the two of us."

"No, what if it had been me captured all those years ago? The dragon needs a friend. You can join us."

Arkan made as if to say no, but the life he had planned when he thought he had lost her seemed foolish now. He wouldn't be able to forget her. If he didn't help her now and she was captured or somehow killed, then he would never forgive himself. He watched as the soft light of the sunrise lit up her features. The exquisite beauty of a new morning blended with the bravery of the legendary lioness goddess on the pin he wore on his shirt. He had sworn to serve Sekhmet. This girl was the living embodiment of the God and he loved her. He would go wherever she would lead him.

Baserius gripped his pen until his knuckles went white. One night. It had taken one bloody night for them to lose the girl. They were a bunch of imbeciles. Fury boiled within him. Not only had they lost the girl, but he'd been ripped away mid-ritual, the sacred rite left unfinished. His jaw jutted forward as he gritted his teeth. Things were unravelling. Without the girl, they wouldn't be able to find the pyramids. Another source of the elixir was gone, and the brethren had seen a ritual uncompleted, but with no consequences.

A hundred years of tradition were in jeopardy.

The catalogue of problems the brothers were recounting was not serving to quell his temper either, only fuel it. The Brother talking carried on, oblivious.

"During the fire she escaped on the yelks."

"This should not have been enough for her to escape. Did you even post a guard next to her tent?"

The priest looked nervous. "We did, but she escaped by digging a hole in the sand. She had to have had help."

"How did she have help?" Baserius' voice took on a silken quality.

"The guard was overpowered by her. She can fight in a way never seen before with just her hands and body. The guard saw another female with her. She was dressed as a nomad."

"Illyara." So that is where she got to. "Didn't you think to check your hirelings for anyone that could betray us?"

"We only had the night to prepare, sir." The priest looked to his friend for help, but none was forthcoming. "We employed no women. She did not travel with our camp."

"So, she must have followed with her tribe. Even the nomads think twice before entering the desert alone."

"You sent someone to follow them and bring them back, I take it?"

The other Brother coughed and answered.

"There were no footprints, and we have collected all the yelks. They are nowhere to be found." He lowered his gaze to the ground.

Baserius thought for a moment, his stare looking through the men in front of him.

"There is no doubt it was the nomads, then. They must think they have their Sekhmet. That is unfortunate. We started that myth to keep them in their place, not to incite them to a revolution." Baserius stood up, forcing the two priests in front to jerk up on to their feet. The pen he had been holding fell to the floor. "I think it is time to bring out our own Sekhmet."

"Is that wise, sir?"

Baserius' head whipped around at the audacity of the man.

"Are you questioning my judgment?"

The man's face turned pale, and he took an involuntary step back.

Baserius ignored him, looking into the far distance once more.

"I believe it is time for our leader to come out of retirement."

The priests prostrated themselves on the floor and then left, the sounds of the camp dismantling outside, disguising their departure. Baserius drummed his fingers on the table's edge. Without Lynsey Walker, the expedition was doomed. There was no point in carrying on. Before they left to return to Ghinari, he would need to implement a more gruelling ritual than planned to keep the acolytes in order. Partly to appease the Gods but also to distract his people. The last thing he needed was anyone thinking.

31 Deceptive Deliverance

The party lasted two more days while the families were reacquainted with each other. Now the important business was dealt with, the nomads showed a side Lynsey was not expecting. She walked through the camp with a permanent grin plastered across her face.

The drink was flowing, and they even accepted Arkan. He seemed to blend in with wherever he found himself. She watched him across the campfire as he threw back his head in laughter. He seemed more relaxed than she had ever seen him. She settled back, bringing the coral blanket tighter around her shoulders. Pico's voice invaded her thoughts.

"YOU KNOW HE LOOKS SO EASY IN THEIR COMPANY BECAUSE OF HIS JOB."

"What do you mean by that?" Lynsey responded, stifling a yawn.

"HE'S AN ASSASSIN. IT WOULD NOT SERVE HIM WELL TO STAND OUT."

Lynsey regarded Arkan again. Pico was right. Maybe it was all an act. She bit her lip. Should she? Could she trust him? What if he was in league with the king? Maybe he followed her to take her back. He did work for the man.

"I'M NOT SAYING HE CANNOT BE TRUSTED, BUT LYNSEY, YOU NEED TO BE CAREFUL. WE DON'T WANT TO SPEND AN ETERNITY BLEEDING IN A BASEMENT WITH A DRAGON FOR COMPANY."

Pico had a point.

The tribes said their farewells to each other in good spirits. On the second night of travelling, Lynsey grabbed a shawl from beside her cushions and stole out of the tent. She paused, holding the tent flap open for a moment to see Illyara mumble in her sleep in the shaft of moonlight. Smiling, she stepped out into the night.

The air outside was cool, and she clutched the shawl tighter around her shoulders. The campfires had been extinguished, and the stars shone in the night sky, undeterred by clouds. There was no sound but the wind and the yelks snorting from where they were tethered.

She stood for a few minutes, staring up at the stars, and then she made her way through the camp.

A few more feet away, she found Arkan lying on a blanket. He was also staring up at the night sky. He showed no sign he knew she was there. Lynsey lay down beside him without saying a word, looking at his profile. She placed her hands under her head and waited. She hadn't talked to him since the night they found each other again. Twisting her neck, she joined him in looking up at the night sky. She was close enough to feel heat radiating off him through his shirt in the cool air.

"Do you know any of the names?" she asked.

"Many of them," he said. "They make you feel insignificant."

Lynsey stayed quiet.

"Have you been avoiding me, Lynsey?" She heard rather than saw him turn to look at her. She swallowed.

"I don't know you," she said.

Arkan sighed. "I would do anything for you. I rescued you once, remember? The king might have put a death sentence on my head. I have no idea if he has. I have risked everything for you."

"You followed me from Ghinari." It wasn't a question, but she had to be sure. This time it was Arkan's turn to be silent as he looked away. After a minute, he spoke.

"I thought you were gone. My career was over." He let out a long sigh. "I didn't know where you had gone, but I needed to leave Ghinari — to disappear."

"What we are going to do is very dangerous." She said, "if you are not sure…"

Arkan moved to lean on his elbow. He was facing her fully now. His long, curly black hair fell forward over his chiselled features. Her skin tingled as Arkan cradled her hand with his. She could feel the heat of his body through their linked hands.

She ran her fingers up his arm, a long lean muscle with fine dark hair growing along his forearm. He didn't flinch.

"Lynsey, I will follow you wherever you want to go. I cannot go back working for the King. I love you."

Lynsey's breath caught in her throat. He'd said it. He clasped her hand tighter.

"Whatever you want, I will do it to prove to you that you mean everything to me."

He seemed so sincere. She felt Pico shift in her mind as a warning. Lynsey wanted to believe him, but the basement room with the dragon was her fate if she got it wrong. She struggled with the idea. Time would tell if he was telling the truth.

The trip back to Ghinari took a few days. They spent the hours talking about their childhoods at the back of the caravan, avoiding thinking about the future. There was no point in confronting him about her fears. If Pico was right, then he would hardly admit to it. She kept thinking of the saying, keep your enemies closer. Her heart told her he was not her enemy, but this was not her world. She had no one to rely on beside herself. She had to choose her friends carefully.

Illyara weaved through her tribe to join them at the back. Lynsey hid a sigh of relief. It was hard trying to hide her confusion, and Pico was not helping. He was the voice of reason in her mind, and she did not want to hear it.

As they neared the city, they joined sparse clumps of people. The people milled together. Voices rose above the din, shouts, screams, grunts of effort, the sound of city life. There was a mixture of men and women, from merchants to the well-to-do. But the closer they got to the gates, they saw people pushed in wooden wheelchairs or hobbling on crutches. The nearer to the great gates they walked, the denser the crowds became.

The nomads drew together to avoid losing each other. She felt Illyara's hand take hers and she grabbed Arkan's hand to her left. It was a good thing that the rest of the tribes had split up. Even with the crowds entering the city, so many nomads in their distinctive garb in the same place would have been suspicious.

Lynsey turned to look at where Illyara was standing to stare at a distant cousin of her friend instead. She squeezed Illyara's hand, still clasped in her own to make sure she was there. All tribesmen who had the ability were invisible to thin down their visible numbers. The yelks were also spaced out in the caravan so they could walk between them without being knocked into and discovered by another traveller.

As they entered the city itself, there was a festive mood among the crowd, and people were singing and dancing on the streets. Men and women were openly drunk, wearing their best clothes. Arkan grabbed the arm of a passing reveller.

"What's going on?"

"The Temple has announced a new festival. Everyone has the day off."

"What is the festival in aid of?"

"Two hundred years since the day that they captured the dragon."

"Has everyone gone mad?" asked Lynsey.

"No," replied the man. "For the first time in one hundred and fifty years, Sekhmet is coming out of the temple. She is old, but they have promised that she will heal the sick."

"How does she do that?"

The man looked at her sideways. "With her blood, of course. It is said that in ancient times, she drank the blood of the dragon and became Sekhmet. She will be at the Temple at mid-day, every day for a week to heal anyone who needs it. I must get my mother." He shook off Arkan's hand and ran off. Arkan let him go.

"They must be draining the dragon. They heard we are coming." Arkan said.

Lynsey watched the man disappear in the crowd. "We have to go see Sekhmet for ourselves and report to the others tonight at the park."

"I agree."

They pulled the hoods of their cloaks up and made their way through the streets, avoiding eye contact with the revellers. Lynsey felt better knowing Illyara was beside her. If Arkan was going to betray her, now would be the time. Her heart raced. She grinned; she had never felt so alive.

"YOU ARE BEGINNING TO ENJOY DANGER, LYNSEY." Pico observed.

"I know. I've changed a lot since coming here." She whispered the next words. "Immortality will do that to a girl."

"IMMORTAL YES, INVULNERABLE NO. YOU KNOW WHAT FATE THEY HAVE PLANNED FOR YOU."

It was a sobering thought. "Yes, I do Pico. I remember."

As they neared the Temple, the crowds grew so thick it was almost impossible to go through. People were pushing and shoving to get to the front, trying to get a good look at the temple steps. Tens of thousands of people had flooded the grand plaza and the streets that fed into it. Many of the people wore robes the colour of sand, gold, and jet. Some of them held rakes, hoes, and shovels. A few had them over their shoulders, as if they had come off their farms to attend the festival.

Illyara's hand slid from her grasp, lost in the surging crowd.

Arkan jabbed through a few people until they stood ten people back from the front, near the edge of the steps. They had a good view but not so close they might come under the Temple guard's scrutiny.

There was a long, low note from a horn.

"It is beginning." He shouted over the noise of the crowd. The double doors of the Temple were thrown open to the sound of the horn. A figure that Lynsey recognised stumbled through on to the steps supported by Baserius and another priest. Lynsey froze, cold running down her spine. She recognised that figure and voice. That was the priest from the dungeon.

"… Sekhmet. I have drunk from the dragon and became an aspect of Sekhmet herself in this world." The woman threw back her head and her hair shone silver in the harsh sunlight. "I was once blond like the lions. This is no more, but I can still heal. Bring forth your sick and they will be healed by the will of Osiris and Sekhmet."

Lynsey rolled her eyes. "She's lathering it on."

"Lathering it?" Arkan's voice was light, and he leaned in to her hood. "What do you mean?"

"You know, laying it on thick, making it more important than it is."

"Healing is not a trivial matter, Lynsey. You can die from a cut."

Arkan looked back at the stage and back at her. "You know if she can do it because of Dragon blood, you could do the same thing, but you wouldn't have to hurt anybody or anything to do it."

Lynsey looked thoughtful. "I suppose so, but I don't know how she does it."

A line of people was forming on the far side of the steps. Families were gathering with their ill members. Nervous-looking people, waiting in line. Sekhmet gestured for the first to come close. A man walked up, carrying his daughter on his back. He set her on a chair before the woman. He spoke to her, his voice a whisper. Sekhmet nodded. The girl's father looked worried. He bit his lower lip.

"You see this child?" her voice was thick and raspy with age. "She has been in a coma for weeks after a carriage accident. The healers could do nothing, but I will heal her. I will first need an offering for my father, Ra, and brother Osiris."

The man nodded and fumbled in his pockets. He offered a coin, and a priest rushed forward to take it.

Yet another priest offered a gold knife and bowl. She took the knife, and he held the bowl under her wrist. She looked up at the sky and started chanting. The priest's voice was weak, but carried across the crowd to the people. She spoke aloud in a language long lost to the world. She spoke words of magic and power.

"What's she saying?," Asked Lynsey.

"It will be old Egyptian." replied Arkan. "No one but the priests can speak that."

"Why can't I understand it, Pico?"

"IT'S NOT ACTUALLY OLD EGYPTIAN. I THINK SHE'S MAKING IT UP."

"Oh."

The woman lowered, then raised her arms to salute the sun and brought her right arm to just above the bowl. With her left, she took the blade and cut her arm. Blood bubbled to the surface of her skin and dripped on to the bowl. As they watched, the arm healed until there was no sign that there had been any damage. She held her arm up to the crowd to the sound of gasps.

The priest took the bowl to the girl, and he nodded to the father who opened his daughter's mouth. Sekhmet's blood was poured in to her mouth, and he closed it again.

A few seconds passed, and then the girl twitched. She coughed and opened her eyes to smile at her dad.

"Father."

A cheer went up in the crowd.

Sekhmet cured thirty people that day. Each one went through the ritual. Lynsey scanned the teeming plaza, packed tight with believers cheering Sekhmet's every move. Sweet incense tickled her nose, and the heat from the torches warmed her skin.

These people believed. They would do anything for that woman right now. If anyone tried anything here, then they would be set upon before they got within a few yards. Not that they could get any closer with all the crowds, anyway.

Arkan took her hand, and they walked away. It was time to join the others. By the time they got to the park, it was already getting dark, but they found the camp. They threaded their way through revellers. The crackling of the fires and birds in the treetops provided a backdrop to the celebration. The park was full of strangers from outlying cities and villages, but they knew the nomads were gathered on the eastern edge of the park near the lake.

They found Illyara waiting with her parents. Everyone seemed subdued.

"Did you go to see the Temple?" Illyara asked, gesturing for them to join her on brightly coloured cushions.

"We did. There is a woman there. She calls herself Sekhmet, like you call me. She healed a few people and made a few more converts. I can't see the city revolting anytime soon."

"We heard. She was there all those years ago when they captured the dragon. Our tribe saw a woman fighter-priest hurt in the fight. They slashed the dragon and his blood cured her wounds when it spilled on her. That is why they captured him. They must have prolonged her life as well as saving it. It is strange she still lives. It was centuries ago. They said Sekhmet looked old though."

"She did. If I didn't know better, I would say she was about eighty. She looked frail, but I think that was an act because she didn't look frail when I met her in the Temple. Anything but!"

"Then the dragon's blood cannot make her immortal, only slow the aging process down. It will mean that she won't be able to fight you very well. If nothing else, if we fail, surely she cannot last that much longer." There was hope in Illyara's voice.

"Two hundred years at eighty? If she would have lived to a hundred, that would be twenty years at the old rate and a lot more at the prolonged rate," said Arkan.

"66.666 YEARS BY MY CALCULATIONS." Pico eagerly supplied.

"She could live another 66 years at least!" Lynsey exclaimed out loud.

"We can't get into the Temple. There are too many people and even when the festival has gone, they've made sure the city is loyal to them." Arkan interjected.

"There is another problem," Lynsey said. "Even if we were to break into the Temple in some way, the dragon wouldn't fit through the door. The Temple must have been built around the Dragon."

"If that is the case, then it will be more difficult than anticipated."

"If only he could breathe fire like in the myths." Lynsey joked. "We need a demolition squad to get him out. Wait." An idea formed in her head. "Do you have explosives here?"

"I CAN SEE WHAT YOU ARE THINKING, LYNSEY." Pico was whirling around her brain like an excited toddler.

Sometimes she forgot he was less than a month old.

"No, there is nothing that will blast the door open, if that is what you mean. We have nothing that will heat stone enough to catch fire." Arkan was laughing at her.

"In my world, when they want to bring down a building, they use explosives. It's a powder that, when you light it up, it explodes."

"Do you know how to make this?"

"No, but I can work it out. I read a lot when I was younger there must be something there that will help me. Those years in chemistry class must have taught me something."

"We need somewhere with very thick walls to mask the sounds when I am experimenting, and we'll need somewhere close to the temple so we can dig under it. Blasting in to the temple to get him out is the only way we are going to manage it. We'll also have to be ready to leave when it happens. I don't think 'Sekhmet' will be thrilled for her source of power to fly away." Lynsey said.

Arkan smiled grimly. "I know of a place that will be perfect for both conditions."

Later that day, Arkan led them to a house opposite the temple. It was made from the same stone and once contained a shop on the ground floor and living space on the second. They entered through the back and moved straight into the basement.

Descending into the dank basement, the reek of mildew and damp earth enveloped them.

"Is this good enough?"

"Perfect." A quick look around the room and she said. "I need a workspace; table, charcoal, saltpetre and sulphur and a pestle and mortar. We'll also need picks, shovels and a lot of luck!"

"I can do most of that. But I'm not sure where to get the Saltpetre from."

"I read you can get it from bat poo?"

"Bats?"

"I sometimes forget we're not on Earth anymore." She went silent to talk to Pico. "Pico, where can I get Saltpetre from?"

"IT'S POTASSIUM NITRATE. WE DON'T HAVE ANY BATS ON THIS WORLD THAT I KNOW OF. ... WHICH ALSO EXPLAINS WHY HE HASN'T HEARD OF BATS. AHA, A WEBSITE YOU BROWSED WHEN LOOKING UP GUY FAWKES MENTIONED THAT IT APPEARED IN CAVES NATURALLY, AND THEY USED IT IN THE AMERICAN CIVIL WAR." Pico showed her the computer screen in her mind's eyes.

"I don't remember looking at that!"

"It doesn't matter. You did look at it and everything you looked at, I can show you again."

"Arkan, you can get the saltpetre from caves. It's a white crust. When you get me sulphur, saltpetre and charcoal, it is important they don't mix. Do you know where to get the sulphur from?"

"Yes, they use it to dye clothes. I'll be back in a few hours."

While Lynsey was rearranging furniture, Mewlli arrived with a pestle and mortar and containers with lids. Behind him were several others, each with a spade and pick. Lynsey pointed to the wall nearest the temple.

"We're going to dig a tunnel into the temple to get to the dragon. We will then blast through the walls so the dragon can escape."

They broke through the foundations within hours. Lynsey wiped the sweat from her forehead. Working in this heat wasn't pleasant, but she had to show that she was prepared to do the hard stuff as well.

True to his word, Arkan returned bearing sacks of what she asked for.

"How did you find the saltpetre?"

"I realised the farmers might have used it for fertiliser, so I took a bag from the warehouse. It shouldn't be missed."

Lynsey picked up a scoop and took a measure of the saltpetre, a pale brown powder. She wrinkled her nose at the pungent smell. It looked like burnt manure. Grinding the mortar against the pestle, she put the finer powder into a container handed to her by Mewlli. She did the same for the other two powders.

"I need a spark to show how this will catch fire."

Arkan brought out a fire drill and produced hot embers. He dropped them into the container and the embers whooshed down to the bottom and worked over the powders in a brilliant dance of red, green, and blue. The powders exploded.

The boys in the corner exclaimed and carried on digging faster.

They dug all night and all morning. They dug until they heard people gathering outside for the Sekhmet ritual. Several of the men took a break and went out to watch while the others carried on. Lynsey worked across the room, combining different portions of the mixture until Pico agreed it was the best they were going to get.

Illyara's brother appeared at the tunnel's entrance, muddy and exhausted with a shout.

"We've done it. We are underneath the tunnel. What now?"

"I need Illyara to do her bit."

32 Ethical Healing

Illyara waited as the people gathered around the temple. She saw some cousins hanging at the back of the throng, but stayed invisible as she threaded her way along the edge. She moved quietly. The crowd was so thick she had to push through. They were so excited they only gave the blank space she occupied a cursory glance. Feet trampled the soft earth of the temple grounds. The silks and linens of those who attended were stained with the dirt of the road. She moved with ease, avoiding the out flung arms and legs of the excited crowd, keeping to the edges until she was near the stone steps.

A metallic smell emanated from Sekhmet's blood in the bowl, pervading the air around the steps. Illyara covered her nose, but she still felt queasy. She crept behind Sekhmet to stand by the door and waited for the ritual to end.

As Lynsey had described to the tribes from the previous session, Sekhmet healed dozens of people, saving the worst for last. This time, it was a man with one leg. The crowd grew quiet. The priests' footsteps rang out, echoing off the temple steps. He had an arm around each priest, and couldn't have weighed much under his rags. Even so, their faces scrunched with the effort of carrying him. Behind them, another priest carried his crutches and handed them back up to him at the top of the steps.

Sekhmet gave a wintry grin. Illyara shivered beside her. There was no concern in the other woman's expression. Sekhmet strode towards the man and bade him sit on a chair brought forward. He pulled up his trouser leg to reveal a stump, long healed over.

"No longer will this man be forced to beg." She cried out. "Behold the power of Sekhmet!"

She slashed her arm once more, filling a golden chalice to the brim. She tottered but waved away a priest who moved forward. Another bowl stood ready, still half-full from the previous supplicant. She closed her eyes for a moment and handed the chalice to another brother standing by. The priest handed the cup to the one legged man. The man looked at the priest and then Sekhmet, swirling the thick and cloying liquid in the vessel. Illyara could see from behind Sekhmet that the blood coated the sides, and she watched as his face contorted in disgust. The man took a deep breath and chugged the blood back in one gulp.

As the man swallowed, a brother splashed the remaining blood from the bowl over the old man's scarred stump. The crowd gasped. The man fell, writhing on the floor of the temple, crying out in agony. As the crowd watched, bone jutted out from his scarred flesh, spurting blood over nearby watchers. New muscle and skin formed to extend over the glistening bone. Within minutes, the leg formed before their eyes. The crowd stood silent. Their eyes were wide with wonder and their mouths hanging open. The entire crowd dropped to their knees. There was no need to say anymore. Sekhmet turned and went inside.

Illyara followed the woman through the Temple into the corridor leading to the basement, keeping close so that she could pass through the door behind her. They passed guard after guard until they reached an ornate wooden door.

The woman stiffened just as she was about to open it, and twisted. Illyara pressed herself against the cool wall. Illyara's pulse roared. Had Sekhmet heard? The woman tilted her head, then shook it, seeing nothing. If she had been visible, she would have been looking at her. She opened the final door and Illyara followed a step behind.

The room was stifling, dark and the smell! Lynsey had never mentioned the stink. It made her want to wretch. It was the same smell as outside in the corridor, but amplified a hundred times. Illyara breathed through her mouth and closed her eyes. Something in the air smelled stale, a mix of rotten fruits, vegetables, blood, and like something had been dead for a long time.

Illyara stayed near the entrance. The blackness of the room temporarily blinding her. She could feel the dragon. The floor was tacky with something wet. As her eyesight cleared, she saw Sekhmet moving with purpose, steel in her hand. She cut at the dragon without hesitation.

His head rose an inch before settling down as if he didn't care. What had they put him through? He whimpered. Bright red blood steamed from his arm, falling on to a deep plate which caught it.

The woman lifted the plate and raised it to her lips. Illyara turned her head away as the woman drank. Her gulps were audible in the stillness. Sekhmet's tongue flicked out, lapping the last drops of blood from her lips. Cloth in hand, she turned and strode for the door. Before she left, she said two words.

"Thank you."

Illyara waited a few more moments before moving. She skirted a table and stood before the dragon before letting herself be seen. He didn't even acknowledge her presence.

"I'm so sorry." She whispered.

That got his attention, and his majestic head swung to look at her.

"I know you can understand me. Lynsey said that you could. I need to tell you we are going to get you out. I know you have been here too long, but with Lynsey, we have a chance to free you. They will come tonight under the floor and they will blast you out. I will go now. Will you be able to fly out?"

The dragon's majestic head shook from side to side, chains clanked on the stone floor through the hay covering it, and he gazed on, still with despair.

"Of course you are chained. Let me help you?"

Illyara took a silver knife concealed in her belt. She pressed the knife into a hole in the lock and twisted. The lock was stiff, but she pressed hard. She let out a sharp exhale in relief when the lock clicked open. Illyara smiled, and she squeezed the lock, just enough so that it looked closed again. She lifted it and ran around his body, doing the same with his legs and tail, until she was back at his neck where she stood up and then stepped back from the dragon, leaving the locks open.

"You should be able to shake your chains off when you hear the first blast."

He nodded as if he understood.

Illyara looked around the room and spotted a chair beside the table. She moved it so it faced towards the dragon, and sat down with her back to the door. She would hear it opening.

"I have to wait until they open the door, so I may as well tell you the history of our tribe since you left while I wait."

The dragon remained motionless, listening.

"We looked for you when you went missing. Our people left the oasis and went roaming. We promised we would never settle down until we found you." She paused. "We searched for a hundred years before we heard about the Dragon Brotherhood. We came here, but we couldn't get to you." Tears streamed down Illyara's cheeks. "It is our eternal shame we could not free you until now."

The dragon shifted until he faced her.

"We travelled and waited. We heard of the first Sekhmet that we think is the same one that hurt you earlier."

He nodded.

"She was powerful and had armies. We could not have rescued you then. The power of Sekhmet has waned. The kings rose to challenge them and were kept in check by bribery and arms, but now is the time when we can defeat her."

Illyara continued, "There is a war with the others, the king is ambitious, the brotherhood is running out of money and we have a new Sekhmet!"

The dragon raised his head. She took it as a question.

"I've seen Lynsey heal. She talks to people in their own tongue and does not realise it. She even looks like Sekhmet in human form with her blond hair. If we fail this time, we do not deserve to."

The door creaked open behind her. Illyara vanished from sight, pressed flat against the wall. She strode to the door and waited until someone came in. It wasn't the woman, but a man carrying a plate full of meat. He laid it before the dragon and sauntered back to the corridor. Illyara followed him silently until she reached the main temple complex and then hurried out of the building.

It took minutes to navigate the road and enter the building that Arkan had found them, and she found Lynsey in the basement filling up mini-barrels with black powder.

"He will be expecting us."

Lynsey nodded and placed a top on to the keg and nailed it shut. She placed her arms on to the new surface and smiled at her friend.

"We are ready, then. We just need to put these barrels next to an outside wall in the temple and kaboom! No more wall. Grolmak should be able to just fly out. I just need some help with taking the barrels down the tunnel."

"I will see if my cousins are available."

Illyara rushed off and sped to the park. She was surprised to find everyone gathered in the main tent. Faroushk was standing in the circle talking, but she heard him with the surrounding muttering. She pushed through until she stood before him.

"What is happening?" she asked him.

"We are going against Sekhmet by doing this."

"What are you saying?"

"We cannot stand against a goddess."

"She is not a goddess." Illyara said.

"Illyara, we saw her with our own eyes: how she healed those people. There were cripples there, people with no legs, yet we saw them grow in front of us."

"That woman is stealing from the dragon. I saw her drink his blood. If she were really Sekhmet, do you think she would age like she has? That is an old woman."

Faroushk paused and everyone looked at him to see what he would do next.

Illyara took over. "This is the only chance we have of defeating the Dragon Brotherhood. She is not the real Sekhmet. The woman is too old, and she is using the dragon for her powers. She is a fraud. The real Sekhmet has no need for a dragon to heal."

The muttering increased until they heard a voice from the entrance.

"I can heal too. If the dragon's blood can heal others, I can too." Lynsey stood in the tent's doorway. Her face was flushed, as if she had been running.

"We shouldn't test the gods." Illyara cried out, but Faroushk overruled her.

"Yes, we need to see this. How can we believe in something that we cannot see?"

Lynsey nodded at her friend, and she subsided. Illyara had never felt more ashamed of her people until that moment.

Faroushk pointed to the corner and called out for Edruter. An old man hobbled forward on a cane guided by hands. "We will see who is the real Goddess."

"Has anyone got a knife?" Lynsey asked.

A few knifes were offered and Lynsey took a small paring knife. She took the goblet that another offered.

Gritting her teeth, she sank the knife into her wrist and let the blood flow into the goblet. It didn't hurt that much; she reflected. The goblet filled up to a third before the gash healed up. She placed the cup in the blind man's hands. They shook, but the man drew his hands up to his lips and drank deeply. Immediately, they saw changes. The white covering his eyes was melting away and leaving the characteristic hazel eyes of their tribe. He was silent for a moment before letting out a shout. The goblet dropped to the floor and his family joined in, hugging him. There were tears in his eyes as he turned back to Lynsey.

"I believe." He said, and then he went off to stand with his wife. Lynsey felt near to tears herself as the old man raised his hands to his wife's face and traced its shape. Illyara knelt before her. One by one, the others knelt until the whole tent was on their knees and Lynsey was the only one left standing.

"We will follow you." Faroushk said, looking at the floor. He then looked into her eyes and smiled. "Sekhmet on Duat. We will follow you wherever it will lead."

There were hundreds of them, and they all believed she was Sekhmet. They looked at her with trust in their eyes. They wanted what everyone did: food, safety, love. She thought about how alike they were to her: their faces tired and lined with weariness, hurt, hope and disappointment. The cut on her arm had faded to a thin red line, then nothing. She examined her arm closer, but there was no sign of the cut she'd made. She let go of the knife and it dropped to the floor with a metallic clink. Lynsey stared at the upturned faces. It wasn't right.

She flew out of the tent. The words kept rolling around in her head. This wasn't right, this wasn't natural. What had she got herself into? She ran hard and didn't stop until she reached the city gates. The sun dipped below the horizon, and golden light stretched out across the fields and hills. Directly behind her, Arkan kept pace but stayed a few feet behind to give her the space she needed.

As Lynsey passed through the gates, she looked at the distant hills. The desert ran on the other side. She watched the red sand shift under the sun, like a living thing that never stopped moving. This was her chance to run away. Some of those people would be dead tomorrow. For what? For a traveller like herself who had been trapped by religious zealots. This wasn't the dragon's world or hers, but shouldn't travellers stick together? The nomads didn't deserve to die, though. It shouldn't be their problem. But they were all trapped in this terrible city, in this awful world.

She noticed Arkan behind her, leaning against the stone walls of the city. His foot was scuffing the ground, scattering the sand. That was Arkan. He professed to love her, and he was standing here waiting for her in this strange city with no protection of the laws she had in her world. He had defied all convention in pursuit of her - even in this strange land, he could have blended into anonymity, but had followed her instead.

Did she love him? Every time she looked at him, her heart did a little flop, her pulse raced, and she dreamed of a life together. This man was an assassin. He might have killed hundreds of people. It was his job. Could she love someone who killed for a living? Was it any different from loving a soldier? Both occupations were dangerous, and it was acceptable to marry a soldier, so why not a government sanctioned assassin? That was what soldiers were, anyway? She wanted a life with him. Did that make her weak? Did it make her shallow to want that?

She shook her head. What was she kidding? She would follow him anywhere. Trapped by the attraction she felt. She couldn't imagine being apart from him and didn't want to.

The plan was risky but not foolish. If it failed, they would be executed and the nomads would be exiled. But, if they succeeded, they would still be exiles and would have to depose the king or he would use the nomads to gain even more power.

A third option teased at the edge of Lynsey's mind, possibilities churning too quick to grasp. Maybe the Sekhmet at the temple didn't realise the dragon was intelligent and capable of feeling pain? Maybe she hadn't wanted to hurt it in the first place. If only she could talk to her!

Lynsey turned to Arkan. "I need to talk to the Brotherhood's Sekhmet."

"Why?"

"I think we should give her a chance to help us. She may not understand what she is doing. If I can talk to her, find out if there is a way to free the dragon without bloodshed. Surely that is worth a shot?"

"Lynsey, I am not sure. Sekhmet needs the dragon to stay alive. She has a vested interest in keeping him. If they have promised a prolonged life to the king, so does he. I don't think there is another way." He moved closer. "You know I care for you and if you feel you need to do this before we commit ourselves to risking the lives of others, then I will support you. That's why I came with you." In the cool shadow of the great wall, Lynsey felt the heat of his body next to hers. She was grateful for his support. She needed to make sure, and this was the only way.

They talked at length for hours about the best way to approach Sekhmet. She never left the temple, but Arkan surmised she must leave the environs of the basement each night. Sekhmet had a suite of rooms away from the other brethren in the outer regions of the Temple. Ladies were not allowed in the Temple, yet the rooms were clearly laid out with a woman in mind. Arkan had seen them when casing out the temple. They would go there.

***

Arkan led Lynsey to a creeping plant to the north of the building. Its long, purple stems were covered in tiny hairs and its small green and lavender-smelling leaves were pointed. He turned and looked back at Lynsey, his eyes burning with fire. Lynsey looked at Arkan, tense and expectant.

"So, what do we do now?" she asked.

"We wait," he said. "I want to see how the guards are positioned."

They waited for a while. The shadow of a nearby tree darkened the window from time to time.

"This is like a game of chess," said Arkan. "I have to figure out where the guards are placed and how best to avoid them while we make our way to Sekhmet. I have to understand everyone's moves, making sure I anticipate them all." He paused. "There are four guards on the first floor and two on the second. The two below are at the main entrance, and the other two are in front of the inside hall. The other two guards are on the second floor, one at each end of the hall."

They waited until the guards walked away. Arkan grabbed a tool and opened the simple lock. Then, they crept through the opened tinted-glass window and found themselves in the pantry, identified by rows of pots, urns, bowls, and bottles lined up on each side of them. Arkan led the way and Lynsey followed behind. There were very few guards on this side of the building. They were concentrated on the front door and around the entrances to the Dragon. The brethren were confident that no one would bother Sekhmet.

The room was crowded with furniture from corner to corner. Ivory walls were covered with colourful tapestries that shifted in the wind from the open window. A large bed took up a small corner of the room. It had a wooden frame, a festive canopy of silk linens, and a hoard of colourful cushions scattered about it. A wood shelf lined with stone statues sat below it, and an open door leading to a bathroom punctuated the right wall. A desk and chair were placed before the window, giving a view of the mountains in the distance.

Lynsey and Arkan waited in the bathroom. It wasn't long before Sekhmet glided in. She closed the door and hung her robe on the back. She was wearing a deep red dress that covered her from head to toe. The dress was made of flowing layers of silk. The material fell in supple folds and rustled like leaves as she walked. Her golden collar gleamed in the light.

There was a bowl of fruit on the desk and the scents of vanilla and cinnamon filled the air. Sekhmet's nails were painted the same crimson as her dress as she grasped an aghera from the bowl. Her silvery hair was tied back in a bun. She sat at her desk and her head snapped up.

"You wanted to see me?" Sekhmet said.

Lynsey looked at Arkan. They came out and saw the woman smiling into a mirror they hadn't noticed.

"Hello again."

"Hello. I'm Lynsey."

"I know who you are. What do you want?"

"Just to talk. Did you know the poor dragon is in pain and understands what you do to him every time you take blood?"

Sekhmet stood up and strode towards them. She stopped at the bed and regarded them with a small sigh. The woman's words were crisp and clear. Her English was perfect. "Did you know we are alike, Lynsey? Lynsey is not a common name on Duat, but then neither is Kathryn. I had to change it to blend in. It is strange here. Don't you think? We spend our lives on Earth just trying to muddle along, meet someone, look after them and die. It's not a life I ever wanted." Kathryn's eyes blazed. Lynsey took a step back.

Sekhmet continued, "Here, life is what you make of it. I came here in the 1820s. I suppose it is a little different now. "

"You are from Earth?"

"Why yes, but from an earlier time. I think we came by very different ways though. How did you arrive?"

"I was struck by lightning and found myself here."

"Interesting, I came here by the way most people did. My father was an

Egyptologist. He was fascinated with the pyramids. I wasn't that struck, but it meant delaying the whole getting married and having children noose. We were promised that we would be shown a pyramid never seen before. Virgin territory, as it were. My father couldn't resist and of course I joined him for company and to be his unpaid assistant. Look, this is going to take some time. Why don't I just show you?"

Kathryn darted forward and grabbed Lynsey's arm. She felt her bracelet hit something metal. Lynsey's eyes widened as she realised Kathryn had a bracelet, too. She felt herself toppling over into darkness.

"Father, can you trust the man?" Lynsey heard a voice say. Lynsey saw an older man standing before her in a crisp, immaculate suit. The older man had a refined air, like he smelled of money and the woodsy scent of pipe smoke. Lynsey couldn't remember a pipe ever smelling like this. She couldn't recall the last time she'd seen a man with a moustache, either.

"We cannot be certain, but he has never let me down before. We need the money. That damned bank will take the house if we cannot pay the death duties. Your debutante ball was a washout, and we have received no offers for your hand. We need to take risks."

Lynsey/Kathryn turned and caught her reflection in a window on the bathroom wall. Her chestnut brown hair was tied up in a knot. Her blue eyes stood out behind spectacles that framed her face, their gold wire rims reflecting the light. Kathryn's dress was covered in immaculate, lacy embroidery, which had been passed down in the family for generations. It looked beautiful against her skin, but anyone would have seen it as old-fashioned even for the 1820s.

Lynsey tried to make Kathryn move but found she was a passenger and all she could do was watch.

"Pico," she called, but there was no response.

"I'm not sure about this, father." Kathryn's voice was clear, but troubled.

"We have no choice." Was his curt reply.

There was a knock at the door, and Kathryn's skirts swished as she went to open it. A slight, short man in an expensive suit stood by the entrance. She wiped her brow with a lace kerchief. The Egyptian heat was too much. The man beckoned them, hurrying. He had a bounce in his step that belied his stature. His thick glasses hung on a gold chain around his neck. He led them out of the room down to some horses waiting outside. The sun beat down on their heads through the wispy clouds that drifted across the sky overhead. There were even more mosquitos out here than in the room. How she detested this place.

"What, no camels?"

Her father gave her a quelling look, and Kathryn subsided. She was used to riding, so she hooked her parasol on to the saddle and hitched up her skirts to get on the horse. They were already moving off by the time she was comfortable. She trotted to catch up to them.

The horse's hooves crunched on the ground, giving her firm footing. She hitched up her skirts and settled into the saddle, adjusting the squabs. The reins felt good in her hands. The warmth of the horse's neck was familiar and reassuring. Her father had let her ride alone since she was ten years old, with only a groom to accompany her. She enjoyed riding bareback without a saddle sometimes, though she had only dared do it once or twice for fear of being thought fast by anyone who saw her.

They rode in silence for an hour over an empty Egyptian desert. The dunes swept inward, their great undulating surface like rolling waves. The horizon was so close that the blowing sand looked like a living thing. They rode in silence through the heat of the day. The air was so hot and still that it felt like her skin was boiling away.

Her imagination could not stop conjuring horrific images of what would happen if they were robbed by bandits here, where no one could hear their screams and their possessions taken from the hotel room. The last laugh would be on them though as they had nothing of value to steal, but they did not know that.

The horses whinnied and crunched over the fine white sand; they left parallel trails of foot marks like a string of squashed caterpillars. After a while, they came upon some men working in the distance, pausing for a moment to look at them. They were soon close, and she saw they had cleared an opening in the sand and erected a cream awning to protect it. Underneath the awning, stone steps led to a corridor that went underground. She looked at her father, whose excitement was contained.

The surrounding people gestured for them to descend the steps.

"Father, where has Felippe gone?"

"He must have been delayed."

"We can't talk to them without him." She said.

"It will be okay." Her father replied. His shirt sleeves were rolled up and his skin shone in the lamp's light they carried. It cast shadows on the walls of the tunnel as they descended farther. The ceiling was low, and she had to make sure there was enough room for her to crawl through. Once they were through the first room, they found a long, low corridor. She was excited, and she tried to calm herself down. She felt her pulse pounding in her ears and dizziness threatened to overtake her. People were depicted fishing, building boats, and hunting together in the carved pictures on the corridor walls. Other pictures showed people cooking and serving food, while others were drinking wine and eating bread near the Nile river, with unfamiliar animals.

They made their way deeper into the tomb until, after what seemed like forever, they reached a treasure room, where silver shone and gold glinted under the harsh light of their lamp. The walls changed colour as they moved on: first white, then gold again.

At a fork in the tunnel, her father pointed for her to go one way and he went another. She was reluctant, but she walked down the incline until she came to a bare room. Kathryn pulled up her lamp and noticed through the disturbed dust sparkling in the lamplight that there were pictures on the wall. She drew nearer to recognise Osiris. His skin was painted green, his body wrapped in sacred linen, and his head crowned with twigs of flax representing rebirth. She touched the green of his skin and some paint crumbled against her fingers. She drew back, horrified at what she'd done.

Suddenly, without warning, the dizzy feeling got worse. A darkening of the senses pulled her away from the familiar. Covering her eyes to blink, she found herself in another place. She cried out for her father, but he didn't answer. She twisted, but it all looked unfamiliar. The room was bigger, with only three walls. She felt frightened, all the more scary for being an unfamiliar emotion.

***

Lynsey felt herself topple again and found herself back in her old home in London. Sickness had wrung her out until she looked like a skeleton with pale, grey skin. Her very bones ached, and she only swallowed small spoonfuls of food because she couldn't eat much. The television was on, but her eyes wouldn't focus on the images. The air was hot and dry, and she pulled the surrounding blanket tighter. God, she felt ill, but she'd turned a corner. The extension on her dissertation allowed her to extend her thesis by a year, and she could finish her degree next year. Things were looking up.

The scene shifted, blurring. Lynsey saw herself months later, waiting alone at a bus stop.

Kathryn was discovering how she had got here, she realised. She saw herself head for the trees and then the lightning strike coming down…

The vision cleared and Lynsey found herself back in the chamber, facing Kathryn by the bed once more.

"So" said Kathryn, looking at Lynsey.

"LYNSEY, ARE YOU OKAY?" Pico's voice sounded concerned.

Lynsey shook off the images and met Kathryn's eyes. "So, you are from a long time ago. You can still stop hurting the dragon. His name is Grolmak."

"I know."

Lynsey looked dumbfounded. For a moment, she was speechless. "Oh, you know, because you got it out of my memories," she said at last.

"No, I know because he told me." Kathryn pulled her sleeve up her arm and the Osiris band became visible. "You are not the only one who can talk to dragons."

Lynsey looked shocked.

"You know he is an intelligent thinking being, yet you treat him like you do?" Lynsey's voice was rising in incredulity.

"Why should that be any different from keeping slaves?"

"You can't do that!" Lynsey cried.

Kathryn laughed aloud. "I think you'll find I have been doing that for over two hundred years."

188

Grolmak was flying in his favourite dream. Light, wispy clouds drifted by in the breeze. The sun shone down on him, making his skin cool wherever the clouds filtered its warmth. Grolmak rolled to let the sunlight bathe his back, then he swooped down to plummet toward the mountain peak. He pulled up at the last instant, soaring upward once more, climbing high into the cloud bank. The clouds wrapped around him, light and airy.

The smell of the mountains, thick with grasses and trees, filled his nostrils. The sun was blistering on his scaly skin and he dived to feel the cool of the wind on his body. He loved it. The feeling was exhilarating. He darted from above to below, from side to side, at lightning speed. His bright green belly flashed as he flew with joy.

All too soon, the joy was retreating, and he felt the hot, dry air of the cavern fill his senses. It was a reminder of where he was. The ache of waking, a gaping and profound loss, the sorrow of memory and losing freedom was painful. He felt his spirits sink as the cramps from sitting in a confined space reminded him of where he was. He kept his eyes closed, trying to recapture the dream of his youth.

Sekhmet was a good distance away from him when he heard her boots. He heard clinking metal and felt air shifting in a way that let him know she was in. Her steps fell into a pattern. There was a certain distance between each step. She placed them so she wouldn't echo. As she walked in, his nostrils filled with the smell of her, a unique mix of sweat and spices. The scent was dark and mellow, like coffee grounds left for days on end.

He thought she could understand him in the beginning, but he must have imagined it. But she had hesitated with the knife, pausing inches from his hide. For a moment, he thought she could. He'd shouted, snarled, he'd ranted, but she'd shaken her head and continued. A brief hope dashed in seconds. He was a fool.

How long had he been here? He had no way of knowing. That girl had been interesting. It would have been better to share his captivity with someone, anyone, even a human. He was not sure if he could tolerate it for much longer. He felt despair and anger, but they faded as quickly as they arrived. Nothing mattered. His misery was complete. He nurtured his hate for his captors, but soon, even that had faded into the background of his mind. Nothing mattered anymore, except his own suffering.

Grolmak cringed away from Sekhmet's cold regard. Her eyes narrowed to slits, scrutinising him like a spider examining its prey. He could feel her breath on his neck as she leaned in close. She didn't even consider him an animal. She didn't even look at him with disdain. He was just a source of blood.

Grolmak had tried to pull away in the past, straining against the chains binding his limbs, but the metal links biting into his scales had always tugged him back. He'd thrashed and twisted, every muscle tense, but the restraints always held fast. He remembered every time the collar clamped around his neck, choking him as he struggled in vain. The collar around his neck shuddered against his bare neck, making him shake with renewed fear.

She talked. Grolmak paid attention.

"... girl is like you. She can heal, but we don't know if she is exactly like you yet. "

That means immortal, he thought. Did it matter? Grolmak slumped, wishing Sekhmet would leave him be. But she continued musing aloud, no longer even addressing him. Then her hand reached out and stroked his side.

"She was here again, you know. Telling me you are intelligent. But we knew that already, didn't we?"

Grolmak stiffened, his eyes swivelled to look at her.

"Oh, yes Grolmak. I've known. It just wasn't important to know. Would it have been easier if I talked to you while taking your blood?" Grolmak felt her soft ape hands slide over his back. She was stroking him! He shuddered but remembered his chains were loose. If she found out...

"I need to know how you came here and how you and the girl can heal together. I am from the same place as the girl, but I cannot heal without your help."

Grolmak snorted.

"I'll see you in hell before I help you." He snarled and tried to bite her. She stepped back easily as his collar jerked against the chain. Luckily it held. He berated himself. He couldn't let her know the chains were loose. She was taunting him.

"You are obviously from a different planet. But the girl, she is from my planet and she has the same abilities as you. It must be the way you both came here."

She wasn't even talking to him anymore. She reached out and touched his side.

Suddenly he was back on ilogac. The sun was hotter than usual, and he was at the Ministry of Weather to warn the Minister.

"You must shut down all energy sources for 24 hours." He said. Grolmak was confused. This was a memory. How was he here? Had Sekhmet sent him back in time?

"We cannot do that. The president will arrive this afternoon. He cannot land without Flight Control." Felar was an officious idiot. The Minister in charge of Energy, he wouldn't do anything that inconvenienced him for a second. Not one to see the big picture. Grolmak bristled.

The stone backless chairs were carved for their appearance rather than comfort. They were hard and uncomfortable, just like Grolmak's current position. The stone cut into the soft underside of his wing, distracting him. The Minister had arrived late and Grolmak's wings were cramping. He should be glad that the Minister had even turned up. Weather scientists weren't high on the prestige list and the scales of his wings were an unremarkable green, the lowest rank of the Iloga. The Minister's high-blue colour denoted that he was of the highest ranks even before he achieved his position. Still, Grolmak clenched his talons tighter around the data crystals.

"You cannot be serious. His space ship will be a sitting duck. " Why couldn't he stop himself from saying those words? He knew what Sekhmet was doing. She was tapping into his memories of the past, memories he thought had been lost long ago.

"This visit has been scheduled for two years. I do not think a simple solar flare should delay his trip." The Minister said to Grolmak.

"A solar flare can wipe out communications on this planet and we have an atmosphere!" Grolmak replied. "You should have told him to delay his visit!"

"He is on his way." The Minister said, "That is all."

Grolmak scrutinised the minister. The blue scales that covered his face shone in the sunlight, which poured from the windows and streamed through the pillars. They had been polished recently. He was a narcissistic leader, obsessed with his own reflection. More interested in himself than his job, he thought. The other Iloga in the room had already turned away, showing there was no talking to them either. Grolmak sighed. He had done everything he could do. It would be a matter of public record that he had tried to stop the ministers' plan. He moved to the nearest pillars and dropped off the floor.

The Ministerial offices were built into the side of the tallest mountain in the province, using the natural wind currents. Grolmak pumped his wings, feeling the pressure of the air. He rose slightly, and he pumped again until he was again as high as he had been. Grolmak looked through the curved windows to where the meeting had been, but the floor was again empty. He shook his head and flew out, clutching the evidence the Minister had refused to look at in his hands. There was one last chance to warn the president to delay his trip for a few days, but it would take hours to get there.

The air was thinner at this altitude and it was difficult to catch the currents but one of his specialities was weather conditions and he knew which way the wind blew.

How could the Iloga be so stupid? If they didn't implement protocols, they would be cut off. They were the furthest outpost. They couldn't do anything to jeopardise their position. Taryk 55 would assume something was wrong when the president didn't call in, but that would take days. Anything could happen. Emergency services would be inactive, schools would be closed. Although he knew someone who would be happy with that. Grolmak's razor-sharp teeth flashed as he thought of his son's delight if the school shut down.

Even if the ship landed safely, the planet would be in too much turmoil to even think about the presidential visit.

Grolmak felt the air around him drop in temperature. A cold front was moving in, changing the climate as he had warned. One of the first signs was a hailstorm. He had to get home. With a flap of his wings, he beat harder against the wind, but the storm was too strong. The squall hurtled toward him, throwing buckets of rain at him. He knew fear as lightning danced in the clouds. He fought against the gusts of wind, but they pushed him back harder.

The gale hurled Grolmak through the roiling clouds. He tumbled end over end as the winds buffeted him from all sides. Rain pelted him in a stinging torrent, blinding him. Thunder boomed, loud. He fought to right himself, but the tempest tossed him about like a leaf in a hurricane. And then he saw it: a bolt of lightning coming right for him. He dug his talons into the cloud, but it was useless. He was helpless. Another lightning strike came close to him, and then everything went black.

"Ah, I see, so you were both hit by lightning," Sekhmet mused. "Lightning strikes thousands each year, yet few find their way here. Some additional factor must be at play." She circled Grolmak, eyes narrowed. "What is the link between you and the girl? There is more to this mystery."

A rkan and Lynsey arrived back at the house to find it empty. Food and gunpowder ingredients were scattered across the table and floor, but it was otherwise deserted. Lynsey turned to Arkan. "They must have gone back to the camp. But they were supposed to stay here." Her voice trailed off.

"I agree. It is indeed strange." Arkan poked his head down the tunnel, but there was no light to show anyone was down there. "We must go back to camp. The rescue must happen tonight or we will have an irate dragon on our hands when he is freed. From your description, that would not be the best option."

They hurried across the city, Lynsey clutching her headscarf against the breeze. There were plenty of people in the streets, but no one gave them any attention. The last thing they needed was for her hair to draw attention to them.

As they neared, the smell of smoke assaulted their nostrils. Lynsey felt fear course through her body,

Arkan led the way back through the yellow sandstone pillars that were carved to look like trees. They threaded their way through the harsh branches, avoiding the rough stone where they could. As they neared the edge of the manufactured wood, he shrugged back his cloak and pulled out his daggers, one in each hand.

Lynsey's hand flew to her mouth, eyes bulging in horror. With a quivering finger:, she pointed at the smouldering ruins that had once been their tents. Black smoke snaked up from the ashes. She grabbed Arkan's arm. "Wait!" Her grip on his arm tightened. He had slipped into that cold, calculating part of an assassin's mind where waiting wasn't an option, but he turned back to face her. Lynsey squeezed his arm forcefully. "Wait."

"What in blazes happened here?" Arkan's hands hung loose, ready to act if needed.

Lynsey scanned the ashes. She released his arm and sprinted towards the charred remains of the tents. "Oh gods! Illyara!" Her voice shot up an octave.

Lynsey raced through the wasteland, the scorched smell of canvas and wool thick in her nostrils. Soot swirled around her feet as she dashed between mounds of ash that had once been tents. Arkan caught up and surveyed the devastation. The fire had torn through the heart of their camp like a vengeful fiend, destroying everything in its wake.

A couple of tents remained standing. Arkan shuddered as the grim truth dawned on him. Lynsey struggled with one tent flap, which swung violently in the wind after being burned free of its ties. She called out again for Illyara as she yanked it open and peered inside. "No!" She sprinted to another tent, only to find it empty as well. "No, no, no!"

As Arkan's eyes adjusted to the scene, he realised what had happened. It was too late for anything to be done about it now. A party of horsemen must have swept in, capturing everyone they saw before they could escape, but not before they had started fires raging through camp, destroying everything they touched.

Lynsey's heart sank and her arms dropped to her sides as she reached the centre. Someone must have found out about their plan. They were gone - all of them.

"There is no blood." Arkan's voice was quiet.

"Sorry?"

"There is no blood and no dead bodies. They are alive. If they wanted them dead, they would have left them here as an example."

A rustle behind them made her twirl to see Mewlli appear near the threaded flap of the nearest tent.

"They took them."

"Who took who?"

"The King's guards they took everyone. I was coming back from the house and turned invisible before they saw me. They have my sister and parents." His voice sounded small.

"Mewlli, it will be okay. We will get Illyara back. We'll get them all back."

Arkan pulled Lynsey aside. "How are we going to do that?"

"We find out who betrayed us, why, and how much they already know. If they don't know about the explosives, then we can still go ahead. It isn't hopeless yet."

Arkan looked at Mewlli, then back at Lynsey, sighing. He considered what she said. If they could find out who betrayed them, then they could deal with it. Maybe there was hope? "They would have taken them to the palace. It is the only place with cells big enough. I can't see why they would want everyone unless it is to find you. If we go after them, they will catch you."

"If it wasn't for me, Illyara and her family would be safe in the desert. They risked their lives for me."

He sighed. "They want to use you to fulfil some prophecy, which the Dragon Brotherhood probably gave them so they could justify their own Sekhmet. You don't really owe them anything."

"I know, but I would have died, well maybe not died, but it would have been a fate worse than death in the desert. I would have been a walking skeleton or something." She shivered. "I don't know how it would work, but I can't die, or rather, my physical body can't die." She rubbed her arms. "I would be continually reset with only my Earth memories. If I die here, my body will resurrect and I will lose my memories of this place, of you."

"That may be true, but it will be dangerous to go into the palace. They will expect us. I can get in to the palace but the cells will be harder—unless…"

Arkan's voice tailed off. "There will be a guard on every corridor on every level."

"We have to try."

"Please." said Mewlli. His voice was small, pleading with his eyes at both of them.

The sun was high in the sky by the time they reached the castle. The streets were empty, and a few of the older buildings were boarded up to protect them from thieves. Lynsey and Arkan skirted the outer walls until they reached a secret entrance. They ducked behind a thorn bush to wait for a patrol to pass by.

"Doesn't the king know about all these security leaks?" Lynsey asked.

"He thinks he keeps trespassers out with a couple of guys standing around the front door. The assassin's guild keeps the entrances secret in case they need them." He whispered. "I bet he doesn't even really think there's any other way in." He pointed at a window hidden by a creeper. "After you?"

The gap wasn't much larger than her shoulders were wide. The space they entered was dark; it smelled musty with disuse. She heard him move farther in, so she reached her arm through to hold on to his shoulder. Arkan led her away from the window. A short hall took them to an inner door; it made a small sound when he opened it. "I wonder how long it's been since anyone came through here," she said; the corridor was silent.

They were halfway down it when the sounds of voices and footsteps came to them through an open door to their left. Arkan pressed her against the wall and they waited for whoever was in the hall to pass. Then he took her hand and pulled her after him into the room. Arkan was already a few steps ahead, so she drew up to stand beside him at the inner door. To her surprise, the door made the smallest sound as he opened it a crack.

Given the musty stench permeating the passage, they peered into the corridor. Lynsey braced herself for an ear-splitting creak worthy of a haunted house. But the ancient door swung open near-silently on its rusted hinges. There was no one there. They moved through the palace.

"I think the best thing to do is to go below the cells and come up through them."

She nodded and followed him down the stairs from the kitchen. It's not like we can storm the gates, she thought.

They made their way down the stairs. The steps were steep, and Lynsey had to keep one hand on the stone wall to steady herself. As they descended deeper, the temperature and noise level decreased until a faint blue light flickered on the wall ahead.

At the bottom, the stairs revealed an enormous cavern with water spreading as far as she could see. Algae glowed in the cave ceiling. Tiny lights twinkled across the length of the cave, glimmering against the blackness like stars in a midnight sky, reflected against the back of rats' eyes as they scurried along the edges - but Lynsey wasn't paying attention to the rodents but at the cavern itself. The reflection against the water looked like constellations.

"This is gorgeous!"

"The king has his own source of water. This was why the palace was built here. I believe it was a village in its own right to start with." He seemed immune to its beauty.

They skirted the wall. Lynsey was loath to touch the slimy stone, but the floor beneath her was treacherous from the water splashed by the rodents. *Were they going to bring the children back this way?*

As they moved up another set of steps, Arkan moved his fingers to his lips.

They crept through another door, which led to a chamber loaded with implements. "Torture". he whispered. She shuddered in response.

There was no guard on the next two doors and they crept through to the cells. The tribe was there, separated into men on one side and women on the other. The children were sitting on filthy straw in cells further along. Ghareg in the nearest cell was the first to see them, and his broad smile told her she had done the right thing.

"The guards are just outside the door." He whispered. Lynsey nodded. Arkan pulled out a set of tools and started with the locks. It opened with ease and he moved onto the next one. The nomads rose and gathered by the door. He put his finger to his lips at each gate. They gathered at the heart of the chamber, and Ghareg spoke. "They took Illyara somewhere else. It was Faroushk who betrayed us and told the guards. He said if there were two Sekhmets, it made sense that the one that was real would be the one who had the most worshippers."

"Where have they taken her Ghareg?" asked Arkan, opening the last cell. His face set in a grim line. The sound of his voice grated through the air.

"The king took her. She is held somewhere else. They were going to kill us one by one until she agreed to give you up and work for them. These people are animals."

36 The Execution

Illyara paced the confines of her cell. She was going to lose everything. She wrung her hands in small, quick movements. There was nothing she could have done. She knew that. *Now that they have us, what are they going to do to me, to my family?* She grew cold at a sudden thought. *How did they even know where we were?* If she'd only turned invisible. Illyara froze, a chill creeping down her spine at the thought. Going invisible was impossible - she would be seen for sure. With one careless act, millennia of secrecy would be lost. She pictured her ancestors' disapproving faces and shuddered. No, she would not be the one to expose their gift, no matter what. Oh, it was impossible.

Why did they separate us? She paused, staring into space. She put out a hand behind her and slid into a sitting position on the edge of the hard bed. *Why would they do that? Why single her out from everyone else?* Sure, she was next in line, but if that was the case, why not her mother or father? They are our leaders! Her mind whirled as she sought the answer. It must be because of Lynsey, she decided.

At least no one had been hurt badly yet. The guards had been restrained. They had herded her tribe along the narrow streets to the palace like cats, but no one was killed. It was more embarrassing than anything; she reflected, feeling tension leave her body. Onlookers had lined the streets, watching and cheering as if their capture were all part of the festivities. Maybe it was a stunt? He could pardon them and claim benevolence. A hoarse laugh escaped her lips once more, sounding harsh in the quiet room. When had the king ever been charitable? She was clutching at straws again and she knew it.

She thought back to when she last saw the king. They were passing under the gate. He was standing above them, visible in the high windows above the stone arch, as they walked under him to the courtyard. She wouldn't have noticed him, but for his yellow overcoat practically glowing against the drab stone framing him. It drew her attention like a lodestone as her gaze rose, following the nearest soldiers' line of sight, up the wall to the half-moon shaped viewing gallery. She watched as his arm rose to point at her. There was a gleam in his eye that made her afraid. Her eyes darted around her family, searching for an exit. She ducked as his finger swivelled to point at her. In the middle of the crowd, her family was packed tight around her. As if by instinct, they shuffled even closer around her to protect her. Her shoulders tensed as she tried to pull away, tried to drag herself backwards through the horde of people moving forwards behind her. She felt hands around her waist pulling into position, ready to drag her away from trouble's path. From the hallway's edge she saw soldiers nod up at the gallery and they pulled her cousins away from the outside, one by one, barging through others. She felt hands like steel traps grip her upper arms. What scared her the most was the image of Faroushk, now burned in her mind, standing beside the king.

Illyara dropped like a stone and the two soldiers lost their hold. She crawled through densely packed feet around her. She darted back on to her feet and turned towards the way they had come, but what was done to protect her was now her undoing. The crush of people on all sides prevented her from escaping. A gap opened to her left, but the guards had already reached her. Their hold on her arms was tighter than before. They would not be fooled by the same trick again. Where their fingers dug into her skin, shooting pains travelled up her arms. She resisted the urge to cry out, clenching her teeth.

They dragged her to the edge of the corridor, shaking off her family, who tried to keep her with them as even more soldiers moved past her to herd her family further on. They took her down a separate fork. She writhed as she heard her mother cry out in despair and then plead for them to leave their daughter alone. She tried to turn—to go back to her. Her feet kicked out at the guards, but they just raised her higher into the air, then pulled her forward with force. Illyara sobbed as her arms strained against their sockets.

She let her shoulders drop, and she breathed low and deep as her mother had taught her to do when she was stressed. Her heart raced, but she kept her breathing steady. She felt her feet slide on the rough stones of the floor. There was no point struggling. She needed to conserve her strength, and try to memorise the way they were taking her.

The walls were getting thicker here; she noticed. The sound of the others had grown faint until she couldn't hear them anymore. In fact, she could barely hear anything but the sound of the guard's chain mail and boots on the floor. How far away were they taking her?

A few more twists and turns and they stopped outside what looked to be a strong metal door.

"Gaoler!" A tall man dressed in dark velvet finery rounded the corner muttering to himself.

He stopped when he saw her hanging between the guards. His face was full of concern and he barked at the guards.

"Come now, the King said she was to be unharmed. This is not how we treat such a valued visitor."

His voice full of concern, he turned to her. "Hello, my dear. We'll just let you in. I have a feeling you won't be my guest down here for long." He fumbled with some keys until the door creaked open. He nodded at the guards and they pushed her through. She heard him sigh and tut at them as she regained her balance. The door slammed, and she rushed to the small window to see their retreating backs through the bars.

Her thoughts returned to the present. Looking around, she realised the cool room had no windows. The only illumination was from a torch sitting on a bracket in the corridor outside. The bars cast long shadows along the floor to the opposite wall. Her gaze switched back to the door. It looked heavy, there would no way of breaking through there. There was nothing in here that could help her escape. She let out a long breath. The floor was bare rock, but at least there was a mattress sat off the ground on a rickety wooden bed frame.

She didn't know how long she waited, perched on the end of the bed, but the gaoler's words gave her hope. It felt like hours before the sound of keys rattling in the lock told her someone was coming. Her head rose and three women entered the room. A lamp and a day-dress draped over her arms were carried by the first to come in. The smaller woman behind carried a bowl of water with some towels and the last carried a box.

The first woman laid the clean dress on the bed. Her expression betraying her distaste at the dirt she saw there. Interesting, Illyara thought, she was not used to these duties then. Illyara ruminated over what that could mean. *What did they want?* The maid pointed to the bowl and the gown. Illyara sighed. There was no point in arguing over such a trivial thing. If she was honest, she wanted a wash more than they wanted her to have one. She wasn't the type to cut a finger off to spite her hand, was she? She inwardly smiled. What would it hurt? She dipped her fingers into the bowl.

When she was ready, the first woman smiled for the first time.

"My lady." She bowed and moved out of the way.

The box she'd noticed earlier was opened by the third maid and a wide-toothed comb was pulled from it. The maid held it towards her. Illyara hesitated for a second. She felt like she should resist but her hair had come loose from its confines and itched from what she hoped was imagined lice. She'd already washed. *What harm could a comb do?* Illyara reached and took it as it wavered in the air. She gave the maid a quick smile. This situation wouldn't be the maid's fault after all. The comb was beautiful. Jewels embedded in gold glinted in the lamplight. As metallic bangles snapped around her wrists, she barely noticed the sound. She looked at the other maid and the empty box on the corner of the bed. She must have drawn it from the bottom of the same box the comb had come out of. The cold metal around her wrists was hard. It made her feel uncomfortable. She pulled at the unyielding metal, but they were tight against her skin. She jerked her arms away, and they jingled in the stillness with the sound of bells. Her eye widened in horror at the realisation. Faroushk! He'd told them of her gift of invisibility!

The door opened, and the women escorted her along narrow corridors. They moved higher within the palace. The bells were so loud! They jarred her nerves in every conceivable way. Her instinct was to go invisible, and she felt herself reach out to their minds, but the bells would still be there. She felt herself move in and out of their minds for a moment before she regained control.

The new chamber was richer. It was not to the standard she had grown accustomed to with Lynsey, but more than she had experienced before they had met. She had time to see that there were again no windows in this room before the lock clicked behind her. She whirled and ran to the door. Trapped again.

There was nothing to do but pace the room from the ornate loor-wood desk to the four-poster bed and back again. Her wrists played a musical melody every time she moved. Every now and again, she tried to push the bracelet off her wrists. The fit was tight and although her wrists were slim, she couldn't pull them through.

What did they have planned? The longer she waited, the more she worried until she was in a panic by the time the door finally opened. The king walked in first, flanked by his special guard on either side. He'd changed and was wearing a striking green embroidered tunic that would not have been out of place at any ball. *Was he trying to impress her? Why?* She watched as he nodded at the men standing beside him. They bowed, closing the door behind them as they went. They were alone. She waited to see what the king wanted.

"You are as beautiful as your friend." The king remarked. He made as if to touch her face, but she flinched and he let his hand drop.

"Faroushk has told me you know where your friend is and that you may help me with another problem that has occurred." Despite herself, Illyara was curious.

"There is a job opening in my personal staff. It appears my assassin has gone missing and I need someone to take his place. Faroushk has said you have an interesting ability that only a few of your tribe have, which could be really useful to me."

"What did Faroushk tell you?"

"Oh come now, there is no need to be shy. Invisibility is a rare skill which your king should know about."

"You are not my king."

"You are in Ghinari, you roam Ghinari lands. That makes you my subject if you like it or not." The king's voice became more dangerous. "If I had known of such an asset in the past, my assassin's guild would have been filled with your people. Unfortunately, you were the only one with the gift we captured."

"What else do you want?"

"I need to know where Lynsey Walker is."

"I would never betray my friends or family."

"Your family is in my cells and you barely know the girl."

Illyara paused. She couldn't give up Lynsey, but what would he do to her family?

He seemed to read her mind.

"I have done nothing to them - yet. They have not been touched, nor will they if you cooperate. There is no need for unpleasantness." He took her hand and gazed into her eyes. "You are so beautiful and if you work for me, I will give you everything you desire, but I need Lynsey for the good of Ghinari."

"Ghinari has kept our dragon locked up for centuries against his will. Our people have starved, your people are starving. How will giving up Lynsey help anyone but you?”

The king raised his hand as if to strike her, but he thought better of it. “I cannot talk to you like this. Maybe Faroushk can talk some sense to you.” He rapped on the door and it opened. The king walked out and in strode Faroushk. He had replaced his usual desert robes with court garb. A green sash complemented his deep purple velvets. He looked into her eyes, but she refused to look into his.

“Illyara, you have to do this.” He urged.

She shook her head and spit back, “How could you betray our family like this?”

He took a deep breath and said, “I’m not betraying anyone. The king has promised us fertile land to the west. All we have to do is serve him and our tribe will have favoured status. We will not have to roam the desert anymore. We will have everything we deserve.”

“I like the desert. It is our home.”

Faroushk looked out toward the east and sighed, “Look at how these people live! They do not want. They do not have to travel days for water or suffer sand storms that can blow the skin off a skeleton in minutes. Ghinarians have easy lives.”

“Faroushk, Are you blind? They do not all have such peaceful lives. Some starve so the rich can get fat. I have lived among them these last few weeks and all they think of is parties and furthering their empire. That is not a life I want for me and my family. We are better than that!” Illyara’s voice strained as her voice raised to convince him.

“We are the chosen to serve Sekhmet. Our duty is to protect the dragon.. Our ancestors so swore and we are so bound.”

Faroushk paced the small space. “Don’t you see? We can break away from our destiny and make a new one? We don’t have to struggle anymore,” he said.

“I would rather struggle with honour and have my principles than live like a dog with no morals. Do you even know what he wants from us? He wants us to kill for him. With an army of invisible assassins, he could take over the world!”

“Is that such a bad thing as long as we are one of the winners? We have whatever we want. We can name our price.”

“It wouldn’t be you who would do the killing. We would be damning our souls to hell.”

“That was uncalled for. Not everyone is born with the gift.”

“You are despicable, Faroushk. You are dead to me.” She turned from him and looked at the wall.

Faroushk was still for a moment and then walked towards the door. “You may not acknowledge me anymore, but if you don’t do what the king wants, he will execute our family, one each day until you do.”

Hours passed and a man she had never seen before appeared by the door and directed her to follow him. They went down long corridors until they were in the courtyard they had arrived in. As they stepped out of the doorway, her eyes stung from the sudden light. She blinked as she held a hand up to shield her face from the glare. In a moment, her vision cleared, and she saw her family, penned into the far corner, surrounded by armed guards. On the left was a platform where a gaoler stood beside another figure, dressed in leather from head to toe. His hair was plaited down his back, tied with a leather thong. He stood leaning on a curved sword. The king was sitting on a chair with some advisors between the platform and her people. She noted Faroushk was there too.

The man that had escorted her pushed her forward to stand before the king. She stumbled on her long skirts, her arms jangling in the stillness as she righted herself. The man let go of her and moved forward to take a scroll from the king's hands. He handed it to the Gaoler's whose voice was strong as he addressed Illyara.

"Illyara, will you recant your treason and give the location of the traitor Lynsey Walker, who claims to be the immortal Sekhmet?"

She felt calm, but her voice resounded through the hall as she spoke with finality.

"I will not."

The man turned towards the king, who moved his hand slightly.

"Then, in the power invested in me, we must put a member of your family to death as an accessory to the crime. One member of your family will be chosen at random and will face death on this day."

The man lifted a blindfold from a table and placed it over his companion's eyes. The other man tied it around his head. He pointed at the crowd. The guard who was nearest pulled out a figure from the crowd. Illyara gasped. Her mother stood there, held by the guard's hand on her shoulder. *Surely, they wouldn't kill a woman?* But she watched as they pulled her towards the wooden structure and made her climb the platform, stumbling over the first few steps. Illyara nearly said something, and the king held out his hand to stop the proceedings. He lifted an eyebrow in lieu of a question. Illyara looked at her mother. She couldn't let this happen! She moved a step closer. Her mother shook her head with a sad smile. No. Illyara understood then that it was her mother who had taught her to never betray your family or a word. If she gave in, then her family would be trapped in service to the kingdom for all time. He would never let them go.

Illyara stood straighter. She wouldn't let them see her cry. The king's arm dropped.

The gaoler took one arm and the other man pushed on the other until her mother was on her knees. They bound her wrists behind her back with rope. The blind fold was taken off the executioner and placed over her mother's face. They pushed her neck over a waiting block. The courtyard was silent, the slight rustling of leaves on the ground from a faint breath of wind was the only sound. They couldn't do this! She looked at Faroushk although it was forbidden to do so, but he was looking in another direction. She went to turn away, but two men behind her grabbed her shoulders, tilting them forward so she had no choice but to watch.

Her mother gave her another smile full of meaning. Illyara knew she forgave her, but it still hurt and it would do for the rest of her life. Illyara's throat tightened, her eyes burning with unshed tears. She dug her fingernails into her palms, gritting her teeth against the overwhelming tide of emotions. She would not let them see her cry, would not give them that satisfaction. They stared at each other, making every second of her life count. The love flowed between them and Illyara felt like her heart was breaking.

A shout came from the surrounding crowd, and she saw her father break through the cordon. He ran towards her mother, who was held by two guards. Behind her father, the king lifted his hand, crooking a finger at one of his royal guards. Without hesitation, the guard broke formation, his boots pounding across the stones toward them. *Why?* The guard's arm darted forward and stabbed her father in the stomach with a dagger. He stumbled, a broad red stain seeped across his white shirt. Her father's body spasmed, hands flying to the hilt protruding from his stomach. His fingers scrambled over the blade, slick with blood, desperately trying to wrench it free. Time seemed to slow down. Her father dropped to the ground with a thud just feet from where they stood. A small cloud of dust rose where he landed, his face contorted in pain and at that instant the other guard swung the evil curved sword down in one swoop and her mother's head rolled off the platform, across the short distance of the floor to stop before her feet. Illyara couldn't believe it. She looked away to see her father's body between her and the king. She collapsed.

37 Shattering Dreams

"We have to free Illyara," Lynsey said, pulling the last child out from behind the bars. She reassured the boy with a touch on his arm before he ran to a nearby woman. "Agreed, but we can't just charge in without a plan," Arkan replied, running his fingers through his black hair. His eyes darted from the far door to Lynsey's. She knew he was right. They needed to come up with a plan before they did anything else.

Lynsey unfastened her cloak and draped it around the shoulders of a young girl shivering beside her. The girl clutched the warm fabric closer as Lynsey surveyed the sea of expectant faces - at least fifty men, women and children all looking to her for guidance.

"His Majesty will have his men hunt us down and kill us," said an unfamiliar voice. "We should get out of here and worry about freeing the dragon later."

"If we free the dragon now, we can escape with him and he can help us free, Illyara," Lynsey countered. She held out her hands to the tribe, pleading with them to understand. "Look, we don't even know where she is being held. We need to leave now and come back for her later."

Arkan stepped forward. "Don't worry about Illyara. I can get us all out of here."

Lynsey nodded, and the group followed Arkan out of the narrow passage. "You lead the way. Arkan and I will bring up the rear. We have to get everyone out fast. We don't know how long we have until someone realises the cells are empty," she said.

Arkan walked the way they had entered, and the others shuffled behind him one by one through the narrow passages.

They made their way through the dim caverns, focusing on not tripping over each other's feet. After two miles of keeping to the shadows, they arrived at a park Lynsey recognised.

"Aren't we near Darianna's house?"

"INDEED, IT APPEARS WE ARE APPROACHING DARIANNA'S RESIDENCE." Replied Pico in a dispassionate voice.

Lynsey sped up to scoot ahead to join Arkan at the front. She matched his pace as they turned into the familiar driveway.

"Won't we be putting Darianna's life in danger?"

Arkan halted mid-step. He was about to say something, then changed his mind.

"Darianna is not who you think she is," he said. Lynsey waited for an explanation, but he said no more.

Rounding the driveway, the house was in complete darkness.

"She's not there?"

"That's what I am trying to tell you. Darianna was in league with the king. She left after betraying you. It is the reason I have brought everyone here. No one will think to look for them here."

***

Lynsey caught her breath in surprise as the last of the tribe shuffled into Darianna's drawing room. She hadn't realised how spacious it was - the entire group of at least fifty now occupied the plush carpet. Arkan flicked the switch for the lights, but they'd been disconnected. He lit some nearby candles as the last of the tribe shuffled in.

"We need to fight!" Ghareg's gentle face contorted in rage. "They know about our gift now. We will never be left alone."

"They still have Illyara and what they did can never be forgiven." Raised another voice.

"We are fighting for our freedom now! Without Illyara, we have no leader."

Lynsey clambered atop a brocade chair, raising her hand for silence. "How many of you will fight to save Illyara?" she called out.

The answering roar was deafening, voices mingling together into a clamour that shook the walls.

"Then it is decided. I will go back to the house by the temple and free the dragon with Arkan. You will need to tell the other nomads of our plan. The explosion will be the signal for you to storm the palace."

Arkan and Lynsey left while the tribes people talked. With a swell of pride, Lynsey noticed the tribe members were deferring to Mewlli, seeking his counsel. The boy stood taller, confidence radiating from him as he took charge. He had come into his own since his sister's absence and was turning into a leader in his own right. His parents would be proud.

As they raced back to the house, Lynsey and Arkan talked over the plan between breaths.

"Does the Temple have the underground lake under it as well?" Lynsey asked.

"It must do."

"I think it would be better to blow the floors so the dragon goes into the cavern. It's not like he can die from a fall. We can follow the water and find another way out. It will be easier than fighting through all the guards."

'That's a good idea,' Arkan said as they entered at the back of the property. The kegs were still there in the basement. Everything was as they had left it. Lynsey was grateful that not all the nomads had been told of the house.

"We'll need to use two barrels in the tunnel to break down to the subterranean level."

Lynsey nodded and grabbed a knife from the table as they entered the basement. Arkan held up the first barrel while Lynsey dug a hole near the bottom with the blade. Black powder dribbled out and Arkan dragged the keg a few feet away to create a fuse. Lynsey rolled a second barrel to Arkan, who was already standing out from the tunnel to receive it. He heaved it

205

with a groan and put it beside the first. Jumping up, he joined the fuse on the floor with a rag to the barrels in the tunnel, creating a bridge. Arkan moved forward with a brand and took a deep breath. "Ready?" Lynsey nodded. She wasn't sure if she was. Neither was Pico, he swirled in dark colours in her mind - and they'd been following his instructions.

Arkan touched the fire to the fuse, and they dived out of the room and ran up a level to the outside courtyard. There was a muffled boom and Lynsey exchanged a look with Arkan. She expected it to be louder, but this was much better. They could, if they were lucky, get away with no one investigating it. They went back to see the damage. The explosion had made a jagged hole in the floor and they saw water rushing in the cavern underneath. Arkan took a rope and tied it to a table that covered the hole. He lowered himself down a few feet and shouted back up to her. "There is a rock we can get to, but we will have to swing to the right. From there, we can get to some tunnels." They tied a couple of gunpowder filled kegs to the rope and climbed down the rope until his feet were on them. He swung the rope until he was close to the rock and jumped off. Holding a keg, he let the other go. He dropped the barrel and took hold of the second as it swung back towards him. "Lynsey! Send down the other barrels." He called up. With a grunt, she lowered the gunpowder kegs one by one down the rope and swung them onto the rock face, where Arkan was waiting. With every movement, she winced at the thought of losing just one barrel. "I've never made gunpowder before, so I don't know how powerful the blast will be. You will need to make sure you are far enough away before they are lit. So many kegs together will magnify the blast." Lynsey warned. Arkan nodded. "We need to know where to put the kegs first, but yes, I value my life, darling." He grinned at her.

"Pico, where is the best place to put the kegs?" Asked Lynsey.

"GO NORTH-WEST UNTIL I TELL YOU." He replied.

"Pico, that won't help down here. I won't be able to tell where I am!"

"SORRY, GO RIGHT AND FOLLOW THE CAVERN WALL UNTIL I SAY STOP."

"That's better." Lynsey replied.

"SAUCY."

"Don't you know it?" She retorted. Pico rumbled with laughter in her mind.

Lynsey pointed down the cavern, and the two worked without talking, dragging the heavy keg through the tunnel. Two minutes' walk later, they found a niche along the wall where Pico said to place the kegs. The space was wide enough for five people to fit side-by-side. They fit fifteen kegs inside and the rest around them.. The space was deceptively large. "Who says women don't have spatial ability?" Arkan looked at her with a question in his eyes. "Never mind, just an ex-thing." He still looked confused, so she changed the subject. "I'll wait twenty minutes for you to get away, then I will light the fuse. Where will you go?" Lynsey asked Arkan.

"That will be long enough for me to reach the nomads. I'll join them in the fight." He grabbed her hips and pulled her towards him. "I love you.

Whatever happens, I will find you."

"I know, and I feel the same way about you. Be careful!" She kissed him and then pushed him back. He pulled her in one last time, but before he could, she said, "Be careful!" One last kiss and then he was gone, disappearing back down the tunnel like a shadow. Lynsey sat down on the cold stone floor and waited for the time to pass by.

"Pico?" Lynsey asked. "If I get blown up, will I survive?"

"THE FUSE IS LONG ENOUGH THAT YOU SHOULD BE FAR ENOUGH AWAY WHEN IT IGNITES," came the calm reply in her mind. "YOU REALISE THAT EVEN IF YOU DO RESCUE THE DRAGON, HE MAY NOT BE WILLING TO HELP YOU?"

"I know. He has been abused by the people here. We should rescue him, whether he wants to help us or not. It is the right thing to do."

"I AGREE. IT IS TIME LYNSEY."

"Wish me luck!"

There was a pause, then the voice came softly in her mind.

"GOOD LUCK."

Lynsey picked up the lamp from the side and removed the glass that protected the flame. She stood up, closed her eyes, and gave a short prayer before throwing the lantern at the gunpowder fuse. It fizzled and looked like it was going to go out before a shower of sparks went up as it burst into flame. She watched it burn for a moment along its length towards the kegs, then ran. A single explosion rocked the world and rained debris down on her. Rocks and splinters of stone hit her and she was thrown forward into the water. The shock of the water took the breath out of her. It was cold. There was a second explosion and more debris fell on her, this time more small rocks. She was sure she was going to die. Water filled her lungs and she couldn't breathe. Panic filled her mind and her arms flailed out. She felt Pico take hold and moments later; she was back on dry rock.

"Thanks Pico."

"I COULDN'T LET YOU DROWN COULD I!"

"Thanks anyway." She stood up groggily but walked toward the temple. Where the roof had been, she could see into the basement where the dragon had been kept. He wasn't there. "Damn! He just left."

"TO BE FAIR, I WOULD TOO IF I WERE HIM." replied Pico.

"Did you see which way he went?"

"THERE IS ONLY ONE WAY HE COULD HAVE GONE AND THAT WAS AWAY FROM YOU. NO, I DIDN'T SEE HIM."

"Right, it's chase the dragon time." She started running with a limp until her leg corrected itself and then she ran as fast as she could.

"Are you doing something?"

"I'm TAMPERING WITH YOUR ADRENALINE LEVELS TO MAKE YOU FASTER. YOU SEEM DETERMINED TO DO THIS SO I'M HELPING."

"Fair enough."

38 Empowering the People

Arkan moved with swift purpose. His feet were light on the ground, making no sound as he stepped over rubbish and horse manure. He chose his steps with a dancer's grace. His clothes were dark and a perfect match for the shadows. With the stealth of a tiger, he slipped unseen across the courtyard and into the nearest inn, the boisterous laughter from within masking any sounds of his passage. His gaze lingered on the entrance. Raucous laughter spilled from the open door. The only light was from candles inside. The stone building itself seemed to breathe in the darkness. No tavern would waste money on electricity.

He kept to the walls and moved from cart to barrel until he reached the stable. The familiar smell of hay and manure assailed his nostrils like old friends and he smiled despite himself. Funny, he was never happier than in a stable. Maybe he should have been a stable boy. He laughed at that. He doubted his father would have found the notion so amusing. The horses caught his scent, nickering softly into the darkness. Their warm, sweet breath drifted over him as he moved down the row of stalls. He pulled the latch on the first stall and saw a beautiful, grey speckled mare. She would be too nervous and gentle for what would become a deadly fight. He patted her neck and whispered to her for a moment until she settled down.

"Not today, darling. You'll have to wait for your owner."

The second horse was perfect. He stood right in the middle of the stall, noble and tall. His eyes were as black as coal. It pawed the ground with its hooves. Arkan smiled with approval. It had fire in its heart. He was as level as a blade and as long as a shadow cast by the moon. He looked around the stall and seemed to size Arkan up. They stood and looked at each other as equals until Arkan reached under his jaw and grabbed a handful of mane, vaulted onto the horse's back and slid to his chest, smoothing his neck all the time. The horse opened his mouth wide and nickered again. He flapped up and down like a bird fluffing its feathers. His big, smooth hooves pawed harder at the dirt floor of the stable. Arkan spoke soothing words into his ear. It seemed to settle the horse down and the stallion stood still while Arkan dismounted to saddle him. Arkan again spoke in low gentle tones, stroking the short silken hair as he went. He continued to move with confidence, knowing that if he didn't, the horse would not submit to his will. Arkan mounted.

They were still. Only the sound of a horse's breath and a neighbouring stallion's hooves hitting the ground filled the silence. Arkan's own breaths echoed in his ears. Neither sure what the other would do, but the horse bowed his head and Arkan gave him a nudge with his knee.

The horse picked its way through the hay, making almost no noise. It had been military trained. There was no other explanation. He was so responsive. It seemed to know what he wanted with the gentlest of commands.

As soon as they were at the door, Arkan uttered one word and they burst out of the stable in a cloud of dust and galloped out.

Out on the streets of the capital, they rode on at full gallop. The horse jumped obstacles with ease, avoiding others.

Arkan reined in his thoughts and focused on riding hard, trying to burn away his thoughts with motion. He travelled down streets he knew like an old friend; streets still filled with festival goers, even this late in the afternoon.

Arkan rode hard, feeling the power of the horse's taut muscles under him. The stallion was a dream to ride, Arkan reflected as the wind whipped through his hair. They sped through the empty streets and out into the desert.

"Woah." he called. Dust kicked up around them like a cloud. He saw thousands of figures lit by campfires in the distance. It had to be all the tribes that had answered the call to arms. What were they thinking, being so visible? The king would have been notified of them within minutes of their arrival. They could not win with a direct confrontation against the king's force! He had to admit, though, that it was impressive to see so many of the tribesmen in one place. He did not know that so many of them existed, never mind that they would answer such a call.

From the few hundred tribesmen that he knew about, their ranks had swelled to thousands. He pressed his knees into the horse and he bolted forward.

By the time he reached the nomads' camp, the sun was starting its downward course. Fires dotted the encampment.

Mewlli was waiting for him amidst the gathering. He was directing people in a cool, confident way he had never seen him do before. Arkan raised a brow. His face was still boyish, but his eyes were all man. Arkan's voice was low, betraying his fury,

"Why are you camped here? They can see you from the gates!"

"It is good that they see us. They should fear us for once."

Arkan raised a brow.

"We have been silent and hidden for too long. Buried in the desert, we have lived like rats. That is not the way we should be living. They don't have the numbers to beat us."

"They have water, armour, swords and, more importantly … gates." Replied Arkan drily.

"That is why we are camped where we are. They will open at the signal. We have people in the city waiting." Mewlli looked different. He stood straighter. He was taking responsibility for the tribe. Arkan was impressed, but he was still untried. He would need support.

"I'd like to join you. If you intend to create a fair society, which is what Illyara wanted, then I will fight with you."

"We do. When we are in charge, water will be shared equally, food will be shared among the needy. No one shall lord it over another."

"Are you the leader now?"

Mewlli smiled at that. "I am the leader because everyone wants me to be. As soon as my people want someone else, I will step down. When we win the battle and free my sister, they may choose to follow her. It is in my people's control, as it should be."

"Laudable. I can't see how that can work."

"You don't need to, my friend. Just know that we will fight for justice, not revenge."

A low rumbling shook the floor under their feet.

"That will be the temple. The explosives have gone off." Arkan replied to Mewlli's startled gaze.

"It is time."

The nomads picked up their gear and marched towards the gate. They could already hear shouting from inside and the drawbridge was raised just as they neared. Mewlli called a halt out of the arches reach. He waited a minute, then the drawbridge lowered again. The tribe strode in across without hesitation, Mewlli and Arkan taking the lead. Ten men appeared next to them, blood dripping from swords.

"Cousin, it is done. There are no more guards on this side of the wall. The next opposition will be at the palace." Mewlli blanched, but nodded, striding on. Arkan smiled, watching Mewlli try to maintain a stoic face as he now faced a battle for the first time in his life. Maybe Mewlli was not as hardened as he would like to appear. The tribe moved into step behind their leader.

Their desert shoes were as quiet as whispers on the cobbled streets. The eerie stillness gave Arkan pause for thought. It felt like the calm before a desert storm. The next few hours would cause devastation. His hands played with his blades out of habit. While this storm wouldn't ruin a crop or destroy houses, this storm would decide the fate of the city. A frisson of excitement coursed through his body. His muscles tightened and his thoughts were hyper. All the training he had gone through his entire life seemed to point to this moment. He looked at Mewlli's face. There was no anger. He was not doing this for the wrong reasons, to gain power or money. He was doing this for the good of his tribe and even the city. This was how it was supposed to be. Arkan noted the low familiar buildings around him. This was his home, and he was helping these people to change it. He dropped back a bit to give himself time to think. Was he doing the right thing? Arkan watched as more people joined them from the back with simple weapons. Kitchen knives were clutched in tight grips along with other household items. It wasn't only the tribes people who had enough of the King's and the Brotherhood's excess. He wondered maybe if Illyara was right. Maybe there was dissatisfaction among the people. He had never noticed before now. Small boys and girls were running around the men and the nomads were shooing them away for them to be scooped up by mothers.

They marched through the narrow streets, then broadened into avenues as they hit the wealthier areas. The people had stopped joining them now, but their ranks had swelled to many more than thousands. They marched in silence, faces grim. No words needed to be spoken - their purpose was clear. As one, the swelling crowd moved toward the palace, the air electric with anticipation. They had one purpose: to topple the king and his family and replace them with their own government. After today, Ghinari would be run by the people, not the Jade King.

39 Kaboom

Lynsey stepped along the wall as close to the edge of the narrow path along the cavern wall as she dared. A long drop to her left seemed to stretch out forever before it met with who knew what. As she moved further along, the jagged spikes of rock to her right grew worse. The smell of dankness filled her nostrils, and she gagged, clinging on to the wall as she shuffled on. A crystal clear cascade of water poured from a small hole in the roof and splashed into a pool below, sending a spray of droplets up into Lynsey's face and causing her to shriek and swear. More water dripped down from the ceiling, sliding past her collar like an icy finger.

"IT'S ONLY WATER LYNSEY." She didn't dignify Pico's remark with an answer, but pulled the collar tighter around her neck. The sooner she was out of here, the better.

She took a single step forward and felt herself kick something hard. Her feet twisted, sending her sliding backward. She grabbed at the rock and it scraped her skin as she struggled to stay upright. Her hand slipped, and she fell into the wall before letting herself slide down it. The sensation of the water running past her feet told her she was heading further into the cave, and that she was heading further down.

"CAREFUL LYNSEY." Pico's voice held a cautionary note. "YOU DO NOT WANT TO END UP IN THE WATER. YOU MIGHT OVERSHOOT THE DRAGON."

"Thanks for the concern, Pico." He was right, though. Her arms healed instantaneously from the rock that bit into her skin, but that cold water would be a whole different ball game. Either way, she wasn't a fan of pain, however fleeting.

Lynsey sighed and continued forward, inclining her head as the roof lowered. Another ten minutes passed and sharp stabbing pains in her neck made her curse again. She rubbed it. Was this tunnel ever going to end?

It was so quiet. Surely she should be able to hear the dragon moving around by now? Maybe she had missed a corridor? Had she gone down the wrong one at the beginning? Doubt set in and she picked up the pace. Soon the exertion made her tired, but at least she was warm.

"Bloody hell, this has to widen soon!"

Not only was her neck killing her, cramp was setting in her twisted back. The path was so narrow; she was almost leaning over the edge of the water to get more headspace. The sharp bits of stone wall to her right were relentless, getting thicker, forcing her to walk sideways, which was making her thighs ache and now the lamp was flickering. She tilted the lamp, expecting to feel the weight shift as the liquid sloshed, but there was nothing. The oil was running out. She groaned. This was all she needed.

"How far do these rivers actually go?"

"PROBABLY MILES, I WOULD HAVE THOUGHT."

"Thanks Pico, great encouragement. Couldn't you at least say you must be getting near now?"

"WHY? THE DRAGON IS PROBABLY LONG GONE. HE WILL BE GOING AS FAST AS HE CAN MOVE. IF WE WANT TO CATCH UP, WE NEED TO SPEED UP."

"The path is getting narrower. He's probably stuck."

"KEEP TELLING YOURSELF THAT LYNSEY BUT JUST A THOUGHT TO CHEER YOU UP THOUGH. WE CAN'T EVEN SEE THE EDGE OF THE OTHER SIDE OF THAT RIVER AND HE WON'T NEED TO STICK TO THE PATH." Pico seemed amused.

"If you can call this ledge a path." Lynsey muttered under her breath.

It would have been quicker if I had fallen into the water. I would have been stopped by his bum, she thought.

"YOU ALSO REALISE THAT I CAN HEAR YOUR THOUGHTS?" Lynsey let out another stream of expletives and she felt Pico swirl in laughter in her mind.

What felt like hours later, she reached the edge of the tunnel. A large cavern came into view. The light from the lantern flickered once more, then died. It clattered on the floor as she let it drop, rolling off into a dark corner of the tunnel. She didn't need it, anyway. Where was the light coming from? She squinted upwards to find herself almost blinded by the sun streaming through a hole in the cave's ceiling, some sixty feet above.

"Oh, great." She breathed out. "That is huge! It has to be some kind of sink hole. If I were a dragon, that is where I would get out."

The sides were of black crumbly mud, and clumps of grass clung on amongst twisted vines, dangling down—just out of reach. Her heart sank. She didn't have time for this and grasped the vines in both hands and heaved her body to hoist herself up. Her shoulder screamed in pain, but she sucked it up to push against the wall with her feet until she could reach higher with her outstretched fingers. Her fingers brushed up against the next curled vine, but it was just too far out of reach.

"USE THE HANDLE OF YOUR KNIFE." came the quiet advice.

Lynsey pulled out her knife and ripped a length from the hem of her shirt, leaving a ragged edge that was a few inches long. If she kept this up, she wouldn't have much of an outfit left. She wrapped the cloth around the blade and then gripped it, protected by the makeshift hilt. It wouldn't be any good if the blade cut the vine she was trying to tease down. Lynsey reached up, using the handle to hook the loop of a vine against the protruding hooks of the hilt. If she could just… She reached up again. The vine doubled up on itself. She pulled on the vine with a gentle tug and it moved an inch closer. She tried again, and it budged another inch. This was going to take a while. Her arm ached already. She tried again a few times until it was low enough that she could jump and grab the vine with her bare hands.

Lynsey gripped the makeshift rope and shimmied up. She felt Pico helping her, taking the strain when she felt she couldn't go any longer. She went to thank him, but thought better of it. Careful, he's already too full of himself, she thought to herself. Besides, he probably already knew, anyway.

Lynsey moved from vine to vine until she felt the heat of the sun on her face. She closed her eyes as the bright sun saturated her vision after the darkness of the cave. She forced them open to blink for a few seconds before her vision cleared. The air smelled rich; full of life and promise. It was like standing in a meadow after a spring rainstorm. She squinted at the sun and allowed its warm glow to saturate her vision again before she stepped out into the full glare of it. The tops of the orchard trees swayed in the breeze; the long grass in between them moved like ocean waves. Shielding her eyes, she glanced around.. She was outside the city walls, in the farming district by the look of it. She could see mountains in the distance through the orchard trees. Down the end of a row, she saw the grey—green bulk of the dragon eating algherai from a tree.

"Grolmak." She called.

He ignored her, but he turned so his back was to her and started eating more rapidly.

"HE'S PROBABLY EATING TO GET THE ENERGY TO FLY." Pico warned.

"Grolmak, don't go!" Running to stand before him, she took in his pale white pallor. As she watched, he was changing. His colour became the mottled brown and green of the trees surrounding him.

"Grolmak, the nomads need your help."

"Why should I care?" He carried on munching.

"Oh, come on, they've waited centuries to help you. They've gathered in the desert in the hope they will free you."

Grolmak's voice was a snarl in her head. "I don't care. I've been a prisoner in that temple for hundreds of years. They could have got me at any point."

"They couldn't. You are asking them to go against an army. As it is, the king now knows about their invisibility and their lives are now in real danger. They have to fight or their people will be enslaved forever."

The dragon paused, juice dripping from his jaws.

"Can you even imagine what I went through?" He said.

Lynsey faltered. He had a point. Then she smiled.

"I can if you will let me? You will have to relive some of it."

He hesitated for a moment, but then his great head lowered to the ground beside her and then it was Lynsey's turn to hesitate for a moment. Did she want to experience this? Her hand shook, but she held her breath and touched her band against the soft leathery hide like Sekhmet had done to her.

She had a moment to register how warm he was before she was back in the Temple basement. It was dark, and she heard chanting. This time it was different from the other memory sharing. This time she was standing in the dark as an observer and she felt the gentle rise and fall of the dragon's breath beside her, watching himself. The heat was like she remembered, even the stench. Bile burned the back of Lynsey's throat as she watched Sekhmet slash Grolmak's arm. She shuddered, ready to break the connection. But out of the corner of her eye, she caught the glimmer of a tear trailing down Grolmak's shadowy cheek. If he could relive it, then so could she.

"They chanted in the beginning." He explained, "but after a while it stopped and only Sekhmet and a select few came. I think she wanted to hide how she didn't age. I don't think even many of the priests knew I existed after a hundred years. She didn't want to share my blood with hundreds of others. The sharing only restarted over the last year."

Lynsey watched as Sekhmet knelt beside Grolmak. She stroked his arm, looking at him with worried eyes. When she pulled out an evil-looking serrated knife, Lynsey gasped. Her gaze fixed on the knife's intricate hilt. Gold thread laced through dark leather, culminating in a dragon's head carved of jade. Its emerald eyes glinted in the torchlight. Underneath the hilt was a bowl positioned to catch blood. Sekhmet looked into the dragon's eyes as if she were talking to it, then slashed at Grolmak's arm. Lynsey yelped. A matching line appeared on Grolmak's arm and she looked down to see one on her arm as well.

"You said we would have to relive the pain." He said. His thought was tinged with sadness. Through their connection, she felt the emotion roll over her in waves.

"Don't you want to get revenge for what they did to you?"

"Of course I do, but they captured me before. What is there to say that they can't do it again?"

"The priests are not fighters anymore. They are lazy, they are used to having their money fight their battles for them. The nomads are marching on the palace. Once the king is defeated, they will move on to the temple. They need to break both systems before the city can be free. If you help them, you will not be the only one. They can win, but they need as much help as they can get."

Lynsey stopped. She felt woozy, as if her blood was draining away and she saw Grolmak felt the same as his body sagged beside her. The scene switched to the next day, and it was repeated. Again and again she relived Grolmak's agony until the pain became overwhelming. His torment battered her mind like ocean waves crashing upon the shore. Finally, it grew too immense - she had to pull back or be swept away. She yanked her arm away from his head and they broke away from the memory.

"There is a girl locked up at the palace who really believes in you. She walked into danger willingly for you. She met you in the basement and then was captured by the palace. You may not be able to die, but she can. Are you willing to have that on your conscience for all time?" Lynsey felt a pang of guilt at the manipulation, but it was true. Her friend's life was in danger. She had to make him help her. Lynsey stood in front of Grolmak, touching his snout.

"We followed through and we rescued you. Can you not find it in your heart to help rescue her?"

Grolmak shook her hand off and took an alghera from the nearest tree. He placed it in his mouth and bit hard, letting the juice explode in his mouth. His eyes rolled in his head in obvious delight at the sensation. He turned back to look fully into Lynsey's eyes.

"I will do this to help them once, but I will not stay here. Once this task is finished, I will never set claw or wing in this place again."

"I understand."

He seemed to regard her for a second. "If you want to get to them quickly, you are going to have to let me take you there."

"How?"

"Climb on to my back and hold on to my neck. I fly quite high to take advantage of the air currents. The fall from that distance would inconvenience you."

"Not to mention painful!" She was sure he was chuckling, but she wasn't Pico. There was no way to tell what the dragon was thinking without the deep bracelet connection, only what he was directing at her.

She scrambled into position on his back. His hide was softer than silk. He rocked his wings and lifted them off the ground, and they rose. He was hesitant, but he was gaining confidence, rising until his wings could support him. The colours of his skin changed from brown and green, then lightened to blue and white as he pulled higher in the sky.

"You are like a chameleon!"

"My people change to mimic the colours of the environment. They say it is the reason we became so dominant on our planet."

"How come you know so much about solar flares and evolution?"

"Why not? Just because I cannot talk like you, you think you are more intelligent than me? I talk through my mind, you talk through your mouth. How is your means of communication more advanced than mine? In my world, only animals talk through mouths. It does not convey emotions or intent in the same way. I don't even know how your barbaric species even became dominant. You are so self-destructive."

He flew around the city gates, but the nomads had already broken camp. They flew lower over the city.

"Where is the palace?" He asked.

"It is in the centre," Lynsey replied. "Why don't you know that?"

"Why should I? I was brought here by cart. I was strapped down with a covering over me. I had no idea what was happening or where I was being taken." Grolmak responded.

"There, that yellow building. They've started fighting!"

The dragon twisted his head to look at Lynsey.

"Do you have any more of those explosives?"

Lynsey shook her head. "There were some in a bag that wouldn't fit into a keg. I remembered something about there needing to be a vacuum, so if it wouldn't fit into a keg, it was pointless putting it into one."

"We should go back and get it."

"There wasn't enough and you couldn't carry that much, anyway."

The dragon laughed. "You drank while making them, didn't you?"

"I might have had a beer or two." Her tone became defensive.

"Put the explosive in the bottle, put a rag and cork in it, and drop it on the enemy."

"Right! Of course! A Molotov cocktail, I've heard about those. Go back to the temple. It was back near the gate."

Grolmak wheeled around in the air and headed back the way they had come. He stayed high until they were near, then dropped like a stone, putting his wings out at the last minute behind the shop.

"There are some stables inside the courtyard. Hide in there until I get back. You won't fit into the door of the shop."

"You like stating the obvious, don't you?" He grumbled as he shuffled off into the building, "You owe me for this."

Lynsey burst into the basement. The table was still there, turned upside down, its legs broken. Looking about, she spotted several bottles wrapped in cloth, still unbroken. She grabbed an armful and put them beside the table. She pulled the table upright and placed the bottles on top. Hurriedly, she grabbed a bag from a corner and poured a black grainy mixture from it into the bottles until they reached the top. Behind her, she saw the corks tossed aside near the door. She still needed a fuse, though. Someone had left their jacket hanging over a chair. Sorry guys, but this is more important. Lynsey ripped strips of material from it and soaked them in oil and put them in the bottle before squeezing the corks back into the bottle one-by-one. She put them into a basket which had been used to deliver the bottles and ran out to Grolmak.

"Can you breathe fire?"

"Why ever would I breathe fire? That would be a strange ability to have."

"Oh. OK." Lynsey rushed back in and found a lamp in another room with a glass covering. She lit it from a cooking fire whose embers were still burning and then rushed back to put it in the basket with the bottles.

"I've got them!"

Grolmak began beating his wings against the ground. His wings flapped at the air, making the stable walls tremble. Hay swirled through the confined space like a plague of locusts. He let out a loose, long, low growl. The sack of coal beside his tail was rattling around his tail as he fidgeted from side to side.

"Let's get this over with."

Lynsey climbed up and perched the basket in the middle of his back between his wings and she clambered on behind them. There was a strap that ran along the top of the basket. She pulled it over her head. And gripped on to Grolmak.

She felt herself lose balance on the shaky scaffolding of the dragon's back and nearly fell off as Grolmak manoeuvred himself out of the building and set off, climbing higher into the sky. She held on to his neck as tightly as she could while he climbed higher into the clouds. Without warning, he turned into a dive, flying faster toward the palace. The high-altitude wind created by his speed blew through her hair as he dived towards the palace.

40 Holding on to Honour

Illyara rolled onto her stomach and buried her face into the thin pillow. They'd killed her parents! Illyara curled up into the foetal position and sobbed painfully. She couldn't stop the tears from running down her cheeks and she didn't want to. She remembered her parents' muffled voices through the white curtain acting as a make-shift wall in their tent. They'd thought she was asleep, but she loved hearing about the places they had visited, and she was comforted by the sight of their shadows cuddling each other.

She closed her eyes and tried to conjure up her father's face and then her mother's face and then Mewlli's face and then tried to recreate their quiet voices as they whispered. The memory of them sitting there, playing guessing games with Mewlli, brought tears to her eyes. She wiped them away as best as she could, trying to wipe away the sadness as well. The memory of them was something she had, but it would never be more than a memory now.

Her parents were still young. They should have been around for years more. She wasn't ready! Not to lose them and not to take over as leader. Neither was Mewlli. How was she even going to tell him? A fresh wave of anguish crashed over her. She buried her face in the sodden pillow as sobs wracked her body. They needed them.

She thought about her father's kind eyes, his gentle smile, the hours he sat talking about religion, philosophy, the tribe. The way they talked problems out as a family. She sobbed into the soaked pillow. She couldn't imagine life without them. A yawning void of loneliness and despair stretched endlessly before her.

The king was a monster. She knew what he wanted. He hadn't said it, but he wanted to use Lynscy's power to live longer. If Sekhmet had lived two hundred years, the king could rule for that long at least. She couldn't be the reason that happened. It wasn't only that. Now he knew about her family's abilities, he would not stop until he controlled all of them. Illyara was under no illusion. If he did this, there would be no stopping him.

Illyara's eyes burned. She felt hate build up in her, rising from deep within from a place she never knew existed. It took over. Her resolve was hardening. Then she remembered her mother's head as it rolled towards her. Her expression was one of love, not hate. She felt the anger dissipate. Her mother had accepted whatever would happen, but she couldn't forgive so easily. She pounded the pillow. If she hadn't come to Ghinari, this would never have happened. If she hadn't insisted on saving the dragon, they would not have been there. A small voice at the back of her head told that she had been right to do it. She could not have acted in any other way. Her breathing was raw and her ribs ached. Illyara fell into a blessed sleep.

She let herself wallow in grief until she realised she did want to stop. She knew she had to grieve, but now wasn't the time. Why did her father run out? He must have known it could have cost him his life. She could almost hear him speaking from a time long ago.

"Let it go, Illyara," he said. "Think of the people. If you accept them, they will accept you. I will die one day and you will have to take control to lead for the good of the people."

Illyara wiped her eyes and sat up. Her arms jangled, reminding her again of the bells attached to her wrists. He was right. She needed to get out, but how? Even invisible, if she took one step near anyone, they would know she was near. Illyara scrutinised the bracelets encircling her wrists, the metal cold against her skin. She gave an experimental tug. The unyielding bands didn't budge. Now she knew how Lynsey felt. Her hands were just too large to slide them off. She let out an annoyed breath, pulling up her wrists to see a small lock. She cast her eyes around the room. It was no use. She had nothing to pick it with, even if the bracelets gave her enough dexterity to do it. She looked at the sheet covering her knees and had a brainwave. With a wiggle and a pull, she tore a strip of sheet away and wrapped it around one wrist, tucking the end in between her arm and metal, using two more strips across the top and bottom of the original strip of sheet, encasing the bells inside it. She used her teeth to pull one end while she tied it with her other hand. Illyara waved her arm, and no sound greeted her. Her eyes gleamed. There was a way out, after all. She tore another length and repeated the process on her other wrist.

There was still the question of how to get out of the room. She couldn't fight like Lynsey; she was nowhere near as strong or skilled. There were no windows, she mused, casting her gaze about - there was no escaping that way. The only way out was through the door. She swept her sleeve over her wet eyes and dribbling nose. She had to at least try. If she didn't, her people were lost.

Illyara scanned the room. She needed a weapon. Her eyes fell upon the table in the corner, and she made her way towards it. The table wobbled as she tapped at it with her finger. It didn't seem very sturdy. The weight wasn't too much for her as she tried to pick it up. It was possible to move it by herself. She grabbed each of the legs and pulled. The table's feet scraped against the stone floor with a screech, but it only moved an inch. Illyara furrowed her brow and gave it another tug. The table was heavy, but she would not let it stop her from getting out of here.

With a grunt of effort, Illyara heaved the table onto the bed. She braced herself and pushed with all her might. The table crashed to the stone floor, splintering loudly. She looked towards the door, but there was no sign anyone had heard. Maybe the thick walls disguised the sound, she surmised. She held up the leg, hefting it in her hands.

She hid against the wall beside the door and moaned. She cried louder, as if she was in extreme pain. The door opened and a guard burst in. He looked around, puzzled at first, then angry when he didn't find her. She swung the leg with all her strength and hit him squarely on the head. He dropped like a stone. She waited for another guard, but there was no one in sight.

Cautiously, she gathered her skirts and stepped out into the deserted corridor. She made herself invisible and walked down the hallway.

41 Mortal Moments

Arkan drew out his knife and threw it. The blade whistled through the air and hit a guard dead centre between the eyes. The man's eyes went glassy, a trickle of blood running from the wound before he fell.

Arkan dashed forward, whirling around a guard, grabbing his knife from another that fell to the ground. He used the knife again in a swiping movement, feeling it hit bone and finding the next guard before taking another knife from his sleeve and letting it fly into the throat of another. Arkan dropped to his knees for a moment to wipe his blade on the man's shirt. He looked up, breathing hard.

The fighting was fierce. He'd never thought the Bardoon had it in them to fight like this. They didn't have the finesse of the guard, but they more than made up for it with energy and skill and they fought for something; their freedom, for their families and for their honour. He would have put money on the guard before today, but the bodies were piling up around him, tribe and guards alike.

Still crouching, Arkan saw a guard notice him a few feet away. A flash of recognition and the man rushed forward, holding up his burnished shield to protect his face and neck. As if they were the only targets on a human body! It was Shalek. Arkan sighed with relief. A loyal king's man, but not the sharpest nail in the coffin. Arkan let out a grim smile as Shalek approached. Forming a quick plan, he rose to his feet while maintaining eye contact with the man on the other side of the shield. He never liked the bully, anyway. He saw the man hesitate and Arkan's smile broadened into a grin. On a deep level, he hated himself for it, but he loved fighting. Even better, he was fighting for the woman he loved. The smile slipped at the thought. Shalek noticed his momentary distraction and pressed forward. The man's arm raised and his eyes narrowed. Arkan raised his right knife automatically and deflected the blow easily, feeling the jar against his bones despite how well he had blocked it with his own knife. His left hand moved up quickly of its own volition and went under the shield in an upward movement. There was resistance and Arkan shoved harder, feeling the blade pierce the other man's formerly pristine uniform to enter the skin and into his heart. The man's expression went slack and he let the body fall.

Arkan moved like a demon, knife flying from his hands with the quickness of a striking cobra. Each hand made coordinated movements, tipping with the force of the blow, twisting with graceful force. The knife moved like an extension of his arm, always coming back to his hand in graceful movements. After half an hour, he felt the battle lust fade, and he noticed bodies falling by themselves around him, clutching gaping wounds out of nowhere.

It had to be Mewlli! Arkan could see why the King would want the Bardoon invisibility skill to serve him. There was a wide space to his left where victim after victim collapsed, clutching arms and legs. He could not see what the boy was doing but knew that the guards were incapacitated by the Bardoon's skill. Good for the boy, Arkan thought. He said he would not kill them, but then he didn't need to, he just disabled them. Imagine what he would be like if he wanted to kill. He had already taken out several of the guards and none of them had even registered a defensive stroke before they lay on the floor.

He rushed forward and deflected a sword with his left knife and undercut with his right. A second sword came in. Arkan chopped under the blade with his right, his arm flaring with pain as the two swords clashed. He ducked under the wild swing of another guard. Any pain was dulled by his other feelings of anger and resolve. He had no problem despatching the guards. He killed without mercy. Years spent on the front line when he was younger inured him to killing in battle. When assassinating a lone target, guilt sometimes pricked at him afterward. But here on the battlefield, there was no room for remorse. Survival drove all else from his mind. The guards were paid well to put their lives on the line, but they also knew that this kind of work came with the territory.

Over the next hour, the nomads pushed back the guards to enter the courtyard. He groaned. There was a fresh wave of guardsmen, but then Arkan grinned and rushed forward with renewed vigour. His face flushed red with effort, veins exaggerated on his forehead, eyes wide and bloodshot. He cut downward, his blade scything through skin, flesh, fat, muscle and bone. He did not feel the resistance of muscle, did not feel the man's spilt intestines slide down his leg. There was a spray of blood and bile. He whirled, half-madman, half-dancer. His blades were deadly, each slice meeting a target. This was what he was born for, what he had trained all those years to do. He was a fighting machine and all he saw was the enemy. Every slash of his sword felt like it was cutting through his last moment of doubt. Everything he hated was represented in those green uniforms. He let go of all his inhibitions, cutting through men like butter. Reached a side entrance, he looked back, panting. He could feel the wet material of his jacket clinging to his back. He felt more alive than he had done in years. The nomads were still fighting, but they could cope with what was left. He moved into the palace looking for the king.

Arkan knew the route to the royal apartments like the back of his hand. At first glance they appeared deserted, but Arkan didn't give them a second glance as he bypassed them to go up the stairs and into the secret anteroom. He found the king sitting at his desk, seemingly oblivious to the fighting going on outside.

"Arkan, you are back. When the fight is over, I will need your services again," he said dreamily.

"I do not think so, your Highness."

The king looked at him unseeing. "I pay your wages, boy, you answer to me."

"When you tried to capture Lynsey, I stopped being on your payroll, My Lord," the last he spat with venom. "What you plan to do is inhuman."

The king sat back in his chair. "What I plan to do would have ensured hundreds of years of peace." The last word was spat with such vehemence it rent through Arkan like a blade.

"Peace with you as king!"

"I have no heirs. It is the only way."

"You have nephews. One of them would become king when you were gone. This has nothing to do with that. This is for your gratification only."

"Arkan, I love you, but you would never make a great king. You are a fighter, not a leader."

"Ruling is not my desire. I would never have saved Lynsey if that was the case! I am not stupid, uncle. There is Jeren or Tyrin."

"They are not suitable."

"They are not suitable because you want to live forever. No one would be good enough. Uncle, you are going to have to leave and never come back."

The king turned and focussed on Arkan for the first time. "You will not kill me?"

"No, I was never comfortable being your assassin. Mother thought that was a good way to be in line for the throne. But I never wanted for that to happen. I have a feeling that no one will be king from now on. You need to go before they break through."

"I cannot do that."

"If you do not, then I cannot guarantee your safety, Uncle. It is only because you are family I am offering you this one chance to escape. You wouldn't allow this for anyone else, but I'm offering it to you now. Take this chance. Please, for Mother."

He smiled at Arkan. "Aren't you worried about what your newfound friends will think if you let me go? I would not tolerate such disloyalty."

"They are not you, and you are not in any position to make threats."

"Arkan, Arkan. I am not making threats. Merely pointing out that your friends may not understand your position. Do they even know we are related? Does your Lynsey Walker?"

Arkan stood. He had not considered that. Lynsey was likely to react badly if she found out that he was related to the King. The Bardoon were inherently a peaceful people. If the king were gone before they reached here, then they would not have to deal with him as long as his threat was diffused. By doing this, he was doing them a favour. He caught the King's gaze.

"It does not matter. What will be, will be? We can only work with what our conscience allows us."

The King looked down at his feet, unwilling to meet the young man's eyes. "Where am I to go?" That question startled Arkan.

Arkan let out a long low laugh at that one.

"Well, obviously not to the islands. You have burnt that bridge with your incessant wars, but you can still go west."

The King opened his mouth then closed it again. He crossed his arms and began tapping his foot, an action that he did when he was extremely agitated or nervous. "That means going through the desert!"

"Take Faroushk." Arkan shrugged; it was obvious that the nomad would be exiled now. "He will no longer be accepted within his family. You two will make splendid companions."

The king nodded, pulling himself up using the corner of his desk. "Faroushk will be in the blue apartments in the South Wing."

Arkan nodded. "In that case, we will pick him up and then leave. It would be better for him if he is not around when the Bardoon arrives."

They strode down disused corridors. Light and dark, the king wore cream robes while Arkan had on his customary black. The sound of screams and fighting outside were getting louder, but the king did not react. The king's face was a mask of passivity, but the tense set of his shoulders betrayed his true feelings. He was striving to maintain a calm facade. It was as if he was strolling to a ball, but the tight way he held his head told another story. Arkan marvelled. The man was about to be banished from the lands he knew as home for all of his life. Everything he had worked for was in tatters, but here he was, walking to his fate as if it were nothing.

The door to Faroushk's rooms was open when they arrived. The heady scent of wine and pipe smoke poured through the doorway. Arkan recognised a voice as he drew closer and he picked up his pace. Faroushk stood by the window, his back to Arkan. The light illuminated his golden silk sleeves that stretched to his feet. His black hair swept across his head, but contrasted with his lined face. Illyara seemed small by his side, her petite body barely reaching Faroushk's armpit, her long brown hair spilled over her shoulders.

"You let him kill mother and father!"

"He would have understood. What I did was for the good of our family. We could have been part of the nobility with lands of our own. We would never need to worry again."

"The price was too high."

"If you had told them where she was and agreed to work for him, there would have been no price!"

Arkan moved to place himself between the pair. The king held back.

"Illyara, the past is the past. You have to let them go."

"He killed my parents." She shouted, then she caught sight of the king behind Arkan.

Illyara rushed forward, eyes blazing with hatred. She raised her hands to hit the king, but Arkan caught her first. She struggled to free herself, but he gripped her. He knew what they had done to her, but she would regret it for the rest of her life if he let her go now. She pummelled his chest with her wrists and he was surprised to see them covered with white cloth.

She saw his look and tried to step back. He let her, knowing he could catch her again if need be.

"They put bells on me. Bells!" She spat out. "Like I am a goat to be tracked. This man is a barbarian. They killed my parents and would have enslaved me to kill." She was looking directly at the king now. "Well, I am ready to kill now."

"He is not worth it. You don't want to kill. It is not your way."

"Give me a knife and I will show you." She hissed.

"Illyara, you will regret it for the rest of your life if you do this. Trust me, it is not easy to kill for the first time. You will be changed forever and you may not like the person you will become."

She ignored him and made to turn away. He relaxed his shoulders. She would come around. He had got through to her, but she stooped and lunged for the dagger, knowing it was there, waiting for her, fastened to his left boot. She moved quicker than he expected.

Swirling her skirts around her legs, obscuring her movements. She grabbed the dagger while his attention was on the skirts. Illyara turned invisible. Arkan went still. Where was she? Of course, she would know about the dagger. He had been too lax in his time with the Bardoon. Then he felt the faintest of air movements to his right. He lunged but caught empty air. She reappeared between him and the king and slashed. The king cried out, clutching his arm. Illyara pulled back, her expression neutral, handing the knife back to Arkan.

"I won't kill him, but he doesn't deserve to get away with no consequence."

Arkan swore an oath and grabbed a shirt hanging over a chair. With his knife, he ripped a bandage from it, wrapping it around the king.

"You are right, but a life in exile will be punishment enough for the man he is. He will have no money, no connections. He will have to start afresh, as will your relative."

Illyara looked at Faroushk, who was eyeing her with fear and no small amount of respect in his eyes. She knew what he was thinking. She couldn't kill for revenge, but she could kill for justice. Tears pricked in her eyes. He had betrayed the family, which normally had a penalty of abandonment in the desert without food or water. What would she do?

Illyara's hands curled into fists, her nails biting into her palms. Oh, how she was tempted - to abandon Faroushk in the desert as punishment for his betrayal. The desire burned within her like a flame.

Faroushk was her cousin. What he did to her parents, his aunt and uncle… Tears pricked in her eyes. She heard Arkan talking.

"C'mon, let's get out of here. The nomads might let the king free, but the people with him will not."

Arkan led them out of a side entrance and they ran out into the city.

Lynsey clung to the dragon's scaly back, holding tight as they soared over the city streets below.

The wind lashed Lynsey's face, its chill bite refreshing after the heat of the battle. Far below, crimson robes billowed around the brethren as they marched, weapons glinting in their hands. She pointed to the ground. "That's Sekhmet," she said. "She's taking the temple guards to help the king."

A deep, angry growl rumbled in Grolmak's throat. "We should bomb her."

Lynsey shook her head and said, "No, we have to help the nomads at the palace first. If they fail, then there will be no point in killing Sekhmet. The nomads will still be hunted by the king."

Grolmak nodded his agreement. Baring his fangs, he clenched his teeth and pressed on. But his claws flexing and eyes blazing betrayed his anger at not engaging his nemesis.

Arriving above the palace, she pulled a bottle out of the basket and dipped the cloth in oil, then into the flame. The Molotov cocktail burst into flame and it shot up to the bottle neck, hissing as it evaporated the liquid inside, singeing her fingers. She yelped at the sudden pain, dropping the incendiary. Quickly, her skin reddened, browned, then healed in an instant. "Thank you, Pico," she mentally called. Lynsey's stomach lurched as her balance shifted. She clung desperately to Grolmak's scales, her knuckles white, as the dragon banked and bucked, first to dislodge the bottle from his hide and then to evade the explosion's blistering heat and deafening roar. She barely saw the explosion fall harmlessly on to the cobblestones when she heard his roar louder than the explosion. "You're supposed to be hitting the guards, not me!"

The courtyard was in chaos, with guards running in all directions. Ignoring Grolmak, she tried again, this time knowing how quickly the fire spread. She held it out as soon as the wick was lit. Grolmak, sensing her intent, swooped down, and she dropped the bottle. It exploded, killing three guards in the courtyard.

Lynsey threw another down with all the force she could muster. It fell toward her foe, landing on the guards. A dozen men screamed as they caught fire, then died. She felt her grip on the dragon's scales slip, then regain itself as she was thrown about his body.

She felt them bank sharply to one side. The explosion of steam and fire rumbled up to her as another bottle hit its mark.

She picked up more bottles, and they fell one by one, exploding and killing the King's men. The nomads and people on the ground cheered as they saw what she was doing.

"I have one left." She cried out.

He wheeled around toward Sekhmet. "They can take care of the rest now. We need to stop the temple guards now."

Lynsey lifted the last bottle in her hands. "No problem," she said, lighting the rag on fire. "Set them up, then knock these suckers down." She drew her arm back and slung the explosive toward Sekhmet. Leaning forward across Grolmak's back, Lynsey peeked over his side to watch the carnage below. The bottle arced through the air, landing in a cart filled with hay, which caught on fire with a whoomph.

"Damn. Let me down. I need to fight her myself." He landed lightly for a dragon in the wide street, blocking Sekhmet's path and Lynsey slid down to stand beside him.

They faced each other the short distance, empty apart from wind-blown sand on the mud road. Sekhmet gave her a knowing smile. Lynsey felt Pico take control of her muscles, feeling them contract and release and repeat. Her hands grasped the two knives peeking out from her boots and he held them, through her body, in the air, adopting a leg-apart stance she had seen so many times in films.

Sekhmet held up her arm, and the guards tapped their spears on the ground. She gestured for them to go after the dragon while she faced Lynsey. "Hello Lynsey. Nice to see you again."

"I can't say the same." Lynsey replied.

"You know we don't have to fight. We are the same. We are both from Earth. You have your immortality. I have mine from the dragon. We have a lot in common. I come from London, so do you."

"I don't think coming from London," Lynsey spat out the word, "means that we have so much in common. I would never trap an intelligent living being and treat him the way you did with Grolmak."

"Oh, you say that now, but you are what, nineteen, twenty? You are also immortal. When I arrived I was twenty and I was thirty before I drank of the dragon. When time's merciless gaze descends on you, you might have done what I did."

Lynsey shook her head. "I would never do that. You are a barbarian. People like you do not exist where I come from."

"Oh, come now, I find that hard to believe. There really is no need to fight."

The dragon was circling around the temple guards now and Lynsey watched from the corner of her eyes as, with surprising speed, he launched and ripped out the throat of the nearest while slashing with his claws at the necks of another. While she was distracted, Sekhmet drew a sword from a scabbard she hadn't noticed.

"However, if you are going to make me fight. I will simply have to defend myself."

"Oh, shut up," growled Lynsey. "You sound like a villain from a spy film."

"As you wish," Sekhmet launched at her. The glittering sword sliced through the air from left to right. Lynsey tried to step back, but Pico took control of their body and caught the blade between the two knives. She whirled and gave Sekhmet a kick in the stomach, which knocked her away.

Lynsey advanced under the control of Pico. She was enjoying herself. Onward to victory! Lynsey thought, trying to hide her excitement behind a mask of boredom. She always wanted to fight, but was usually either hopeless or just not allowed to take part. Here she was, fighting with no effort.

Sekhmet tried again, but Pico parried and hit her twice, first on the shoulder and then on the face, first with their fist and then with the flat of their palm.

"Careful Pico," Lynsey said. "Don't get too confident."

"SORRY, I THOUGHT YOU MIGHT ENJOY THAT."

"You weren't wrong."

Sekhmet circled around Lynsey. She heard Grolmak fighting someone toward the end of the line. It sounded like there was a whirlwind in there and every once in a while she heard a scream and whoever had been fighting Grolmak fell silent. Then several footsteps running away as fast as they could.

Lynsey saw Sekhmet glance behind her with what could only be genuine fear on her face.

Lynsey's face was flushed. "Grolmak is winning, isn't he?" she asked. As they continued to circle around, she saw Grolmak, a twin whirl of fangs and claws.

"How did you capture him that time? He can clearly defend himself." Curiosity filled Lynsey's voice.

"A stray arrow." the thought implanted itself in her mind. "She didn't catch me. It was the arrow by one of her companions who I killed. She just took the credit."

"Oh, so the almighty Sekhmet takes the credit for capturing the dragon, discovers the healing power of the dragon's blood and creates the brotherhood. Wouldn't it have been better to create a sisterhood?"

"Don't be silly, that wouldn't have worked here." Sekhmet replied.

"I suppose not."

"Stop circling each other and fight." Growled Grolmak.

"Shall we?" Lynsey asked.

Sekhmet threw herself at the younger girl. Her skill was impressive. She fought like a berserker, slashing her sword as if possessed by a spirit. Lynsey was thrown backwards by her ferocity but came back quickly, slamming her blades against Sekhmet's chest, causing hundreds of cuts, but Sekhmet healed them as fast as Lynsey could cut them. Again, Lynsey was thrown backwards by the force of her attack, but she quickly recovered and slashed back, her eyes narrow and angry. Sekhmet's wounds continued closing, and Lynsey soon tired beneath the onslaught of blows. Pico took over again and had to fight for their lives. Lynsey ducked and rolled and came back at her, but she was still unharmed. Sekhmet laughed at her reaction.

"Do you think I would enter a battle without drinking dragon's blood?"

"What do I do Pico? She just won't go down."

"IT WON'T LAST FOREVER, IT'S FOREIGN TO HER BODY. WE JUST HAVE TO WAIT IT OUT."

Lynsey's body tensed as Pico took control, surging them forward. Their blades sliced toward Sekhmet in a flurry of strikes. They battled back and forth, but Sekhmet was tiring under the onslaught.

"IT'S HAPPENING, SHE'S GETTING TIRED." Pico's thought was exultant. He renewed his effort. Lynsey's muscles burned with fatigue. How she wished she was anywhere but here, locked in this endless battle. The surrounding sounds faded, and she felt the dragon watching quietly.

"Anytime you want to butt in, be my guest." Lynsey panted, ducking under a vicious thrust.

"Oh, I don't know, you seem to do doing well. I want to see her suffer before she dies." Came the lazy thought.

"Grolmak!"

"Okay, okay."

Sekhmet looked warily at the dragon and edged away from the open path. The dragon showed his fangs and chuckled with a low rumble. Lynsey stepped forward, aiming a thrust at Sekhmet's stomach. Just as Lynsey was about to attack, the dragon lunged forward and took a chunk out of Sekhmet's torso.

"This is for all the times that you pretended you couldn't understand me, for when you tortured me unnecessarily and kept me cooped up for two hundred years!"

Lynsey rolled away, and the dragon launched at Sekhmet. Sekhmet gave one last scream before her throat was ripped out. He spat it out on the floor and casually ripped the woman's head from her shoulders. Blood poured from Sekhmet's stump as she fell to the ground with a heavy thud, eyes still open in death. Her head hit the ground with a sickening squish.

"Survive that!" He said. Turning, he gripped Lynsey's hand gently with his talons. "Shall we help the others?"

43 Tomorrow's Hopes

There was no sign of the king. The fighting continued into the night, but the palace was reclaimed by the middle of the next day. All guards were lined up next to the dais. Mewlli walked down the line, taking their oaths to serve Ghinari and rescind the king. Their voices were quiet and their uniforms dirty with grime and blood. They had fought well in defence of their king and it was hoped they would serve the city well in the future.

A footman was reading from a long scroll at the bottom of the steps leading to the dais, which was hastily put together by a vote of the people in the hall the night before. The tax on water was rescinded and the food stores of the king were handed out in celebration. Freedom of speech and trade and the right to live without fear of harm unless the law was broken. All laws were revoked and new laws would take their place. Lynsey noticed a few were being read out next. They were probably worried some criminals were going to take advantage; she thought.

They were in the main ballroom where Lynsey had first met the king. Tapestries depicting battles hung from the walls. Flax, woven into yards of cloth, gave the room a warm glow. Someone had pushed the large table which had dominated the room to one side, leaving room for several smaller, but long tables for people to eat at. The mix of people was heartening. While the hall previously had been filled with lords and ladies, who had all escaped at the onset of fighting when there was no one to stop them, there were no nobles here now. Lynsey twisted her neck. "Pico, can you see Arkan?"

"He's not here Lynsey. Maybe ask Illyara if she's seen him?"

Across the room, Illyara looked up and saw Lynsey looking back. Illyara smiled brightly and waved. Lynsey laughed and ran across the room to embrace her friend.

"Illyara!" she said. "I'm so glad you're here. Do you know where Arkan is?"

"He's gone." Her friend looked uncomfortable, seeing the panic in Lynsey's eyes. "Sorry, I think you may have misunderstood." Her eyebrows drew together. "Arkan went with the King willingly. He escorted the king out of the city. He said he would try to follow you later wherever you go. Did you know he was related to the King?"

Blood drained from Lynsey's face. Her stomach flip-flopped.

"No."

"He stopped me from killing the King, but I'm glad. He should have told us, though."

Lynsey's green eyes narrowed in anger. "Why did you let them escape?"

It was going to be a long time before she forgave her friend, but they both knew that there was no right decision. If they had killed the king, an heir would claim the empty throne.

Illyara gathered Lynsey in her arms and comforted her. "Arkan went with him to make sure he went. It wasn't really the King's fault. He was doing what his father and his father's father before him had done. There was no one to tell them differently. He was like a little child, really. He will go to the Western Empire, where they will probably welcome him. Arkan knew that. If he tries to raise an army, he will have to go through the desert. No one knows the desert better than us. If he comes by water, we will have a warning. He is no threat now. Arkan didn't betray us. "

Doubt gnawed at Lynsey. Why had Arkan concealed his family link to the king? Unease slithered through her at the thought of what else he might be hiding. She shifted, suddenly uncomfortable. Then she remembered about Illyara's parents and felt bad that she hadn't thought about what her friend must be going through.

"I'm sorry about your mum and dad, Illyara."

Illyara's eyes dimmed, their brightness fading.

"They will always be remembered. Mewlli will organise a day in remembrance of their lives. Our people see them as heroes for their sacrifice."

"Mewlli? Why won't you be doing that?"

"I can't stay here. This place has too many memories. I would like to come with you? If that would be agreeable?"

"How did you know I was leaving?"

"Everyone knows who you are and what you represent. You can't stay here. Someone will always try to take advantage of you." Illyara took a strand of Lynsey's hair. "It is beautiful, but you must admit that it stands out here."

"You are right. I will go with Grolmak. We have heard of a people in the islands who may have come from our world a different way from the Egyptians. Maybe they can send us back to our worlds. We have to try."

"I understand. I too want to travel, to explore. In the time I have spent with you, I've lived more than in my entire life. Mewlli will look after our people. Our aunts and uncles will advise him as they did our parents. Mewlli is more suited to this life than me, anyway. He has grown up a lot over the last month. He is like a different person, but one I respect." She looked for her brother across the room, but he was already heading towards them.

"Thank you, sister." Mewlli replied, smoothing down his purple tunic. "I'm sorry to see you go, Lynsey. Why won't you stay to help us build a fairer society?"

"Surely you realise I don't belong here? I need to find a way home. If I can get here, then there should be a way home."

Mewlli nodded. "You know, I had to try." He turned to Illyara.

"Sis, are you sure you want to go with Lynsey?"

"I am. I need some time away."

"I miss them too." Mewlli replied.

"I know, but you seem much better suited to this. Look at you. Less than a month ago, I was worried about you following me in the desert. Now I think you can rule the tribe. We have all changed."

"Do you want an escort?"

"No thanks, we need to travel light. All we need is a pair of horses and some provisions to take us to the port. We can take a ship to the islands from there."

"The islands? We know little about them."

"Well, it can't be more dangerous than this place." Lynsey joked.

"You are indeed right," Mewlli grinned and wandered off.

The room was filling up. More and more people were squeezing in to see what was happening. Mewlli stood on the dais.

"Ladies and gentlemen, we have done it! We have overthrown the rule of the Jade King and Dragon Brotherhood! We are free citizens of Ghinari! No one will ever rule us again!" The people roared their approval.

"Mewlli seems to have it all in hand." Lynsey shouted over the noise.

"He's a good kid." They walked out of the palace into the courtyard. The bodies had been taken away, but the vultures were still circling. The tang of blood still permeated the air, metallic and cloying like the lingering smell of doom.

"I suppose all births are gruesome."

Illyara laughed. "You could say that."

Two horses stood in the centre of the circle with panniers loaded with supplies on them, with a little cart behind them filled with vegetables. Their hooves tapped in unison, the squeak of leather and clinking of metal echoing through the yard.

"Why do we have so many vegetables?" Illyara asked curiously.

"it is for me," growled the dragon. "I have been forced to eat meat for the last two centuries. I can eat what I like now. No more meat, no more blood. Are we ready? I want to leave this place!".

"The Dragon is a vegetarian," Lynsey translated. "And he's getting a little impatient to go."

"Wait, a moment Lynsey." Pico warned.

"What is it Pico?"

"I have been looking into your code. I can make a very small adjustment that will turn your hair to a different colour. Would you like that?"

"I told you to stop messing with my DNA!" Then she paused. "Actually, can you change it to a dark brown like Illyara's?"

Lynsey felt her head turn to look at Illyara.

"Easy." was the reply. Her hand grabbed her hair and brought it to her eye. As Lynsey watched, her hair darkened until it was the same shade as her friend's.

"No one will recognise me now," said Lynsey with a grin. "Not if they've never seen me before."

Illyara's eyes widened when she turned to look at Lynsey.

"Gorgeous, we could be sisters." She giggled. "We are going to have such fun!"

Note from the Author

Hello, from Wales! Thank you for taking an interest in my novel. I wanted to spend a few minutes to talk about the writing of this book.

You'll notice that the story is in British English. It begins in England before moving to the Egyptian colony. This influenced my decision to write in my home dialect. I wanted to create an immersive experience from the perspective of Lynsey Walker.

The story is a 'what if' scenario. What would happen if the Ancient Egyptians had colonised a planet and called it Duat? What would happen if a modern-day Londoner found themselves transported to their planet to the receiving station, long after it was abandoned? That was my starting point.

This book was written around 9 years ago for NanoWriMo (National Novel Writing Month.) The earliest draft appeared on Wattpad first, and then a few chapters on my website. Please don't go looking for them on the Internet Archive. They were really early drafts while I worked out the story kinks!

As this was written so long ago, AI wasn't available when I wrote it. However, I have put it into AI to check its structure, and asked for some pointers for improving it. I'm a bit of a pantser when writing, which can make the structure a bit wobbly. I'm happy to report that AI gave it a thumbs up, but then again, it may be biased, as one star of the novel is an AI! You guys will be the ultimate arbiter of Lynsey's story.

If you spot any errors, feel free to let me know at my website CeriClark.com. You might wonder why Ceri Clark, when the author is Ceridwen Hughson. Well, they are both my real names. I was born Ceridwen Hughson and married into the Clark clan. All my fiction will be put under my Ceridwen Hughson name to separate the novels from diaries, password books, tech manuals and the like.

If you enjoyed my epic tale of AI, assassins, dragons and desert kingdoms, please leave a review where you bought this. This is a standalone novel, but I've left it open for sequels if enough people like the characters and want to know what happens next. I have a few ideas! Don't forget to let me know if you want more of this story! I'm always happy to get helpful feedback.

Until next time,

Ceri Hughson (or Clark, I answer to both).

Baker Eleri hoped returning to her late aunt's seaside cafe in Wales would provide a fresh start. But her new beginning is haunted by strange whispers, and a mystical silver locket that washes up on the beach.

When Eleri enlists the help of her childhood friend Gareth to unravel the locket's secrets, their investigation reveals her family is cursed by two star-crossed lovers from centuries past. Eleri and Gareth have until Christmas Eve to break the curse...or risk losing each other forever.

Passion ignites as they race to decipher the curse's origins and discover the truth behind Eleri's ghostly premonitions. Dark supernatural forces seem determined to tear them apart and doom Eleri to her ancestors' cursed fate.

To defeat the ancient evil, Eleri and Gareth must trust in the power of their bond and believe love can conquer any darkness. But on this enchanted Welsh coast, nothing is as it seems. Will forbidden desires lead to a happily ever after...or a haunting heartbreak?

This contemporary paranormal romance filled with Celtic lore is set in the seaside town of Aberystwyth, Wales. With a determined heroine, charming love interest, quirky locals, and just a touch of magic, Whispers of the Past will appeal to fans of ghostly love stories with depth.